KNIGHTS OF
THE RANGE

Also published in Large Print
from G.K. Hall by Zane Grey:

Arizona Ames
Under the Tonto Rim
Black Mesa
Blue Feather and Other Stories
Shadow on the Trail
The Lone Star Ranger
The Vanishing American
Wildfire

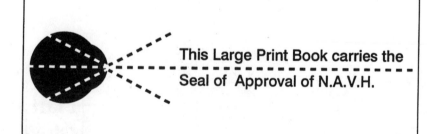

This Large Print Book carries the
Seal of Approval of N.A.V.H.

KNIGHTS OF THE RANGE

ZANE GREY

G.K. Hall & Co.

Published in 1995 by arrangement with the Golden West
Literary Agency & HarperCollins Publishers.

This novel is a work of fiction. Names, characters, incidents,
and dialogues are products of the author's imagination and are
not to be construed as real. Any resemblance to actual events or
persons, living or dead, is entirely coincidental.

G.K. Hall Large Print Western Collection.

The text of this Large Print edition is unabridged.
Other aspects of the book may vary from the original edition.

Set in 16 pt. News Plantin by Minnie B. Raven.

Printed in the United States on permanent paper.

Library of Congress Cataloging in Publication Data

Grey, Zane, 1872–1939.
   Knights of the range / Zane Grey.
     p.   cm.
   ISBN 0-7838-1166-7 (lg. print : hc)
   1. Large type books. I. Title.
  [PS3513.R6545K55   1995]
  813'.52—dc20   94-37506

KNIGHTS OF THE RANGE

CHAPTER 1

Colonel Lee Ripple sat on the porch of his ranch-house in eastern New Mexico, facing that famous fan-shaped scene that lay between the great timbered escarpments stretching down over the green and gray terraces to the vast rolling plain below, through which the Old Trail followed the shining way of the Cimarron into the purple distance.

It was the grandest scene in all New Mexico, and the sad blue eyes of the cattle baron lingered long there before shifting round to the west, where a splendour of range empire unfolded to his gaze. A million acres swept and waved on all sides to the silver slopes, and these in turn sheered up to the black-belted mountains with their snowy peaks.

"Wal, Kurnel, I heahed you, shore, but I'd like to get oot of takin' you serious," said Britt, the rancher's foreman, who sat on the porch steps.

"Cap, you must take me seriously," replied Ripple, in slow grave speech. "Another spell with my heart like this last one will kill me."

"Aw, I cain't believe it," rejoined Britt, stubbornly, despite the something convincing in his employer's tone and look.

"I know, Cap. I thought this second attack would

do for me. My heart has acted queer for a long time. But that spell in San Antonio was the first bad one. I consulted a doctor. He told me to make my will and get ready. But scared as I was, I didn't obey. I went on to New Orleans after Holly, and fetched her home without tellin' her aboot it. I just couldn't tell her."

"No wonder, boss. Thet would have been plumb hard on the lass," replied Britt, wagging his lean, hawk-like head. "You sent her to thet school when she was eight years old. An' you went to see her half a dozen times in these nine years she's been gone. An' when you was fetchin' her heah to Don Carlos' Rancho, the only home she ever had — to tell her you was aboot to die — Aw! thet would have been cruel!"

"You're right," agreed the Colonel, bitterly, as he spread his hands with a hopeless gesture. "That mawnin' when I met her and told her I had come to take her home she was so happy, so radiant. I couldn't kill her joy. . . . But now, Britt, she must be told at once."

"Why, boss? You know how onsartin life is. *Quien sabe?* You might live long yet."

"Yes. It's possible. But not probable. And I want her to make her choice while I am living."

"Choice of what, Kurnel, if I may make bold to ask?"

"Whether or not she will live heah or go to her Mother's people in Santone."

"Holly will never leave Don Carlos' Rancho," said Britt, quickly.

8

"Did she say so?" asked Ripple, eagerly, his gray eyes full of soft warm light.

"No. But I'd gamble on it. These few days Holly has been here she's been plumb loco aboot the ranch. Why, she has been wild with joy. Boss, she's like a freed bird. An' she loves it all, particular the hawses. She's crazy aboot hawses. An' she's never been in a saddle yet. Think of thet, Lee Ripple. Heah's a girl of sixteen, granddaughter of old Don Carlos, the greatest of all the old hawse-breedin' dons — an' she's never straddled a hawse."

"I know — I know, Cap. Don't rub it in. I always meant Holly to have all the West could offer. But first I wanted her to get an education. The years have slipped by. . . . So my lass loves horses — What did she say?"

"Wal, the lass has yore blood in her, same as thet of the Valverde. She asked me how many hawses we had. An' when I told her aboot four hundred thet we knowed of she squealed with joy. Swore she'd ride every one of them. . . . Lord, I see my troubles. But I'll teach Holly to ride. I shore won't leave thet to these saddle rowdies."

"Britt, you make me hope," returned the Colonel, feelingly, as he lay back in the great rocker. "I always wanted a son. But I never loved Holly the less for that. . . . If she lived on heah, and learned to run this ranch under your wise eye, and some day married one of these saddle rowdies — I could die happy."

"My Gawd, boss!" expostulated Britt, heatedly. "Why'd you ever send Holly away to make a fine lady oot of her if you wanted her to marry one of these firebrands?"

"Cap, could Holly do better? I mean if this lucky cowboy is one of the breed we know so well. Not a Texan! Holly is half Spanish and you know Texans will be long forgettin' the Alamo. . . . He must be of good family and have some little schoolin'. For the rest, I don't care so much. Holly could make most any cowboy take his place in the makin' of the West. . . . They are the salt of the earth, these wild range riders. Without them there would never have been this cattle business growin' by leaps and bounds, destined to tame the frontier. You know, Britt, even better than I do. For five years you've handled these hard-ridin', hard-drinkin', hard-shootin' devils of mine. And you have loved them."

"Wal, mebbe I haven't loved them like I ought to have," rejoined Britt, regretfully, surprised into feeling. "But, Kurnel, it just makes my blood run cold, to think of Holly alone on this big ranch."

"Cold! — Your blood should run swift and warm at the very thought. It will be wonderful. Holly looks Spanish, but she is American. She has her mother's beauty. But *my* brains. I have no fear for her, Britt. . . . If she only chooses to stay! . . . With you to train Holly, teach her to run the ranch, watch over her — she would not be alone. I'm not afraid to risk it."

"But I am, boss," declared Britt, tragically. "I

almost wish you hadn't fetched her home."

"Nonsense, old timer. My girl has loved you all her life. It was you who nicknamed her Holly. You danced her on your knee and helped teach her to walk. You can't go back on her now. You must take my place as her Dad."

"Kurnel, I'll do my damndest. . . . But lookin' ahaid, in the light of this lovely lass growin' up heah into a woman, I don't like the times."

Colonel Ripple made a slight, violent gesture, as if a motive prompted by passion had been quenched by will.

"Nor do I. That is somethin' I have put off, and like this other must now be talked over. Yet the reason is simple. . . . Look there to the south, old timer. That is the grandest outlook in the West, if not in the whole world. Kit Carson sat right there and said so. Lucien Maxwell did the same, and you know his pride in his old Spanish grant and the beauty of his sixty square miles of ranch. St. Vrain tried to buy this ranch from Don Carlos. Chisum, Murphy, the Exersall Company, and that English outfit who bought the Three X's — not one of these cattle kings has the West under his eyes as I have. Not one of them has the protected grazing-lands. . . . Look down over the Old Trail and the Cimarron. Peaceful, lonely, eh? The Kiowas and Comanches are my friends. Look at the buffalo. All those black patches down there are buffalo. . . . And now look around to the west, Britt. No range like that in all this broad New Mexico. Look at the cattle. Do you remember

11

when we drove in heah first? It seems long. But it's only seven years. Seven years! They were heaven compared to the years of the war, and long before. . . . You know my story, Britt. How I came through heah in 1855 with a caravan on the way to Santa Fe. How I won Carlotta Valverde and took her back to Texas with me. How old Don Carlos cast her off and did not forgive her for many years. . . . Look at my herds of cattle dottin' the range. Like the buffalo. Fifty thousand head, so you say, and half a thousand horses. I could sell ten thousand head — twenty thousand head and be rich. . . . What is wrong with the times, Britt?"

"Wal, you ain't told it all yet. Go on."

"Oh, I know what you're drivin' at. . . . But listen, Cap. The war is long past. Texas has come through, and her cattle have built this empire. Just as the trappers did, the gold-seekers had their day, so had the freighters. The caravans are slowin' up, Britt, and those that roll by down there on the Old Trail are loaded up with pioneers. A new day is dawnin' — the day of the settled West."

"Shore. But a hell of a lot can happen in a day, Kurnel. Yore hope is father to yore belief. . . . This heah year of our Lawd, seems fine an' fair to you, Kurnel, 'cause white men an' red men alike, ootlaws an' robbers, all the good an' the bad of the plains air yore friends. As the house of Don Carlos was open to all, so has yore house been. . . . But I say, fer you if you live, an' fer all of us who live heah, the hardest an' bloodiest, the wust times air yet to come."

"Kit Carson said that years ago. But I never believed it. And his prophecy has not been verified."

"Yes, Kit swore thet, settin' right heah where I set now. . . . Kurnel, I reckon men like you an' Maxwell an' Chisum know more aboot cows than anythin' else. It's men like me an' Carson who have vision. We never was blinded by great possessions."

"Britt, I bow to that vision," replied Ripple, solemnly. "I always feared, but I drove fear from my mind. Let us grant, then, that the worst times of the frontier are to come. Tell me what they are and how they will work."

"Wal, it's as simple as when Carson seen through it. But only been long in comin'. . . . Fust, take the buffalo. The huntin' of buffalo fer their hides has begun. We old Texans always feared this. It means such war with the Indians as has never been seen on this frontier. Yore friends the Utes, the Kiowas, the Comanches, the Cheyennes, the Arapahoes, the Pawnees, all the tribes will go on the war-path. Thet means turrible bloody times, fer the settlers have come pourin' oot West thick. Texas will see the wust of thet, because the buffalo on their rangin' from south to north an' back again air most on the Texas plains. The hide hunters will concentrate in the Pan Handle, or under the *Llano Estacado* or between the Brazos an the Rio Grande. An' the plains Indians will fight to the death fer their meat. They live on buffalo. It will be a fight to the finish between the buffalo hunters an' the Indian tribes. The Yankee army could not lick the red men. Not in a million years! Look at the Custer campaigns. I heahed thet Carson, an' Buff Belmet, an' other scouts have advised these army men to lay off the Indians. But they will blunder right on to be massacred. . . . The pioneers you talk aboot cain't lick the Indians. An' if the buffalo hunters don't lick them this West will shore become unhealthy damn pronto."

"I gather that, Britt. All the same I'd say the hide hunters will break the power of the allied tribes and drive them off the plains."

"My guess, too. When this hide huntin' movement gets goin' strong there'll be many thousands of hunters. An' all keen, hard-fightin' men, armed with heavy rifles an' with wagon-loads of ammunition. They'll do fer the Indians, I reckon. But it will be a hell of a fight with the chances not all agin the Indians."

"Agreed. We'll pass, however, on to that future period when the red men's power will be gone. What is the next catastrophe you predict?"

"Wal, no less than the hey-day of the rustlers."

"Cattle thieves!" exclaimed the Colonel, contemptuously. "We've always had them, Britt. Texas before the Civil War had her cattle raids. Mexicans, Indians ran off cattle. And the white raider developed. You had him when you were trail drivin' the herds up to Dodge an' Abilene. But what did that ever amount to? Hardly any more than the beef every cattle outfit appro-

14

priates wherever it happens to camp. We lose some cattle heah, so the boys say, but not a tenth — not a hundredth of the yearly increase."

"Right, Kurnel, so far as you go," drawled the foreman. "Listen, boss, an' I'll tell you how I figger. Durin' the last year a lot of tight-lipped, cold-eyed strangers have rode into New Mexico. Mebbe you haven't seen this much. But I have talked with men who have seen it an' who didn't like it. Jesse Chisum is one. Thet old Texan with his Jingle-bob brand has a far eye fer everythin' aboot cattle. If you rode to San Marcos or Fort Union or Sumner, or over Pecos way to Roswell an' Lincoln, you'd shore get a hunch. Wyomin', Nebraska, West Kansas, East Colorado, an' of course Texas, air sendin' a good many riders oot our way. Riders thet don't give names an' don't ask questions an' don't take kind to curious Westerners! Some of these may be what you called the cowboys — salt of the earth — but the most of them air bad. Thet is to say hawse-thieves, rustlers, bandits, desperadoes, the genuine bad men an' genuine four-flushers, ootlaws, all of them, an' thet ain't countin' the riff-raff from the East an' the ruined rebels from the South."

"Britt, I'm not so blind as you think," protested Colonel Ripple. "I've noticed somethin' of what you say. However only what might be expected with this westward movement."

"It's more than might be expected. New Mexico is as wild as Texas west of the Pecos. There is no law, except the law of the six-shooter. It has

15

a bad reputation. Please observe, Kurnel, thet most of these pioneers keep right on travellin'. New Mexico will be the last of the states frontin' on the Great Plains thet will be settled. This in spite of the finest grazin' lands in the West. . . . Wal, heah is what's goin' to happen. Cattlemen like you an' Chisum, followin' in the footsteps of Maxwell an' St. Vrain, air goin' to grow powerful rich in cattle. In three years the Ripple brand will show on the sides of eighty thousand haid of cows. Think of thet! An' thet ain't countin' what you sell. Wal, this will give rise to such rustlin' of cattle as was never dreamed of before on the ranges. It is inevitable. It will last ten years or more. You see this government buyin' of beef fer Indians on the reservations, an' thousands more thet must be counted in as time goes on, will furnish a market thet rustlers cain't resist an' cattlemen cain't stop fer a long time. Then there's the railroads. It ain't no hell of a drive to Dodge from heah or Las Animas either. The longer the drive the shorer the market. . . . An' there it is, Ripple, all in a nutshell."

"So help me heaven, you are right!" ejaculated the rancher, in concern. "Hey-day of the rustler! . . . Britt, with your usual perspicuity you have seen ahead to an unprecedented and dubious future for the cattleman who operates on a large scale. . . . All right, suh! If you see that clearly you will be equal to meetin' such a situation when it comes. I'll never see it, worse luck. But Holly will be in the thick of it — perhaps unmarried. That

16

freezes me inside. . . . Britt, you've been Texas Ranger and Trail Driver, both of which callings, peculiar to the great Lone Star State, should fit you to deal with bad men at a bad time. You have always been a genius handlin' cowboys. . . . How do you aim to meet this situation?"

"Wal, I'll admit thet's been a stumper," replied Britt, with a dry laugh.

It was something he had pondered over during many a lonely ride on the range and many an hour in the darkness of the bunkhouse while the wind moaned in the cedar trees outside.

Britt gazed thoughtfully down over the green-gray terraces to the far ribbon of silver meandering across the plains to blue obscurity, and he knew that that scene was good, always soothing and strengthening to the lover of the open. He always looked to this southward scene when the one to the westward had given rise, as now, to a troubled mind. He loved the spur of cedared ground from which this unparalleled view lay open, and likewise he loved the gray escarpment walls as they widened and heightened toward the plain below, and the aloof mesas and the sandy arroyos and the dark canyons, and all that wild and rugged beauty which at length softened into the vast blue prairie. But even if this eastern steppe of New Mexico had not been inspiring and all-satisfying, Britt would have loved it for Holly Ripple's sake.

When he looked back at the cattle empire, however, he was actuated by mingled feelings of pride, of achievement, of dismay, and over all a sense of fatality in the sublime reach and sweep of the range. The insulating mountains might temper the winter winds and send down never-failing streams upon the grazing lands, and protect the rich bunch-grass and gamma-grass which were so fattening for the herds, but no rock walls could ever keep out the parasites of the rangeland. For a cattleman that scene had a pastoral and intimate beauty wholly dissociated from the wilder one to the south. A hundred thousand cattle dotted the endless pastures. A winding yellow road led down to San Marcos, a green circle of foliage from which the white and gray houses of the town gleamed in the spring sunlight. Far across and leagues away showed the dark patch that was Fort Union. Lincoln was a tiny speck in the distance. But northward the red spot which marked Santa Fe shone plainly over a hundred miles away. With its color and legend of three centuries of occupancy by the dons and padres it had power to cover this broad land with the drowsy languorous atmosphere of the Spaniards.

But all that had only a momentary charm for Britt. With his hawk-eyes he was seeing the deeds of the day at hand. San Marcos would lose the sleepy tenor of its way. The saloon, the dance-hall, the gambling den would soon ring with the revelry attendant upon the payday of the cowhand. Half-nude girls with pretty faces and shadowy eyes and hollow laughs would waylay the range-rider upon his infrequent visit to town. Pale-visaged and thin-lipped gamblers, with their broadcloth frockcoats and wide brimmed, flat-crowned hats, would shuffle their cards with marvelous dexterity of long, slim, white hands. And groups of dark-garbed, dark-horsed riders, proceeding in close formation, with something inimical about them, would pass up the wide street. The bark of six-shooters would become too common to attract interest, except when the town flocked out to see some gunman forced to draw upon a drunken, notoriety-seeking cowboy, or when the flint and steel of real killers struck sparks face to face.

Britt saw the raw wildness of Hays City, Dodge and Abilene enacted on a smaller scale, yet with an equal lawlessness. There might not ever be another Wild Bill Hickok, at whose vested star so many desperadoes and outlaws had shot vainly and too late. But there surely would rise to fame emulators of Buck Duane and King Fisher and Wess Hardin and Ben Thompson, those famed and infamous Texas exponents of the draw. And perhaps there might arise one who would dwarf the achievements of any of this quartet. And lastly Britt saw, with something of a grim and sardonic humor, dark slack forms of men, terribly suggestive swinging from the cottonwoods in the moonlight.

"Wal, Kurnel," he said, finally, "I reckon there's only one way to meet what's comin'. An' it is to scour the country fer the damndest ootfit of cowboys thet can possibly be found."

"Britt, the outfit you're runnin' now are far from bein' lambs. I could name half a dozen others that

19

are bad. But not one of them could buck such a rustler gang as you expect to develop heah on this range. . . . I don't quite grasp what you mean by damndest."

"I shore know, boss, an' the idee grips me. Reckon I've pondered over it a good deal. I want riders so hard an' wild thet they cain't hold a job fer long. Fact is, Kurnel, I never hired a cowboy thet I couldn't have kept on, if I'd stood fer his tricks. My idee is to pick my men — I've a few in mind now — an' make this job so attractive thet they'd stick. Shore I'd have to stand fer hell itself. But I could do it."

"Britt, I agree you can handle cows and men. Your idea is great. There's only one drawback. My daughter. Think of that young girl, lovely, like an unfoldin' rose, innocent, full of fire and joy, as mistress of the hardest outfit of cowboys ever thrown together in the West. . . . My God, Britt — think of it!"

"I been thinkin'. It'd been better fer us, an' Holly, too, if she hadn't had them nine years in school. But thet cain't be helped now. If you are keen to have Holly live her life oot heah, keep up the great house of Ripple, thet's the way to do it — an' the only way."

"Would you risk it, if Holly was your child?" queried the rancher, hoarsely.

"I shore would. Holly is no ordinary girl. She will rise to the occasion. . . . Run yore herd an' yore house — wal, by thunder! I'll bet on her!"

"She shall choose," shot out Colonel Ripple,

strung with emotion. "We will tell her the truth and let her decide. I have been tortured between the devil and the deep sea. I want her to live here. Yet if she prefers San Antonio or New Orleans, I shall not let her see my disappointment."

"Boss, you'll shore never be disappointed in Holly. I reckon, seein' how het up you air, thet we'd better call her oot an' get it over. But I'd rather face a bunch of ridin' Comanches."

"*Holly!*" called the Colonel, his rich voice ringing.

As there was no answer from the house, Britt arose to go in search of the girl. All the rooms in the front of the wonderful old Spanish mansion opened out on the arched porch. Britt went through the wide hall to the patio, where his spurs clinked musically upon the flagstones. But the girl was not to be found near the sunny fountain, or among the roses, or in the hammock under the dense canopy of vines. Britt went into the living-room, and halted a moment in the shadowed light. Then from the porch came a gay contralto voice. He went out, lagging a little.

Holly stood beside her father's chair. And Britt had a tingling recurrence of the emotion the girl had roused in him when he saw her first after her arrival from New Orleans: a strange yearning to be young again, to be the very flower of fine, noble manhood, handsome, gifted, rich, worthy.

"Howdy, Holly," he drawled. "I was oot lookin' fer you."

"You old hawk-nosed, hawk-eyed devil! What

have you been putting into Dad's head?"

Britt laughed and found himself forthwith. Holly Ripple had a regal air. She looked her aristocratic Spanish lineage. Her great dark eyes and her exquisitely pale skin came to her from the Castilian Valverdes. But Britt had only to hear her to know that she was American, and Lee Ripple's daughter, and that she belonged to the West.

"Lass, I reckon it's been yore Dad puttin' things into my haid," replied Britt, and resumed his comfortable seat.

"You both look like owls," said the girl, and she slid on to the arm of her father's chair.

"Holly, dear, it's only fair that you learn at once the serious side of your home-comin'," replied the Colonel.

"Serious?" she asked, with a puzzled smile.

"Indeed it is. Back me up, Britt."

"Wal, lass, I reckon it's nothin' to make you feel bad," said Britt, feeling his way and meeting squarely those compelling eyes. "You're oot West now. You've been heah three days. An' it's just sense to tell you pronto what we air up against."

"Ah, I see," Holly rejoined, soberly. "Very well. Tell me. I left Don Carlos' Rancho a child and I have come back a woman."

"Holly, look down there," spoke up her father, pointing to the grazing lands below. "All those black dots are cattle. Thousands of cattle. They are mine. And all I have to hold them is a wavy brand from shoulder to flank. A ripple! . . . Times are changin'. We expect the wildest years this sec-

22

tion of the West has ever known. When we came back from Santone by stage, you saw Indians, soldiers, cowboys, pioneers, rough men galore. You saw buffalo by the million, and cattle and horses almost as many. In short, you rode across Texas and you saw wild life. . . . But nothin', my daughter, compared to what you will see heah in New Mexico the next decade — if you stay."

"*If I stay?*" she echoed, with a curious intentness.

"Yes. Because I meant it to be a matter of your own choice," he went on, swiftly. "Rustlers — that is the western name for cattle-thieves — and a horde of hardened men of differin' types will ride into New Mexico. There will be fightin', Holly. . . . Now, for instance, suppose I happened to be shot. What —"

"Oh, Dad!" she cried, poignantly.

"Holly, the chance is remote, but it might happen. Suppose I were shot by rustlers. What would you do?"

"Do! — I'd hang every rustler in this country," exclaimed the girl hotly.

Britt met the piercing eyes of the rancher. Holly Ripple had answered to the subtle call of the Texan.

"All right," went on Ripple, a little huskily. "Now, say for example that I — I didn't get shot, but just passed — on, you know. . . . Died. . . . Holly, listen. That, too, might happen. It's natural. I'm gettin' on in years and I've led a strenuous life. . . . Well, suppose that happened.

23

. . . Would you want to stay on heah at Don Carlos' Rancho?"

"Yes, Dad," she answered quietly.

"But, listen, child. You will have wealth. You — you could go to your mother's people. I have no near relatives, but those I have would welcome my daughter. . . . Holly, the time has come to make your choice."

"It was made — long ago. I hate cities. I don't care for crowds — or relatives, either. I was cooped up in school. I am free now — *free!* . . . I was unhappy there — I love it here. . . . Dad, I will never, never leave."

Britt saw the long, dusky lashes close over tear-filled eyes. Ripple bent over to kiss the lustrous dark hair. Under his tan a pallor showed and his jaw quivered. Britt turned away to gaze down the valley. Holly had seen through her father's attempt to disguise the truth.

"Then — that is your choice — Holly?" the rancher resumed, presently.

"Dad, there never was any choice. There was only — home. My West! I have never forgotten a single thing."

"My beloved — I am ashamed," returned the Colonel, with agitation. "I should have known you would be like Carlotta. I imagined you might. . . . Well, never mind what, since it can never be. . . . Holly, in the days to come you will learn how I run my ranch — how I keep *open* house for all. Never have I turned away anyone from Don Carlos' Rancho. Indians, outlaws, wanderers, travellers, all have been welcome heah. That is why no white or red hand has ever been against me yet. . . . When the time comes, Holly, will you preserve my open hand to all?"

"I will, Dad."

Ripple clasped her in a close embrace, then turned a working visage and beaming eye upon his foreman.

"Britt, you old rebel, you know my child. And I'm thankin' God that when I have to go you will look after her. . . . There, Holly. Our serious talk is over."

"Not yet, Dad," she murmured. "I have my turn. There are some questions I want to ask you."

"Ah! — Fire away, daughter," he replied, gayly, but it was easy for Britt to see his perturbation.

"Dad, I know hardly a word of Spanish," said Holly, softly, with her eyes downcast. "It was forbidden me at school. I did not realize until I got home. Your Mexicans speak Spanish to me. The living-room I remembered so well has all been done over, refurnished. The beautiful rooms you have given me — the same. Everything new, beautiful, costly. But not a trace of Spanish color or design."

"Holly, that is easy to explain," returned her father, frankly. "I wanted you to be American. That is why I kept you away at school so many years. If I had brought you up heah, in the Spanish environment which pertained until recently, you would have been all Valverde. I was not a Catholic. I respected your mother's religion, but I did not

25

want you to have it. I wanted you to be American in education, creed, manner and spirit."

"Dad, was that any reflection upon Don Carlos Valverde?" queried Holly, with proud, dark eyes upon him. There was something passionate and alien in her that could never be wholly eradicated. And Britt, who loved her as his own, felt glad this was so.

"No. I had a high regard for Don Carlos, and these early Spanish families. Both Kit Carson and Lucien Maxwell married into them."

"Were you ashamed of my — mother?"

"Absolutely no, my child. I was proud of her beauty and quality."

"Did you love her?"

"Holly, I think I may say yes with an honest heart. But, dear, when I met Carlotta I was a wild young Texan, a gay blade in love with every pretty face I saw. It is hard to confess to you that when I became infatuated with your mother, I did not go to Don Carlos honorably and ask for her hand. I knew only too well that he would have raged and thrown me out. Carlotta was hardly more than fifteen. . . . I — I ran off with her. But I married her in San Antonio. As I grew to love her more I regretted havin' been the cause of estrangement between Carlotta and Don Carlos. She was an only child. In time he forgave her. You were born soon after that. Then followed the happiest years of our lives. Don Carlos left Carlotta this ranch. After the war I drove a cattle herd up from Texas, and have prospered ever since."

26

Britt liked that frank confession of the Colonel's, and when he saw Holly's reaction he thought it was well. If there had ever been any brooding doubts in the girl's mind, they were dispelled then and forever. She embraced her father.

"Thank you, Dad," she whispered. "It's all right now — except you mustn't frighten me again."

The moment seemed sweet and far-reaching for Britt. All was well that ended well. This home-coming of Holly Ripple had been fraught with dismay as well as dread. She had been an unknown factor. But now the old ranger revelled in the faith he had doggedly held in the girl he himself had named.

"Lass, I never told you how I come to call you Holly," he said, as the girl sat up again, to smile with wet eyes. "I had a sweetheart once an' thet was her name."

"Sweetheart? — Cappy, you used to call me that when I was little. I'm horribly jealous. What was she like? Did you — run off with her as Dad did with my mother? Please tell me."

"Some day," replied Britt, rising, and he patted the glossy head. "Kurnel, I've seen a few happier days than this, far away an' long ago. But not many. Shore you will be long heah with us. What fun you'll have teachin' this big-eyed lass to handle hawses, to shoot an' rope, to run the cowboy ootfits ragged, to be mistress of this great house an' do honor to yore name! An' I — wal, I'll go ahaid with my plans."

"Plans! What plans, Cappy?" queried the girl.

"You began that speech sadly. You grew really eloquent. Then you end with that hawk-eye glinting and with news of plans. If I am to become mistress of Don Carlos' Rancho, I shall be your boss. Oh, what a dance I'll lead you! . . . But come, tell me. Do your plans include a party to celebrate my return?"

"Holly, that shall be my job," interrupted her father. "I will give such a party as was never seen heah in New Mexico. And every year thereafter, on the anniversary of that date, you must repeat it."

"Oh, glorious!" she cried, rapturously. "My first party."

"Britt, bring on your wild outfits!" sang the Colonel, keen and glad-eyed. "Bring on your riders, rangers, cowboys, outlaws, desperadoes, gunmen, and killers! Don Carlos' Rancho shall flourish many a year!"

"Wild outfits! — Cowboys — desperadoes — killers?" echoed Holly, mystified, her great eyes like dark, glowing stars.

"Holly, it is Britt's plan to surround you with the wildest and most dangerous outfit of men ever gathered on a western ranch," announced the Colonel.

"Oh-h! — But why?"

"Wal, lass, the idee is to save you an' yore cattle when the times grow bad," interposed Britt.

"How perfectly wonderful! . . . Don Carlos' Rancho! Holly Ripple's outfit! . . . Dad, I shall fall in love with every single one of them. That

28

is the penalty you must suffer for penning me up with books. Nine long years! And I was born on the range! . . . Cappy Britt, henceforth Old Hawkeye, you will need your keen sight. Bring on your wild cowboys!"

Britt paced his slow, clinking way down the flowered path toward the bunkhouse. Hard upon his excitation followed a pensive sadness. Only he realized what lay in store for Holly Ripple. Let her enjoy the girlish freedom she had been denied. Let her ride and laugh while her father was with her and the days burned with all the glamour of a New Mexican summer. For the shadow on the horizon would soon loom into dark groups of horsemen, strange, silent, formidable; and the languorous serenity of Don Carlos' Rancho would be gone.

CHAPTER 2

Two eventful and fast-flying years later, almost to the day, Cap Britt sat his horse on the high slope above the mouth of *Paso del Muerte,* and with grim, bitter revolt in his heart, forced himself to admit that the evil times of his prophecy had come.

"They been comin' ever since the Kurnel died," he muttered darkly. "Slow but shore! . . . Wal, by Gawd, I didn't get my hard ootfit none too soon."

Britt gazed down across the eight miles of rolling gray rangeland, and on up the long slope to Don Carlos' Rancho, standing like a picturesque fort, red and green on the high divide between the two great valleys. Holly Ripple was there on the porch, no doubt at this very moment with glass levelled upon him. It was that powerful glass which had brought about the present critical situation. He had a string of several hundred horses ranging up *Paso del Muerte,* among which were a number of the fine blooded Ripple stock. And the day before Britt had sent three of his riders over there to report on this drove of horses. They had not returned. For riders to lie out a night or several nights was nothing for the foreman to concern

30

himself about. But early that morning Britt had taken a sweep of the range with the glass. And he had picked out one of those dark compact bunches of horsemen that were no longer rare on the range. They had disappeared up the pass. If they were not rustlers they were horse-thieves, a distinction with a difference. Holly Ripple had been unconcerned about the increasing loss of cattle, but highly indignant at the stealing of some of her thoroughbreds. Britt's big outfit of cowboys was scattered all over the range for that day on various jobs. When he rode down at Holly's order he expected to pick up some of the cowboys at White Pool; at least Stinger, Beef Talman, and Jim, who should have been there. But they were not there. Whereupon Britt had climbed the slope to the pass alone.

Dobe Cabin, in a grove of green and white aspen trees, lay beneath Britt in the mouth of the wide canyon. A substantial fence of peeled poles stretched from slope to slope. That bunch of riders who had roused the foreman's suspicions had left the big gate open. Presently Britt espied dust clouds far up the winding pass, and soon after that a line of horses coming at a jogtrot. Britt waited until a number of dark riders on dark horses appeared; and then he dated the war on the Ripple range from that moment.

"Wal, it had to come, so why not right now?" he soliloquized, somberly, and headed his mount down the slope. Arriving at the fence he got off his horse and closing the big gate he awaited developments with watchful vigilance and active mind. Britt scanned the slopes for some of his riders. He was going to need them presently. Horses and cattle grazed below, and under the mesa a few shaggy black buffalo had strayed up from the south. Britt was hard put to it to decide whether to ambush the raiders or meet them out in the open. In the former case he was pretty sure to be shot in a brush with eight or ten desperate men, but in the latter there was a chance that wit and nerve might serve him better. The question of letting these riders go unchallenged did not occur to the old Texas Ranger.

Dobe Cabin had been the home of a settler who had been murdered by Utes. A fine stream of water babbled down out of the pass; the aspens were out in their spring dress of fresh green, every leaf quivering in the still air; white-rumped antelope edged up the slope; wild turkeys were gobbling from a lofty wooded bench. Britt recalled the legend of *Paso del Muerte*, which concerned the massacre of some Spaniards by Apaches a century and more ago. It might have happened on a beautiful, serene, sunny New Mexico morning such as this. And he had a premonition that those bygone days of the old *padres* had been tame to those that were still to come.

Britt heard the bony crack of unshod hoofs on the rocks beyond the grove of aspens. Then gleams of brown and gray and black showed through the leaves. Soon horses appeared slipping leisurely between the slim white tree-trunks. Some splashed

32

into the brook to drink while others trotted out of the grove into the sunlight. The foremost shot up long ears and halted with snorts. Others coming from behind forced them onward. Presently the band, sighting and scenting Britt, sheered to one side, and trooped to the left. Stragglers followed to join the main bunch.

The foreman climbed up on the high fence and sat on the top pole next to the gate. Shrill whistles from the driven animals would certainly acquaint the raiders that the advance had been halted. Britt counted two score and more of horses that had been selected from the stock by men who knew horses. These were all young, notable for thoroughbred points and the fact that they were unbranded.

"Cuss the luck!" growled Britt. "Another showdown. Stock we haven't time to brand is just lost. Thet's all. If I had twice as many cowboys I couldn't put an iron on all the colts an' calves thet belong to us."

The horses stopped at the fence, stood head on for a while, and then began to graze toward the slope. Britt saw the riders before they discovered him. There were eight in sight. He rather inclined to the opinion that more were yet to come. Voices came clearly to him.

"Bill, somethin' turned the dogies."

"Gate closed."

"Look thar!"

"Who'n hell's thet?"

After a trenchant pause one of the riders answered: "Thet's Cap Britt, foreman of the Ripple outfit."

Britt recognized that surly voice as belonging to Mugg Dillon, one of his cowboys.

"Ride ahead — you," ordered one of the group, sharply. "Take a peek in thet cabin."

Dillon rode on out of the aspens and up to the open door of the cabin. Peering in he called gruffly: "Nobody hyar."

Then the riders advanced, separating in a manner which told the Texan much; and in this formation they rode to within a hundred paces of the fence. Dillon fell in behind them. Britt's swift eye took in many significant points. These men were superbly mounted on dark bays and blacks. They were heavily armed. A harder looking gang Britt had not seen on the range. Whatever else they were, they surely were cowmen. Britt needed only a glance to link the lithe, easily poised riders, all evincing the incomparable saddle-seat of cowboys, to the stone-faced, matured type of range-rustler and horse-thief.

"Hyar, Dillon," rasped the leader, a swarthy man whose features were vague in the shadow of a wide sombrero. The rider called made haste to get out in front. "Come on an' introduce me to your boss."

"Easy, Bill," cracked a dry voice from the line. "Thet hombre was a Texas Ranger."

Warily the leader urged his horse all of fifty steps toward the fence. Dillon lined up beside him. At this distance Britt gathered from the cowboy's ashen face that he was in a predicament from which there seemed to be no escape. Britt had never seen this man Bill. He had brawny shoulders and unkempt hair low on his thick neck. The foreman could catch only a gleam of rapacious eyes.

"Dillon, is this your boss?" he queried, gruffly, without looking at the cowboy.

"Yes."

"Howdy, Britt."

"Howdy, yoreself," rejoined Britt, curtly.

"Enjoyin' the scenery roundabout?" went on Bill, sarcastically.

"Not particular, leastways not in front."

"Reckon you shut the gate on us."

"Wal, it's our gate."

"You can open it pronto."

The foreman vented a short dry laugh, but vouchsafed no other answer.

"What's the idee, Britt?" went on the raider.

"I seen a bunch of our hawses comin' an' I didn't want them to get out."

"Your hosses? — How you goin' to prove thet? They ain't branded."

"Wal, I reckon I cain't prove it. But my ootfit knows 'em an' they'll be comin' pronto."

"Hell you say," retorted Bill, flashing a plainsman's gaze across the range. "Only one hossman in sight."

"Mugg, where'd you leave Stinger an' Brazos Keene?" inquired Britt, coldly.

"Boss, we left Stinger fer dead. An' the last I seen of Brazos he was ridin' hell-bent fer leather up the pass," replied the cowboy, hurriedly.

Dillon had been the last rider taken on by Britt for the Ripple outfit, and he was an unknown and doubtful quality. Britt knew his status would be defined shortly.

"Mugg, how come you're ridin' with these gents?" drawled the foreman.

"I — he . . . boss, I jest had — to," burst out Dillon, disconnectedly. He was not yet old enough at this game to face death coolly from two sides. Britt knew he was guilty.

"Bah!" ejaculated the raider, scornfully, and with a back sweep of his gloved left hand he struck Dillon from his saddle. The cowboy fell, and bounded up hatless, a cornered wolf. His horse plunged away dragging the bridle. "Britt, save me the trouble of borin' the yellow pup."

"Mugg, I reckon I wouldn't bore you for double-crossin' me," drawled Britt, ponderingly. "But these air Miss Holly's hawses — an' some she puts store in. What air Brazos an' Jim goin' to do aboot this deal?"

"Britt," interposed the raider, "I don't mind tellin' you thet Brazos took a flyin' shot at Dillon an' creased him, as you can see if you look close."

"Cowboy, fork yore hawse an' ride," said Britt, contemptuously, after verifying the raider's statement. Dillon bent over to pick up his sombrero.

"Suits me," said Bill, laconically. "But fust open thet gate."

Dillon had no choice but to comply and Britt

36

likewise had no choice but to sit on the fence and take this humiliating procedure. He had himself well in hand, though an unwonted heat boiled beneath his skin. Britt knew his job. His life was worth more to Holly Ripple than that of this insolent raider, and all his men. Nevertheless it galled the Texan to withhold his hand.

"Thet feller's comin' fast," spoke up the raider after Dillon had opened the gate.

Britt did not turn, but he had an uneasy premonition. Certainly no single rider in his outfit would be bearing swiftly down upon that doubtful group.

At this Britt wheeled so quickly as nearly to lose his seat on the fence. His sudden dread was verified. Scarcely two hundred paces distant came a black clean-limbed racer with Holly Ripple in the saddle. "Good Gawd!" groaned the foreman, in sudden distraction. Then, cupping his hands round his lips he bellowed stentorianly: *Holly, turn back! Hawse-thieves!*

She did not hear, however, or did not heed, but came up swiftly, a striking figure on the racer.

"Britt, you ain't flatterin', but I'll pass it over," remarked Bill, tersely.

In what seemed only a moment, and one fraught with acute concern and uncertainty for Britt, the fleet-footed black slowed down and plunged to a gravel-scattering halt at the gate. Britt had seen his young mistress many times to thrilling advantage, but never like this. She had not taken time to don her riding-garb, yet she sat her saddle astride, as the black, silver-mounted *chaperejos* proved. A thin jacket, buttoned tight, emphasized the slender voluptuousness of her form, as did the red spots in her cheeks the singular creamy whiteness of her beautiful face. Magnificent eyes, black as the wing of a raven, blazed levelly out upon the men. This was the first direct contact of Don Carlos' granddaughter with the riff-raff of the ranges.

"Whoa, Stonewall. Steady," she called to the spirited prancing horse, and she raked his flanks with her spurs. "Britt, is it — a raid?" she queried, pantingly.

"Wal, this gent heah contests our ownership of these hawses," drawled the foreman, with a mildness he was far from feeling.

Holly rode inside the fence toward the raider chief.

"Dillon, close the gate," she ordered, and the cowboy obeyed with no less alacrity than when he had opened it.

"I am Holly Ripple."

Bill awkwardly doffed his sombrero, exposing a lean head of dark hair streaked with gray, a swarthy face which, but for its curious awe and smile, would have been a seamed bronze cast of evil.

"Howdy, Lady of Don Carlos' Rancho. I sure am glad to meet you," he replied. He appeared dazzled, not by the pride of that little regal head or the imperious contralto voice, but by the ravishing charm of this descendant of the dons.

"Who are you?" she asked.

"Bill Heaver, at your service, Miss."

"What are you?"

"I reckon I'm a little of all pertainin' to the range," he replied, with a broad grin. He had been momentarily impressed by her fearlessness, but that had passed.

"Were you driving these horses?"

"I sure was."

"They belong to me."

"You can't prove thet, Lady. Not by unbranded stock on this range."

"Yes, I can. At least I can prove I own some of them. . . . I've ridden that roan. I know that bay. . . . That sorrel is two years old. There's a scar on his left flank where the cowboys started to brand him and I stopped them. . . . The pinto there I called Paint-brush. Most of these horses have been in the corrals at the ranch. I know them. I never forget a horse I've looked at closely."

"Well, Lady, all thet makes no difference. They're not wearin' a brand. Thet's all a hoss-dealer reckons with."

Heaver replaced his sombrero, hiding the telltale ghoulish eyes. But not before Britt had caught the birth of a hot glint, like a spark. The raider had succumbed to Holly's allure. It was an old story to Britt, though this man was the first desperado to face Holly with it. Britt's hand slipped to his gun. If driven far he would kill Heaver, and any other of the band that threatened, and then depend upon intimidating the rest. All of the raiders had ridden up close, to surround the principals in a half circle against the fence. It was here that Britt discovered the presence of two new riders, one of whom, hanging a little back, struck him as somehow remarkable among these conspicuously formidable men. But Britt had only time for a glance, as Heaver was urging his horse toward Holly's. What was the hardened lout up to? Holly had not sensed any peril in the moment. She had expressed anger at this deliberate theft of her horses, but no other emotion. Britt knew to his sorrow that the girl had never yet felt fear. This situation, however, was deplorable, and might easily lead to a catastrophe. Already it had passed out of Britt's control. If Heaver grew ugly and answered to the leap of passion, Britt must take a desperate chance, and he grew cold and steely at the certainty of its enaction.

"So you're the famous Holly Ripple?" queried Heaver, with a subtle voicing of his change to something intimately personal. Holly caught it, and was reining her horse aside when the raider stretched out a long arm and caught her bridle near the bit. "Hold on, my proud *Señorita*. Suppose you come in the cabin with me where we can have a little private confab about these hosses."

"You insolent ruffian! Let go that bridle." Holly supplemented her sharp words by lashing down with her quirt. The leather thongs cracked on Heaver's bare wrist. Cursing, he let go in a hurry.

"You half-breed wench! I'll —"

"Heaver, you fool! Look out for Britt!" interrupted the cool dry voice of the raider's subordinate.

"Aw, to hell with him! You watch him, Covell. If he winks, bore him."

Before Holly could get out of his reach, the raider seized her arm so fiercely that he almost unseated her. The red spots left her cheeks. Suddenly Holly appeared to realize the actuality of brutal affront, if not real peril. She made no move to wrench free.

"What do you mean?" she demanded, with incredulous amazement.

"For two-bits I'd pack you off to the mountains," he answered, thickly.

"You — wouldn't dare!" gasped Holly, shocked out of her poise.

"The hell I wouldn't! — But I'll let you off easy. . . . With a little lovin'! Thet proud white face will go red from rubbin' stiff whiskers. Haw! Haw! . . . Come on. We're goin' in the cabin."

"No!" she rang out.

One powerful pull dragged Holly out of her saddle on to Heaver's hip, but her far foot caught in her stirrup.

"Britt, stop him!" she cried, struggling frantically. The horses began to plunge.

In one leap Britt cleared the space between him and Dillon. He snatched the cowboy's gun from its holster.

"Open the gate," he hissed, and with two guns extended low he wheeled to take his only chance.

Heaver had hold of the girl and her bridle as well. The black was rearing, and the raider's horse plunging. Heaver was at a great disadvantage in trying to hold Holly and draw her horse close so he could release her foot from the stirrup. The action of the horses and Holly's furious struggle to free herself prevented Britt from getting in a shot at the outset of this fracas. He dared not fire for two reasons — fear of hitting Holly, and realization that if he killed Heaver while her foot was caught she would fall and be dragged. Suddenly Holly's foot came free. The raider swung her clear, evidently oblivious to Britt's rising gun. But as Britt had three horses between him and Covell he appeared momentarily protected from that quarter.

"Stop!"

A piercing command halted Heaver. It even shunted Britt for an instant from his deadly intent. Then from behind Britt and to one side a horse plunged in with screeching iron hoofs that sent sheets of gravel flying. Before he slid to a halt his rider leaped clear and with a single bound confronted Heaver and his men. The rowels of his long spurs kept up a whirling tinkle. This member of Heaver's band was the striking newcomer whom Britt had glimpsed hanging in the background.

"Frayne!" expostulated the raider, with a rising inflection of voice that had vast significance for Britt. He knew men. For twenty years he had observed and heard desperate characters of the frontier in meetings that were critical.

"Let her go," came the command, in icy staccato notes.

"Wh-what?" stammered the raider chief, his swarthy face burning dark red.

"Heaver, you heard me!" Frayne's lithe form sank perceptibly, but even more significant were the quivering, claw-like hands that lowered as perceptibly over the big blue guns sheathed low on his thighs.

"My Gawd — Man! — What's eatin' you?" yelled Heaver, hoarsely, and his red visage turned a dirty white. He lowered Holly to the ground and dropped her bridle. Hurriedly she snatched it up and dragged the black away out through the gate, where she mounted.

Heaver leaned forward, shoving his huge sombrero back with nervous hand, showing his hard gray face beaded with sweat.

"Frayne, you buckin' me?"

"What's the sense of more talk?" queried the other, derisively.

"But talkin' is on the cairds," went on the raider, hoarsely, his voice losing its tremble for a gathering might of rage. "This hyar is the second time you've bucked agin me. I'll allow you had some reason, leastways this time. But I was only tryin' to scare the gurl."

"Liar!"

"Well, at that I might have hugged an' kissed her till she swallowed her high an' mighty talk. . . . What was it to you, anyway? I've seen before you was kinda touchy about wimmen. Holly Rip-

43

ple sort of got you, huh, the pretty black-eyed hussy of a half-breed?"

"Shut up, you dirty foul-mouthed dog! Miss Ripple is a lady, which is something you can't appreciate. Leave her out of this."

"Hellsfire! . . . Frayne, I'll allow fer your stand, if you're so testy over a gurl. But I let her off. An' you'll lay off more insultin' talk — or we're through."

"Heaver, you're dense. When I called you we were through."

"Aha, we air, eh? All right. It's damn good riddance," fumed the leader.

"You're not rid of me yet."

Uncertainty ceased for Heaver. He changed again, not subtly, but with sudden hard realization that the breach was irremediable and something dire hung in the balance. Turning to Covell he cursed him roundly: "————— ! This comes of your takin' on men of his lone wolf stripe. I *told* you. . . . An' now, —— you! Show yellow or come in!"

Britt wrenched his gaze from the infuriated Heaver to the man who had opposed him so strangely. In a flash then he caught the drift of events. This Frayne loomed as inevitable as destiny. Seasoned as Britt was, he felt galvanized through with the man's terrible presence. Among hordes of Westerners, desperadoes, outlaws, he would have been recognized then as one of the few. He epitomized the raw wild spirit of the frontier. His lips curled in a snarl, his white teeth

44

gleamed, his eyes were slits of gray fire. All his features combined to express an appalling power. And Britt had seen that power expended by more than one implacable and unquenchable killer.

"Frayne — I savvy," choked out the raider chief, in hoarse passion. "But why you forcin' me?"

"I don't trail with your kind," replied Frayne, deliberately. "You lied, same as you lied on the other deal. . . . I didn't like the way you worked on Dillon to make him betray his outfit. We rode out here to steal a bunch of unbranded horses. But that wasn't enough. When chance threw Miss Ripple in your way, out bristled the dirty dog in you. . . . You insulted her, pawed her off her horse. . . . You would have carried her off . . . leaving your men to fight this Texan. You'd have made your men accomplices in a crime that Westerners never forgive. You'd have put that stigma on *me*. . . . Now, Bill Heaver, have I made myself perfectly clear?"

"Per-fickly — clear — Frayne," returned Heaver, haltingly. He drew a long deep breath that whistled with the intake. Then blood and arm and voice leaped simultaneously. "*Covell!* Bore him, men!"

Britt's sight was not swift enough to catch Frayne's draw. But there the big blue guns were, spouting red behind puffs of smoke. Then followed the crashes, almost together. Covell's gun was out and half up when it exploded. But his face was fiercely blank and he was swaying backward when

45

his gun went off. Heaver sagged in the saddle as his horse lunged away, to unseat him and throw him heavily. Then Covell fell. Neither man moved a muscle. Both had been dead before they struck the ground.

The other horses were hard to control. Iron arms dragged at their heads. Frayne had the riders covered. Perhaps the action of the horses favored Frayne in his intimidation of these men. None of them drew. As their mounts were pulled to a standstill Britt lined up beside Frayne with his two guns ready. The tension relaxed.

"You fellars ride. Pronto!" called Britt, seizing the moment.

Frayne's left gun took a slight suggestive swerve toward the gate. As one man the raiders spurred their horses, almost running down the pale-faced Dillon, and galloped away toward San Marcos.

"Fork yore hawse, Mugg," called Britt. "This range won't be healthy fer you heahafter. You shore got off easy. Take yore gun."

While Dillon hurried to leap astride Britt ran out the gate to where Holly hunched stiff over her pommel. The marble whiteness of her face, the dark fading horror of her dilated eyes, the palpitating of her heart attested to the strain she had come through.

"Holly, it's all over," said Britt, fervently, as he grasped the gauntleted hand that shook on her knee. "Brace up. We're shore lucky. Mebbe I won't scold you good when we get home!"

"He drove — the others away," she panted, lifting her head to sweep the range with flashing glance.

"Wal, I sort of snicker to say he did," drawled Britt, talking to ease the contraction of his throat.

"That devil — and the other man, Covell . . . dead?"

"Daid? — I reckon they air."

"He killed them for me?"

"Holly, lass, it shore wasn't fer anyone else. . . . Come oot of it now. You had nerve. Don't collapse now after it's all over."

"He saved me — from God only knows what," she whispered in awe.

"Yes, he did, Holly. I cain't gainsay thet. I'd had no show on earth if he had sided with Heaver. Shore I'd have killed Heaver, an' then more of them. But I'd have got mine pronto. An' thet'd left you at their mercy. . . . Holly, fer Gawd's sake let this be a lesson to you."

"I must thank him — talk to him. . . . Go back, Britt. Give me a few moments. Then bring him to me."

Britt sometimes opposed Holly when she was serene and tractable, but never in her imperious moods, or when she was stirred by emotion. Naturally she had been poignantly upset. Still he did not quite like her request and he was in a quandary. As there seemed to be no help for it, however, he hid his dismay and hurried back inside the enclosure.

He found Frayne leaning against the fence, one boot hooked on the lower pole. He was rolling a cigarette. Britt made note of the steady fingers. Frayne had shoved his sombrero back. His face was extraordinarily handsome, but that did not surprise Britt nearly so much as its utter absence of ashen hue, twitch, sweat, dark sombre cast, or anything else supposed to show in a man's features immediately after dealing death. It was indeed a baffling face, smooth, unlined, like a stern image of bronze. Frayne had all the characteristics of the cowboy range-rider, even to the finest sombrero, belt, dress and boots, which but for their dark severity would have made him a dandy.

"Got a match, Tex?" he inquired, civilly. His intonation was not that of a Southerner. Nor would Britt have accorded him western birth. Nevertheless the West had made him what he was. Britt had not seen his like.

"Shore. Heah you air," replied the Texan, producing a match.

"Hardly needed you in that little set-to," he said, as he lighted the cigarette. "But thanks all the same."

"You're darn welcome," grunted Britt, feelingly. "It was shore a bad mess. . . . Did you see me dancin' aboot tryin' to get a bead on Heaver?"

"Yes, I was afraid you'd hit Miss Ripple. That made me run in sooner than I might have. I was curious to watch Heaver. Stranger to me where women are concerned."

"Wal, I seen thet, an' I heahed you," rejoined Britt. "But yore reasons don't concern me. It was

48

the result. Shore you saved me from gettin' bored and Holly Ripple from wuss than death. . . . Seems sort of weak to thank you, Frayne."

"Don't try. It was nothing."

"Wal, the girl wants to thank you. Come on oot."

"Thanks, Britt, but I'd rather not."

Holly, riding outside the fence on the grass, passed so close that she could not have failed to hear the cool speech of the raider. She turned in the gate, and rode up to the men. A wave of scarlet appeared to be receding from her face. Frayne stood out from the fence, and removing his sombrero, inclined his head.

"May I ask your name?" she queried, composedly, though to Britt's astonishment, her usual poise had gone into eclipse.

"Frayne. Renn Frayne," he replied. He was courteous but cold. The immeasurable distance between Holly Ripple and an outlaw of the range might have been imperceptible to Heaver, but not to this man.

"Mr. Frayne, I — I am exceedingly grateful for your — your timely interference."

"Don't mention it, Miss Ripple," he returned, flipping his cigarette away. After that first direct glance he did not look up at her again. "I want no thanks. You only distress yourself further — coming inside near these dead men. Go away, at once."

"It was sickening, but I am over that. . . . Thanks in this case seem so silly. But won't you accept

49

something substantial?"

"For what?" he retorted, and his wonderful gray eyes, clear and light as crystal, and as soulless, turned to fix upon her.

"Evidently you place little store upon your service to me," she replied, pride gaining ascendancy.

"And you want to pay me for shooting a couple of dogs?"

"You make my duty difficult, Mr. Frayne. . . . But I do want to reward you. Will you accept money?"

"No."

She stripped off a gauntlet to take a magnificent ring of Spanish design from her finger and proffered that to him with an appealing smile.

"Won't you take this?"

"Thank you. I don't want it."

"Would you accept one of my thoroughbreds?" she persisted, hopefully.

"Miss Holly Ripple," he said, as if stung, "I am Renn Frayne, outlaw, rustler, gunman. This day made me a horse-thief. I have not a dollar to my name, nor a bed to sleep in, nor a friend in the world. But I cannot accept pay or gift for what I did. You could not reward such service any more than you could buy it. Not from me."

"Forgive me. I did not understand," she replied, hastily. "But your — your kind have been unknown to me. How was I to know that a desperado — all you called yourself — could be a — a gentleman? You are a knight of the range, sir." Plaintively she appealed to Britt. "What can I do,

50

Cappy? He has placed me under eternal obligation."

"Lass, I reckon you'll have to let it go at thet," replied Britt.

"Miss Ripple, I am rude, but I don't misunderstand you," said Frayne. "If you must do something for me. . . . But first — Haven't you any more sense than to ride out on this range alone?"

"I — I do as I please," retorted Holly.

"Then you ought to have a lesson. I've ridden all the wild ranges. And this is the worst. You are a headstrong little fool."

"How *dare* you?"

"I call spades spades, Miss Ripple," he rejoined. "It may do you further service to listen to the truth. You are a spoiled young woman. If Heaver had packed you off to the mountains, as he and many men like him have done before with girls — you'd soon have learned that blood, wealth, pride could avail you not at all. You would have become a rag. Heaver would have made you wash his feet."

"Sir! . . . Pray do not make me resent your service to me."

"That is nothing to me. But have you no father to hold you down?"

"He is gone — and my mother, too." In spite of herself, Holy seemed impelled to answer him.

"It's easy to see you have no husband. But surely a sweetheart —"

"No!" A crimson tide blotted out Holly's lovely fairness.

"Small wonder then. Well, Miss Holly, if I were your father I'd spank some sense into you. And if I were your sweetheart, I'd beat you good and hard."

Holly's individuality seemed to have suffered a blight. Her great eyes opened like midnight gulfs. In mute fascination she stared at this stranger to whom she owed so great a debt and who, all in the same hour, dared to flay her as no one had ever dared.

"You're a child, too," he went on, as if astounded to contriteness. "Well, I'll tell you how you can reward me. Promise on your honor never to ride out on this range again without men to protect you. That'd save you and your friends bitter grief. And for me it would mean one good deal to chalk up against all the bad ones."

"I — promise," she replied, tremulously.

"Thank you, Holly Ripple. I didn't really think you would. . . . Shake hands on it, man to man. . . . There, we're quits."

"Do you trust me?" she asked, strangely. "Do you think I can keep it?"

He studied the beautiful face apparently blind to its charm, and impervious to the lure of her femininity, as one to whom the thought of attainableness had never occurred.

"You would never break your solemn word," he said, with finality and turned to Britt. "Take her home, Tex. You'll send some boys down to plant these stiffs?"

"Shore will, Frayne. You better search them."

52

"Not me. And I mustn't forget to tell you that your boy Stinger might still be alive."

"If Brazos Keene got away from Heaver he's right back with Stinger now. Cowboys don't come any nervier than Brazos."

"Brazos Keene. Wonder where I heard that name. He got away, Britt, believe me. They was all shooting at him. A chip off the old Texas block. Watch that lad, Britt."

"Wait — please wait," called Holly, as Frayne turned to look for his horse.

"I thought we were quits," he said, dubiously.

"Not yet. I have something more to ask of you."

Britt cursed under his breath. Almost, but not too late, to send him aghast and quaking the girl had come to her sweetest self. A man would have to be anchored like the rocks not to be drawn by those eyes of velvet blackness, shining eloquence of her strong and passionate soul.

"Make it *adios, señorita,*" Frayne said.

"You have no money, no bed, no friend in all the world."

"I told you. It is unkind to remind me."

"What will you do?"

"The same as many a time before. Ride on."

"Not back to Heaver's men!"

"No."

"You'll ride on alone, until loneliness drives you to other men like them?"

"The truth is bitter, Miss Ripple."

"Renn Frayne, you do not belong to such gangs."

"I did not once, but I do now."

"You do *not*."

"Why, may I ask?" he queried, wearily.

"Because of something noble in you. Because you killed to save a girl from harm!"

"Well, I shall remember how Holly Ripple romanced over me," he rejoined, with the ghost of a smile.

"Will you work for me?" she asked.

"Miss — Ripple!" Frayne ejaculated, at last shocked out of his indifference.

"Will you ride for me?"

"Girl, you are mad," he burst out, incredulously. "You ask *me* — Renn Frayne — to ride for you?"

"Yes. . . . Britt, don't stand there like a gaping idiot. Tell him I need him, and why."

"Wal, Frayne," exploded the Texan, "it ain't a bad idee. I've got an ootfit as wild as they come. With you at their haid we'd weather these comin' years."

"Man, the girl has you locoed."

"Thet may be. But it ain't the question. I reckon she means this. Turn yore back on ootfits like Heaver's an' raise yore hand fer Don Carlos' Rancho."

Frayne shivered and by that slight reaction he betrayed himself. His brazen boast of irremedial ill-fame was nullified.

"My God, you ask me this?" he besought, huskily, a hand going out to Holly as if to warn her.

"I beg of you."

"But I am a thief!" he blazed.

"Yes, and you hate it," she flashed, poignantly.

"Heah's yore chance, Frayne," interposed Britt, at last inspired. "I've known a heap of bad men turn oot good. Thet's western. Air you big enough fer the break?"

"Miss Ripple, I'd be a liar if I denied the — the wonder of your offer. Only — it's unbelievable. I'm new to this range, but the Texas Pan Handle, Kansas, all the ranges north, scream at me for listening to you."

"I don't care what you've been," she went on, passionately. "It's what you are *now*. . . . Those ranges are far, far away. Forget them. Bury that past. Fight for my rancho, my cattle, my horses, for *me!*"

Like a drunken man Frayne staggered back against the fence. Britt quickened to the most complex and moving situation of his experience. If this man had been utterly bad, he could not have remained so.

"I will never ask you one question," went on Holly. "I'll exact only one promise."

"What?"

"That as long as you stay with me — and I hope it will be always — this, this dishonesty you confess will be as if it had never been. . . . Do you promise me?"

"I swear it. . . . But how can you trust me?"

"I made you a promise. You said I would never break my word. . . . Can I do less than trust you, Frayne? Here's my hand."

Blindly he reached out to take her ungloved hand

in his, and bowed his face over it.

Holly gazed down upon his lowered head. Britt had seen many lights and shades in those splendid Spanish eyes, but none ever so soft and strange and mystically lovely as those that shone there now. It had taken an outcast of the range to reach Holly's wayward heart. For two years Britt had watched her varied obsessions in the cowboys of Don Carlos' Rancho. She had been Lee Ripple's American girl, but her light and fickle fancies had been Spanish. Britt sighed over the inevitable, yet his love for Holly stormed his convictions and routed them.

Frayne lifted a cold face, from which emotion had been erased, and released her hand.

"Take her home, Britt. I will follow," he said, composedly, and stalked toward his grazing horse.

CHAPTER 3

Holly Ripple's school life in New Orleans, from her ninth to her sixteenth year, had been one of comfort, luxury, restraint, so that when she was launched upon the wildest range on the frontier, soon to become sole mistress of Don Carlos' Rancho with its great herds of cattle and droves of horses, she most certainly needed the pride and spirit that had been born in her.

Britt had trained her ceaselessly and faithfully during these past years. She cared nothing for cattle, but as she loved horses he had taught her to ride them like an Indian and to know them. She developed a superb physique, strength, skill, endurance, and a daring that had cost her foreman much dismay and anxiety. But Britt could not perform miracles, and the hard life of the range failed to blunt the soft feminine characteristics which had been fostered upon Holly during the impressionable forming time of adolescence. Perhaps the wise Colonel had intended this very thing.

Naturally Holly had seen much rough life on the range. Curious, interested, thrilled by everything, it had not been possible to hold her back. The old caravan trail from Santa Fe to the Mississippi ran across her land. A Mexican village, the inhabitants of which were in her employ, nestled picturesquely below the great ranch-house. A branch post of Horn's Trading Company was maintained here, where trappers came to sell and red men to buy and trade. Troops of dragoons stopped there on their way to escort caravans. From spring until winter the caravans passed, always camping in the cottonwood grove along the creek. Wagon-trains from Texas made the most of Don Carlos' Rancho.

In two short years much of western life had unrolled before Holly's all-absorbing eyes. Half a hundred cowboys had come and gone. Many a wild or drunken cowboy had bit the dust or dug his spurs into the earth on her range. Fighting was the breath of their lives. Holly had seen the beginning or the end of innumerable brawls. She had been known to stop fights. On more than one occasion she had unwittingly ridden upon dark slack forms of men swinging by their necks from trees. She had viewed a brush between soldiers and savages; she had seen stagecoaches roll in with bloody drivers roaring and dead passengers with the living; she had been present that very spring when a cattleman and rustler shot it out fatally on the street of San Marcos.

But the raw terrible spirit of the frontier had never closely touched Holly Ripple until this bright May morning when an outlaw had killed two of his comrades to save her.

Holly rode away from that scene sick to her marrow. She had watched the encounter on her nerve.

Every word and every action had been etched indelibly upon her consciousness. Anger at the boldness of these horse-thieves had given place to fury at their leader, and then to fright such as she had never known. If she could have saved the lives of Heaver and Covell by lifting her hand, she would not have done so. The West of her birth welled up in Holly that day. Afterward pride upheld her while she answered to irresistible and incomprehensible impulse in persuading this lone-wolf outlaw to become one of her riders.

Upon facing homeward with Britt, the trenchant thrill of this impulse faded away. And then the ghastly business of what had threatened her, and the blood and death which had followed, resulted in a cold misery in her vitals. Only the interest in the strange man who had saved her kept Holly from reacting to that aftermath as might have one of her tenderfoot schoolmates in New Orleans who used to faint at the sight of blood.

"Holly, you air pale aboot the gills," spoke up Britt, solicitously, before they had ridden far. "An' you ain't settin' yore saddle like you'd growed there."

"I'm sick — Cappy. Ride close. . . . But I'll get over it."

"Shore you will. Grit yore teeth an' hang on, Holly."

"Please don't scold me — for riding down alone. You were right."

"Wal, lass, I'll not scold you now, anyway. But I hope thet will be a lesson to you."

"It will be. I'll never be headstrong again. . . . I promised *him*. Oh, he was ruthless, insulting. But no common sort!"

"Holly, our new hand 'peared to be a lot of things — one of which was chain-lightnin'. My Gawd, but he was quick! . . . Holly, I've seen a few of the great Texas gunmen draw. Frayne would have killed any one of them today. Wonder who he is."

Holly was silent. She did not want to know. Frayne repelled her even more than he fascinated her. What had possessed her to such a rash and inconsidered offer? Did she already regret it? Had gratitude and pity prompted her wholly? At length she turned in her saddle to see if Frayne was coming. No horseman in sight on the grassy plain! She felt relieved. He might not follow. Then hard on this thought stirred a vague and disturbing fear that he might not keep his word. Next instant she championed him with self-accusation. He would not lie. Shame edged into her conflicting emotions. Cold, ruthless, indifferent, insulting outlaw! No man had ever dared to so criticise her. Holly rode on unaware that her sickness was gradually succumbing to stronger sensations.

"Cappy, was I wrong?" she asked, at length.

"How so, lass?"

"To offer him work? . . . To trust him?"

"Wal, thet's a stumper. Fust off I was scared stiff. But I'm hedgin', Holly. If Brazos an' Cherokee an' the Southards take to Frayne I'd say his acquisition might turn oot great fer Don Carlos' Rancho."

"You wouldn't be afraid to trust him?"

"It seems onreasonable, but I reckon I wouldn't," replied Britt, thoughtfully.

"Is he — coming?" she asked, hurriedly.

Britt glanced back over his shoulder to scan the rolling range. As he did not reply immediately, Holly grew conscious of a blank restless merging of relief and regret.

"There he is, just toppin' a rise," answered Britt, at length. "Didn't see him at fust. We might have knowed thet hombre —"

But Holly did not hear any more of Britt's drawl. She suddenly grew deaf and dumb to all outside stimuli. Her sickness and conjecture vanished in a rush of startling glad certainty, which as quickly affronted her. Holly, in consternation, and with a sinking of her heart, tried to take refuge in the thought that this had been the most exciting and upsetting day of her life. But an uneasy, unstable sense of weakness remained with her.

"Holly, there's a caravan in," spoke up Britt, eagerly, pointing toward the long grove of cottonwoods, above which rose columns of blue smoke. "Fust from Las Animas this spring. Must be Buff Belmet. He'll have loads of stuff fer us."

"Yes, indeed, and high time. Let us ride over to greet him," replied Holly, suddenly animated.

The afternoon sun shone on a natural scene of rangeland that never failed to awe and delight Holly. High on the gray-sloped, green-topped hill blazed the red of the old mansion. She could picture Don Carlos there in the days of the Spaniards, monarch of all he surveyed. It was hers, that indestructible home, vine-covered and weather-stained, a monument to the friendship between Don Carlos and the Indians, and likewise for her father's day. No enemy had ever darkened that open portal. No man of any degree had ever been turned away from that door. Holly had kept faith with father and grandfather. She prayed that she might still do so in this wilder day yet to come.

Soon the galloping horses reached the zone of cottonwoods, and then the wide clear brook babbling over gravelly bars. In the long half-circle on the other side, the caravan had halted for camp. How the great broad-wheeled, boat-bodied, gray-canvassed prairie-schooners thrilled Holly! They not only represented the forerunners of the western empire, but they seemed to be bridges across the plains to civilization. There were scores of these immense long-tongued wagons. Sturdy oxen were grazing away across the open; rolling mules were lifting the dust in many places; a hundred brace of horses had taken to the grass, while many were being unhitched. A dozen huge fires were burning. Red-shirted men stood out conspicuously among a horde of others, and all were busy as ants. The camp shone with color and hummed with activity. It was a scene of a kind which never palled on Holly.

As Britt and Holly rode up to the first group, several men advanced to greet them. Holly recognized a sturdy, bearded freighter who boomed at Britt, and then the magnificent Buff Belmet,

scout and plainsman, a friend of her father's, and
famous across the frontier. At the age of ten he
had driven one of these great wagons. He had lost
mother, father, brother and childish sweetheart on
his first trip across the plains. At twenty he was
a leader of caravans and a noted Indian fighter.
And now at thirty he had the lined stern face,
the piercing half-shut gray eye, the wonderful
poise of the frontiersman to whom all had happened except death.

The greetings were as between friends long separated.

"An' air you still single an' fancy-free, Miss
Holly?" queried the grizzled Jones.

"At least, I'm still single," replied Holly, with
a laugh.

"What's the matter with these young ranchers
an' rangehands out hyar?"

"Tom, it's a case of too many to pick from,"
drawled Britt. "How many wagons this trip? You
shore come heeled."

"We left Las Animas with thirty-eight," replied
Belmet, "an' we picked up twenty on the way.
Jest as well, otherwise we might had more'n a
brush with some Kiowas on the Dry Trail."

"I seen yore decorations," replied Britt, pointing
to the feathered arrows that stuck out in grim sug-
gestiveness from the wagons. "Look there, Holly."

"I saw them long ago," she replied, her eyes
dilating.

"Now aboot my supplies, Buff?" inquired the
foreman.

"Six wagons, Cap. I'll leave them hyar for your boys to unpack, an' pick them up on my way back from Santa Fe."

"Fine. We shore need them. An' Miss Holly has been frettin' more aboot —"

"Now, Cappy, don't betray my vanity," gayly interrupted Holly. "Even if all my pretty things did come I'll never be vain again."

"Wal, Miss Holly, you don't 'pear your usual bloomin' self atall," chimed in Jones.

"No wonder, Tom. She had a scare oot on the range today. An' believe me, I had one, too," replied Britt, seriously.

"Friends, I've had a scare for every one of these," said Belmet, putting his finger to the white hairs over his temples.

"Britt, this hyar New Mexico was gettin' hot last year," interposed Jones, wagging his head. "Buff will agree with me, I'll bet. You're in for hell."

"I'd rather not give Miss Holly another scare today," rejoined the scout.

"I'll tell you aboot it," said Britt. "You know, Buff, how things happen right oot of a clear sky. This would have been plumb bad but fer a queer deal." Whereupon Britt briefly told the story without mentioning Frayne's name.

"Miss Holly, ain't you ever goin' to grow up?" queried Jones, reprovingly. "This range ain't safe fer a girl no more."

"I fear I discovered that today."

Belmet shook his eagle head in grave portent.

"It's comin', Cap. I told Colonel Ripple thet years ago. Too big an' wild a range. Too many great herds of cattle. In Maxwell's day beef was cheap. He couldn't give it away. But this is a new era. The range offers easy pickin' fer rustlers, an' food markets. All the bad outfits will flock into New Mexico."

"I had thet figgered, an' I'm goin' to meet the situation with an ootfit of my own."

"Thet's the Texas idee, Cap. You'll give them a run for your beef."

"Buff, did you ever run into or heah of a fellar whose handle is Frayne — Renn Frayne?"

"Frayne? I know him. Not likely to forget him, either. Cap, I was present in Abilene some years back when Frayne made your Texas gunman, Wess Hardin, take water."

"No!" ejaculated Britt, incredulously.

"Hard to believe, an' thet's why it's not generally known. But I saw it. Frayne bluffed Hardin. Dared him to draw. An' would have killed him, too."

"Wal, I'll be darned. Who is this Frayne, Buff?"

"I don't know who he is, but I can tell you *what* he is."

"Go ahaid. Miss Holly an' me air shore interested. It was Frayne who did the shootin' today."

"You don't say? . . . I met Frayne first time after the war. Young fellar, footloose an' wild, with a hand for guns. He was a cow-puncher. He became one of many hard-shootin' hombres. I heerd of him often after thet, but never seen him again until thet time in Abilene. Then he was classed with the best of gunmen. An' you know, you could count them on the fingers of one hand. Let's see. That was three years ago. After thet he killed Strickland's foreman, an went on the dodge."

"Crooked?"

"No. It was the other way around, as I heerd. Strickland was a power in Kansas. An' any one who bucked him had sheriffs an' jails to reckon with."

"Like Chisum?"

"I wouldn't class Chisum with Strickland, except as a hard driver of men."

"What was yore idee of Frayne?"

"Wal, I reckon some different from thet of most of the youngsters I've met along the Old Trail. Most boys of good families didn't last long. The Englishmen — an' there was a sight of them — an' still comin' — petered out pronto. They didn't adapt themselves. They got snuffed out. But Frayne had the stern stuff of the Texas cowboy. He lasted. An' I'm glad to hear he done you a service."

"Is Frayne an ootlaw?"

"I reckon so, back in Kansas. An' probably Nebraska, Wyomin', Colorado. But I wouldn't call him an outlaw here in New Mexico. 'Cause there ain't any law yet."

"Wal, last summer we inaugerated what hawse-thieves an' rustlers fear wuss than a gun — the rope," declared Britt, forcibly.

"Cap, has it occurred to you thet Frayne would

66

be a whole outfit in himself, if you could hire him?" asked Belmet, thoughtfully. "I reckon you couldn't, though. Anyway, Miss Holly wouldn't have a bad hombre like Frayne around the ranch."

"Wouldn't I?" rejoined Holly, hiding her nervous embarrassment. "I thought of it first and asked him."

"Good! You are wakin' up to the needs of the range," declared the scout. "It takes bad men to cope with bad men on this frontier."

"We've got him, Buff," added Britt, with satisfaction. "An' since I seen you last summer I've added Brazos Keene, Cherokee Jack, Tex an' Max Southard, an' two or three other tough nuts to our outfit. Now with Frayne it shore beats any bunch I ever heahed of. I'll be obliged if you'll spread thet news all along the Old Trail."

"You bet I will," replied Belmet, emphatically. "I'll lay it on thick, too. . . . Miss Holly, I shore feel sorry for you. But it's the way to tide over this rustler wave."

"Britt, I know you was a Texas Ranger, an' a Trail Boss, but can you handle an outfit like thet?" asked the bearded man with Jones.

"It'll be the job of my life, but I'll do it."

"They'll fight among themselves over Miss Holly," declared Jones, quizzically.

"Wal, thet's up to her," laughed Britt.

"Gentlemen, it may amuse you, but it's not funny to me," interposed Holly. "But thank you for the advice — and come up for supper. We shall want to hear the news."

67

"Miss Holly!" expostulated Belmet, aghast. "It's awful good of you. . . . Look at us ragamuffins!"

"Come as you are, Belmet. At six o'clock sharp."

"Wal, be it upon your bonny head, Miss Holly. . . . I almost forgot to tell you. There's a man with us who claims to know you. He's in the Texas crowd. I didn't get his name. We heerd about him from the women folks in thet train. They gossiped. Handsome rich southerner — suitor of yours when you was in school in Orleans — comin' to visit you, an' all thet sort of talk."

"I have no personal friends or acquaintances in the south," replied Holly, dubiously.

"Wal, accordin' to the caravan gossip this gentleman was more'n a personal acquaintance," went on Belmet. "I didn't take much stock in it. But rememberin' how you're run after by so many adventurers, I reckoned I'd better tell you."

"Indeed yes. Thank you, Belmet. . . . Come to supper, surely. I must go now."

When Holly was halfway home Britt caught up with her. "Wal, lass, you look fagged. Rest a couple of hours, an' throw off all thet's troublin' you."

"I wish I could. Today seems to be a cloud on the horizon."

"Wal, thet cloud will come an' go. . . . I see some of the cowboys ridin' in. An' there's our new man pokin' along. Holly, I'm glad Belmet gave Frayne a better rep than he gave himself."

"I was glad, too. Still, it was bad enough."

"Holly, you're right. An' at thet Buff had no line on Frayne these last few years. I take it Frayne

68

finally went to the bad. It always happens thet way. But mebbe nothin' will come of it. The West is awful big an' in these times you cain't separate bad from good. We can afford to be charitable."

"Will you please ask Frayne to supper?"

"I was aboot to give you a hint. Let's impress him powerful fine fust thing. . . . Shall I set him next to you?"

"By all means. . . . Britt, I've worried about Brazos."

"Wal, you're wastin' yore feelin'. Thet boy will be ridin' in pronto."

"But Stinger is dead or wounded!"

"So we heahed. In either case Brazos will fetch him in. . . . Now, Holly lass, leave it all to me. If I cain't pick up Brazos with the glass I'll send some of the cowboys after him. . . . You go sleep a while an' forget this mess, an' then make yoreself prettier than ever before."

"Cappy! — Why so unusually — pretty?" inquired Holly, curiously, with a smile.

"Wal, thet Frayne was as cold as a daid fish," declared the Texan, resentfully. "He looked at you once an' didn't see you atall. An' thet was all he looked."

"Indeed, he was not flattering," observed Holly, conscious of a quickening of tired pulse. "But he had just shot two of his own comrades."

"Nothin' atall to Renn Frayne. I reckoned thet he was a Westerner who had no use fer wimmen. You run into one now an' then. I don't recollect you ever bein' so sweet to any man. An' the damned hombre not only never seen it but insulted you to boot. It riled me."

"Cappy, it will be good for us. You have spoiled me," she rejoined, thoughtfully, and rode on in silence to the corrals.

Rest and sleep and the image Holly saw in her mirror gave her back her poise, but did not eliminate from her mind the somber sense of that day's catastrophe.

The great dining room was exactly as it had been in Colonel Ripple's day, when red men and white men of high and low degree met at his table. Don Carlos' rich and lavish hand showed in the heavy dark furniture, in the polished stone floor with its worn rugs, in the huge carved stone fireplace, and the stained adobe walls with their old Spanish weapons, the painted frieze, and the huge rough-hewn rafter that centered the ceiling all its length.

Holly's guests arose at her entrance. Every seat had an occupant except the one of honor to her right.

"Be seated, friends," said Holly, in the words of her father's custom. "Eat, drink and be merry."

Belmet occupied the seat next to the one which Holly had intended for Frayne. His absence affected her as had his affront out on the range, despite the fact that her reason made excuse for the mood of a man who had just shed his fellow-men's blood. Conchita Velasquez and the Mexican women of Holly's household sat upon her left. Britt faced her at the end of the long table, and the seats between were occupied by the invited guests and by others who took advantage of the standing Ripple hospitality. Among the rough-garbed, bearded freighters and teamsters a young man, conspicuous because of the difference of his attire, at once caught Holly's eye. She recognized him, and acknowledged his elaborate bow. Embarrassment, and something of anger, accompanied her recognition. This fair man, whose sharp, cold, handsome features proclaimed him about thirty years old, and whose black frockcoat and gaudy waistcoat and long hair characterized him as a gambler of the period, was no other than Malcolm Lascelles, a Louisianian, whom Holly had met in New Orleans, during the concluding year of her school. It was a shock to see him at her table, recalling her girlish indiscretion.

She had met him by accident, and then, resenting her loneliness and longing for freedom, for adventure, for love, she had been so foolish as to steal out to meet him again and again. Upon learning that Lascelles was a gambler and adventurer, she had regretted her folly and ended the acquaintance. Lascelles had persistently annoyed her with attempts to re-establish himself in her esteem, thereby getting her into disgrace with her teachers. For Holly this had its good side, for the principal wrote to her father, who hastened the advent of her departure for home. Holly had never heard from Lascelles and had almost forgotten the incident. But here he had turned up, at her own table, an older man with whom the years had played havoc, whose hungry eyes betrayed that he had been hunting for her, and intended to make her remember. Holly suffered a moment of dismay. She was to blame for this. Whatever had been in her mind — to imagine she had been in love with this Lascelles?

The supper was served by a troupe of Holly's Mexican girls in native costume, and it was a bounteous one. The table groaned with savory viands and steaming vegetables and luscious fruits. At the outset the burly members of the caravan were too hungry and too glad to be present for any consistent merriment. But by the time the wine was passed around they made up for their lack.

In the succeeding hour Holly heard all the news from the towns on the Mississippi, from the cattle centers in Kansas, from the camps and posts in the plains, and from the forts. Not the least of this information consisted of reports of Indian attacks on the vanguard of the buffalo hunters, the advance of the railroad, the increase of travel westward, the renewal of soldier escorts for the caravans south from Las Animas, the hold-up of stagecoaches, all of which attested to the spring quickening of activity on the frontier. And the best of it was a marked rise in prices for beef, the increase in markets, owing to the pushing westward of the Santa Fe Railroad.

"Hard times for railroad construction are about over," said Belmet. "Last December the work crossed the Colorado state line. That was well within the ten years of grace allowed the builders by the land grant. Rails will reach La Junta by 1873, mebbe, and Raton the year after, mebbe."

"Holly, thet's great news," exclaimed Britt. "When the Santa Fe crosses New Mexico we want 75,000 haid of cattle heah."

"Cap, you can breed them on this wonderful range," said the scout. "But keepin' them long enough to sell — thet'll be the rub!"

When the supper party broke up Holly was standing with Britt, saying goodbye to Belmet, as Lascelles presented himself. Looked at through more mature eyes, he did not revive even a hint of the old girlish thrill. Still he had a semblance of southern grace.

"Holly Ripple, we meet again," he said, with gallant bow. "I have long dreamed of this moment. May I present my compliments? You have changed from the girl I knew so well at Madam Brault's school in New Orleans. From pretty girl to lovely woman!"

Holly did not offer her hand and she met his eyes with level gaze.

"I remember you, Mr. Lascelles," she said. "Are you not lost, away from the boulevards of Orleans? What are you doing on the frontier?"

"Holly, I have never ceased to search for you," he returned, boldly. "You alone brought me West."

"Indeed? I am sorry. You must have overrated the silly flirtation of a pent-up school girl. You are welcome, of course, at the table of my father. But I have no wish to renew the acquaintance."

73

"Holly, I'd like to meet the gentleman," interposed Britt, in his cool drawl.

"Mr. Lascelles, this is my father's old trail comrade, and my foreman, Captain Britt."

Holly moved toward the door with Belmet. "Thet'd shore took the hide off the impudent fellow if it hadn't been so thick," observed the scout. Holly went out on the porch with him. The last group of guests were thudding down the path. Stars were shining; the peep of spring frogs came plaintively from the ponds; a cold tang of mountain air made Holly draw her wrap close about her bare shoulders. She bade the plainsman goodnight and went into the living room, to turn up the lamp. Cedar logs burned ruddily on the hearth. She thought again of Frayne. Presently Britt entered, with his keen eyes gleaming unwontedly.

"Say, Holly Ripple, air you responsible fer that flash gambler showin' up heah?" he demanded.

"He says so."

"Has he any hold on you?"

"None whatever."

"I heahed you tell him. An' shore I shouldn't need more. But he ruffled me, lass. I must be gettin' testy in my old age. . . . Dog-gone-it, I'm the only dad you got!"

"Cappy, you are indeed, and I love you. Don't waste concern on Mr. Lascelles."

"Wal, he tried to make oot there was somethin' between you. Kind of brazen, or thick-haided. I told him he'd had supper at Don Carlos' Rancho, an' to slope. All the same if I don't mistake my figgerin' men you'll heah more aboot this kid flirtation."

"Cappy, you don't mean this man will take advantage of that indiscretion of mine to — to —"

"I shore do," returned Britt, as Holly hesitated. "The damn fool thinks you air — or was — sweet on him. Reckon it's a bluff. He's an adventurer an' 'way down on his luck. He fetched his pack up heah, an' I had to give him a room. Another instance of yore Dad's famous hospitality to anyone! I cain't throw him oot."

"No, indeed. . . . But it might prove annoying. I certainly don't want to meet him again."

"Wal, how air you goin' to avoid it, if he stays heah? Remember thet army officer who bored you half to death?"

"You might try the same remedy," said Holly, with a little laugh.

"Brazos! — Holly, I must say thet when you air sick of a man you reckoned you liked — wal, you show yore Spanish. It wouldn't never do to give Brazos a hint aboot this gambler."

"Did Brazos get back?" asked Holly, quickly.

"Yes, before supper. Mad as a wet hen because he had to pack Stinger on his hawse, an' walk ten miles. How thet boy hates to walk!"

"Oh — Stinger! Is he —"

"Shot up some, but nothin' to worry aboot. . . . It happened thet Frayne seen Brazos comin' an' packed Stinger in. Frayne said he knowed gunshot wounds, an' thet this wasn't bad if dressed proper. Which he proceeded to do. Done it swift an' slick,

75

too. I shore get a laugh oot of those cowboys. Brazos said, 'I'm dawg-tired an' I don't care a damn if he croaks. An' I'm gonna bore Mugg Dillon!' . . . Then Stinger looks up at Frayne an' asks, suspicious like, 'Who'n hell air you, stranger?' An' Frayne says easy an' cool, 'Renn Frayne' . . . Thet bunkhouse went as quiet as a church. They'd heahed of him. Cowboys air a curious lot. They never fail to talk whenever they meet riders or go any place. An' they never forget an' they tell each other. Some of our new boys have rode the Pan Handle. Ride-'em Jackson is from Texas. They've heahed of Frayne an' have talked aboot him, same as of every bad hombre on the range. It worries me."

"Did you tell Mr. Frayne that I invited him to supper?"

"I shore did, Holly. He just refused, short an' sweet. I was sort of stumped, an' told him when you invited people, same as yore Dad before you, an' Don Carlos before him — why, they just come plumb glad. Then he says: 'Thank Miss Ripple for me, and tell her I appreciate the honor, but that I do not want to come.' "

"Britt, is Frayne a criminal, with good instincts?"

"No criminal, believe me, in the sense you mean. No low-born man could ever look straight at you like Frayne does. . . . An' I shore don't believe he was ashamed to come."

"Could it have been because he shot his comrades?"

"No. Frayne wouldn't think no more aboot shootin' them than jackrabbits. Holly, you'll have to swaller it. Heah's an outlaw you've been gracious to. An' he just plain snubs you. I reckon, though, thet it'd mean nothin' to you except fer thet absurd old custom of yore Dad's, an' one you think every man should kow-tow to."

"It's not absurd, Britt," protested Holly, spiritedly.

"Be reasonable, lass. What could an old Spanish law of hospitality or the pleasure of a great pioneer mean to a man who survives only by eternal vigilance?"

"Survives? I don't understand you."

"Renn Frayne is a hunted man. By officers perhaps, but mostly by men who want revenge fer the killin' of friends or relatives. Or by genuine bad men he has got the best of. Or by the bluff bad hombres or wild cowboys who'd like the fame of killin' him."

"Oh! — Frayne is indeed to be pitied," murmured Holly.

"Look at his hands next time you get a chance. Kept careful as yores, Holly. I'll bet Frayne never chops wood or digs post-holes. He keeps them hands limber an' soft so thet he can handle them guns swift as lightnin'."

"I can excuse his rudeness," concluded Holly, and bade her foreman goodnight.

Holly was at breakfast in her room when she heard a familiar clinking step out upon the path.

She was expecting Britt, but this step was quicker and more vibrant than that of the old Texan.

"Mawnin', Cap," spoke up a lazy resonant voice. "How's our Lady of the Rancho?"

"Howdy, Brazos," returned Britt, who evidently had arrived first. "Haven't seen her yet this mornin'. She's late. But yesterday knocked her oot, I dare say."

"Who's the flowery-vested caird-sharp I jest met?"

"Name's Lascelles. From New Orleans. Dropped in heah yesterday with thet wagon-train. Used to know Holly when she was at school. She confessed she'd flirted a little with him before she found oot he was a gambler. An' he pestered her after thet. It was plain last night thet he meant to take advantage of the early acquaintance."

"Wal, you don't say," drawled Brazos, in a tone that sent little shivers over Holly.

"Yes, I do say," rejoined Britt, testily. "Doggone! We never know what's goin' to bob up. Lascelles fetched his pack. An' I had to give him a room. If he hangs aboot heah it'll be unpleasant for Holly."

"How you know thet?"

"She told him plumb oot thet she had no wish to renew the acquaintance."

"Ah-huh. Holly can shore tell a fellar. . . . What you gonna do aboot it?"

"Reckon I'll give Lascelles a hint to leave with the wagon-train."

"Holly won't like thet. It ain't Ripple hospitality."

"But the four-flusher might set down to live heah. Thet's happened before."

"Shore. But if Holly doesn't like the galoot he wouldn't be around long."

"I savvy. You'd set in a little game of cairds with him, huh? An' then we'd have to plant another stiff back on the hill. Brazos, you're just plain devil."

"See heah, boss. Haven't you forgot thet little confab you had with me when you persuaded me to ride heah?"

"No, Brazos. But I hate to distress Holly. She was game yesterday. All the same thet blood-lettin' made her sick. . . . Besides, dog-gone-it, I don't want you to get any wuss name on the range. I like you, Brazos."

"You don't say? Nobody'd ever notice it. Wal, there's some hope of me likin' you, Cap."

Holly finished her coffee rather hurriedly, and went through the living room to the door. Britt was sitting on the porch steps, looking up at his tall companion. Brazos Keene was the youngest, the wildest, the most untamable, yet the most fascinating and lovable of all Holly's cowboys. His slim, round-limbed rider's figure lost little from the ragged garb and shiny leather; his smooth tanned face, fresh and clear as a girl's, cleancut and regular as a cameo, his half-shut, wild blue eyes and clustering fair hair, all proclaimed his glad youth and irresistible attractiveness, without a hint of his magnificent lawlessness and that he was a combination of fire and ice and steel.

"Howdy, Texans. Come right in," invited Holly, gayly.

"Mawnin', Lady," drawled Brazos, doffing his sombrero.

"How air you, Holly?" asked Britt, rising uncovered.

"My dreams were troubled, but I am fine this morning."

"Thet's good. You was so late I . . . Wal, I cain't waste more time. The wagons air heah, Holly. There's a whole wagonload fer you. Jim said 'Shore we know spring is come!' . . . Boxes, bags, an' what not? Where'll I have the boys pack this stuff?"

"In the patio by my storeroom. Have the boxes opened, Britt."

"All ready fer you in less'n an hour," returned Britt, stepping down. "Adios, Holly." . . . Then he looked at Brazos, as if prompted by an afterthought. "Say, cowboy, rustle along pronto."

"Aw, boss, I have a report to make," complained Brazos.

"Wal, cut it short an' leave oot the smoke," concluded Britt, curtly.

"Come in, Brazos. I'd rather not see the frocked gentleman who is loitering around."

"Thet pale-faced gent! — Britt told aboot him," said Brazos, and following her into the room to her desk he took her hand. "Holly, you never was in love with him?"

"No. I don't believe I ever imagined that. But I was pining for company — for masculine company, I confess. Then I was mad at my teachers. I met this Lascelles and I was a foolish girl. It was an adventure. I flirted with him — a little."

"Holly, you never let him kiss you?"

"Gracious no! Nor allowed him to hold my hand as you are doing now. . . . Brazos, promise me you won't pick a fight with Lascelles."

His imperturbability lay only on the surface. Holly felt the throb of his sinewy hand and the blue flame of his eyes.

"Promise me," she repeated, imperiously.

"Why should I, Lady?"

"Because you are more to me than just one of my cowboys."

"Yore word is the only law I know. . . . Holly, do you care anythin' aboot me atall?"

"*Si, señor,*" she replied, smiling, and gently endeavoring to remove her hand.

"When I fust come to this rancho you liked me a heap, Holly. An' it kept me straight. You rode with me more'n any of yore riders. My land, how jealous they was! An' I got my hopes up, Holly."

"Hopes of what, you foolish boy?"

"Wal, thet you'd love me — an' marry me some day," he replied, with a soft frankness that touched Holly with contrition.

"Brazos, I do like you a heap. I am proud that I have kept you straight. But I do not love you."

"Aw! . . . Thet night at the *fandango* — last

summer. You let me kiss you!"

"No, Brazos."

"But, Lady, you made no fuss. An' you didn't run off or — or slap me."

"Brazos, please be honest. You kissed me, not by force, but by surprise."

"My Gawd, girls air strange! — Holly, how aboot my puttin' my arm around you thet night in the buckboard, when I drove you home from San Marcos?"

"Yes, you did. I was very foolish, Brazos — and cold, too."

"Then it never meant nothin' atall," said Brazos, with pathos. "Not even at first?"

"Brazos, I asked you to be honest," replied Holly, earnestly. "So I can be no less. . . . I never quite understood myself. I did have a — a sweet, romantic feeling for you. I did. But I had had that before. It didn't last. And I've had it since. For that young army officer who came here wounded and we cared for him. It didn't last, either. I am a fickle jade, Brazos. It must be my Spanish blood. But I do really love you, Brazos — as a sister. And I want you for a brother. I'm a lonely girl."

"Shore. But I don't want to be yore brother," he replied, stubbornly. "I want to be yore husband. You need one, Holly. You'll never leave Don Carlos' Rancho. You ought to marry a cowman. Yore Dad would have wanted thet. An' I'm as good as any of these ridin' gents an' better than most. . . . If you'd marry me — you'd come to love me some day. An' I wouldn't ask you to be my — my real wife till then. I could take care of you, Holly."

"Brazos, dear, you do not grasp the situation. I don't love you that way. I never will. . . . Why you're not yet nineteen years old. And I am! . . . I feel like your mother. You're only a boy."

"Boy! — Holly, I'm as old as Britt, in the ways of the range. An' this range is yore home. An' if you can believe me or Tex or Britt or Buff Belmet, it's gonna get powerful wild pronto. Holly, ain't a man in the ootfit who wouldn't give an eye to save you what Frayne saved you. He's a darn good-lookin' chap, educated, an' was somebody once, as anyone could see. Buff Belmet knows the frontier. It's only fair fer me to admit thet the ootfit took to Frayne. We're scared of him, shore, but if he only takes to us he'll be a round peg in a round hole."

"Brazos, I hope Frayne and all of them are as loyal and gallant as you," rejoined Holly, feelingly. "Then I'll have the outfit Britt has dreamed of. And Don Carlos' Rancho will be the home for me that Dad prayed it would be."

CHAPTER 4

Late one afternoon in early June, Britt rode wearily across the valley toward Cottonwood Basin where he expected to find a third group of his cowboys in camp. Weeks on end his outfits, widely separated, had been branding calves. That day Britt had ridden to White Pool and from there to Ute Flat. He had had worry enough without bad reports from these places, and he had been tired enough without this added ride across to the basin.

Yet despite the mounting burden of Britt's responsibilities, he was as sensitive as ever to the open range. He faced a half circle where for thirty miles his keen vision could distinguish cattle as thick as scattered bunches of sagebrush. Off toward San Marcos a group of riders headed toward the little town. They might be cowboys, but Britt inclined to the conviction that they were not. Down the vast green slope a stagecoach rolled along, streaming dust behind. It was due at the trading-post below Don Carlos' Rancho that night and the driver, Bill McClellan, was not letting any grass grow under the hoofs of his six horses. The run from Santa Fe to Las Animas had taken on greater risk these days.

But there was another side to Britt's state of consciousness, and this was a revivification of pleasure and even exaltation in the beauty and wildness of his surroundings. Holly Ripple had been the cause of such sentiment in an old Texas Ranger, who had slept on the ground half his nights for twenty years. She rode with him almost every day and it was impossible not to see the West through her young and vivid eyes.

The range appeared limitless. Don Carlos' Rancho was only a red dot on the green divide to the east. The roofs and trees of San Marcos blazed gold in the sunset. The basin was bisected by a shining ribbon. All the rest, beyond, was level plains and rolling land, and ridges and valleys, leading to the lilac-hazed mesas, to the rosy foothills, and the dim purple mountains.

A last flush of sunset bathed the valley in dying fire as Britt rode across the belt of cottonwoods to the camp. Evidently the cowboys had knocked off for the day. A small knot of cows and calves was working out toward the black-spotted range. Along the bank of the creek several score of horses grazed. This was Jim's *remuda*. They waded knee-deep in luxurious grass and flowers. The Mexican cook, Jose, stooped over his campfire and steaming pots. Cowboys stretched at length, their shoulders propped against packs. Riders were straggling in from the range.

Britt dismounted to greet Jim, the cowman in charge. He was a tall, stoop-shouldered, sandy-mustached range-rider of uncertain years. His dust-begrimed face showed the marks of sweaty fingers.

"Howdy, boss. Jest in time fer grub."

"I'm shore needin' some — an' water, say! — Shades of old Texas Land!"

"You look it. Hyar's a good cold drink. . . . Reckon you rid over from Ute Flat?"

"Yes, an' White Pool, too."

"Then you'll hardly be ridin' back to the rancho tonight?"

"Have to. But I'll eat a bite an' rest some. . . . It's been a real warm day."

"Humph! If you ask us, boss, we'll say it's been hot."

During the interval before supper while Britt walked a little to ease his cramped legs, the cow-boys bestirred themselves languidly. They were tired, quiet. Some went bare-breasted to the creek; others importuned Jose for hot water.

"Skylark, if I'm as black as you, I'm a nigger," said one.

"You're blacker'n me, Laigs, but washin' won't make you handsomer," was the reply.

"Come an' geet eet," called Jose.

Presently Britt found himself seated amidst Jim's outfit, eating as heartily as any hard-worked rider among them. From this group Britt missed Brazos Keene, and Mugg Dillon. The latter, of course, he had not expected to see. But where was Brazos? The magnificent Skylark, his clean thin visage as red as fire, stood up with pan in hand; Laigs Mason, the little bow-legged, homely clown of that outfit, sat on a pack, finding it awkward to get his knees close enough together to hold a pan; the Nebraskan, Flinty, bent his hard face over his supper; Tennessee, the sallow-faced, tow-headed southerner, knelt on one knee to eat. Santone, swarthy and beady-eyed *vaquero,* helped Jose at his tasks.

For a while only the sound of grease sputtering in the iron oven, the sizzle of fresh beef frying, broke the hungry silence. Twilight marched down over the range from the hills, and soon after that coyotes began their hue and cry. Cows lowed and calves bawled. The lonely night began to creep on.

Britt was not by far the first to finish supper. "Wal," he said, at length, "thet was good. Jose is the best cook in the ootfit. . . . Gimme a smoke, somebody."

"Boss, how's tricks over White Pool an' Ute Flat way?" asked Jim, at last finding a seat. One by one the cowboys clustered around, lighting their cigarettes.

"Good an' bad. Hell of a new crop of calves, an' a lot of activity to offset it."

"Activity?" queried Jim.

"Thet's what I said."

"Ah-huh. An' same for Ute Flat? Some movement of steers an' a lot of burned hair not by the Ripple outfits, huh?"

"Exactly, Jim. . . . You don't 'pear bustin' to make yore report."

"Boss, I'm bustin' all right, but not with good news."

"Where's Brazos?" returned Britt, quickly.

"He ought to be hyar before dark," rejoined Jim, evasively.

"Come oot with it," snapped the foreman.

"Laigs, will you tell the boss what come off?"

"Cap, it was like this," replied the bow-legged cowboy, sitting up. "Day before yestiddy me an' Brazos run onto some rustlers drivin' a bunch of steers thet wore our mark. This was way up at the head of the Cottonwood, I reckon fifteen or twenty miles from hyar. Brazos acted plumb sore, so I reckoned he'd been expectin' it. Wal, there was four of the rustlers an' one of them was Mugg Dillon. We yanked out our rifles. But they seen us pronto an' rode off toward San Marcos. After a bit they slowed up, seein' we didn't follow. We rode back. Brazos rode slower an' slower, till finally he stopped. 'Laigs,' he says, 'I'm waitin' hyar till dark an' then I'm ridin' to town.' Wal, you know Brazos. All I said was I'll go with you. 'No, you go back to camp an' report to Jim. An' if the boss should ride in tell him I went after Dillon, but he's not to let Miss Holly know.' "

"Damn thet cowboy!"

"No use to damn Brazos," interposed Jim. "He an' Stinger have shore got it in fer Dillon. I don't know jest what made them so sore, outside of his double-crossin' us."

"Stinger never said a word to me," rejoined Britt. "I couldn't pump much out of him."

"My hunch come from somethin' Frayne said."

"Frayne?"

88

"Shore. He thinks Brazos an' Stinger were on to Dillon — thet they ketched him before an' trusted him not to go into another low-down deal."

"Wal! . . . A hawse deal?"

"No. I reckoned it must have been cattle, but Frayne didn't think so."

"When did Frayne tell you this?"

"Weeks ago, jest after he started ridin' with us."

Britt pondered a moment, darkly revolving in mind what risks Brazos might have incurred while trailing Dillon. Finally he voiced his concern: "If Brazos doesn't come back tonight go after him — some of you."

"Boss," interposed Laigs Mason, coolly, "if you'd seen Brazos you wouldn't be worried. I savvy thet hombre. He's the nerviest fellar on this range, but when he takes chances he's got an even break."

"All right, Jim. What else?" went on Britt, gruffly.

"We been hyar seventeen days, an' shore slapped our irons on a sight of calves," replied Jim, complacently. "Jest about cleaned up this basin. But we had help, an' thet riles me some. Sewall McCoy's ootfit hung in this neck of the woods till the other day. We jest know his men was brandin' calves whose mother had a Ripple brand on her flank. We seen a hundred an' more thet had new burned Bar M's on them. The boys was partickler not to drive any cows over hyar but ours. McCoy's ootfit didn't round up a bunch, as is our way. They jest rode everywhere, brandin' every maverick in its tracks. Shore we might have got a few calves not really ours. But damn few. . . . An' to be short an' sweet, I don't like this McCoy cattleman nor his ootfit."

"Sewall McCoy? So he's rangin' over heah. Jim, how many cattle has he on this range?"

"Couldn't say. But I'd swear not more'n five thousand haid."

"Wal, while you an' yore boys air ridin' around, make a count of McCoy's an' any other brands. We got too many cattle an' too many calves. I'll recommend thet we sell a bunch to the government beef-buyers an' make a big drive to the railroad."

"Thet's a good idee, boss. It'd give us a chance to get a line on what's bein' bought an' shipped. Countin' the increase this year, we're runnin' sixty thousand haid."

"Thunder an' blue blazes!" snorted Britt. "We can't handle them. We could sell to the posts, an' reservations, an' to eastern markets, over an' over again without makin' a hole you could see in our herd."

"Shore. But we're havin' help in makin' thet hole," remarked Jim, impressively. "Rustlers drove a good big herd off toward the Purgatory last week, an' you can bet your life most of them steers belonged to Miss Holly."

"Et ees so, señor," corroborated the *vaquero,* puffing a cloud of smoke.

"Not *mucho malo,* but. . . . Hello, what's thet?"

"Hoss comin'."

90

"Thet's Brazos. I know his trot," added Laigs Mason.

"Wal, I shore hope so," returned Britt, peering into the gathering gloom. Presently a horse bobbed black against the gray. Jim threw some bits of sage on the fire. It blazed up brightly. Soon the horseman entered the circle of light.

"Who comes?" shouted Jim.

"Brazos," came the harsh retort.

Then in the flare of fire Britt recognized the striking figure of his favorite cowboy. Laigs Mason, who got up, was the only one to stir. Brazos stepped off. With a few swift violent pulls he loosened the cinches, then one powerful sweep of arm flung saddle and blanket to the ground. Slipping off the bridle, he slapped the wet horse, to send him cantering off in the darkness.

"Pard — you all right?" queried Laigs, haltingly. At that moment there emanated from Brazos something inimical to approach. He tossed his sombrero at Mason and stood bare-headed beside the fire, over which he held lean brown hands that quivered slightly. His fair hair stood up, shining like a mane. His face appeared ghastly gray, out of which slits of glittering eyes swept over his comrades.

"Aw! . . . So you're heah — Cap," he jerked out, in colorless voice.

"Howdy, Brazos," replied the foreman.

Laigs approached to place a hesitating hand on his friend's arm.

"Hey you —— ! Lay off!" exclaimed Brazos.

91

"Thought thet wing hung kinda funny. Hope it ain't broke."

"Gun-shot. Nothin' much. But sorer'n a burnt thumb."

"Pard, you look peaky. Ain't you hungry?"

"I don't know, Laigs. But I haven't eaten anythin' since I left."

Britt interposed with a dry query: "How aboot whiskey, Brazos?"

"Nary a red drop, boss," replied the cowboy, wildly.

"Three days? Gosh!" ejaculated Laigs, with concern. "You must be starved."

"I cain't eat, pard."

"But Brazos! . . . You gotta try. I'll rustle some soup — an' a biscuit."

"Got the makin's — anybody?" asked Brazos, hoarsely.

"Hyar, cowboy. Jest rolled one," replied Skylark, sitting up. "Ketch."

He flipped the cigarette accurately, but the nervous Brazos failed to catch it in the air. Stooping he picked it up, and at the same time a bit of half-burned stick, with which he lighted it, and puffed clouds of smoke. Then he sat down on a pack, and with expulsion of deep breath appeared to relax. No one spoke to him. Laigs, who brought a plate and cup, handed these to Brazos without speaking. The cowboy took a few more pulls at his cigarette, then spat it out. He sat motionless a moment, gazing into the fire. Then he seemed to remember the food and drink which he held.

But at first they must have been tasteless and repellent, for he could hardly force them down. At length, however, hunger manifested itself, and he ate what Laigs had fetched him.

"Brazos, lemme see your arm?" asked Mason.

"Get some hot water. You'll have to soak my sleeve off. It's all caked."

Britt's heart warmed anew to this wild youth. Yet on the moment dismay dominated his feelings. Brazos was no uncertain quantity: his actions could be fairly well forecast. Britt got up to stroll away into the darkness, revolving in mind what to say to Brazos. And he recalled the last argument he had had with Holly anent the managing of these cowboys. Britt seemed to feel that the time was ripe to put her plan to a test. Returning to the campfire he found Brazos stripped to the waist, his slender powerful white torso shining in the light. An ugly red bullet hole showed in the upper part of his left arm. Britt bent over to scrutinize it closely. It was a superficial wound.

"Clean as a whip, boss," said Mason, deft and businesslike. "It won't be nothin'."

Brazos sat indifferent to pain, if he felt any, intent on the fire. Britt resumed his seat. Skylark appeared to be the only curious one, though he did not manifest this vocally. As always, Britt was amused and thrilled by these cowboys. Of all western types he admired them most. He had vision to see that they, more than trappers, traders, goldseekers, freighters, soldiers, and pioneers, should be given glory of being the empire builders. With the buffalo-hunters, who were going to subjugate the Indian and drive him into the waste places, these cowboys, with their rolling herds of cattle, would be the true and the great freers of the West.

"Wal, Brazos, it won't hurt you none to talk," drawled Britt, mildly, after a long interval of silence.

"Cap, now I'm back again with the ootfit, it ain't easy to say what I had in mind," replied Brazos, soberly.

"Shore, I savvy. But I'm leavin' pronto, an' I reckon you might as wal get it off yore chest."

"Did Laigs tell you I quit my job?"

"No."

"Jim, did he tell you?"

The tall cowman shook his head as he removed the cigarette from his lips. "Laigs talked a heap, but he didn't tell thet."

Brazos turned to the comrade who was bandaging his arm. "You —— !"

"Pard, you'd quit before more'n onct an' come back. So I jest kep mum about it," explained Mason.

"Dog-gone! I used to ride with boys thet you could depend on," complained Brazos, bitterly.

"What'd you quit fer, Brazos?" asked Britt.

" 'Cause I knowed you'd let me oot if I didn't quit."

"Wrong, cowboy. I wouldn't let you oot, no matter what you did."

"What's thet?" demanded Brazos, swiftly, as for

94

the first time he turned from the fire to face Britt.

"You heahed me, Brazos."

"But I don't savvy."

"Wal, since you been oot on this round-up, Miss Holly has laid down the law to me. I convinced her thet we had the greatest ootfit of riders ever got together under one brand. But the hell of it was to hold them, to make them pards, to stand one an' all loyal to her. . . . Brazos, an' the rest of you — listen. Miss Holly took thet responsibility off my hands."

Every cowboy sat up, cigarette suspended, eyes intent on Britt in the firelight. Brazos' stern pale visage worked with a voiceless question.

"You bet, boys, Miss Holly has a big idee. She sees these bad times ahaid. She knows she's dependent on her ootfit. You all know she could sell oot fer million, leave this hard range, an' go live a life of luxury an' comfort. But she won't do it. She is Ripple's daughter, an' she'll carry oot his dream of a great cattle kingdom. To do thet she must have such in ootfit as I have roped in heah. I reckon Miss Holly cares a heap fer you-all, collectively an' singly. Yore bad records don't phase her. Wal, every last one of you knows in his heart whether he's worthy of thet or not. But what concerns her now is not yore past, but yore loyalty to her."

"What's she mean — loyalty?" queried Brazos, hoarsely.

"Wal, mebbe this will explain. I called you boys Rowdies of the Saddle. Thet was Kurnel Ripple's name fer his ootfit. But Miss Holly doesn't like it. She calls you her Knights of the Range. . . . I reckon there ain't a one of you so ignorant thet he never heahed what a knight is. . . . Wal, loyalty means you'll stand by her in these bad times, fight to save her rancho, her herd, an' if necessary — die for her."

"My Gawd!" burst out Brazos, as if to himself.

"Miss Holly is boss of this ootfit an' you're beholden to her," went on Britt, driving his appeal home. "I cain't let any of you go. An' she wouldn't. She doesn't care what you do so long as you're loyal to her."

"Cap, thet means not to steal from her — not to stand fer a pard double-crossin' her?" queried Brazos, with ringing passion.

"You hit it plumb center, Brazos."

"Cap, *I* did," cried Brazos, poignantly.

"Did what, you locoed cowboy?" demanded Britt, fiercely. "Don't tell me you stole from Holly Ripple!"

"Stole? *Me!* — God, no! But Dillon stole an' I ketched him. I made him swear never to do it again. I trusted him. Stood fer it! Never told you! An' the —— lowdown skunk double-crossed me."

"Tell Miss Holly. She will forget thet, Brazos."

"But thet wasn't loyalty."

"Not to her. But it was to Dillon. Mark my word, cowboy, she will forgive you. But *tell* her yourself."

"I hate to, wuss'n poison. But I will."

"Fine!" ejaculated Britt, with intense relief. By

96

that he knew Brazos would reverse his decision to quit. The cowboys settled back to more comfortable positions. Laigs Mason finished his task of bandaging, and helped Brazos get back into his spirit. Conversation lagged again. All this excitement and talk without a word about the fate of Mugg Dillon! Jim ordered the Mexican lads out to guard the *remuda*. The noisy coyotes ventured close to camp, to snarl and snap over bones thrown away by Jose. Wolves bayed out on the range and the bawling of cows attested to the merciless carnage enacted out there. The night settled down black and starry. Britt felt that he must start for the rancho. Yet he liked to linger there around the campfire, among these hard-faced youths. Meanwhile he watched Brazos, trying to read that worthy's mind.

"I forgot, Jim," suddenly Britt spoke up. "Rustle oot this week an' then home. Thet's my orders to all the men."

"I was wonderin'," replied Jim. "Next Wednesday week is the anniversary of thet great party Kurnel Ripple gave Miss Holly nigh on three years ago. We ain't heahed nothin', but I reckon the party will come off. This would be the third."

"It'll come off, bigger'n ever," Britt assured Jim. "Some of you was there last year. Wal, this time Miss Holly is givin' a dinner to her ootfit before the party."

"You don't say?" ejaculated Jim.

"There!" shouted Laigs Mason, suddenly vehement, shaking a finger in Brazos' face. "I told you. Now you'll miss thet grand purty."

"Miss nothin'," growled Brazos. "Shore I quit. But I'm gonna ask Miss Holly to take me back. . . . She wouldn't have it without me."

"Haw! Haw! . . . If you ain't the conceitednest cowhand on this range!"

Britt got up to join in the laugh that broke the restraint and established something of a genial atmosphere once more. He took advantage of the moment.

"Wal, somebody fetch my hawse. I'll be rustlin'."

"Boss, shall we send some one with you?" asked Jim.

"Brazos, do you want to come?"

"Aw! . . . Not jest yet."

"Wal, never mind then, Jim." After a moment, as he stepped to his horse, which Santone had led up, Britt gazed hard at his crippled cowboy.

"Say, Brazos, I reckon I'm to figger thet bullet-hole in yore shoulder jest happened you know — oot of a clear sky," he drawled.

"Cap, I don't get shot oot of a clear sky," retorted the cowboy.

"Wal, then?" But there did not seem to be an answer forthcoming. Brazos stiffly arose to his lofty height. Then Britt launched sharply at him: "Did Mugg Dillon shoot you?"

"Hell no! — Thet hombre never even got his gun oot," replied Brazos just as sharply, and with that he stalked away from the campfire.

Britt had his answer. His glance at Jim cor-

98

robrated his interpretation of Brazos' curt reply. A cold wrench tugged at Britt's vitals. Dillon had been a fine rider, a good chap, except when under the influence of strong drink. The bottle and evil companions had ruined him. A common story on the ranges! Britt sighed as he mounted.

"Adios, boys," he said. "Keep yore eyes peeled, an' rustle in on time." Then he rode out into the dark, lonely, melancholy night.

It was Holly Ripple's bad luck — and Britt averred that anything untoward for Holly simply multiplied itself for him — to have an east-bound caravan, a troop of dragoons, two tribes of trading Indians, and a band of trappers, all arrive at Don Carlos' Rancho the weekend before the great party.

This would have augured ill at any time, but the fact of Holly's cowboys all riding in, after a month out on the range, made the situation unmanageable.

The Horn brothers, traders, had always contested the Ripple right to the land upon which their post was situated. Holly objected strongly to the saloon and gambling-hall they maintained, but she did not want to force them off or interfere with their business because there were many advantages in having the trading-post and store near at hand. Caravans and stagecoaches all stopped overnight at the post. Britt had always advised Holly to make the best of it, and so far only ordinary brawls had been the outcome. But this was different. Britt was mightily concerned. All three of his outfits had ridden in late on Friday, and they had clamored for their wages. He had the money to pay them, but was afraid to do it. With Holly's annual party only a few days away he was at his wit's end to meet the situation.

Saturday morning Britt had breakfast and a conference with Holly, after which, fortified by her forceful instructions and the money for her riders — both of which he intended to keep to himself if possible — he strode valiantly into the big bunk-house. This was a long structure of adobe, with kitchen and store-room at the back, and in front a single hall-like room, running the full width of the house. It contained twenty-odd bunks in rows of three, one over the other, built out from the wall, very roomy and comfortable. A huge, open fireplace centered the back wall. From a rough-hewn rafter hung a large lamp, under which stood an enormous table.

As Britt entered, the room appeared to blaze and roar at him. Red blankets and every variety of colorful cowboy accoutrements, and a score of clean, tanned, freshly shaven faces, leaped at Britt. His entrance, however, stopped the babel of voices.

"Mawnin', men," he said, cheerily, and gazed around the room, trying to be casual. The cowboys sat and lounged and lay everywhere. Brazos, as usual, was the center of observation, and this time it was in the middle of the floor, where he sat cross-legged like an aborigine. The ruddy-faced

Beef Talman inclined his large bulk on the table; Stinger, pale but bright-eyed, dangled his bow-legs from a bunk; Cherokee, the Indian, leaned straight and dark against the stone mantel; Handsome Gaines straddled a chair.

Before Britt could survey half of his outfit, Brazos, in his inimitable manner, claimed attention.

"Cap, what the hell do you think of a cowboy who throws his sombrero on the floor, hangs up his spurs, an' sprawls aboot with two heavy guns hangin' low on his thighs?"

That was a long speech for Brazos. A dancing devil beamed from his blue eyes. Britt had only to hear him and get one glance at his fair and brazen face to know that Brazos was in his happiest and most bewildering mood.

"Wal, I reckon thet cowboy is some oot of the ordinary," replied Britt, with a laugh. "Sounds Texan to me. Who you mean, Brazos?"

"There's the dog-gone hombre," rejoined Brazos, pointing.

Renn Frayne sat in a chair, tipped back against the windowseat. He was in his shirtsleeves, and for the rare moment, a slight smile gave charm to his leonine features. The whole outfit, except Brazos, had taken to this outlaw. He had been a cowboy for years; he possessed all the qualities that cowboys admired or revered or strove to attain; and his notorious renown sat lightly upon him. Britt caught a twinkle in the half-shut gray eyes, and he felt anew that Frayne was vastly more than what he had claimed to be — a lone wolf of the ranges. He liked the young, fair-haired firebrand, and he understood him.

"Brazos," he began, coolly. "The way you asked Britt that sounds friendly. But really it's not. It's a slur. You're always giving me a dig. I must rub you the wrong way."

"Yu do, Frayne," replied Brazos, flushing as red as an embarrassed girl. Frayne had at last called his bluff.

"All right. That's frank. I'm glad you came out in the open. You're always bragging about putting the cards on the table. Just why do I rub you the wrong way? Can it be because I always pack two guns — that I am Renn Frayne — and you, like an ordinary fool cowboy who's quick on the draw, want to try me out? I'd be ashamed of you for that. And I don't believe it. You're a wild youngster, Brazos, but you are genuine. I like you. I never did you a wrong, or even hurt your feelings, which I know are damned sensitive. So come out with it. What have you against me?"

"Wal, Frayne, since you push me — not a —— thing," rejoined Brazos, with a hint of contempt for himself, as if he had been driven. "I reckon I'm a cross-grained cuss."

Britt felt that he alone understood Brazos' strange antipathy for Frayne, and that the cowboy had lied. Holly Ripple's only too evident interest in the most notorious of her men was responsible for it. Frayne, of course, had no inkling of this, and Brazos imagined his secret was safe. Britt welcomed the by-play and hoped it would clarify the atmosphere.

"Brazos, the last thing we want in this outfit is a disorganizer," went on Frayne, earnestly. "You never were that kind of a cowboy. I trailed cattle for ten years. I know the game. I know cowboys. And I'm telling you that never again in the West will there be an aggregation such as Britt has gotten together to ride for Miss Ripple. The day will come when you'll be proud of it. I'm proud now to be one of you. Like Britt, I see what's coming. We're older, Brazos, and we look forward. There's just going to be bloody hell on this range. Some of us will stop lead. But our outfit must not break up from internal strife. It must *not*, Brazos. Can't you see that?"

"I see it better'n I did," said Brazos, the blue flame of his eyes on Frayne, as if to pierce through the man's cool, earnest mask. "Shore we mustn't fight among ourselves. . . . Frayne, I'll come clean before the ootfit. I apologize fer naggin' you. But don't misunderstand thet naggin'. I never had no hankerin' to mix draws with you, Frayne. Not me! . . . An' heah's my hand, if you'll shake."

Frayne's chair crashed to the floor as he moved to meet Brazos halfway. The meeting of this gunman and cowboy held more for Britt than the smoothing out of a rough discord in the outfit. The cowboy's subtle search for a motive behind Frayne's impassive refusal to be insulted, for his eloquent appeal for harmony, struck Britt as singularly thought-provoking. Brazos had the keen intuition and perspicuity of a lover. Why should Renn Frayne, one of the marked bad men of the plains, prove so strong and eager to keep Holly Ripple's great outfit of cowboys intact? As Frayne never looked at Holly, or spoke to her unless addressed, as he had never sat at her famous table or been in her house, and as his indifference had become so marked as to excite comment among his companions, it followed then that his stand was simply that of a man.

"Brazos — Frayne," sang out Britt, happy for whatever had corrected this rift, "I'm shore glad to see you shake hands. An' I'll bet the ootfit is, too."

"Boss, give us some *pesos* an' we'll go drink to them, an' to an outfit thet can't be busted now," called out some cowboy unseen by Britt. The voice sounded like Rebel McNulty's, young brother of the famous Captain McNulty, of the Texas Rangers.

"He coppered the trick, boss."

"Wager a whole month back before we rode out."

"Britt, we're plumb busted."

"Aw, come on, Cap, an' be a good fellar. We all need boots an' pants."

The clamor grew until Britt threw up his hands.

"Boys, I have the money right heah, but . . ."

That was a blunder, as Britt deduced by the ensuing uproar. Nevertheless he waved them back and held his ground until they quieted down.

"Wait! — Brazos, Frayne, Jim — I leave it to

104

you. Is it safe to shell oot yore wages jest four days before Miss Holly's party?"

"I reckon so, Cap," grinned Brazos, slyly.

"No," declared Frayne.

"Boss, I hate to have this pack of range dawgs snappin' at me, but dog-gone if I'd pay them till after the party," added Jim, vehemently.

But these few older heads availed nothing against the young bloods who were hot to spend, to buy, to drink, to gamble. Britt, driven to succumb against his better judgment, drew a chair up to the table, and hauled forth rolls of greenbacks and a handful of gleaming gold.

"Listen, you dumb-haids!" he yelled. "Miss Holly made me take this money. I didn't want it fer another week. But she insisted. 'Pay my cowboys,' she said. 'But tell them thet if any one of them comes to my party drunk I'll never speak to him again!' . . . There! Thet's the kind of mistress you have. Do you want yore wages now?"

"Who's gonna get drunk?" asked the irrepressible Brazos, with his beautiful smile.

"Line up, then, an' let's get it over," called Britt, slapping the table. "With two months' wages comin' you can all afford to pay each other what you owe."

Brazos got his first, and with the gleeful face of an imp, he clanked for the door.

"Hyar, Brazos," brawled Laigs Mason. "You owe me ten *pesos*."

"Chase him, Laigs," said Britt, as he paid the cowboy.

It was noteworthy that the brothers Tex and Mex Southard, half-breed *vaqueros*, asked for only *"Cinco pesos,"* each; and the lithe Cherokee, with a smile breaking his sombre bronze, said: "Me take ten dollar." When they had all rushed out, eager as boys released from school, Britt discovered Frayne leaning on his knee, with his foot up on the windowseat. He was watching the cowboys make down the slope for the village.

"Frayne, come get yore money," called Britt. "What was yore wages?"

"Miss Ripple did not speak of any," rejoined Frayne, as he turned. "She just asked me to ride for her, and I agreed."

"Shore. She overlooked it. Thet'll annoy her. But I won't tell her. . . . How much, Frayne? I'm payin' the cowboys forty. Jim gets more, an so I reckon you should, bein' older."

"Suppose we just pass the wages up."

"What?" queried Britt, dumbfounded at the idea of a cowman not wanting his wages.

"I have plenty of money," returned Frayne, his voice cool, his face impassive. "My needs are few. I'm through with drink and cards. So never mind wages for me, for the present, anyway."

"Miss Holly won't like thet," declared Britt dubiously.

"You won't tell her."

"But Frayne! . . . See heah, man, you're not gonna ride away on us?"

"I gave my word."

"Excuse me, I forgot. . . . But it's not regular.

106

. . . Frayne, have this yore own way. I don't savvy you, atall. Think a heap of you, though. Thet was shore fine of you to slap it on our smart-alec Brazos. You jest hit me right. I'd like to get better acquainted with you."

"Well, why don't you? . . . . I've an idea, Britt. These boys will go on a tear. Some of them will be drunk for Miss Ripple's party. I won't go myself, but I'll see they're all sober. I'll get Cherry to help me. The day of the party we'll hunt out every drunk or drinking cowboy, and dump him into the creek. It's cold as ice. Then we'll tie them in their bunks."

"Frayne, you do have idees," drawled Britt. "Thet's a darn good one. It'll work, an' Miss Holly will be tickled. . . . But what's this aboot yore not goin' to her party?"

"I'd rather not, Britt."

"Why in hell not?"

"Look here, old timer, do I have to tell you that? I'm no roistering cowboy. I'm a man with enemies. This rancher, Sewall McCoy, is one of them. He made an outlaw of me. And he's the crookedest cattleman I ever knew."

"Hell you say," snapped Britt, deeply stirred. "Thet's news, most interestin'! But what's it got to do with yore comin' to Holly's party?"

"McCoy might come. Everyone on the range is invited, you know. Or some other enemy of mine might bob up."

"Ah-huh. An' you'd have to draw?"

"I would. Even at Miss Ripple's table."

"All right. We'll chance it. You're comin'. I won't see Holly hurt."

"Nonsense, Britt," ejaculated Frayne, his composure broken. "How could it possibly matter to her?"

"Wal, it does. Yore attitude to Holly has already hurt her."

"How do you know that?"

"I knew before she told me."

"Vain little Spaniard," declared Frayne, with heat. "Britt, are you sure you understand your mistress? . . . . I've heard all about her affairs. Don't get me wrong, old timer. Miss Ripple is as good as gold, as proud as her mother, as fine as the Colonel must have been. But she's a spoiled girl. She is a flirt. She is like a princess. She wants *all* these cowboys to adore her, bow down to her. Well, *I* won't do it. I daresay she made a sort of hero out of me. But I'm no hero, nor a romancing cowboy to be made eyes at. I've forgotten who I was, but I'll never forget what I am. Is that plain, Britt?"

"Plain as print," retorted the foreman. "You figger Holly right, as she *was*. But thet girl has changed lately. I wouldn't swear it's permanent. An' I wouldn't swear you had all to do with it. Only you shore had somethin'. . . . An' I'm remindin' you, Frayne, thet so far as her respect fer you is concerned, an' mine, yore past doesn't count. I'm remindin' you thet this is New Mexico in seventy-four with hell aboot to pop heah. What we need oot heah is men. What Holly Ripple will need sooner or later is a man. She's blood of the West. A few years now an' this wild frontier will slow up. If you live, an' if you air loyal to Holly — which means turn yore back square against yore past — you'll have as good a chance with her as Brazos or any other cowboy. An' from cowboys Holly Ripple will choose her mate!"

Frayne turned aside a slightly paled face to bend it while he lighted a cigarette.

"Old timer, why do you tell me that?" he inquired, with voice a little deepened.

"Wal, I'm concerned fer Holly's happiness. Since she came home from school she's had a dozen flames fer boys, like a Mexican señorita. But they never lasted. Whatever she feels aboot you, it's different. Mebbe she's jest piqued at yore indifference. If you know women atall you'll understand thet."

"No man can understand a woman. Still, you may be right. She might be young enough and crazy enough to be piqued. I doubt it. But no matter what she feels — I am an outlaw — a gunman with a bloody record that must grow bloodier before this West sees any law. The odds are all against me living that long. . . . Now do you see my side, Britt?"

"Yes. An' I reckon you're right," replied Britt, gruffly. "All the same you come to Holly's party — at least thet dinner she's givin' fer the ootfit."

"Very well, Britt, if you put it that way. . . . I'll come."

CHAPTER 5

Once or twice each spring of late years the trappers would come down out of the mountains with the Indians to sell their pelts.

Horn's Post had seen the day when thousands of them came to barter. But the glory of the trapper had faded long ago. Perhaps a score of white men, and a hundred red men, comprised the motley crew which visited Don Carlos' Rancho that Saturday in early June. The trappers were a greasy, bearded, rollicking lot; and the Indians a hungry, silent crowd with the prospect of the reservation in their somber eyes. The beaver were almost gone from the mountain streams.

Britt was one who sympathized with the red man. He sensed the romance of Carson's day, when the eastern demand for beaver hats made the fur hunters rich. Indians never depleted any natural resource. But the white trappers were the advance guard of that greedy army of adventurers who must strip the streams and hills.

Across the half-mile-wide trail from Horn's Post, a large flat adobe structure, cracked and crumbling of wall, was the Indian encampment. Ponies and dogs, squaws in their beaded and fringed buckskin, braves lolling on their colored blankets, a few tepees of painted hides, packs and pelts and fires — all these gave the old Texas Ranger a sad inkling of the past. Below the village in the wide bend of the creek the gray groups of prairie-schooners, the droves of oxen and horses, the movement of burly teamsters, some how harmonized with Britt's conception of the past glamour of the trappers' era. The day of the caravan, too, was passing. In a few more years, when the steel rails reached Santa Fe, the great white rolling ship of the plains would be gone.

On Britt's way to the trading-post he encountered an army sergeant who hailed him as an acquaintance. Britt remembered the ruddy Irish visage, but could not place the man. They chatted. The sergeant belonged to Gen. Mackenzie's Fourth U.S. Cavalry bound for Fort Union and other points in southeastern New Mexico and Texas. They were making trails, and expected some hard Indian campaigns in the near future.

"Did you travel west along the Old Trail?" queried Britt, ever eager to add to his information of the day.

"Yes, from Fort Lyon," replied the sergeant.

"How aboot movement of cattle?"

"Shure more than last summer. Las Animas reminds ye of Dodge."

"Wal, you come up fer supper an' tell us all aboot it."

Before Britt got much farther on his way he was accosted by a young man whose apparel proclaimed him not long in the West, and whose dissipated face told the common story of many a ten-derfoot.

"Are you Captain Britt, foreman for the Ripple ranch?"

"Yes, I'm Britt. What can I do fer you?"

"My name's Taylor — Lee Taylor. I'm from the south. Miss Ripple will remember me. She knew my sister. I used to call at their school."

"Ah-huh. Come in from Santa Fe?" asked Britt casually, studying the young man. Long used to reading faces, he reacted unfavorably to this one.

"Yes. Up from El Paso."

"Hawse-back, caravan or stage?"

"Came in the stage."

"Had kinda a rough time, eh? What you want of me? A job ridin'?"

"No. I'd like to borrow some money. Don't want to call on Miss Ripple in these rags. I'll get money from home eventually."

"Wal, I'll ask Miss Holly aboot you. An' if she knows you, why shore, I'll help you oot. . . . Come in heah an' meet the ootfit."

Britt led Taylor into Horn's saloon. At first glance he thought all his cowboys were there lined up at the rude bar. Brazos met him, surprised at his entrance and curious as to his companion.

"My Gawd, boss, air yu lost?"

"Say, Brazos, cain't I take a drink myself once? . . . Heah, meet Lee Taylor, from the South. Says he knows Miss Holly. . . . Taylor, this is Brazos Keene."

Britt conveyed a good deal more with a look

112

than by words. He had no compunctions in turning the stranger over to Brazos. If Taylor was all right, which he certainly did not look, Brazos would grasp it quickly. Britt was getting tired of strangers imposing upon Holly's generous hospitality. Lascelles was still up at the ranchhouse, to Holly's annoyance and Britt's helpless rage.

"Wal, dog-gone! Another old beau of our Lady's," drawled the devilish Brazos. "Come on, Mister Taylor, meet the ootfit. . . . Cap, will yu have one on me?"

"Don't care if I do. An' I'll set them up once, anyway."

"Gosh, fellars, the world's shore comin' to an end. Heah's the boss, an' he's thirsty."

"He looks guilty to me," declared Skylark, with a keen grin.

"Boys, meet Lee Taylor, from the south," announced Britt, glad to relinquish the stranger to the tender mercy of his cowboys. And he lined up with them, amused at Skylark's perspicuity. In truth he had more than one sense of guilt. Frayne had always had the power to excite him, thrill him, upset him; and that colloquy in the bunkhouse weighed hauntingly on Britt's conscience. His feeling had gotten the better of his judgment, which seldom happened, and never except pertaining to Holly. He needed a bracer. On Frayne's account he was glad to have had the talk. It gave more light on this fascinating complex outlaw. But it might have been a hasty and inexcusable exposure of his own conjectures. His love and concern for Holly often led him to impulsive speech. On the other hand, when he cudgeled himself with reproach, he had, to uphold him, certain acts and words of Holly's. If he could have been cold and calculating they might have betrayed more. As it was, he feared Holly liked this indifferent Renn Frayne far more than was good for her happiness. In view of Frayne's attitude, which Britt felt bound to admit was honorable and fine, a wild and hopeless infatuation on Holly's part would be deplorable.

Britt partook of a good stiff drink, and then he had another. They stimulated him to the extent of eradicating the oppression of vague trouble that had weighed upon him.

As Britt shook off the happy Brazos and turned to go out he met Ride-'Em Jackson, the negro of the outfit, with Bluegrass and Trinidad, two more of his cowboys.

"Boss, we is sho lookin' fer yo," declared Jackson.

The red-headed Trinidad, and the sharp eagle-eyed Bluegrass, hailed Britt with glad hands, and both gabbled at once.

"You needn't squawk at me," said Britt, producing his roll of bills. "Come over heah."

"Boss, doan gimme all dat," objected Jackson, his black face and rolling eyes ludicrously expressive. "Dis hyar Goge Washington Jeffersun Jackson sho nebber could keep it mo dan ten minnits."

"Good, Ride-'Em. You got sense in yore woolly

haid," declared Britt. "Jest ride in?"

"Dis hyar minnit. An' I'se got news."

"Bad news?"

"Yes, suh. I reckon — orful bad fer Missy Holly."

"Hawses?"

"Yas, suh."

"Wal, report to me at the bunkhouse in half an hour."

Britt went out through the trading-post, lingering to watch the unaccustomed scene. Perhaps the most interesting place on the frontier was a trading-post during a big day. Dancehalls, gambling-halls and saloons had more of raw drama and wildness of the period, but the trader's emporium had the life, the vividness, the atmosphere and business of the West. Here Mexican *pesos* and American silver dollars jingled on the counters, and rolls of gold coins went into the greasy buckskin of the trappers. Lean, half-naked, befeathered and painted savages sat and lounged around the great barn of a room, waiting to market their packs of hides. A dozen or more rugged white trappers held the floors, haranguing like auctioneers. Horn Brothers were close buyers. They knew these trappers dared not ship consignments of pelts east. And the trappers, earnest, desperate, knowing their day was past, argued with bulging jaws for a living wage. Fat squaws and comely maidens, with their coal-black shining hair hanging down their backs, fingered the dry goods and gazed longingly at the colored candy. Counters were piled high with merchandise; rows of shelves sagged under the weight of countless cans; the odor of tobacco vied with that of dried pelts. A swarm of flies buzzed in the warm air.

Of late a habit of procrastination had grown upon Britt. He was conscious of it, believed that in a measure it was deliberate. He hated to think — to get down to facts and figures. If he had been alone, with only that bunch of fire-eating cowboys, if he had not the responsibility of Holly's future on his hands, he could have revelled in the near prospect of the cattle crisis.

Repairing to the bunkhouse he jotted down his payments to the men, and then figured carefully details of the two cattle drives he would advise Holly to sanction right after her party. The rise in price of beef was unprecedented, and it had two sides, one of them cardinally serious.

Presently Renn Frayne sauntered in leisurely, thoughtful of brow and smouldering of eye.

"Howdy, cowboy. Whar you been?" asked Britt, closing his account book.

"Didn't you see me trailing you around?" was the laconic answer.

"Nope, I never did."

"Cap, you are a worried man."

"Hellyes."

"I don't blame you. It's Miss Ripple, of course. An old Texas Ranger like you wouldn't wink an eyelash about cattle or rustlers, or a tough outfit."

"Shore. It's Holly — bless her heart! I'm the

116

only Dad she's got. . . . What'd you see down at the post?"

"Getting lively. By tonight it'll be going strong. Reminds me of Dodge and Hays City. But tame."

"So you know Hays, eh? Ever run up against Wild Bill?"

"I saw Bill shoot five cowboys in a row, across the street, and he never got a scratch. But they were drunk and had buck-fever beside."

"I used to trail-drive up oot of Texas. Them was the days. Dodge 'peared the wust town to me. . . . Wal, everythin' is haidin' west. We'll think we're back in Kansas pronto. Jackson has some bad news fer me. It jest keeps on comin'."

"Britt, was it a good plan to draw all your riders in off the range?"

"No. Miss Holly's orders."

"It'll cost her plenty."

"I'm not so shore, Frayne. Everybody inside of a hundred miles will be heah. It's an open invite, you know. Old Kurnel Ripple's idee."

Ride-'Em Jackson came trudging in to interrupt them. Walking did not appear to be his best method of locomotion. His shiny black face was wet with sweat.

"Hyar I is, boss."

"Set down, Jackson, an' get it off yore chest."

"Yas suh," he returned, with hesitation, rolling his eyes at Frayne. "Howdy, Marsh Frayne. How yo is?"

"Shoot, Jack. I'm able to help Cap bear up under your bad news."

117

"Boss, dem hosses was gone."

Britt cursed under his breath, though he had expected no less. It was not the loss of a score and more of good stock so much as verification of the closing in of a net about Don Carlos' Rancho. Since the Heaver raid all of the Ripple thoroughbreds had been driven into the pastures and corrals. This bunch of many remaining out on the range had been left in Cedar Draw, an out-of-the-way place.

"We tracked 'em tree days, an' den we gibe up," went on the negro.

"Hawse-thieves, of course?"

"Yas suh. Dey sho nebber runned off by demselves. De tiefs rode shod hosses. Blue an' Trinidad disagreed wif me aboot how many dey was. I made oot fo shod hosses, an' one of dem was a little hoss carryin' a heavy man."

"Which way did they go, Jackson?"

"To de souf. We tracked 'em till we could see Seven Rivers. Den we reckoned we'd better mosey back."

"Ha! I rather snicker you reckoned correct," retorted Britt, sarcastically. "Frayne, do you know the Seven River country down on the Pecos?"

"No. Only by hearsay."

"Wal, thet's Chisum country. The old reprobate. Boss cattleman of the West! An' boss cattlethief, too! He laughs an' owns up to it. Frayne, I reckon Chisum has his Long Rail brand on a hundred thousand haid of stock."

"No!" ejaculated Frayne, incredulously.

118

"Des thick as bees, Marsh Frayne," corroborated the negro. "I rode for Chisum an' I knows."

"Wal, Jackson, I hope thet's all."

"Yas, suh. But it ain't, suh. I sho ain't tole yo nuthin' yet. . . . Fust camp we made comin' back Chisum's top ootfit rid down on us. We sho was scared, boss. But dey wuz friendly. A plumb dozen riders, boss, an' Chisum's top riders. I knowed 'em. I'd rid with dem. Russ Slaughter was haid of dat ootfit. Only ornery Slaughter in all dat Texas familee. . . . Wal, Russ tole 'em dey had quit Chisum. Dey wuz goin' in de cattle game demselves. Russ says, 'Jack, what yo want to ride fer thirty dollars a month when yo can git a hundred?' — An' I asks Russ how. An' he says dere's half a million hed of cattle in de country an' no law. Railroad market payin' forty dollars a hed, an' government buyers givin' ten an' no questions ast. . . . Russ talked till he was red in de face. We sho didn't want to tro in wid dem an' we was sort of flabustered."

"Jack, thet was a fix. How'd you get oot of it?"

"Wal, suh, I says to Russ — 'Yo knows I'se turned ober a new leaf, an' I'll be dawg-goned if I'll quit. Missy Ripple has been good to me an' I sho gonna stick.' . . . Blue an' Trinidad talked like one man. Dawg-gone they did! An' they says, 'I'se not gibben up providin' a husband fer Missy Ripple.' . . . Russ looked ugly an' talked ugly, which I ain't gonna squeal to yo-all. 'Cept he said, 'Say, if all yo heah boot the little lady is so, dere's a chance fer any hombre to grab dat million.'"

119

"Ride-'Em, what did Blue an' Trin say to that?" quietly asked Frayne.

"Marsh Frayne, you know Blue. Thet Kaintucky boy got kinda pale, but he kept mum. Russ hed been hittin' de bottle an' anyway, he wuzn't acquainted wif Blue. I was scared 'cause it looked like Blue might bore him. But Trinidad he got redder'n a beet an' busted oot, 'The —— hell yo say? Shore yo come ober to Don Carlos' Rancho, an' try dat game yoself, Russ Slaughter.' . . . An' Russ laughed kinda mean. 'Why not?' he says. 'If niggahs, Injuns, ootlaws, all hev a show with Holly Ripple then sho a white cowman can buck his luck. We'll come to de party an' look yo all over.' . . . Den dey rode off an' Blue hed a hell of a time keepin' Trin fum trowin' his rifle on Slaughter. An' we rustled home. Dat's all, boss."

"Jackson, keep yore mouth shut aboot this," replied Britt, authoritatively. "Hurry back to Bluegrass an' Trinidad an' tell them my orders air they're not to tell the ootfit."

"Yes suh. I'se rustlin', suh," replied the little negro, and bolted out of the door.

"Frayne, what you think of thet?" queried Britt, meeting the outlaw's piercing gray eyes.

"It never rains but it pours."

"Slaughter's ootfit will come, shore as Gawd made little apples. They'll use Holly's party as a blind to look over the lay of our cattle. I don't know what could be wuss than their quittin' Chisum. I remember Maxwell tellin' Kurnel Ripple why he was sellin' oot. He knew."

"Britt, didn't you get the significance of that nigger's report?" asked Frayne, cuttingly.

"Hellyes!" retorted Britt, heatedly. "Thet aboot Holly. . . . I've heahed it before. But Frayne, these hard-nut range-riders have vile minds an' vile mouths. If only Holly would get married! Thet'd stop all this crazy courtin' an' gossipin'. . . . Slaughter will come an' he'll have the gall to make up to Holly. Thet needn't bother us. She can take care of herself. But if Blue or Trin get drunk they're liable to squeal what Russ said aboot Holly. If Brazos heahs it! — He'll draw on Russ at fust sight."

"Why Brazos?" queried Frayne, with cold detachment. "Why not Blue? Or someone else?"

Britt gave Frayne a sharp glance and threw up his hands. He paced the floor for a few minutes, while Frayne leaned in the doorway gazing out.

"Frayne, gimme yore angle on this idee," spoke up the foreman, presently. "After Holly's party I'd like to drive all our cattle this side of Cottonwood Creek, an' hold them fer a while heah in sight of the ranch. Then cut oot as big a bunch as would be safe to drive to Las Animas. An' do the same in the fall."

"I'd advise that very thing. Only we can't drive all the Ripple stock along the Cottonwood. But if we bunched the cattle closer and put out a night guard we would cut down rustling. And I'd say the more Miss Ripple sells now the less she'll lose."

"My sentiments. I'll advise thet strongly. . . . Now, Renn, I'm lookin' to you fer help. Our prob-

121

lem is to hold these cowboys. Can we do it? What effect will Russ Slaughter's quittin' Chisum have on them?"

"You may pay the penalty of hiring the riff-raff of the ranges. They're most bad, these cowboys, and some of them as bad as Slaughter. I'd say in the ordinary run of things your outfit would break under this deal. Then, of course, you'd suffer an enormous loss, perhaps ruin. It has happened before."

"I savvy thet. We must make this oot of the ordinary."

"There's a chance Miss Ripple might reach those boys so all hell couldn't change them. You know cowboys. Tell her to double their wages and give them freedom. Put them on their honor. I know that's funny, Britt. But do it. If they can be made to see that she relies on each and every one of them to beat these rustlers and save her rancho — why, it's as good as done."

Britt cracked his hands together with the sound like a pistol shot.

"Renn, thet night at the supper, will you have a talk ready fer the boys?" flashed Britt.

The outlaw waved the proposition aside.

"Unbeknown to Holly, I mean," went on Britt, eagerly. "She's preparing a talk. Of course she'll call on me, an' perhaps Brazos, though if he knowed it, he'd die of fright. But you can, Renn, an' I'm appealin' to you. Surprise Holly an' the whole ootfit. I declare I'd never get done thankin' you."

"Old Timer, you are back to the wall," said Frayne, with his rare smile. "I'll do it, Britt. I'll take the hide off these cowboys."

Sunday was a lonesome day for the foreman, who likened himself to an old hen that had lost most of her brood of chickens.

Frayne, Tex and Mex Southard, Santone, Ride-'Em Jackson and Cherry were around when Jose called them for meals. But the rest of the outfit had succumbed either to liquor or to games of chance, or according to Santone, to both these failings of cowboys. Britt did not have opportunity to consult Holly about his plan to drive a big herd of cattle to the railroad. Holly was engrossed with the details of her coming party and dance, especially with the speech she intended to make to the cowboys. She was going over her books, and her father's papers and correspondence.

Britt kept track of the boys through Santone and Jackson, and by patrolling the beat between the bunkhouse and the corrals and the crowded Mexican street with its concentration around Horn's place. Nothing of any moment had occurred in the way of brawls. The cowboys were jolly and prodigal of their two months' wages.

On Monday the east-bound caravan pulled out with its wagons about half loaded. The departure of sixty-odd teamsters thinned the ranks of the crowd. But before that day had advanced far the vanguard of visitors to Don Carlos' Rancho began to arrive. By Tuesday, which was the date for the great *fiesta,* the ranchhouse was full of guests from all over the surrounding country. San Marcos, Cimarron, Raton and Lincoln were represented to the extent of practical desertion of these frontier towns. Sewall McCoy rode in at the head of his contingent of cowboys. Various groups of hard-faced, intent-eyed men arrived to keep to themselves.

About noon on Tuesday Britt thought it high time to inaugurate the proposed treatment of cowboys under the influence of liquor. It developed that Frayne and Cherokee would not want for help. Skylark, who had marvelously sobered up on Monday, and Talman, Stinger and Jim all wanted to be in on the ducking of the inebriates. Cherry and Santone hitched up and drove a big wagon into the village, where Frayne and Britt were ready to receive them. Bluegrass and Trinidad were carried out and dumped into the wagon. Rebel and Handsome Gaines were located, and hilariously took the proceeding as a ride in their honor; Flinty and Tennessee had to be tied hand and foot, a procedure which brought a frightful chorus of profanity. The triumphant cowboys in charge drove toward the bunkhouse, followed by a crowd of whites, Indians and Mexicans.

Brazos Keene and his faithful Laigs had been dead to the world for many hours. They were rudely awakened and hauled out of their bunks.

"Wot you hombres up to?" Brazos bawled, furiously. They promptly roped him and carried him out like a lassoed bull.

"Boss, wot ya gonna do?"

"Brazos, you forget the party tonight."

"No I didn't neither," he protested. "Me and Laigs come home early last night."

"Wal, you're too shaky to suit this vigilante ootfit. . . . Pile him in, boys."

"———— !" roared Brazos, "I'll kill somebody fer this."

Laigs Mason was more complaisant.

"Wasser masser?" he asked, stupidly, leering around at his captors. "Wash Brazos raisin' — hell aboot?"

"Laigs, come oot. We're takin' you on a little hay-wagon ride."

"Dawg-gone!" babbled Laigs, staggering between Britt and Frayne. "Shore nice of — you fellars. . . . Brazos, no cowboys ever hed sich frens."

"Haw! Haw!" yelled Brazos, fiendishly. "Laigs Mason, you'll wake up pronto. . . . All yore fault. Didn't I want to come home? — Jest one more little drink!"

"Rustle Cherry," ordered Britt, climbing up on he seat beside the driver. "Down over thet stony flat to the creek. . . . Drive like hell. . . . Frayne, you boys keep 'em in the wagon."

Cherokee drove the wagon at a gallop over ground covered with loose boulders. If cowboys hated anything it was to be jolted. They were bumped and tossed about. When one of them tried to jump or fall out he was promptly thrown back by Frayne and his allies. That ride down to the creek was hard enough even for the sober cowboys who could hold on. Cherry drove down upon a gravel bar to the edge of a green clear pool about three feet deep.

"Brazos first," yelled Britt.

They dragged the flaxen-haired cowboy out of the wagon and threw him in. Brazos went under, and then bounded up with incredible speed.

"Aggh!" he bellowed. And the shock was so great that upon plunging back he went under again. Floundering and rolling he got up to wade out, like a drenched shivering dog, and as sober as he had ever been in his life.

"Come mon, Laigs. Take yore medicine," he shouted, bouncing around on the bar.

When they rolled Laigs out upon the gravel he sat up with his solemn blinking eyes beginning to show some intelligence.

"Wash thish, boys?"

"Grab hold and swing," called Frayne. Britt and Santone and Skylark also laid hold of the cowboy, one to each arm and leg, and they swung him, once, twice, three times, then let go. Laigs was small and light. He went far, and fell with a tremendous splash. And when he came up like a spouting porpoise his breathless yell was echoed by the ruthless captors. That water must have been as cold as ice water. Laigs made terrific haste to plunge out. When he got ashore he was sober, and madder than a wet hen.

"I'm g-gonna cut out s-somebody's gizzard," he shivered. He presented such a ridiculous figure

126

that the cowboys yelled in glee.

"Take those guns," called Frayne, as they dragged out the limp Bluegrass.

"Frayne, how's Blue goin' to take this?" queried Britt, dubiously. "He's from Kentucky, you know!"

"He'll take it wet," declared Frayne, with grim humor. "In with him, boys."

Bluegrass went in like a sack of lead and sank likewise. As he did not immediately burst up with a great splash Britt yelled frantically for Brazos and Laigs to drag him out.

"S-say, I — I wouldn't wade in thet water even fer you, boss," declared the Texan, laboriously climbing into the wagon.

"Laigs! Pull Blue oot! Rustle!"

Whereupon the obliging Mason plunged in and rescued Bluegrass, pulling him out on the bar, where he presented alarming symptoms of unconsciousness.

"He's all right," declared Frayne. "I'll look after him. He's coming to now. Throw the rest of them in!"

Splash! Splash! Splash! went the remaining cowboys in succession; and with their bawls of shocked sensibilities and the infernal glee of Skylark and his helpers, they made the welkin ring.

Britt forgot to keep track of Brazos and Laigs. But in a moment more they made their presence known. Brazos lashed the horses and drove them at breakneck speed off the bar and up the slow slope.

"Wait fer us, boss," yelled Brazos, from the wagon-seat. "We're gonna come back with another load."

"*Stop!*" replied Britt, in stentorian tones.

"Go to hell, Cappy, you an' your baptizers," shouted Laigs, gleefully. "We'll be back."

"Wal, Brazos turned the tables on us. We'll have to walk," declared Britt.

"I'll bet he'll come," said Frayne. "We'll have to wait till Blue recovers."

"Aw, Brazos will be heah pronto. Didn't you see thet devil in his eye? He's shore up to suthin'."

It developed that Bluegrass must have opened his mouth under water and had almost strangled. Frayne rolled him on his face, pounded and pumped his body, until signs of life returned. His pale features took on a shade of red, and he opened his eyes to stare at the faces bent over him.

"There, you're all right now, Blue," spoke up Britt, with relief. "Air you sober?"

"I reckon. . . . Who thought I needed a bath?"

"We all did. Brazos an' Laigs got theirs fust. Look at Trin, an' the rest of yore pards."

But Blue did not laugh. He sat up shivering. "Whose idee was this?"

"Mine," rejoined Britt, fearing the reaction of this hot-blooded Kentuckian.

"He's a liar, Blue," spoke up Frayne, with a laugh. "It was my idee. I've seen it worked before. . . . You forgot we were all to be sober for Miss Ripple's *fiesta* tonight. I was afraid some of you boys wouldn't be. So we ducked you."

"Frayne, I'm holdin' you responsible."

"Sure. But don't be a damn fool, Blue," returned the outlaw, easily. "Take a joke when it's on you."

"Joke hell! I'm froze. I'm a bag of ice-bones. I'll catch numonia an' die."

"All you need is a rub-down and a sleep. Then you'll be fine."

"I'm gonna call you out for this," said Bluegrass, doggedly.

Britt silenced the cowboys who were about to remonstrate with Blue. He divined that Frayne was equal to the occasion.

"Blue, that'd be a poor return for the favor I've done you."

"Favor! — Jest what favor, Mister?"

"Why, sobering you up. And saving your good name with Miss Ripple. If you get sore I'll have to shoot your arm off — or worse if you get ugly. That would put Miss Ripple against me. I was only working for her, for your good, and for all of us."

"I don't care a damn," yelled Blue, now red in the face. But he did care. "You gotta show me you can beat me to a gun."

"Blue, we took yore guns off an' you bet we'll keep them," interposed Britt. "Swaller yore medicine, boy."

"Did you duck Brazos?"

"Wal, I should smile we did."

"An' how'd he take it?"

"Yelled murder. But he stole the wagon, an drove off, leavin' us heah to shank it back."

129

Bluegrass gazed from his partner Trinidad to the other shivering cowboys, and his face began to work.

"Dog-gone-it! Do I look like them?"

"Wuss. You lay in the mud. An' you better let me wipe it off."

"All right. . . . Frayne, I lay down. But I'll play some orful trick on you, by thunder!"

"You're welcome, Blue," replied Frayne, heartily. "I knew you were a good fellow. . . . Boys, you all want to take this to heart. If we don't pull together as an outfit, like brothers, like men with their backs to the wall, Miss Ripple will be robbed poor. And we'll be disgraced in our own eyes forever."

Skylark called from the bank: "Brazos' drivin' back, hellbent fer election."

The cowboys, except Frayne and Blue, trooped behind Britt up the slope, all voicing anticipation. Sure enough there came the bouncing wagon behind galloping horses and leaving a cloud of dust.

"Wonder who thet son-of-a-gun has got?" demanded Britt, with vast curiosity.

"I'll bet ten bucks I know."

"Gee, look at thet wagon!"

"Boys, you can gamble Brazos would figger up suthin' great."

"Thet hombre always laughs last."

To Britt's amazement the horses did not fall and the wagon did not break to pieces. Brazos, whooping, his face like that of a red imp, drove down and slowing the team, brought them with a fine flourish to a halt on the wide bar. He leaped out. His audience was not slow in reaching the tail-end of that wagon. Britt saw Laigs Mason astride a man dressed in black. There was another man in the wagon. Brazos laid hold of his heels and hauled him out to drop him on the sand, like a sack of potatoes. This personage was Lee Taylor, whose visage attested to a debauch.

"Heah yu air," sang out Brazos, and with a remarkable exhibition of strength he lifted Taylor aloft, above his head, and giving vent to an Indian yell, threw him into the pool. Whatever the Southerner's condition on the moment of hitting the water, it was certain that when he lunged up in a great splash and floundered ashore he was not under the influence of anything but exceedingly cold water.

Blue of visage, shaking as one with the ague, drenched and dishevelled, Taylor fronted Britt.

"S-so this is h-h-how you let your ruffianly cowboys treat a gentleman?"

"Only fun, Taylor. An' at thet you needed it," replied Britt, dryly.

"Say, who's a ruffian an' who's a gentleman?" queried Brazos, menacingly. The diabolical fun in him suffered a blight. Britt quietly pushed Taylor back to the rear.

"Let him up, Laigs," shouted Brazos.

Britt wheeled in time to see the gambler, Malcolm Lascelles, arise clumsily from the floor of the wagon. His frockcoat and flowered vest were spoiled by contact with dust. His wide, flat-crowned sombrero was not in evidence. His handsome face was streaked with dirt and distorted by rage.

"Step oot, Mister Lascelles," invited Brazos, sarcastically.

Lascelles jumped down, his action proving that his equilibrium was not perfect.

"Britt, what's the meaning of this outrage?" he demanded.

"I don't know, Lascelles. We treated Brazos an' Mason to a duckin'. They stole the wagon an' drove away. Why you're heah I don't savvy, but it wasn't from order of mine."

"Damnable outrage!" fumed Lascelles. "These drunken louts of yours —"

"Take care, Lascelles," interrupted Britt. "I warn you."

"But this range is free. A man has a right to his liberty."

"Shore. But there's no law heah. An' if a man doesn't measure up to what the frontier expects, he's liable to lose not only freedom, but life."

"You're one with your crew," snarled Lascelles, malignantly. "I am Miss Ripple's guest — an old friend — and you dare insult me."

Brazos stepped up. "Boss, I reckon this is my deal," he interposed, coolly.

"It shore is, Brazos. But you're sober now. Use your haid."

Laigs Mason edged his ludicrous little misshapen form in beside Brazos. His homely face expressed

132

an untamed and unabatable fidelity to his partner.

"Don't weaken, Brazos. This caird-sharp stinks of rum."

"Shet up. Lemme do the talkin' heah," snapped Brazos, and then he fastened those piercing half slits of eyes on the gambler.

"Lascelles, my idee was to duck yu along with yore southern gent friend," said Brazos. "Reckon I don't often explain my actions toward any hombre who makes me sore. But I'm tellin' yu. Miss Holly ast us to be sober today. Thet's why Frayne an Britt hashed up this duckin' idee. Wal, it is a plumb good one — an' I'll be —— if I'm gonna let her see yu at her party drunk —"

"I'm not drunk," protested Lascelles.

"Aw, you're a liar. Yu been drunk fer a week. Right now as Laigs heah swears, yu stink of rum. An' my idee was to give yu a cold bath. Gonna take yore medicine?"

"No, you heathen rowdy. Don't you dare lay another hand on me."

"Ah-huh. . . . Wal, my idee grows a little," returned Brazos, with a cool insolence that Britt had learned to gauge. "I jest happened to remember how yu fleeced Laigs oot of half a month's wages."

"I did not. My game is square," declared Lascelles, stoutly, though he paled slightly. No doubt he had been long enough on the frontier to find out what was meted out to crooked gamblers.

"How aboot it, Laigs?"

"Pard, I couldn't swear I seen him, 'cause my eyes was pore," admitted Mason, frankly. "But Sky seen him hold oot on me, an' Ride-'Em seen him, too."

"Boys, is thet so?"

"Yes, it's so," declared Skylark, curtly.

The little negro rolled his big eyes till the whites showed. He was reluctant. He remembered the southern attitude toward his race. But he was also loyal.

"Brazos, jest how slick Mistah Lascelles is I dunno. But I sho seen him pull tricks thet Laigs hisself can pull when he's sober."

"Lascelles, now what?"

"You're a Texan. Can you believe a nigger against a white man?"

"Yu bet yore life — when I know the nigger. Jackson isn't a liar. Cowboys don't lie — when they're in earnest."

"You're as low-down as they are," retorted Lascelles, yielding to a passion that perhaps did not rightly interpret the cowboy's coolness. "That's the last straw, you take a nigger's word to mine. I'll shoot him. And I'll recommend to Miss Ripple that she discharge you."

"Fine. You'll get a long way, 'specially with thet first bluff," rang out Brazos. Then with incredible rapidity he launched a terrific blow upon Lascelles. Following a sharp, solid crack the gambler fell backward to measure his length in the pool. All save his head went under. In contrast to the others

134

who had been immersed in that icy current, his motions were slow and deliberate. When he strode ashore, his right hand inside his coat, all the cowboys except Laigs sheered to either side of Brazos. Britt himself leaped instinctively out of line. All saw Lascelles' white supple hand close round something which could only be a gun. Gamblers seldom packed a gun on their hips, but they always had one, or a derringer, up their sleeves, or inside the coat, concealed but easy to draw. And there stood Brazos and Laigs, unarmed.

"Look oot!" warned Britt, reaching for his weapon, which he had left on the table in the bunkhouse. The moment was terrible. Out of a clear sky the thunderbolt!

"Lascelles, don't draw!"

Even the maddened gambler stiffened at Frayne's voice. Britt suddenly relaxed with a strong revulsion of feeling, and the sweat broke out all over his cold skin. And he knew what to expect before he turned. Frayne leaned back against the wagon with a gun levelled low.

"Let go. . . . Come out."

Lascelles' hand dropped limply from under his coat, and with a repulsive face, dirty gray and livid white, he stepped out of the water.

"Hawses comin'," shouted Brazos.

In the soft sand of the bank a group of horsemen had drawn close without being heard by the tense spectators or participants in that drama.

"Russ Slaughter!" added Bluegrass, trenchantly.

Britt swept his gaze away from Frayne and Lascelles. At least ten or more riders were heading down under the cottonwoods, with a swarthy leader in front. Several more horsemen hung back on the bank with a string of pack-mules. Slaughter at the head of his followers walked his horse leisurely down on the bar, far enough to take in the situation. Then as Frayne stepped out from the wagon Slaughter halted so sharply that his companions' horses collided with him. Like so many range-riders Slaughter had the visage of a beast of prey. It would have been impossible to determine his motive, but to be on the safe side Britt gauged him as an enemy. Frayne could be trusted to read this man the same way.

" 'Scuse us fer ridin' in on you," drawled Slaughter. "We seen the wagon as we wus crossin' above . . . Howdy, Blue. . . . Wal, there's my ole nigger cowboy, Jackson. . . . An' Trinidad too, wet as a drowned rat. . . . I take you, sir, to be Britt, foreman of the Ripple outfit."

"Yes, I'm Britt, but you'll excuse me fer the minnit."

"Who are you, rider?" queried Frayne.

"I reckoned everybody had heerd of Russ Slaughter, an' would shore know him on sight."

"Never heard of you," returned Frayne, curtly. "Would you mind shutting your jaw until I get through with this card-sharp?"

"Wal, it's none of my bizness, but I don't like your talk. . . . I reckon you're this coal hand, Frayne, huh?"

136

"If you don't like my talk — lump it," deliberately rejoined Frayne, with the nerve of a man who had no fear.

"Yeah?" returned Slaughter, insolently. His oscillating red eyes had swiftly grasped the general absence of guns in that group, except in Frayne's case.

"Lascelles, you're played out here at Don Carlos' Rancho," said Frayne. "If your card-sharp tricks weren't enough, your gall in taking advantage of the Ripple hospitality and using it to press your absurd suit upon Miss Holly, would be. Send for your pack and get out. That's all."

"An' see heah, Lascelles," added Brazos, passionately. "Yu seen I hadn't a gun. Yu'd shot me but fer Frayne. . . . Wal, —— yore cheap soul, go fer thet gun next time we meet."

"Lascelles, thet's clear enough," interposed Britt, forcefully, wanting to lend his authority to this expulsion. "I advise you to leave pronto."

Lascelles flung his hands with a gesture of hopeless rage and impotent defeat. Then he started to stalk off, his back to Frayne, who still held that ominous gun forward.

"Hold on," called Slaughter. Then he addressed Frayne and Britt. "If you're through, I reckon you've no objection to my talkin' to this Lascelles?"

"Wal, it's a free country," answered the foreman, not heartily.

"Who air you, stranger?" asked the Chisum cowman, fastening hard eyes upon Lascelles.

"My name's Lascelles. I'm from Louisiana."

"Gambler?"

"I play cards for pleasure."

"This fellar Frayne called you a card-sharp."

"He's a-a-er . . . That's not true. The cowboys lost and put up a job on me."

"What's thet talk about your imposin' on Miss Ripple?" queried Slaughter, with a crackling laugh.

"More balderdash," retorted Lascelles. "I'm a guest here. Everybody in the West knows of the Ripple brag. All welcome! Stay as long as you like! No man ever turned away from that Ripple door! — That would be enough. But I knew Holly Ripple in New Orleans. . . . We were sweethearts. Her father took her away. I got here finally to try to win her back. And these jealous —"

"Stop the —— liar!" burst out Brazos, flaming of face.

"Wal, by ——, thet's interestin'," drawled Slaughter. "I've heard a sight aboot thet little lady. Sweet on you, Lascelles?"

"Yes, she was."

"Jest what you mean by sweet?" went on Slaughter, his evil mind betrayed in tone and look.

Brazos' harsh appeal to Frayne caused Lascelles to turn, and suddenly he read something in Frayne's menace that the arrival of the Slaughter contingent had disrupted.

"No gentleman ever kisses and tells," he responded.

"Haw! Haw! Haw! . . . But come out with it,

Lascelles. . . . Hellno! — Keep yore mouth shet."

Frayne had taken a forward stride, his gun going to a level with his eye. It quivered and froze.

"Another word about Holly Ripple and I'll shoot out your teeth," hissed Frayne.

"Lascelles, you'll need your teeth," interposed Slaughter, as cool as if disaster did not impend. "You can keep — thet fer my private ear. . . . How'd you like to throw in with my outfit? We're footloose. Got plenty of money an' big deals on buyin' an' sellin' cattle."

"I'll do it," choked out Lascelles.

"You're in. Come on. Send fer yore pack an' camp with us tonight," rejoined Slaughter, motioning his men back and wheeling his horse. He turned in his saddle.

"Britt, I'll see you at the *fandango*," he said, jeeringly.

The foreman was glad indeed that he did not have a gun on him.

"Frayne, we'll meet again," called Slaughter, from the slope.

The outlaw's piercing gaze did not leave the retreating Lascelles until he passed out of sight with the horsemen under the trees. He might not have heard Russ Slaughter's taunting last call.

Brazos' first move, after being relieved from that restraint, was to boot the southerner in the rear. "Taylor, get oot. Go along with them. An' Gawd help yu if yu run into me again!"

The frightened young man, ashen of face, and dripping water from his bedraggled garments, hurried up the slope to disappear in the direction of the village.

"Brazos! You're plumb loco!" remonstrated Britt.

"Who'n hell ain't? — Mad? I'm so —— mad I could bite nails. Look at Laigs, heah! He's spittin' fire, but he cain't talk. Look at Frayne. White in the face by Gawd! Look at yourself, boss. You're green. All 'cause we got ketched with our pants off. No guns! — Cap, if yu ever rustle my gun again, fer any reason whatsoever, I'll hate yore guts."

"I'm sorry, Brazos. But cool down. Mebbe it's better we weren't packin' our hardware. What do you say, Renn?"

"Britt, I haven't swallowed so much in years," replied the outlaw, breathing heavily. "I'd say — let's never be caught unarmed again."

"Boss, you'll bust the outfit wide open," claimed Mason. "Course we-all know it's on account of Miss Holly. What you-all say, fellars?"

"You needn't vote on it," interrupted Britt, harshly. "My fault! Old Ranger thet I am — thet girl makes me wax in her hands. But boys, she's no squeamish woman. She's got guts. She's jest afraid some of you cowboys will be shot."

"Shore she is, bless her heart!" rang Brazos. "But we're gonna get bored anyhow. An' I want my guns an' my chances."

"Boys, after this you're wakin' an' sleepin' arsenals," ordered Britt, grimly.

"*Whoopee!*" bawled Laigs Mason.

"All the same we're gonna use our haids," concluded Britt.

Brazos turned to Frayne and thrust out his long arm and quivering hand. His boyish face lost its tense cruelty and bitterness in a warm and beautiful smile.

"Shake, Renn."

The outlaw made haste to comply, for once somewhat flustered.

"Yu saved my life. Thet gambler would have bored me. I seen murder in his eye."

"Struck me that way," rejoined Frayne, as Brazos wrung his hand. "Bad mess. I was afraid I'd have to shoot Lascelles. Slaughter's an ugly, contrary cuss."

"He didn't quite savvy yu, Renn," went on Brazos. "But I did, shore. An' I was itchin' to line up beside yu."

Britt placed a clasping hand on the grip of the two men. "Thet should make you friends."

"Pards, if Renn will have it," replied Brazos, his strong, wild spirit visible in his blue eyes.

"Brazos, I would only be too glad. But —" Frayne's piercing gray eyes, fine and glad yet doubtful, strove to read the cowboy's mind.

"There ain't no buts — leastways no more."

"Frayne, take him up. Brazos is a true blue Texan," interposed Britt, in earnest zeal. "Cement this proffered friendship. It'll save the ootfit."

"Frayne, I never had one damn thing against yu — but — but —" and here Brazos hesitated and grew as rosy as any girl.

"But! There you are, Brazos," replied Frayne, hastily. "I know what it is, you darned locoed cowboy! I'll take your word. . . . Don't give yourself away in front of this bunch of hard eggs!"

"I shore will, Renn," retorted Brazos recovering his cool ease. There was something winning about him then. "I never had a damn thing against yu — but — but this. . . . Fust off I was afeared Miss Holly l-liked you better'n me. An' now I know it."

"Brazos! — You sentimental jackass," retorted Frayne, his anger vying with other and more powerful feelings. An unfamiliar ruddy tinge showed under his tan. "You are wrong. . . . But I appreciate what it cost you to come clean like this. . . . I'm with you for life, cowboy."

"Laigs, yu pop-eyed geezer," ejaculated Brazos, roughly, perhaps to hide more emotion, "shake hands with our new pard, Renn Frayne."

CHAPTER 6

Holly had barred herself in her room for an hour's relaxation and rest after the long preparation for her party. This day was the third anniversary of this event inaugurated by her father on the occasion of her birthday. She was twenty years old; she was wondrously happy about innumerable things and unhappy about only one.

There came a knock on her door, accompanied by Britt's familiar voice: "Holly, don't disturb yoreself. But you ordered me to report."

"Yes, Cappy. . . . Oh, I hope. . . ."

"All's well. The cowboys air sober, fine, happy like a lot of colts, an' shore prancin' aboot."

"All of them?" called Holly, with eagerness.

"Lady, thet applies to every single last one of the ootfit."

"Thank Heaven! . . . And you, Cappy?"

"Shore. But you'll have to thank Renn considerable," drawled the foreman.

"Renn?" thrilled Holly.

"I said Renn. Thet's Frayne's first handle, you know," replied Britt, with a touch of dry humor.

Holly hesitated a moment, conscious of a suspension of breath, and a heat in her cheeks.

"Why must I thank — Renn?"

"Wal, I'll tell you some other time. *Adios, señorita.* . . . Be shore you're not late."

She heard his clinking steps pass through the livingroom, and out on the path. Holly sat up on her bed, dreamily stirred, aware that the last hour was at hand, and then arose to gaze out of her window. The sun was tipping the high mountain wall in the West. Splendor of scene and glory of color held Holly enraptured. The open range rolled away from Don Carlos' Rancho, a wild and purple world, so vast that the specks of cattle, the threads of roads and trails, the dots of distant ranches and towns appeared lost in an immensity of space. The sun sent shafts of gold down upon the white peaks. Long scattered stretches of cloud, like islands of rose in a golden sea, lay above the bold horizon. All the shadows under the clear bulk of the mountains were of an obscuring purple. And even while Holly gazed it seemed that the purple sheen was encroaching upon the gold-fired empire of grass, softening, enveloping, changing with magic alchemy.

The loveliest sunset of the year, so far, Holly thought, had come upon her birthday, as if to honor her party, and remind her of the incomparable beauty of New Mexico. Below the ranchhouse the Mexican village, the wide flat between it and the cottonwood-bordered creek, bathed in the glow of sunset hues, glittered and flashed with the activity of the most colorful day of the year on that range. At the village it was *fiesta* day. Indian camps, cowboy camps, rancher's camps, covering of a wagon-train shone brightly gold; horses grazed everywhere, as if that grassy flat was a huge pasture; far out along the creek the dark spots of outlaw and stranger camps, significantly far apart, attested to the drawing power of the Ripple invitation to all.

When Holly's father had inaugurated this annual entertainment, which was merely a grand festival embodying the principles of hospitality that he had held for years, conditions on the range had been very different. The one drawback now, Holly admitted, was the presence of many undesirables who came out of curiosity or for other motives inimical to the courtesy that made it possible for them to be present. Someday, much as Holly hated to think of it, she would be compelled to change her father's hospitable policy. It was Britt, supported by Clements, Doane, Haywood, and other ranchers with experience and standing on the frontier, who was accountable for this drastic change in Holly's mind. She had never dreamed, until lately, that she could ever go against her father's wishes. Another factor was the annoyance, not to say actual distress, fostered upon Holly by fortune-hunters such as Lascelles, and that ne'er-do-well brother of a schoolmate, Lee Taylor, both of whom had made her virtually a prisoner in her own home. Then there were others, Westerners, especially Sewall McCoy, whom Britt called Holly's rival rancher, who had been persistent in flattering but most unwelcome attentions since their arrival at the rancho.

145

Holly cast all thought of them aside, as well as doubts about this annual birthday *fiesta*. Then she thought of Renn Frayne, and that was different. Britt had used the outlaw's first name. Renn! Holly liked the sound of it. She recalled that she had put its owner out of her mind of late. But this time she seemed to surrender to Britt's insidious hint. Frayne had somehow subdued those wild cowboys. Holly left her window. She paced the floor. There hung the exquisite gown, with its soft folds of Spanish lace, which she must be putting on presently. Would Renn Frayne like her in that? No — Would he even see her? Long had Holly's pride suffered over his indifference, all to no avail. The more proof of his callousness to her beauty, the more he fascinated her. Holly had a sudden attack of honesty. It was no use to lie to herself any longer. Would Renn Frayne admire her in the beautiful gown? Would he ask her to dance? It shocked Holly to realize that for her the success of this long-prepared-for party depended upon the response of an outlaw, whose notorious fame had gradually dawned out of the eastern ranges. For weeks past she had feared that her feeling for Frayne was actually and dismayingly serious. Then, not long ago, had come a climax, a change that caused her as much shame to recall as when it had first burned over her. One day, riding up to Horn's Post, she had gone in to encounter Frayne most obviously attentive to Señorita Conchita Velasquez. There were several pretty girls in the village, but Conchita was by far the prettiest,

146

as well as the most seductive and irresistible. All the cowboys, even Brazos, had run after her, and it was Holly's opinion that the dusky-eyed maiden, like the majority of her soft-voiced, voluptuous kind, was not absolutely unattainable. Holly had reproved Brazos for dallying with Conchita. It had seemed a far stranger, and somehow stingingly shameful thing to catch Renn Frayne flirting with the girl. Holly had ridden home furious with herself, thinking one moment that she loved Frayne and the next that she hated him.

"But Conchita is distractingly pretty," mused Holly, now trying to be fair to Frayne, as she had been to the other cowboys. "She's a seductive creature. If *I* were a man I'd be crazy about her. . . . But Frayne — Oh! *he* wouldn't —"

Holly dared not go on with this thought, for she divined that to do so would result in the realization that Frayne might very well find Conchita as attractive as the other cowboys apparently found her. And this was a contingency Holly felt she wanted to escape, not that she could not be woman enough to excuse Frayne, but that it must lay bare the mysterious and mounting tumult of her own heart.

"*Quien sabe?* My party tonight may tell me much," soliloquized Holly, soberly. "So much that I may never give another."

Whereupon she admitted her maid Roseta, and called Ann Doane, who, with her father, was a guest at the rancho. Ann was a buxom girl of seventeen, rosy-cheeked and blue-eyed, a daughter of the frontier. In the pleasant bustle that ensued, the introspective and troublesome thought went into abeyance.

"Ann, how many of your beaus will be here?" asked Holly, mischievously.

"Laws! All of them, Holly," ejaculated Ann, with a giggle. "And I'm shore scared stiff."

"Why? You should be delighted."

"Holly, I'll tell you if you promise to keep it secret," whispered Ann, tensely.

"Of course I promise."

"It's this, Holly — Oh, it's awful to confess. . . . Last night I — I promised to marry Skylark."

"What? — My cowboy Skylark?" exclaimed Holly, in delight.

"There's shore only one — an' he's the hombre."

"Ann! — How perfectly splendid! I'm happy to hear it. I congratulate you. Skylark is one of my — my steadiest boys."

"Well, you know, Holly, that isn't so terribly steady," rejoined Ann, sagely. "Sky is all right. I'm not flustered about his bad habits. I'll settle *them*. . . . What worried me is that I took up with him before I ended off with some other boys."

"Dear! That is awful. Ann, you don't mean any other of *my* cowboys. Not Brazos?"

"Not that flaxen-haired devil! Or I *would* be scared. Brazos never no more than chucked me under the chin once, an' said if I got lonesome he'd ride over. These other boys are from over our way — an' well, they're not crazy aboot any of the Ripple ootfit. There'll be a fight, but I swear

I'll keep it from happening here at your party. Holly, I'd never forgive myself if I didn't."

"Ann, we women have to forgive much, don't we?" sighed Holly. "Last year at my party there were three fights — one of which ended in gunplay down below."

"Shore I remember. But thet's pretty good, I reckon. Sam Price was not shot seriously. And he shore deserved a licking. You were away so long at school. This is the West, Holly. My Dad says it's going to be the hellbentenest West thet ever was."

"So does Britt," laughed Holly. "I'm trying to prepare myself for war. But I *hate* the idea."

"There'll be war over you tonight, if I don't miss my hunch," declared the Western girl. "Holly, you never looked so — so lovely. These hombres will go mad."

"Do you think so, Ann?" murmured Holly, intrigued by the startling idea.

"I know it. Holly, you're a year older, different somehow, more of a-a — Oh, I can't tell you."

"Ann! You don't mean this gown. I'm afraid to look in my mirror. . . . Arms, shoulders all bare! My — Oh, I feel naked. It's an indecent gown, Ann."

"Oh, I wouldn't go so far as that," remonstrated the girl, loyally. "It's cut pretty low. But, Holly Ripple, you're a grand dame."

"Ann, if it's really — so bad — I'll lose my nerve," faltered Holly. "I had it made in Santa Fe. I never tried it on. I was afraid I'd try to

149

alter it here. I've the dress I wore last year."

"Holly, you may feel queer when you see yourself, but you can't never change now. Not for this *fiesta!* . . . Roseta, what do you say? Doesn't the Señorita look grand?"

Roseta was volatile, passionate and incredibly flattering, without a hint of what Holly feared.

"Et ees so, La Señorita, she ees so lovely. And her dress? . . . *Que bonita! Que hermosa!*"

When eventually Holly stood up to view her image in the mirror she uttered a little cry of shocked amazement. Following that came another emotion, one she sought to shunt aside before it dominated her completely enough to make her appearance in this gown impossible. She sustained more girlish vanity than fear, more womanly pride than shame. She soothed the still small voice of conscience which had haunted her, for she knew her father would not have sanctioned this Spanish gown. At that moment she loved her little regal head, with its rich black hair so beautifully and elaborately dressed. Excitement had given her face a pearly pallor. She hardly recognized those dark, turbulent eyes, such indicative masks of her troubled and passionate heart.

For an endless moment she gazed, divided between widely separated impulses, with a strong leaning toward that in her which was American and which her father had fostered and developed. But the throb and beat of her Spanish blood conquered. The flashing thought which swayed Holly was that Renn Frayne should see her thus, cost what such folly might. Then the swift fire of scarlet neck and face stung her with the bitter and terrible truth — she loved this outlaw. An instant later she was as pale as marble, true to the proud Castilian race of Valverdes as well as the indomitable spirit of her pioneer father.

Holly viewed herself anew, with eyes unbiased by a shameful secret.

Her glossy hair, circling in a loose knot low on her neck, and held in place by a huge jewelled comb, appeared almost too heavy for her small head. She had been wise in choosing the Spanish gown of shimmering sequins and ebony lace, if she were bent on conquest as well as to do grace to her ancestors.

When it lacked but a few minutes to the hour for her to appear in the living room to meet her cowboys, Britt again knocked at the door.

"Holly, how air you comin'?" he asked, anxiously. "The boys air quiverin' like a bunch of race hawses."

"All ready, Cappy. Come in," replied Holly, gayly, motioning to Roseta to open the door. Britt appeared, spic and span in a new dark suit. "How do you like me, old friend?"

Britt's eyes popped. They expanded to help in a smile that satisfied even Holly's insatiate vanity. His first effort to speak was a failure. Then he exploded: "My Gawd! . . . My lass, not only do you make me young again, but you break my pore old heart."

"Ah! Cappy! Why break?"

"Wal, I reckon with love an' joy. . . . You're changed, Holly. No little girl no more!"

"Thank you. If I please you I shall please them. . . . Are they all there? I'm intensely curious — and I — I don't know what else."

"Holly, you won't know thet ootfit. They been trained to the minnit."

"Trained?" asked Holly, eagerly.

"Shore. By Frayne, with me helpin'. But I forgot. I wasn't to give thet away. . . . If I don't miss my guess you'll think thet ootfit has been used to dressin' up slick an' dinin' off silver all their lives."

"Darlings!" cried Holly. It would be just like that inimitable Brazos to inspire his comrades to a cool easy nonchalance which no person or no event could disrupt. "Go back now, Cappy. I want to make an effective entrance. . . . Oh, I feel like a schoolgirl."

"Wal, you look like an empress," replied Britt, and went out.

The door let in the commingled sounds of footsteps, gay laughs and voices. Holly heard the twang of a fiddle, the mellow chord of a guitar. Supper for the multitude was to be served simultaneously with that given her cowboys, the former in the dining-room and patio, the latter in the living room.

"What-have-I-forgotten?" gasped Holly. "Oh, my notes! . . . Pray for me, girls."

When Holly entered the brightly lighted, brilliantly colored living-room to see that group of keen-faced standing men, she received from them, or from some inexplicable source, a welling trenchant emotion that completely vanquished her nervous qualms. Advancing to the head of the table she stood a moment behind her chair, smiling down the lines of intent faces. Frayne stood at her right while Brazos was on her left. Britt's place was at the foot of the table. Nineteen in all! Holly counted them with eyes that did not see clearly.

"Good evening, gentlemen," she said. "If my father were only here this would be the happiest hour of my life. Nevertheless, I am very happy. . . ."

Frayne stepped to draw back her chair, and as she took her seat he bent over gallantly: "Miss Ripple, may I say no fairer lady in King Arthur's day ever sat to do honor to her Knights."

"*Frayne!*" Holly's amazement and delight inhibited the confusion which threatened her poise. Though she blushed she did not otherwise betray herself. "English Knights! Why not the gay Spanish *Caballeros?*"

Brazos had heard Frayne and was not to be outdone. "Holly, you shore look grand. You make me want to die 'cause I cain't have you an' stay on livin' jest to see you."

"Flatterers! I'd know you were cowboys if you were strangers and I was blind," replied Holly, stirred to laughter. And she looked down the lines of shining faces. They were all there, somehow inexplicably dear to her, the sombre Cherokee, the black rolling-eyed Jackson, the *vaquero* Santone, and the half-breed Southards, her knights as well as the cowboys of her own color. Holly felt a name-less strength steal over her. The last of the Ripples had no family. These were all she had — her range riders, wild characters from all the wild ranges, and in that hour she loved them.

The long table with its white linen and silver, its burden of fruit and food satisfied Holly's critical eye. When her guests were seated it was the signal for the Mexican maidens, garbed in their colorful gowns, to enter with steaming dishes. Holly had hoped for comfort and happiness for her cowboys, so used to hard fare in all kinds of weather. She was to have her wish. There was an utter lack of embarrassment, and the cool, devil-may-care audacity of cowboys who had been made to feel at home, to be glad, to be themselves in the presence of their mistress. Their garb differed with an infinite variety, yet all was new. Frayne, like Britt, wore a dark suit with white shirt and collar that emphasized the eastern manner that sat becomingly upon him. Holly had not yet looked directly at his face. Brazos, always strikingly handsome, surpassed himself this evening in a new blue blouse with wide collar, around which he had gracefully knotted a red scarf. He was the only one minus a coat, in lieu of which he wore a new beaded and fringed buckskin vest. It was open, and the left side bulged noticeably. Holly had an instant suspicion.

"Brazos, what have you in your pocket?" she asked.

"Aw Lady!" Then he looked across the table

at Frayne. "What'd I tell yu galoots? It jest cain't be done."

"What can't?" asked Holly.

"Foolin' you."

"Brazos. Have you a — a bottle or a gun inside your vest?"

"Wal, what do yu think, Holly Ripple?" he queried, fastening those eyes of blue fire upon her.

"I hope it's a gun," Holly made haste to reply.

"Don't you know it is?"

"Yes . . . but I forbade that, too."

"Wal, I'm not the only one."

His gaze directed Holly's to Frayne, who drew back both lapels of his coat, to disclose the shining black butts of guns, one on each side. "Britt's order, Miss Ripple."

"Oh! — You are all armed?"

"Yes."

Brazos interposed, leaning to speak low. "Holly, we gotta sleep in our hardware from now on. An' it's a grand idee."

"Whose?"

"Wal, Frayne's fust; 'cause he always plumb refused to be without his guns, an' if he hadn't packed them today you'd be conductin' a funeral 'stead of a grand party."

"Brazos!"

But as the cowboy only smiled in his cool exasperating way Holly appealed to Frayne.

"Child, it's nothing for you to bother about," he replied with a smile.

"You call me child?" asked Holly, firing. "This is my twentieth birthday. I am your employer."

"Granted. But, nevertheless," he rejoined, with a baffling halt and an inflection which might have meant that his retort proved her to be a child, or that he considered her an adorable one. The latter interpretation made Holly's face burn and routed her anger. These cowboys were hopeless. Holly beckoned imperiously for Britt. He came swiftly around the table to bend over her.

"Cappy, the two gentlemen nearest me call me a child," she told him.

"Wal! You don't say?" Britt returned, not feeling sure whether to laugh or be concerned. "In some ways I'll back them up. You air a child. But not tonight. This evenin' you shore air the distractionest woman in the whole wide world."

"Thank you. . . . Britt, I discovered Brazos had a gun inside his vest. Then Frayne showed me the butts of two guns inside his coat. Are all the cowboys armed thus?"

"Indeed they air, Holly."

"But that is expressly against my orders."

"I know, lass. An' I'm sorry."

"Why have you disregarded them?"

Britt stiffened slightly under her unusual severity.

"Won't you trust me to know what's best, an' let me explain some other time?"

"Tell me now."

"This mawnin' somethin' come off thet showed how even an old cowman an' ranger like me can

156

be too soft," replied Britt, swiftly. "It was Frayne's idee, this mawnin' to — wal, to sober up some of the boys thet needed it. The idee was to haul them down to the creek an' duck them. All of us left our guns behind 'cept Frayne. We had a heap of fun duckin' these sleepy cow-hands. Did they wake up pronto? Wish you had been there, Holly. . . . Wal, one of these red-head boys took it plumb serious. Mad at fust an' then devilish. While we was fetchin' Blue — aw! there I go, givin' him away — this cowboy an' his pard jumped in the wagon an' drove off lickety-cut. An' —"

"That was Brazos Keene and his shadow, Laigs Mason," observed Holly. She had read Brazos' serene countenance.

"I didn't say so. . . . Anyway, they fetched back young Taylor an' Lascelles, both the wuss fer liquor. Brazos throwed — Oh, Lord, there I go again! — Wal, Brazos throwed Taylor in. But Lascelles turned oot ugly. He wasn't drunk. I reckon thet gambler doesn't go so far. He shore resented the ootrage, an' he made Brazos sore. He made *me* sore, too, blurtin' oot thet crazy claim of his on you. Wal, to make it short Brazos soaked him an' piled him into the water. Lascelles came oot, his face like ice, an' with his hand inside his coat, where he had a gun. He had seen thet Brazos and Laigs was without guns. We split to get to either side, all except Laigs, who stood his ground by Brazos. . . . Miss Holly, if it was plain to all of us thet Lascelles meant to kill Brazos, how do you suppose Brazos felt? — But Frayne stopped Lascelles' draw."

Britt, evidently having warmed somewhat to this recital, paused a moment, during which Holly turned to Frayne. She might have spoken then but for a slightly weary or bored expression on the outlaw's face. Britt had to humor his child employer! He had to tell what men did not tell outside of their circle.

"Jest then down on us rode Russ Slaughter with his Chisum ootfit of hard-nuts. Aboot fourteen strong. He was plumb curious an' if that was friendly, I'm oot on my figgerin'. But Frayne shut him up pronto, an' then proceeded to tell Lascelles he was through at Don Carlos' Rancho. Jackson an' Skylark testified thet Lascelles was a card-sharp, who'd stoop to cheat a drink-befuddled cowboy. . . . Frayne told Lascelles to get oot. . . . Wal, then Slaughter took a hand at questionin' Lascelles. I didn't like this atall, because I could read Slaughter's dirty mind. We all seen what he was drivin' at. Lascelles, the skunk, brought up yore name an' thet flirtin' he put sich store on. An' shore he'd have insinuated somethin' wuss if Frayne hadn't sworn to shoot oot his teeth, if he opened his trap again. . . . Wal, thet bluffed Slaughter. He offered Lascelles a chance to throw in with them an' Lascelles jumped at it. Thet's all, Holly. I meant to tell you in the mawnin'."

"Never wait to spare my feelings, at any time," returned Holly, composedly, though she had passed from hot to cold during this narrative.

158

"Thank you, Cappy. Go back to your seat."

Holly sat there inwardly shaking. Except for Brazos, and perhaps Laigs Mason beside him, and Frayne, none of the cowboys had apparently paid any attention to this colloquy. They were intent on the most gorgeous repast of their lives. Holly watched them a moment while she fought her emotions.

"Lady, please don't let thet spoil yore party," appealed Brazos, earnestly. "It wasn't nothin'. Course it might have been plumb bad — fer me, if Frayne hadn't been there. But he was there."

Brazos' emphasis of finality seemed to intimate something inevitable about Frayne. Holly's intuition was swift to catch in Brazos' look and voice the absence of former hostility toward the outlaw. That warmed away the cold terror and sick confusion within her. Impulsively she laid her hand upon Frayne's as it rested momentarily on the table.

"Again — Frayne?" she said, without betraying agitation. "You increase my debt."

"Miss Holly, don't overrate these things," he replied, kindly, and he gave her hand a strong pressure, while his hard face softened. "It is a tough job for an orphan girl who had to spend half her life in school. You are game, Holly Ripple. Let this twentieth birthday see your eyes open wide to the violence of this range! Listen to Britt. Let him give us leeway."

Holly was so strangely affected by the clasp of

159

their hands that she scarcely made coherence of his words. She nodded her thanks. Then she addressed herself to the sumptuous meal, and by forcing her thoughts upon her speech, she gradually drew away from the confounding fact that the mere touch of Renn Frayne's hand could make her weak.

Evidently the cowboys had been fasting for this supper, or if not they had prodigious appetites. Holly could not deny the evidence of her eyes. Laigs Mason was a little fellow, but he stowed away so much food that Holly feared he would do himself harm.

"Heah pard, you'll founder," whispered Brazos.

"Say, you ain't passed up some second an' third helpin's," rejoined Laigs, in fierce remonstrance. "I ain't had nuthin' yet."

But there appeared to be remarkably little conversation. Cowboys were not much given to talking even in the bunkhouse during the meal hour. At last, however, even Laigs brought his gormandizing to an end. The wine was poured and all the lean faces and keen eyes turned toward Holly.

Holly rose, sure of herself at last and revelling in this crucial hour. The room grew silent. But from the outside came a ceaseless hum of voices and music, of constant tread on the porch and in the patio. A coarse laugh from some rowdy jarred into a Spanish love song. Holly took time to allow her sweeping glance to rest upon every face at her table. And when she looked up from Frayne's piercing eyes she seemed shot through with some-

160

thing strong and sweet, a gleam of encouragement to do her best.

"Gentlemen, Westerners, my cowboys:

"In any case I would have addressed you tonight, as I have done twice before, and as my father used to do all the years that he employed riders. But my purpose tonight goes far beyond just a repetition of the Ripple hospitality. It is to make an appeal to you. It is to inaugurate a change in policy of the running of Don Carlos' Rancho. It is to place clearly before you the certain danger of loss, the grave danger of ruin, which Britt has made me see. Particularly it to emphasize what a splendid part you are unconsciously playing in the opening of the West. And to tell you what a wonderful thing you are doing for the last of the Ripples.

"Despite what Britt says, I know cowboys. I was born among them. I returned from school with eyes keener to see them, with mind sharper to understand their strange, hard, lonely, violent lives, with heart bigger to forgive, to tolerate, to sympathize. My father called cowboys 'Rowdies of the Saddle.' That was a felicitous name. For cowboys are all that the name rowdy implies — wild, rough, bold, often killers, many worthless except to ride and rope and break, yet withal true to that spirit which developed them. The West needed cowboys. The empire of cattle, now in the making, will never be made without you hard-riding, hard-drinking, hard-shooting cowboys. My father did not go quite far enough in his eulogy. That is my happy task tonight.

161

"But first let me delve back a little into the past of this glorious West, into the history of the ranges. You cowboys of the 'lone prairee,' who have stood endless watches in the dead of night, under the white stars, in sleet and rain and sand, in bitter cold and the hot blast of summer, who have ridden from the Rio Grande to the Black Hills, from the big river to this last and greatest cattle-range, who have slept nine out of every ten nights on the hard ground of plain or desert or upland or mesa, who know the West as none but the Indians know it, perhaps you still do not know the West. You know its romance but do not think of its history; you know its cruelty but you do not consider its destiny. And to have you see this tonight, its past and its future, its greatness and your own greatness, is the main purpose of my address to you.

"That Old Trail down there crossing my rancho: to you it is a half mile lane of furrows, so poor a trail that you choose to ride your horses aside, so bleak and waterless and ghastly a road that you hate to put a horse to it. Well, my friends, that Old Trail connects three civilizations to this wild and primitive range. It is the main artery of the West. Over it men have toiled in blood for three hundred years.

"The white man's love of gold, gain, power, adventure account for the Old Trail. Spaniards were the first to set their mailed feet upon the plains of America — the intrepid *conquistadores*. *Alvar Nuñez de Vaca*. You cowboys, if you know your Spanish, should like that name, for Alvar

Nuñez means Cow's Head. I daresay Laigs Mason will call some of you Alvar Nuñez from this day. In 1528 de Vaca started from Florida with many men, but before they went far his party was reduced to three companions. They were lost for eight years before they met men of their own race on the Mexican border. They were the first white men on earth to see what they called 'the hump-backed cow,' no other than your old pest, the American bison — the buffalo. Can you imagine these ragged and miserable Spaniards wandering along, suddenly to be confronted by the huge, shaggy, black and tawny buffalo? Gentlemen, surely that was a tremendous moment.

"The Spaniard Mendoza, a Governor of Mexico, fired by stories of fabulous gold, sent men out to verify de Vaca's claims. They found some pueblos on the Rio Grande, but they augmented this into the 'Seven Cities of Cibolo,' the El Dorado of the Spaniards. Coronado was sent with three hundred Spaniards, all of high degree, and eight hundred Indians. It was a great retinue doomed to failure. They rode and walked, starved and died of thirst, fought the savages, but they never found Cibolo. Coronado was the first to see the Grand Canyon of the Colorado. He left the first horses that ever roamed the Great Plains.

"Next came the Spanish friars, the wonderful padres who marched not for gold or gain, but to plant their religion in the minds of the savages. In 1591 De Soto got as far north as the Zuni pueblos. In 1598 four hundred Spaniards under Onate left Mexico with many wagons and thousands of cattle. It was through Onate that our Santa Fe was established in 1609. Then began the early days of the Old Trail. The Spaniards wanted to be let alone. But they had to have a market to buy and sell. In 1690 the French-Canadians, the fur hunters, began to edge into New Mexico. With the trappers, marching west with their pack-mules, laden with whiskey, guns, beads, bright goods to trade to the Indians, the Santa Fe Trail became known to the world — our Old Trail down there along the Cimarron and the Cottonwood. The fur trade expanded. The trappers were friendly with the Indians. There was no war. Americans began to mingle with the French. The era of the great fur trade lasted for nearly a hundred years. . . . My friends, there will be trappers here at my party tonight. Ask one of the white-haired old fellows to tell you what the trade was when he took to it as a boy. That must have been a grand free life. It used to thrill me to sit beside Kit Carson, when I was a child, and listen to his stories. Still Carson only knew of that magnificent early day from the old trappers who had seen some of it. When Carson ran away West as a boy, the plains were black with millions of buffalo and thousands of wild horses.

"After the dwindling fur hunters came the Forty-Niners, the gold seekers, streaming across the plains for the bonanzas in California. They, next to our thoughtless government, incurred the hostility of the Pawnees, the Utes, the Comanches, the Arapahoes, the Apaches, of all our Western tribes. And scalps of the white men dried in the sun on the wigwams of the Indians.

"Next came the freighters and the day of the caravan. The wagon-trains! The canvas-covered prairie-schooners! They hauled supplies to the forts and to Santa Fe, to Taos, to Las Vegas. But Santa Fe was their great objective.

"Most of you here tonight have seen Buff Belmet, the scout and caravan-leader, who hauls from Las Animas and the end of the advancing railroad. Think, my cowboys, of that trail of steel! You are responsible for that. No Santa Fe line would ever have been built but for cattle. The rails march on. Next spring they reach Raton. In a few years they will reach Santa Fe. That indeed will be the end of the Old Trail.

"Buff Belmet told me the story of his life. It is marvelous. In 1855 when he was eleven years old he left Independence in a caravan with his father and mother. Before he had travelled half way to Dodge, he had lost his mother, and he was driving one of the great ships of the plains. The romance and adventure of the caravans made Belmet a scout. His father was killed, as were his old friends and comrades; he was wounded countless times, but bore a charmed life. His childhood sweetheart was lost to him for years, and that added to his hatred of the red man. But Buff found his sweetheart a few years ago, in 1869, the year that Carson died — found her still young, beautiful, faithful.

"Following the freighters with their mile-long caravans came the pioneers, the settlers. The end of the Civil War spilled a horde of ruined Southerners, of rebels, of outcasts from the East, of fugitives, wanderers, criminals, adventurers — and the day of the desperado was at hand.

"Then, my cowboys — the cattle herds! You all know that story. The Trail Drivers from Texas, with their unparalleled heroism that made my father's native state an empire. Hundreds of thousands of cattle up from the Rio Grand — herd on the heels of herd — ten miles a day over grass and rock and sand, across the Texas rivers, often in flood, fighting Indians, rustlers, drouth and heat, the icy blizzards, the electric storms, on and on and on to Dodge and Abilene! Oh, my cowboy friends, grasp the truth of that day to your bosoms! It was great. Britt was a Trail Driver. Frayne has ridden the Chisholm Trail. They will tell you as I cannot.

"1867, '68, '69, '70, '71, '72, '73 and this year of our Lord 1874 — and we have a million cattle grazing from the Cimarron to the Pecos. No law! Rustlers raiding every day and more coming. Cowboy outfits betraying their bosses. They are leagued with the rustlers. Many have quit work to take up the profitable stealing. Stock buyers from the East meet the cowboys at the railroad — and ask no questions. There are dishonest officers in the government post. They buy beef for the reservation Indians. They pay five and ten dollars a head — and ask no questions. What do

166

you suppose the government pays them a head?

"Thus is ushered in the day of the rustler. He flourishes on all ranges, but he will be freest, boldest, bloodiest, richest — and therefore last longest on this New Mexican range. This is Britt's prophecy. It was my father's. It is now mine.

"To conclude now, my cowboys. This then is the situation today along the Old Trail. To meet it Britt has gathered together the wildest outfit possible in the West. You come from all points except further west. I doubt if there is one of you who could not cut a notch on his gun if you were that kind. I'd hate to know *all* you are guilty of. Some of you are — or *think* you are — lady killers! — *I* don't need to be told that. My state of feeling toward you all is not easy to define. In some way, I think I — I love every single one of you. My grandfather built this home. He had a hundred *vaqueros* on this *hacienda*. My father loved his 'Rowdies of the Saddle.'

"Once upon a time there was a good King. He gathered an outfit of great fighters and put them to noble tasks — to redressing human wrongs in his dominion, to driving out or killing the robber barons who oppressed the weak. I am bold to hope, to pray that *my* outfit of fighters will deserve my name for them — Knights of the Range. I beseech you — do not imagine that I ask this for myself. But also for the other ranchers in this beautiful and wild valley, for the poor settlers and their children, for our good neighbors, the Mexicans. But mostly, for the West — our West — and because it is something great to do.

"From this night you are free as the wolves out there. You will have no restraint. You can drink, gamble, fight, kill — if you must. Your wages will be doubled, and those of you who are alive and with me after this rustler-war is ended, will be given an interest in my business, or helped to start one of your own. — Only I ask you, I pray you, don't break out and take undue advantage of your freedom. Try to see your importance in this vast, incomprehensible movement westward. Don Carlos' Rancho is only a speck on this range. Try to be proud of your place. Try to be serious about it. Oh, I know that *what* you are *now* is solely because of the life of the frontier. You may have been bad, but you are not to blame. You could not be good, tame, gentle — all that women like in men — and make this range habitable. Lesser cattle outfits will take their cue from you. . . . And so I dare to believe you will earn — the name I have — bestowed upon you. . . ."

Holly's voice failed at the very end. She sat down in a breathless silence. To her amazement, the cowboys sat like stone images. Then Brazos jumped up with a yell that rang from the rafters, and the others followed suit. For a few moments pandemonium reigned.

When the noise had died down Britt stood up, to tap lightly on the table. Instantly all the eager taut faces turned his way.

"Miss Holly, an' gentlemen," he began, in the dry drawl that presaged something inimical in motive or word, and he transfixed his men with those bright and twinkling eyes. "We have with us tonight a boy who is in a class by himself. In an ootfit which contains many bad hombres, an' which hasn't one thet is not a great rider an' roper an' gunner, this boy stands oot conspicuously, not only fer these qualities, but fer many others, prominent among them bein' his gift of gab. He has been known to talk cowboys deaf an' dumb. I know of one instance, back in Texas where he talked a sheriff oot of arrestin' him. . . . An' thet, gentlemen, is shore talkin'. . . . Gawd only knows the misery among girls this boy's silver tongue has wrought. . . . Wal, it behooves me on introducin' this paragon among riders of the range to prepare you, no doubt, fer a speech thet never was made before, an' never will be again. . . . Friends. . . . Brazos Keene!"

A short, sharp roar rang around the table. Holly punctuated it with her high, sweet trill of delight.

Holly calculated that everyone present, except herself, had entertained the idea that Britt had Frayne in mind. Certainly Brazos himself was the most surprised cowboy who ever had gotten himself inadvertently or otherwise into an awful predicament. Obviously he had never made that kind of a speech in his life. His comely face turned as red as a beet and then as white as a sheet. He sustained a more violent shock throughout his lithe frame than if someone had shot at him from behind.

"My — Gawd!" he gulped, his face beginning

169

to work, and he fixed eyes of agony upon Holly. "Cap cain't — mean *me!*"

"Indeed yes, Brazos," replied Holly, beaming upon him.

"Aw! — No!" groaned the cowboy, turning to his faithful partner. But before Laigs could betray him, which the devilish grin on his face surely presaged, the other cowboys called with the caustic and trenchant originality and wit characteristic of them.

"Come mon, you curly-haired darlin' of the range."

"Brazos — who ever heerd of you afeared to talk?"

"Cowboy, you're the talker of this ootfit."

"We're shore expectin' Washington's Gettysburg speech to be skinned to a frazzle."

"Fork yore hoss, pard, an' rustle."

"Brazos, yo sho only gotta be yo own self."

"You *grande señor.*"

"Brazos, you might as well warm up, 'cause Conchita is here tonight, an' thet black-eyed little dame is shore layin' fer you."

This from Skylark about finished Brazos, whose expression was that of an innocent cowboy against whom a diabolical plot had been concocted. More cutting remarks were forthcoming, and then Laigs Mason had his say.

"Pard, the honor of the ootfit is at stake. Who'd ever think thet Brazos Keene had lost his wits. . . . Wal, if you can't talk sing 'Lone Prairee'!"

Brazos, goaded to desperation, again appealed to Holly.

"Shore, it's a low-down trick," he said, huskily. "Aw, Holly, say yu wasn't in with them?"

"No, Brazos," she replied, earnestly. "I'm absolutely innocent. But now I'm thrilled to death. Show them, Brazos."

"Gawd help this heah ootfit from now on," replied Brazos, as if he were destiny itself.

CHAPTER 7

Brazos escape from his chair and rise to his lofty height were as remarkable as they were funny. There might have been a rope around his neck, tight over one of the rough-hewn rafters above, and hauled upon by some of these grinning imps who revelled in his anguish. He came away so heavily that he might have been glued to his seat.

Once upon his feet he had to look at his hostess, and then upon his gleeful and expectant comrades. It was Holly's conjecture that he did not see any of them clearly. Brazos' remarkable eyes were round, bewildered, starting from his head, and his face baffled description.

He bowed low to Holly, then jerkily to the others.

"Our — Lady," he began, in a hoarse whisper, "an' yu — fellars . . . Yu — we — I . . . Yu-all join — me-all join yu . . . this orful occasion — I mean grand — in honor of pack of hound-dawgs . . . yu — we . . . er, my. . . ."

As Brazos floundered hopelessly for more words there came suddenly from under the table a solid cracking thud. Holly did not need to be told that Laigs had kicked Brazos on the shin. She nearly

choked trying to contain her dignity. Brazos'
breath puffed. His expression of fright and distress
changed to a physical distortion of acute pain.

"*Aggh!*" he yelled.

"Fer Gawd's sake, pard, be yoreself," burst out
Laigs, with a passion of loyalty. His love for and
pride in Brazos had transcended even the cowboy
passion for fun.

His importunity reacted with subtle and incredible power upon Brazos.

"Aw!" groaned Brazos, "shore yu had to pick
oot my bum laig." Then he stood erect to face
them all differently. Holly sustained a deep and
poignant thrill in the surety that Brazos would find
himself.

"Fun is fun, boys, an' yu've had it at my expense. But I savvy thet Miss Holly gave us this
supper fer more'n a good time. It must hev took
lots of study to read up all thet aboot the Spaniards,
an' those thet come after. . . . Fer me, pards,
the Old Trail will hev a different meanin'. An'
range-ridin' a bigger job. An' belongin' to Holly
Ripple's ootfit aboot as close to heaven as I ever
expect to get.

"Pards, my folks was fine old Texas stock. I
never had much schoolin' — yu know how hard
it is fer me to write my name — an' I run away
from home 'cause I was jest no good. All thet a
cowboy can do except gettin' himself killed I've
done. But, so help me Gawd, never since I run
away till this heah minnit, hev I had any thought
of a cowboy havin' respect fer his callin'. It sort

of seeped through my thick haid — the real an' strong reason why Our Lady is callin' to us so sweet an' earnest. An' it dug deep into me, boys. Heaven knows we air an ignorant lot, 'cept in case of Frayne, an' mebbe Skylark, who shows human intelligence sometimes. But to find oot — an' 'specially from Holly Ripple, daughter of a great Southerner, and the great Don Valverde, thet what we air is what the range made us an' what she needs — why, fellars, there ain't words enough, leastways not in my dictionary, to tell how savin' an' upliftin' thet is.

"An' so, cowboys, heah's where Brazos Keene lays his cairds down as never before in no game. My pards of Texas Pan Handle days air daid. Since then I never had one 'cept Laigs heah. Yu all know why I took on Renn Frayne. . . . Wal, heah's where I take yu-all on. My pards! When a Texan makes a pard of a nigger somethin' big has happened. I'm sinkin' race prejudice an' all thet other damn selfish rot. We've got a common cause, men. . . . I never was in an ootfit thet didn't hev a disorganizer, an' a rustler or two, an' a mean gun-toter who ached to try you oot.

"Wal, if I've been any one of these things, after tonight I'll never be no more. Yu-all know yore inside thoughts an' feelin's. Yu shore can see Miss Holly's wonderful offer to yu. An' none of yu is such an ignoramus as not to see now the wuth of the cowboy to the West. But if any one of yu — or two of yu — or three should double-cross Our Lady an' disgrace her ootfit — they'll have to draw on me — an' Laigs heah — an' shore our latest pard, Renn Frayne."

Amid stamping and vociferous applause Brazos sat down, white and rapt of face. When the uproar subsided Holly leaned to Brazos.

"Oh, Brazos," she whispered, with agitation. "I knew you would not fail. You were splendid."

Suddenly Holly became aware that Frayne had touched her hand. She turned, quick and vibrant.

"May I speak?" he asked, with his slight smile.

"Oh! — I would be delighted. . . ."

Frayne stood up, striking of form and face, piercing-eyed and stern. There would be no humor from this outlaw. He bowed to Holly.

"Miss Ripple, our gracious and lovely hostess, Our Lady, as Brazos so truly said, on behalf of all of us I thank you for this hospitality, and particularly for your magnificent and generous spirit."

Then he bent his gaze on the uplifted tense faces, down one side of the table, to the absorbed Britt, and up the other side to Brazos.

"The rest of my few remarks will be addressed to you, as man to man. To you Britt, you old leather-backed Texan trail-hound, to you Jackson, you black-faced, nose-biting horse-driver, to you Cherry, you Indian buckaroo, to you half-breeds, to each and every one of you rowdy cowboys! If what I say pinches your foot in its high-heeled boot, grin and say you like it.

"But before I make implications which at any other time and place would hurt your feelings I shall tell a little about myself. I am an Easterner. I have been on the frontier fourteen years, since I was twenty. Many ignominies have been fastened upon the name of Renn Frayne, which is my own. But that one which made me a fugitive from justice was false. As a boy and young man I hated cities, crowds, work. I wanted adventure. The West called me. I landed at Independence in 1860. From buffalo hunting I drifted from one thing to another. I shot a cheating gambler on a steamboat — and that started me on the career some men unfortunately must be intended for. During the Civil War I was a soldier for a while. I killed an officer at one of the army-posts — over a woman — and I deserted to hide out with trappers in the mountains. After the war I became a cowboy and rode the eastern ranges for years. The Pan Handle, Nebraska, Wyoming, eastern Colorado, but mostly Kansas. The time came when I couldn't ride into Old Dodge, or Hays City, or Abilene, or Newton, without smelling smoke of my own gun. Finally I shot Sutherland, a big cattleman. It was the most justifiable killing of all. He was one of those cattlemen who operated in two ways, one open and honest, the other hidden and crooked. There are many such rustler-developing cattle kings. There are two right here in New Mexico. Sutherland had powerful friends, and they egged on the gunfighters, the two-faced sheriffs, and the tough cowboys to put me out of the way. I became an outlaw, with a price on my head. When some clique exposed Sutherland, laying bare his crooked

176

dealings, they forgot to remove the price from my head. It has never been removed and if I went back to Kansas I'd have to shoot my way out. That's the bad thing about being a marked man who is quick on the draw. . . . Lastly I've trained with some hard gangs, of which Heaver's wasn't a marker to others. . . . . Rustler! I'm bound to admit it. But, men, you all know the status of cattle on the range. It is hard to define the line between branding and stealing. To appropriate beef wherever you found it has been a universal custom. To round up a bunch of cattle, not your own, drive them off their range, sell them for a fourth of their hoof value — that is cattle-stealing. In weak defense of all of us who have transgressed thus I can only say that the easy custom, the unfailing fact of cattlemen all accepting small losses, have been to blame. The cowboy hasn't had a fair chance to be honest.

"But horse-stealing is another matter. A rancher will stand to lose some cattle; he raises Cain when he loses horses. My one offense, which I am ashamed to confess, was the Heaver deal in which we drove some two score of Miss Ripple's thoroughbreds. Britt blocked that drive. I never felt right after Heaver double-crossed me about that deal. He didn't say we were after horses, and I was into it before I realized. Then I hated him. . . . Well, he got shot for his deceit, and that saw the beginning and end of my career as a horse-thief.

"When I threw in with your outfit I promised

Miss Ripple that I would be honest. That promise I shall keep. . . . Boys, I wonder if you can appreciate it when I tell you that I sleep at nights, that I no longer hear steps upon my trail, that I *know,* absolutely, I will never dangle by my neck from a cottonwood. It will not be many years now before the noose will supersede the gun — in execution of rustlers.

"In our case there is no use, no sense, no reason for us to steal from our employer. We are a lucky outfit. Chisum's top bunch of riders have left him cold — Russ Slaughter and his outfit. They look bad and they might go far — unless they run foul of us. Slaughter did not know that he missed it today by a hair. If he had soft-soaped Lascelles into opening his vile trap again — well, pards, there would have been two less for you to contend with. You all know as well as I that Slaughter quit Chisum because he saw big money for the next few years. Jackson tells us Chisum is a hard boss. He pays little and drives his men. Moreover he's not above making them do a little rustling. Except for the uncertainty of life Slaughter is figuring all right. He and his outfit will be very much better off going on their own hook. Or I should say their own guns! And there's the rub. Guns make life uncertain. Guns in the hands of Brazos Keene and Laigs Mason and Cherokee and Mex Southard — or any of the Ripple outfit, not to forget our Texas Ranger boss — *and* your humble servant here speaking — guns in these hands make life most damned uncertain, all of which is to say that if

Slaughter's outfit go to rustling on this range they will not last long.

"But gentlemen, that is not so important, in my mind, as what Britt called inside rustling. You're bound to respect a bunch of hard nuts who go out in the open and steal cattle, and fight on sight. It's the gang that has inside help that I'm leery about. You know what I mean. A big cattleman, outwardly honest, mixed up in all that's doing on the range, but secretly in league with one or more crooked outfits, and with some crooked boys in his own outfit. This was what always ruined the cattle business in Kansas, when cattle were cheap and plentiful. Sutherland was such a man. And, men, as sure as I stand here tonight, that kind of rustler will develop here soon, if he is not already here. . . . Savvy, men? He may be here now.

"Well, such a leader, with his large holdings, his many deals, his influence, *and* his crooked cowboys, is what we must expect and prepare for now. Some of you boys will be approached. Attractive propositions will be made you. This big fellow will want a spy, a scout, or two, even in the camp of Don Carlos' Rancho. There is the case of Dillon who was just weak, dishonest, and ignorant. He was a damn fool. A likeable cowboy, so I've heard, full of fun, lend you his last dollar, or stand your watch, or nurse you when you were sick — but when under the influence of whiskey he was a poor, easy, yellow dog. He deceived Brazos, because Brazos is kind-hearted and likes everybody. . . . Men — that fool break of Mugg

179

Dillon's *cost him his life!* And I say if there is one among you to whom life is not sweet he had better ride away pronto — or else cultivate a keen and passionate desire to live. Otherwise Don Carlos' Rancho will be the last place for him.

"Now, comrades, a last word. The deal ahead of us on this range is hell. Some of us — half of us will get killed. But it appeals to me because of the right — which I have disregarded for so long — and because a thoroughbred Westerner, a game kid, a *girl,* refuses to go back on her father's wishes, on her ranch, and her cowboys. We can not go back on her. It would be too lowdown.

"Pards, from now on we are a pack of lone wolves. We ride the range together. We are no longer good fellows, to talk, to drink with cowboys of other outfits, or strangers. We reverse the old habit of cowboys. And always one of us, or two of us will keep the others from drinking too much. . . . Now, gentlemen, please stand up!"

As Frayne's ringing voice ceased, the cowboys, with scarcely a sound, rose erect, most of them pale and all of them stern. Frayne's cold, harsh facts and arguments had told.

"Britt has asked me to propose a toast," went on Frayne. "We will drink to — Holly Ripple and her Knights of the Range!"

When Holly fled from her cowboys to her room, with her hands over her ears pretending to shut out their thundering applause, she knew herself to be a deceitful creature, because she should have pressed those white members over her tumultuous and bursting heart.

Before Frayne had ended his talk Holly knew that she loved him. She fled now because she had to be alone a few moments or go mad. Safe in her room, barred in, behind closed curtains she paced swiftly to and fro, in a torment that was rapture. She knew now who and what he was. Had he come out openly with his ignominy for her sake, as much as to impress her men? He was finer than she had dreamed. Cold and hard as rock! Like Nemesis he had faced those rowdy wild cowboys, to convince them of the inevitable law of right itself, of how great they might become in loyalty to her, in chivalrous friendship among themselves, in unrewarded and unsung duty to the empire in the making.

Holly made no compromise with herself. She flung doubts and moods to the four winds. She loved Renn Frayne, and her happiness depended on winning his love. It would not have mattered now if he were really bad. She had to be his wife. But he was not bad — not in the sense that she had feared. She believed him, she loved him, and her heart sickened and froze at remembrance of his past indifference. That did not last. He had killed a man over a woman. Then Holly knew the real horrible pangs of jealousy. But Frayne could not have been more than a boy.

"Oh, what shall I do?" she whispered, frantically. "No mother! No woman friend! . . . I am twenty. . . . My party — all the range here! . . . I must go out there — smile — talk — dance — be Holly Ripple — when I am so terribly in love that I'll die — if — if he —"

But as she passed the mirror and caught her reflection in it, some instinct, deep and strong and female, stirred in her. Holly sat down on her bed, there to face this catastrophe as she had faced the future on the day of her father's death. From some unplumbed depth welled strength. In a few moments she was again outwardly composed. She had had her fight, and it was more terrible than that of loneliness. She was a Ripple of the South, she had the pride and passion of the Valverdes in her veins. She could not kill pride. She knew her vagrant moods, her temper and spirit. She had to change them or suffer horribly through them. As it did not seem reasonable to expect that she could change her nature she accepted suffering. It would be her portion. Renn Frayne would be hard to win. Holly slew her vanity; nevertheless, as all was fair in love she would use her beauty, even to lowering herself to the wiles of a Conchita Velasquez. All these lonely frontier men were hungry for women. This very night her cowboys would surround her like a pack of wolves. Why could not Renn Frayne be human? She would be happy with so little. His protection, his presence, his kisses. . . . She realized then that she had yearned for them. Vague fancies, yes, but seen now in this hour, how different, how sweet and terrifying!

"He called me a thoroughbred Westerner — a

game kid — a girl who refused to show yellow," soliloquized Holly, as she arose, exalted and unquenchable. "All right, Renn. That is my star and my anchor. You never dreamed — that then you won yourself a friend — a sweetheart — a wife!"

Holly swept out to capture Britt and a cowboy, who happened to be Skylark. With their assistance she addressed herself to the task ahead — of greeting her guests. They were soon joined by the Doanes; and Ann, merrily attaching herself to Skylark, went along with them.

The dining room and living room were being stripped of all furniture, except lights and decorations, to prepare for the dance. A horde of strangers, Indians, Mexicans were being served in the patio. Outside on the porch and in the front of the house were groups of men who held aloof. Holly instructed Britt to invite them through the main hall to the patio, where they too would be served. Cowboys were everywhere. Bevy after bevy of Mexican girls, pretty and graceful in their brilliant colors, paraded to and fro, dusky-eyed and coquettish, waiting for the music to start. Holly had engaged all the musicians in the valley, and as they were lamentably few in number she would have been short but for Mexicans with their guitars. The two big rooms would accommodate a hundred or more dancers, and the wide stone-floored L-shaped patio porch a like number. There were seven American girls present, beside Ann and herself, and perhaps two score of Mexican girls.

There were also two decidedly pretty Indian maidens. They were outnumbered ten to one by the male contingent, avidly ready to dance.

"How many here tonight?" asked Holly, breathlessly.

"Thunderin' big crowd. All of five hundred, countin' the Indians," replied Britt.

"Say, boss, hev you taken a peek out in front?" queried Skylark.

"Shore, but I forgot them."

"Almost twice as many as last year. Oh, how lovely!" cried Holly, delighted. "If only all goes well!"

"Lass, you've done yore part. Leave the rest to us. I'll take my stand at the front door. An' some of the boys will take turns at the back. No rowdy drunk or armed will get in."

A whooping howl and a rhythmic stamp from the dining room drew Holly to the door with her companions. The cowboys were lined in a half circle around the little negro Jackson who was engaged in some incredibly active and ludicrous movements. One of the fiddlers was sawing violently upon his instrument. Upon Holly's entrance the hullabaloo ceased.

"Jackson, what in the world were you doing?" queried Holly, most interested and curious.

"Missy — Ripple —," panted the colored cowboy, wiping the beads of sweat from his shining black face. "Dey done provoke me — dese heah white trash. Dey bet me — I wuz a swamp niggah

184

— wot couldn't dance — an' I was sho showin' 'em."

"Very well. Show me. I will be judge," replied Holly.

"Nix, fellars," shouted Laigs Mason, in alarm. "Ride-'Em is the jumpin'-jackinest darky thet ever come out of Texas. Take thet bet back."

"Yo cain't take it back, Laigs, 'cause I'se put up my money. . . . Come arustlin' dere, Mistah fiddler. I'se rarin' to go."

With the music and the beating of time with hands and feet by the cowboys, Jackson flung himself into violent motion. Holly became aware then that, funny as he looked, he had a remarkable ability to keep time, not only with his pattering feet but with all his body, even to the rolling of his eyes. Music, clapping, stamping, and the shouts of the cowboys, increased in intensity, swiftness, and volume. Suddenly Laigs Mason, evidently unable to resist the combination, flung himself into action with the negro. Laigs was as small in stature, as bowlegged, and is clownish as Jackson. No doubt he was bent upon out-doing the negro. But he was far from being such a master as his comrade. Finally the speed and fury of the dance precipitated Laigs to the floor, amid a roar that Holly feared would lift the roof. It likewise proclaimed Jackson the victor on two counts.

"You win, Jackson," said Holly, when she could make herself heard. "You are a wonderful dancer. . . . Mason, may I inquire what that was you were doing?"

185

"Aw, Miss Holly," protested Laigs, "I was jiggin', too."

"You did very well indeed. Perhaps Brazos or Frayne would like to try you out. I'll be glad to back you."

"Not much," yelped Brazos. "I'm a lady's dancer," while Frayne smiled his disinclination to compete with Mason.

"Fork ober, yose gennelmen," spoke up Jackson. "I'm collectin' mah bet. . . . Two-bits, suh, fum every dawg-gone one ob yo."

"Boys, get your partners," called Holly. "Dancing will begin in ten minutes. I shall ask one of you to start with me."

Brazos led a charge of eager cowboys toward Holly. She fled, while Britt and Skylark blocked the door. Holly had long ago made up her mind whom she intended to choose. Her sudden flight had its inception in fun, perhaps a little coquetry, and assuredly, as the moment arrived, in strange lack of courage. She raced from one place to another, announcing the dance, sending girls and boys in flocks to the big rooms. When she returned to the dining room, a score and more of couples were waiting with bright eyes and restless feet.

Holly glided in, once more mistress of her feelings and of Don Carlos' Rancho. She espied her choice, Renn Frayne, evidently paired with Conchita Velasquez. But Brazos was present, also, and she might have been mistaken. Nevertheless sight of Frayne, subtly less cold and formal, with this Mexican belle who had never before appeared so

186

alluring, with the vivid contrast of her beautiful white arms and shoulders to her dusky eyes and raven hair, brought to Holly the staggering fact that here was a rival. Holly went directly up to Frayne.

"Renn, will you start the dance with me?"

For once his reserve, his poise, was shattered. Most obviously amazed, embarrassed, he turned red and stammered! "Why — er? — I — I'm sorry. . . . I've asked Conchita."

Holly gazed straight up into his gray eyes.

"Did you not know I would ask you?"

"Miss Ripple! . . . I — I never dreamed of that. Why should I? — Please excuse me."

Holly turned her back upon him. Brazos was beside her, with that same cool, audacious smile. He had come to her rescue.

"Lady, I had them hombres all figgered," he drawled. "An' I waited fer yu. But at thet I ain't so turrible flattered to be second choice."

Holly waved her signal to the musicians and slipped into Brazos' arms, to be whirled away upon the floor. All cowboys could waltz, but Brazos was the best she had ever danced with. And the sudden pleasure of the moment edged into the hot pain of the jealousy she could not control.

"Old Faithful Brazos," she murmured.

"Shore. I'm the only one of thet ootfit who luves yu deep, who's been true, who'd die fer —"

"Brazos, did you say true? I just happened to remember. And I called you Old Faithful Brazos."

"Wal, I would die fer yu, wouldn't I?"

"I'm quite sure you would. Brazos, but be *true* to me. Oh, cowboy, that's different."

"Dawg-gone-it, Holly. You never give me the tiniest little hope."

"Of what?"

"Thet you'd marry me."

"Brazos! — I'd have to love you first. . . . Don't hold me so tight. If you must hug me, wait till — the floor is full."

"Wal, I'll wait, but I shore must," replied Brazos, breathing heavily.

"Then I'll never dance with you again."

"But I'm the best dancer."

"Yes, you are. But I don't care."

"Look at Frayne," whispered Brazos, gleefully. "Said he hasn't danced fer ten years. Shore looks it. But Conchita doesn't 'pear to mind. She's wrapped up in him. . . . Look, Holly."

"Thank you, I don't want to," replied Holly, dreamily. "I'm very happy as I am. . . . Is Renn hugging Conchita?"

"Wal, if he ain't she is him. . . . Holly, thet Mexican dame is after Renn."

"Indeed. Is that an unusual proceeding for Conchita?"

"No. But Renn is kinda shy aboot gurls. He's plumb decent, Holly."

"I'm glad to hear it," murmured Holly.

"Conchita will hev Renn eatin' oot of her hand in no time."

"Jealous, Brazos?"

"Aw, Holly, yu make me mad. I don't care

nothin' atall aboot Connie. An' I do aboot Renn."

"Brazos, you are growing remarkably chivalrous lately. — What do you want me to do?"

"Wal, you might give Renn a hint."

"Impossible, my cowboy."

"Then dawg-gone-it — she'll get him."

"And you'll lose her!"

"There — them sons-of-guns have stopped fiddlin'. Gee, thet was a short dance. But nice, Holly. Only you made me forget to hug yu. . . . Do yu reckon yu could give me another chance?"

"Not tonight, Brazos."

"Aw wal! — My Gawd, Holly, you're lovely tonight. Yu jest go to my haid."

"Brazos, your head is not very strong."

"Wait! I cain't say nuthin' when thet ootfit corrals yu," he whispered, detaining her. "Listen. Heah, darlin', is where Brazos plays the game. . . . Thet fellar Frayne is so in love with yu he cain't be natural."

"Bra-zos!" she gasped, collapsing inwardly.

"Wal! — Don't grab me like thet, if you're so all-fired. . . . Aw, 'scuse me, Holly. . . . I seen through Renn. He's all bluff aboot yu. Thet cold, mean, standoffish way of his is 'cause he's afeared yu'll see he loves yu wuss'n we all do. . . . Now Lady, play yore cairds."

"Nonsense!"

Brazos, with something warm and bright that almost dimmed the piercing devil of his eyes, relinquished Holly to one of his comrades, which one she had no idea at the moment. Holly danced dizzily, with her cheek on the broad shoulder of her present cavalier, who turned out to be Tennessee, the enigma of her cowboys, whom she knew least. When presently he in turn let her go to Bluegrass, Holly had still only partly recovered. Brazos was a fiend, but he could not have told Holly that unless he believed it. He had, however, guessed her secret. Brazos' virtues of magnanimity and generosity were as great as some of his other qualities. He was making up for unjust dislike of Frayne. But he was wrong. Frayne did not love her. He did not even like her yet. Holly beat down the ecstasy of her rebel heart with her own convictions.

The dance went on. Holly did ample duty by her cowboys, dancing with all who claimed her. Twice Frayne had his opportunity, but did not avail himself of it. Once she caught his gaze, when he must have imagined himself unobserved, and the lightning of it was something she dared not believe in.

The rooms crowded with other cowboys, with ranchers, and strangers. And eventually Sewall McCoy approached Holly. He was a large, square-shouldered cattleman, over forty years old, handsome in a bold rugged way, heavily jowled and possessed of the hard eyes and thin lips characteristic of so many rangers. Holly did not like McCoy, but as Britt had suggested that she talk with him and draw him out she was ready to dance with him.

For so heavy a man he danced well, except that he presumed upon his opportunity. Holly had a way of circumventing these range men, and she kept McCoy from crushing her. He was a man of some education, of large means and influence; and he had already proposed to Holly twice. She had become used to offers of marriage on short notice. It was a Western way. There was no time for courting. Long distances made a general social life impossible. Once a year range folk met, and that was about all.

"Miss Holly, I've been anxious to see you," began McCoy.

"Yes? What about?"

"Well, several things, all important, and all hangin' together. Do you recollect that little offer I made you last year?"

"Offer? I'm afraid I've forgotten."

"Flatterin'. — I asked you to marry me."

"Oh, that! Pray excuse me, Mr. McCoy. I thought that was over."

"No doubt. But I'm makin' it again. Third an' last time. They say a third time is the charm. How about it, Holly?"

"My answer is the same. Thanks for the honor you would do me — but no."

"Why not?" he asked, rather arrogantly.

"The main reason a woman refuses a man is because she doesn't love him."

"Holly, there are reasons why you'd do well to waive that."

"Indeed. And what are they?"

"This range is changin.' You're runnin' thirty thousand head —"

"Fifty thousand, Mr. McCoy," corrected Holly; and in that very moment her woman's intuition placed this cattleman in the same category as Sutherland.

"So many? Well, your man Britt never was any good at countin' either or grades. But no matter. This range is in for some long tough drill with rustlers. Your outfit has a bad name. This man Frayne is an outlaw — a notorious gunman. Britt picked him out of a band of —"

"Wrong again, Mr. McCoy. *I* picked him."

"You did? I'm surprised. . . . When cattle stealin' gets bad Frayne an' some more of your disreputable outfit are goin' to be suspected. I am your nearest neighbor. Our cattle run together, at least most of my ten thousand head —"

"Mr. McCoy, you have a little less than five thousand branded stock on this range."

"Sure, a lot of mine hasn't had the iron yet," he added, hastily. "I've been short of riders. But now I've got the best outfit on this range. If you throwed in with me we'd be too strong for any combination of rustlers. An' my outfit would give yours a respectable name. We'd dominate the range. This Chisum bunch — they're footloose. Slaughter has got somethin' up his sleeve. He made me a proposition, which I won't consider till I get your answer."

"You are threatening me," returned Holly, and stopped dancing on the spot, which happened to be just outside of an alcove where Britt and Frayne stood talking with Doane.

"Not at all," protested McCoy, nettled and uneasy. "I'm just talkin' sense. . . . What's your answer?"

"No."

"Very well. You may regret it."

"Never," rejoined Holly, spiritedly, in a voice that carried to her men. "Mr. McCoy, I shall back my disreputable outfit, as you called it, to the very limit. Throw in with Russ Slaughter, as you threatened. That has a suspicious slant — just as suspicious as your hint that some of my men are dishonest. . . . Mr. McCoy, I resent your blackguarding my men. You force me to break for the first time my father's law of hospitality. . . . Please leave my house!"

Stunned, his heavy visage gray in hue, McCoy gave Holly a baleful look and strode through the dancers like a jostling bull. The music ceased. Holly moved to confront Britt. Outwardly calm, burning within, she gave Britt her hands, but she looked into Frayne's impenetrable face.

"Good Gawd, Holly!" ejaculated Britt. "We heahed you. What possessed you to lace it into McCoy thet way?"

"Rage."

"Wal, shore. You needn't tell us thet. You're as white as I never seen anythin'. An' yore eyes, lass!"

"Can I speak before Mr. Doane?"

"Shore. Doane is my friend as he was yore Dad's."

"Renn — McCoy insulted you," said Holly, with

a passion that made her thoughtless. Frayne made no reply. "He tried to strengthen his offer of marriage by claiming that you and others of my men were crooked. He hinted of a big secret rustler combination for whose deals my outfit would be blamed. He said throwing my outfit in with his would give mine respectability."

"What was thet aboot Russ Slaughter?" queried Britt, sharply.

"McCoy said he'd consider throwing in with Slaughter — if I refused his offer."

Britt stroked his chin gravely, while his keen eyes went from Doane to Frayne.

"Oh, I lost my temper," cried Holly, beginning to see something seriously amiss.

"Lass, I shore couldn't have answered McCoy better, an' neither could Frayne heah — unless he'd flashed a gun. . . . Renn, back me, will you? Holly is upset."

"Miss Ripple, you could not have handled the situation better," replied Frayne, with respect and admiration. "But tell us. How did you make that tight-jawed cattleman give himself away?"

"I don't know. I didn't do anything. . . . Let me think. He smelled of whiskey. He tried to hug me. He began at once to make his proposal. He was excited."

"Plumb easy," concluded Britt, with a wry smile. "Doane, keep this under yore sombrero. But think a heap. An' keep close tab on everythin' over yore way. . . . Holly, I'll leave you with Renn."

To be left thus with Frayne would have been disturbing enough to Holly, even if she had not been profoundly moved. Besides Frayne's eyes pierced her.

"Like father, like daughter. If I could only have known him — ridden for him years ago! . . . Miss Holly, it's easy to understand why you are what you are."

His flattery was impersonal. But any praise from this man, with the fine allusion to the father she had worshipped, would have affected Holly then. A dreamy, seductive Spanish waltz suddenly thrummed from the guitars. Holly drew Frayne out of the alcove.

"This is our dance," she said, and swayed into his arms. He could not see her face, which was hidden on his breast, nor her heart, which was more of a traitor. She did not care if he did feel it throb. She did not know nor care whether he danced well or ill. All Holly felt then was his strong clasp, under which she sank to the irresistible sweetness of this trance. Sooner or later it lost dominance over her mind, and she awakened to the subtlety and allurement which she had sworn to practice upon this man.

"Are you enjoying yourself?"

"I am now."

"Didn't Conchita — amuse you?"

"She did more."

"Did you hold her as — closely as you are holding me?"

"I beg your pardon. I didn't realize. . . . Yes,

I must have. Conchita has a way of dancing you off your feet and out of your head."

"Have *I* not that, Señor?"

"No doubt, to these boys with sagebrush in their heads, instead of brains."

"But not to you?"

"No."

"If it had not been for your one and only compliment — a moment ago — my birthday party would be spoiled."

"Must you chatter such party nonsense? — Be sincere, Holly, or be quiet."

She was quiet for a few rounds among the whirling couples. Then all too soon the waltz ended.

"You are pale — dizzy," he said, solicitously, as he released her. "It is long past midnight. You have danced steadily."

"That will be the last. And I had to steal it! — You would not have asked me. You alone!"

"Santone did not ask you. Nor Mason, nor Jackson, nor the Southards. Why do you persist in expecting more from me?"

"Let us go out a few moments," she replied, and led him into the patio. Dancers and strollers were numerous along the wide porch, and every bench had its couple, but at the lower end, where the patio opened into the garden, there was the seclusion Holly desired.

"Is this garden walled in?" asked Frayne, peering into the gloom of foliage.

"Yes. You can enter only from the patio. Why?"

"Miss Holly, has it not occurred to you that

some of your guests are thieves, outlaws, rustlers? You are surrounded by men who hate your cowboys — who would stop at nothing. . . . It astonishes me — your nerve or your blindness, I don't know which. A splendid tribute to you, this turnout. But I disapprove of this free-for-all hospitality. It will lead to annoyance to you, or more. Yet you seem not to see it. You are a grand lady on this range. Still in my opinion to laugh, talk, dance — flirt under such circumstances is most unwise."

"Renn, I want to be happy," she explained, poignantly.

They walked on in silence, out into the garden, down a moonlit, rose-scented path. Their slow footsteps gave forth no sound. At a curve in the path Holly heard a familiar voice, and she halted. Above it sounded the sensuous melody of a Spanish love song from somewhere beyond.

"What has leetle Conchita done that her beeg señor ees no more sweet — he has no kees, or hug for her tonight? . . . No!"

Holly would have recognized that pleading voice without its self betrayal, and she turned to leave when Frayne detained her. "Hold on," he whispered in her ear. "I'd like to hear some more."

"But Renn!" whispered Holly, in expostulation. "It's not nice — to listen."

"I reckon not. But wouldn't you like to?"

Holly's "no" was not a miracle of truth, but it would have actuated her had not Frayne put his arm around her waist, which made it impossible for her to move, even without the slight restraint.

"Connie, you're no good," drawled Brazos. "You're like all the rest of them."

"Ah no, señor! You theenk bad of Conchita when her heart beet only for her magneeficente Brazos."

"I'll bet you let Frayne hug an' kiss yu."

"Frayne? — That so-cold Señor, who no speek Spanish — who dance so steefly. . . . Si Señor, he hug Conchita, but he not know it. An' he never think of kees. He no love Conchita!"

"You black-eyed kitten! If you lie to me!"

"Conchita no lie —"

"Come heah," replied Brazos, masterfully. A low soft murmur ended in a succession of audible kisses. "Dog-gone-yu, Connie. If you didn't cock yore eye at every cowboy on this range, I reckon I'd marry yu."

Frayne lifted Holly clear of the ground and carried her noiselessly back up the path for some distance before he let her down. Then he drew her on to the arched, vine-covered entrance to the patio.

"Risky, sneaking on Brazos that way," he remarked. He relaxed from his tenseness. His face changed magically and grew convulsed with mirth. "Gosh, if I could only — tell the outfit!"

"Don't you dare," broke out Holly, loyally, though she sensed a queer burning within.

"I won't. But, Holly, wasn't it — rich? — The jealous son-of-a-gun! Sore at poor me. — Why,

198

honest, the girl almost fooled me. She said the same things to me. She rubbed her cheek against mine — her lips. She got her hair in my eyes. She just melted in my arms."

"But you hugged her!" exclaimed Holly, with all a schoolgirl's senselessness.

"Good heaven! Of course I did. I'm human. And that little Mexican lass is devastating. But no more! I'm on to her now. The darned little hussy! She's as much of a devil as Brazos. . . . Holly, didn't you nearly burst?"

"Yes, but not with mirth."

"What do you mean?" he queried, changing.

"Renn, I was jealous."

"No! Not really?"

"I'm afraid so."

"But just because . . . Brazos is your favorite cowboy, I know. . . . You wouldn't be seriously jealous of that pretty Mexican?"

"Not on his account," replied Holly, with a significance wholly lost upon Frayne. He threw off something in relief. What had suddenly clouded his mind? Holly grasped it. He knew Brazos as she did not know him, and his perplexity, his obvious consternation had undoubtedly come from the impossibility of telling her. Britt had once informed her that cowboys did not possess morals, a sweeping statement which Holly had disbelieved. She grew perturbed, and struggled against an insidious reasoning that Frayne held her innocence sacred.

"Take me in," she said, worn out with physical

and mental strain. The stars burned white and remorselessly down upon her. That Mexican with his love song! The music thrummed and throbbed; and the great house seemed riotous with mirth and sound. Holly had had enough. She clung to Frayne's arm through the gay bright rooms to her own door, which she opened.

"Good night, *Caballero*," she said, softly, holding out her hand.

"Holly, let me apologize."

"For what? — Your not wanting to dance with me?"

"No. That absurd misunderstanding — about your jealousy."

Holly smiled her forgiveness, and denied herself little in one fleeting glance before she closed her door.

CHAPTER 8

Holly awoke late and lay thinking. The golden sun sifted through the vines over her window, spreading lace-like shadows and bright spots upon her bed. In broad daylight she could not retrieve the thoughts and feelings under which she had strained last night. It seemed impossible to give credence to some of them. What had she done — what had she said? Nothing compared to that which she had determined upon! Would she ever be able to cultivate the beguilement of Conchita Velasquez?

She passed from a vague and unsatisfactory review of her experience and conduct for the evening to an impersonal contemplation of her birthday party. It had undoubtedly been a huge success. There had been no fights, so far as she knew. But she never knew half that went on. Frayne's somber intimation that the gay and sumptuous party had been held over a powder magazine had been a warning she must heed in the future. How easily her house could be made the scene of as bloody a fight as had ever occurred among cowboys!

When her next birthday rolled around Holly would break her father's rule, to the extent that only those who received invitations could be present. It might be wise, also, to close her house at once to strangers. Lascelles and Taylor had virtually forced her to remain a prisoner in her room. The good old tranquil days of southern hospitality and Spanish atmosphere were gone forever. The era of the settler and the rancher had begun.

Holly had her breakfast, sitting up in bed, listening to the chatter of the Mexican maids, who pronounced her party *una fiesta grande.* Many of her guests had departed early. And some had never gone to sleep at all. They lived thirty, forty, sixty and even hundred miles away, which meant long drives and dark camps before they reached their homes. This was a fact about the range that Holly deplored. She had visited San Marcos, but the towns farther west, Lincoln, Fort Sumner and Fort Union, Santa Fe, Taos and Las Vegas, she had never seen. Britt did not approve of Holly riding in stagecoaches.

"My party is past — maybe the last one," said Holly, to herself, as she slipped out of bed. "Now what? I haven't a thing to do. There are many things I ought to do. . . . One that I can't — I can't. . . . But I shall!"

She had peeped out of her window, down upon the grassy pastures, the wide green and gray stretch to the line of cottonwoods, and around to the corrals and the cabins. That was never a lonely scene, but this morning it appeared even more than yesterday active and colorful with horses, Indians, riders, wagons and buckboards on the move. The scene in front of the bunkhouse decided Holly at once to go down. Cowboys on foot and on horse-back, to the number of a hundred or more, excited her curiosity. Her boys must be up to something. She hesitated a moment, checked by a thought, but as it appeared to be a friendly gathering Holly hurriedly donned her riding outfit, and quirt in hand she ran out. She did not inquire into her eagerness, her keen scent of the warm, sage-laden air, her mounting thrill at the purple range, with its thousands of cattle. She did not inquire into the unusual precipitancy of her blood, the sense of youth and life and happiness, the joy of un-plumbed anticipations. Holly's thought, as she ran down the path, was a rebellious one that Britt was not going to hold her in any longer.

When Holly emerged from the trees she saw mounted riders and cowboys on foot in groups beyond the cabins. She recognized some of her own boys at the far end of the long bunkhouse porch. As their backs were turned they did not see her. Holly gained the door, which was open, and from which issued a voice she knew.

"Aw, hell, Cap, don't *tell* me nothin'," Brazos said, harshly.

"But I do tell you. Frayne's hunch is to watch Talman," rejoined Britt, sharply.

Holly knocked on the door with the handle of her quirt.

"May I come in?"

"Thet you, Holly? . . . Yes, come in, now you're heah. I'm shore glad Jose cleaned up this messy place."

Holly went in to meet Britt, who for once did not brighten at sight of her. Brazos slipped off the table to greet her. But his moody face broke to the smile it always wore for her.

"Mawnin', Lady. Yu shore look top-notch after yore all night *fandango*."

"Brazos, I'm sorry I can't return the compliment."

Britt interposed nervously, if not testily: "Holly, what'd you bob down heah for? You go right back to the house."

She laughed at him. "Who are you talking to? . . . What's going on?"

"Wal, thet Slaughter ootfit sent word they had a hawse they'd bet no cowboy of yores could ride. I reckon it'll delay range-ridin' fer the time bein'."

"I hope you'll disprove that. Have they ever heard of Jackson?"

"Shore not, Holly, else they wouldn't be so gay."

"Too good to miss," interposed Brazos. "We'll lead them on an' win every dollar they got."

"Britt, what is this I heard you tell Brazos, as I got to the door?"

"What? . . . Aw, nothin' much. I forget," returned the Texan, coolly. But he did not deceive Holly.

"Will you tell me, Brazos?"

"Shore. I'd tell yu anythin', if I remembered. But I cain't keep track of my own talk, let alone Britt's."

"Call Frayne," returned Holly, shortly.

They stared at her.

"Do you hear me? Call him, or I shall go out after him."

Britt went to the door and halloed for Frayne. Brazos gave Holly a cool scrutinizing glance. She smiled back at him, not so coolly, but with an intelligence he must have grasped. Quick, heavy steps sounded on the porch.

"Come in. Miss Holly is heah an' sent fer you," said Britt. Frayne came in with his sombrero in his hand, the same inscrutable man that had so long baffled Holly. He bowed without speaking.

"Good morning, Renn. . . . Britt has just lied to me. And Brazos has lost his memory. Before I ask you some questions I want to tell you something, which I mean for them to hear as well. . . . From now on I am boss of this ranch. Britt treats me as a little girl he used to dandle on his knee. He thinks he's my Dad and that I'll never grow up. Brazos is a slick hombre who thinks I'm as easy to fool as — well, Conchita, for instance. They try to keep everything unpleasant or serious or bad from my ears. This I will not tolerate any longer. . . . Have I made myself quite clear?"

"Indeed you have, Miss Holly," rejoined Frayne, in surprise. Both Britt and Brazos were dumbfounded, as well as ashamed.

"Very well, now, Renn, for the questions. You wouldn't lie to me? You wouldn't keep things from me?"

"Why wouldn't I?"

"Because of last night."

"I don't understand."

205

"It is personal, of course. I always trusted you. But after your talk to my men last night, I shall have absolute faith in you."

"You win, Miss Holly," he said, with his fleeting smile. "Certainly I will never lie to you."

"Thanks, Renn. . . . What is this hunch of yours to watch Talman? I heard Britt tell Brazos."

"Last night Britt and I divided our time in watching. With McCoy and Slaughter in the house we did not feel at ease. Anything could happen. Slaughter got in with a gun inside his vest, a fact he didn't think any of us knew. He approached some of our boys and got a cold shoulder for his pains. But McCoy got to Talman. They did not go out together. McCoy went first, then Talman. They met outside."

"Did you — follow?" asked Holly, breathless with interest.

"No. It might have been nothing. Yet again it might have meant much."

"What time did that happen?"

"Late. After you had said goodnight."

"Frayne, you would not have given Britt a hunch to watch Talman, if your suspicions had not been aroused."

"Hardly. But I never took to Talman, somehow. It's my habit to study men. That seems to have been inborn. The need of self-preservation developed it strong. Talman is a queer duck. He's one of the few cowboys I've met who loves money. He's greedy. He's a great horseman. He makes friends, yes, but not pards."

"Did Talman come back?"

"No. And if he slept at all last night, it was little. It happens that I know eyes. It has saved my life more than once."

"Therefore you advised Britt to watch him?"

"Yes, Miss Holly."

"Well, Britt, this is what you and Brazos were quarreling about when I stepped to the door?"

"I reckon."

"But why the quarrel?"

"Brazos wouldn't heah. My idee, of course, was to tell him an' have him watch this cowboy."

Holly turned to Brazos, who sat with downcast gloomy face. "Brazos, it may be nothing. We must respect Frayne's judgment. Still he may be over-zealous. And your watching might prove Talman merely thoughtless, which heaven knows you all are."

"Dog-gone! I *hate* it," ground out Brazos, with passion.

"What? You mean spying on a comrade? So would I."

"No, Lady, I don't mind thet. It's the idee I hate. I've knowed so many pards who turned oot to be jest no good atall."

"That is bitter, Brazos," said Holly, earnestly. "But listen. I am dependent upon my men. Why, for all, even my life and more than life. . . . Suppose I lost Britt and Frayne. How would *you* handle this case?"

"I wouldn't discharge Talman. Thet'd tip off these schemin' ootfits. I'd want to ketch their drift.

207

I'd watch him, with Laigs to help me. Thet's all."

"But you would not listen to Britt."

"I was stallin'."

"Do you want to be let out of this distasteful job?"

"Not atall, Lady. Fust off I was huffy. But no more. I hope to Gawd I can prove Talman straight. It'd shore be tough to find another Dillon in the ootfit."

"I hope so too. Now, boys, go back to the riding contest. I'll stay and watch out of the window. I'd like to bet, too."

"Wal, we'd shore like to hev yu," replied Brazos, changing as if by magic. "Hev yu got any money in them togs? It'll be a cash deal, believe me."

"Brazos! — Wouldn't you trust me?"

"I would, but I don't know aboot —"

Britt extracted a heavy wallet from his coat.

"What'll you bet on Jackson?"

"Five hundred. And give him half if he wins."

Brazos smothered a whoop, and instead of letting off his exuberance in that way, he danced a jig.

"Lady, yu shore air a thoroughbred," he declared, suddenly getting tense and businesslike. "Heah, get yore haids together. . . . Jackson would ride a bat oot of hell fer thet much. We cain't lose. . . . Now heah's the deal with this Slaughter ootfit. They started it. We didn't even encourage it. But they galled us pretty deep. My idee is they must have a hell-buckin' broncho. They reckon they can clean us oot. All right. We'll bet easy fust off. We'll back Laigs, an' course he'll get piled. Then we'll back, say, Blue, fer a little money. To egg them on, see? — Then I'll get sore, an' fork thet varmint myself. It'll be a bluff 'cause I cain't ride nothin'. We'll be het up, then, an' we'll flash our rolls, an' bet every damn *peso* we got on Ride-'Em. It'll be highway robbery, an' thet bunch will yell murder. . . . How's my idee strike yu-all?"

"Brazos, it strikes me fine," replied Holly, warming to the youthful face, the flashing blue eyes, the mobile lips that expressed such glee.

"Wal, so long as Slaughter throwed this in our faces I kinda am fer it," drawled Britt.

"Great idea," declared Frayne, keenly. "I want a chance to look this outfit over."

"They're yellin' fer us. Aw, I hate to do this. Come on."

"Miss Holly, you can see very well from this window," said Frayne, as Brazos and Britt started out. "Would you mind dropping the bar, after I close the door?"

"Renn! Are you afraid I'd be kidnapped?" exclaimed Holly, jokingly.

"Hardly that. But you will be seen. These men are hard, curious, insolent."

"Oh, you don't want me annoyed?"

"That is putting it mildly."

"I'm curious myself. I want to see this Russ Slaughter."

"He's not much to look at. I'd say a big tawny wolf, just come out of winter quarters, ragged and rough, with hungry eyes."

"How thrilling! I shall come out."

"You are a woman — that is to say, hopeless, incomprehensible," retorted Frayne, retreating into his shell. "No wonder Britt is growing gray. You won't listen to sense. You are a contrary little devil. Come on out. Slaughter will insult you, if not by word then by look. And I'll kill him."

"Renn! Don't — don't be so harsh," faltered Holly, subdued. "I was only teasing. I'll stay in — and bar the door."

Holly did not at once take her seat at the window. Renn Frayne seemed to magnify in one man all the ruthless qualities of the frontier. If her attempts at coquetry were to be met thus she would not progress very far. Thoughtful and subdued, she found herself to be merely an instinctive natural woman. Her spirit rose rebelliously at the proof of what a stern look and a few cold words from this man could do to her. If they could make her as weak as water, what would happen to her if Renn Frayne took her in his arms, as Brazos had done, as other cowboys had tried to do.

"Oh, dear! Why do I think such — such insane things? . . . If he did — and I was not so — so mad with joy that I'd faint. . . ."

A yell from outside directed Holly's feelings into another channel. She drew a chair to the window and sat down. The edge of a crowd of cowboys, Indians and Mexicans was not many rods from the bunkhouse. The crowd split with wild shouts, to let out an ugly beast of a horse, upon the back of which Laigs Mason sat precariously. No ordinary horse could make Laigs look like a tenderfoot. It was a dark buckskin in color, ragged and hairy, with wild eyes and steaming nostrils, humped in a distorted ball on four legs, which bounded as if on stiff springs. Such swift and violent bucking Holly had never seen. All at once Laigs Mason went flying to the ground, whereupon there arose wild mirth, punctuated by shouts and jeers. The buckskin, having gotten rid of his burden, ceased his gyrations. Standing still he was indeed a horse to tantalize any boastful cowboy. He was big, rangy, exceedingly muscular and uncouth, with an ugly head and untamed eye.

This time Holly was witness to the laying of more wagers, and to the assault of the Kentuckian upon the catapult of the Slaughter *remuda*. Blue was a fine horseman, but he lasted only five jumps before he was thrown. He was hurt and angry, too, as was indicated by his yell, almost unheard in the din, and by the fist he shook at Brazos.

Holly revelled in Brazos then. Since last night he had fallen from his pedestal, but she still loved him as a perfectly real, wild, terrible cowboy, the type of the age. Brazos simulated fury. He hopped up and down like a flea on a hot griddle, flung his arms, tore his curly hair, and otherwise demonstrated his rage at defeat. When the noise subsided he yelled:

"Lay yore bets, fellars. I'll ride thet ornery cayuse myself — or die tryin'. — But ask fer odds, boys. This ain't no ordinary hawse. Russ Slaughter has jobbed us. It's a dirty trick. He's got a circus hawse. . . . Lead him heah. . . . Aha, yu fire-eatin', smoke-snortin', iron-jawed mule — you're shore gonna be rid!"

Brazos was not only a magnificent actor, but also, according to Britt, the equal of any rider who ever straddled a horse; always excepting Ride-'Em Jackson who was in a class by himself.

The tremendous exhibition that Brazos boasted of did not materialize. He manifested none of his skill and made the poorest show of any of the boys. Holly noticed, however, that he chose a nice grassy plot to be thrown upon. Picking himself up, he apparently had sustained a surprise and shock.

"Dog-gone! Thet ain't a hawse," he complained. "No long-laiged rider could ever stay on him."

"Naw, nor any short-legged ones in your outfit," jeered a rider, striking for his superb seat in the saddle, his hatchet-face and tawny fringe of beard.

"We call yore bluff, Slaughter," returned Brazos, ringingly. "We got pore riders an' pore hawses heah, but we shore got plenty of the long green. Give us two to one odds an' we'll bet yu again, whole hawg or none."

Slaughter was suspicious, but his clamoring men overruled his objection, or whatever his gestures and voice implied. They crowded to take all bets offered by the Ripple cowboys. Slaughter was not proof against the sight of so much money, and he got off his horse to elbow his way into the crowd around Britt, who was holding stakes. The time required to get all wagers made attested to the large amounts and the importance of this last contest. But at last it was done. Slaughter and most of the visiting cowboys got back in their saddles, their lean, dark faces hungrily expectant.

"How aboot it, Slaughter?" yelled Brazos. "Any more money to bet?"

"All we got is up, Keene, an' you'll never smell it."

"Cowboy, take thet saddle off," called Brazos, to the rider who had charge of the bucking horse.

"Hey, you don't put no other saddle on him," objected Slaughter, as his cowboy looked up dubiously.

"We don't want no saddle atall," announced Brazos, swaggeringly. Whereupon in another moment the saddle was stripped from the restive mustang.

"Throw him. We want him on the ground," ordered Brazos.

"What's the idee?" yelled Slaughter, belligerently.

"Lay yore hawse down," returned Brazos, curtly. "Our man wants to fork him from the ground. If he cain't ride him yu win."

Accordingly two of Slaughter's cowboys roped the horse, stripped him, and threw him on his side. Brazos promptly seized the bridle from the one who held it and knelt upon the head of the horse.

"Slip them ropes loose," shouted Brazos. "All right, Jack, come arunnin'."

The little bow-legged negro appeared as if he had come up out of the ground. "Heah I is," he rolled out, and ran to the prostrate horse. He strad- dled the animal. "Gimme dat bridle, Brazos. I done hate to do dis." He appeared to wrap himself around the horse and to bend flat, almost to the ground. Brazos also bent over, evidently to see. Suddenly he leaped and backed with a wild yell. On the instant, with a horrid scream the horse raised himself spasmodically with a cracking of hoofs. Like a burr Jackson's body appeared stuck upon him. Holly had seen Jackson perform this trick before, though never so clearly. He had sunk his teeth in the nose of the horse, which made it impossible for the animal to get its head. And when they came up together the horse had his head high, turned back in a distorted way, with the little negro like a leech upon his neck.

"Look oot!" bawled Brazos, leaping aside, as the frantic beast began to lunge. Riders and those on foot scattered like quail. The great horse, frenzied at this attack, plunged all over the space before the bunkhouse, amid a din that made the former noise insignificant. It took a few moments for the intelligent beast to realize that lowering his head to pitch was impossible. He screeched like a demon. He scattered dust and gravel. And at length he bolted straight across the level. The angle of his head made him run in a circle, so that in short order he was back from where he had started. And right before his backers he quit as obviously as any horse could have done without balking.

Jackson let go his cruel hold, and sliding off threw the bridle. His grin showed his wide mouth and big white teeth.

"Whar yo-all wuz, pards?" he boomed.

To Holly's amazement her cowboys did not break into a pandemonium, as was usually their wont at any coup. Brazos strutted like an Indian chief to meet his black jockey. The other cowboys stood lose around Britt. Slaughter and his men were dumbfounded.

"Come hyar, nigger," yelled Slaughter.

Instead of complying, Jackson replied: "What yu want, boss?"

"How'd you ride thet hoss?"

"Sho mah own bizness."

The cowboy who had again taken charge of the prize horse called out: "His nose is bleedin'. Thet nigger bit him — hung on by his teeth."

"Hell! Can't I see?" rasped Slaughter. "Jackson, you rode fer me onct. How come you never showed us thet trick?"

"Wal, boss, I wuz only a nigger in yore ootfit."

"Ahuh. Wal, you'll be a dead nigger fer this outfit — some day."

"Sho. We'se all gotta die — an' some men's gonna get hunged by de neck," declared Jackson, sarcastically, as he slipped out of sight among his comrades.

"Take your medicine, Slaughter," rang a voice from among the group around Britt, and the tone of it made Holly start.

Brazos sheered off to come between Slaughter

and Britt's group. "Haw! Haw! Haw! — Slaughter, we Ripple ootfit haven't any hawses or riders or nothin'! Like hell we haven't! . . . Yu come over to make a friendly bet, didn't yu? Wal, yu got it an' yu lost it."

"Right. We got trimmed plumb good. I ain't kickin', Keene. But I'll have you know it wasn't my idee."

"Wal, whoever had it, shore blew some greenbacks our way," drawled Brazos.

"Jest two-bit change fer us. Plenty more where thet come from," replied Slaughter. But when he turned to his men he was not so boastful. "Get the hell out of hyar!"

It was noticeable that Slaughter, as he turned to ride away with his men, veered somewhat to the left, and when opposite the bunkhouse window, where Holly sat, halted to light a cigarette. But when he looked up, directly at her, Holly knew that had been a ruse. He was not too far away for the expression of his eyes to be discernible. Holly unwittingly caught their hard brightness before she could avoid them.

"Howdy, girlie," he called. "You might keep me from throwin' in with McCoy."

Holly left the window, nonplussed at the ruffian's declaration, until she interpreted it through the evil meaning in his eyes. It revolted her to realize that the time had come when she was not safe from insult even on her own ranch, in front of her cowboys. But hearing steps on the porch she stifled her sickening sensations. At a

216

hard knock on the door she slipped the bar and opened it. Frayne and Brazos stood there, as if they were her judges.

"Holly, did thet hombre see yu?" demanded Brazos.

"Certainly. I was in plain sight. They all saw me."

"Why didn't yu duck when he rode by?"

"Brazos, I am not in the habit of ducking."

"Wal, it'd be a darn good one fer yu to learn," complained Brazos. "I wasn't lookin' jest then. Too busy grabbin' my money from Britt. But Renn heah says Slaughter spoke to yu."

"He did. I heard him," corroborated Frayne, quietly, his penetrating gray gaze enveloping her.

"Yes. Did you hear what he said?" asked Holly, with a laugh. She was not so sure she could deceive Frayne. These men breathed something that stopped her heart.

"Only one word. 'McCoy.' . . . It was quite far and he spoke low."

"My vengeful *caballeros,* it was nothing."

"Holly, you claimed the absolute truth from me," declared Frayne, sternly.

"Why, of course," replied Holly, lightly. Yet she could not but thrill at the raw wild youth of Brazos, at the ruthlessness of Frayne. If she told them the truth they would call Slaughter out, kill him, and precipitate a bloody battle she wanted to put off as long as possible. It could not be put off forever.

"Holly, you're gonna lie to us. To me an' Renn
— yore best friends on Gawd's earth!" protested
Brazos.

"No!" exclaimed Holly. "I'll tell you some day.
When you come back from Las Animas after the
drive."

"Probably just as well," rejoined Frayne, briefly.
"If you told us now we might not make your cattle
drive to the railroad."

"Renn!"

"He heahed Slaughter mention McCoy. What
aboot him?" added the persistent Brazos.

"Well, I can tell you definitely that Slaughter
is going to throw in with McCoy."

"What'd I tell yu, pard?" hissed Brazos, with
a lightning simulation of the draw. Frayne con-
tinued to pierce Holly with eyes of doubt and con-
demnation, and some other disconcerting thing
that she found it preferable to avoid. A clamor
of voices outside and a stamping of boots preceded
the advent of Britt, who ran into the house, his
hands full of bills, his eyes full of mirth.

"Hey, gimme elbow-room, you Injuns," he protested. "Every man will get his money. I wrote
all the bets down."

Ride-'Em Jackson confronted Holly with great
shiny black orbs, full of worship.

"Missy Ripple, I sho nebber seen so much
money in all mah life. Wid yu backin' me dat way,
why I sho could have rode de debbil. . . . I'se
tellin' yu — dat money yu staked me is goin' to
mah ole black mammy."

Not so many days after the event of the year, the grassy triangle below Holly's ranchhouse shone red and white with thirty-five hundred head of steers ready for the drive to the railroad.

It was early morning with sun hot and the range blossoming in flowery meadows, the cottonwoods and willows full-foliaged. The mountains burned purple up to the gradually lessening snow patches. Down to the east, where the Old Trail wound along the ribbonlike Cimarron, the descending range rolled and rippled out to the vast gray of prairie.

Brazos had just bade Holly goodbye, a cool and nonchalant Brazos as always, but somehow stronger in earnestness and less sentimental. He left Holly thoughtful and sad. She knew and he knew that some day he would depart never to return.

Britt, brisk and businesslike, came in with Frayne for final instructions.

"Wal, they're pointed, Holly, an' all you got to do is wave yore scarf."

"Frayne, whom did you choose to take besides Brazos? Of course he would not go without Laigs," asked Holly.

"Santone, the Southards, Jackson, Cherokee. Eight of us in all," replied Frayne. "Not enough for so big a job. But we must not leave you short here."

"Who on the wagon?"

"We'll take turns driving."

"No *remuda?*"

"Only a few extra horses, which we'll drive ourselves."

"You are saving. . . . What's the count, Britt?"

"Three thousand, five hundred an' sixty-two. Brazos had less. But Renn an' I tallied the same."

Holly wrote the number down in her note-book. "Here's the mail, Frayne, and my several orders for supplies, which you may look over at your leisure."

"What are your instructions about selling?" queried Frayne, anxiously.

"No different from Britt's. Has he not told you?"

"Yes. But let's go over it again. This is a new job for me."

"Take the best offer you get."

"Shore thet'll be no less than forty dollars a haid," interposed Britt.

"What is the lowest I can accept, provided conditions fluctuate?"

"Frayne, I want to get rid of cattle. You need not advertise that. Hang out for a good price, but if compelled, take any offer."

"Very well. I don't anticipate any save the present top price. Have you written instructions to deposit checks, mail them east, or bring them back?"

"No, you are to take cash. And wait if it has to come by express."

"Cash!" ejaculated Frayne, aghast. "Britt did not tell me that."

"Wal, I wanted Holly to take the responsibility,"

explained Britt. "I disapprove, but Holly's boss."

"Please — Miss Holly!" exclaimed Frayne, almost entreatingly.

"Please what?"

"Don't put such a burden on me. — Just think! — Figure it out. Allowing for losses in any way — even a little rustler raid — I'll sell out for over one hundred and forty thousand dollars."

"What of that? We need cash. Britt agrees now is the best time. Trail conditions will grow worse. When we sell again we'll make deposits."

"Holly, you'll trust me — *me* — with all that money?" queried Frayne, hoarsely, white to the lips.

"Certainly I'll trust you," replied Holly, evenly, finding his level gray gaze of pain exceedingly trying to meet squarely.

"Thank you. . . . But you — shouldn't. . . . That's a fortune. How do you know I'll not steal it — and run off."

"Renn, it'd be worth that much to find you out," she rejoined.

But he did not catch the significance of that. "How do you know the half-breeds and Cherry won't murder me?"

"Don't insult them, either, Renn. But they need not know. Tell Brazos."

Frayne turned to Britt with twitching lips. "Old Timer, can you beat this? For two-bits — if it was anyone else but Holly Ripple — no — I wouldn't take the risk."

"Risk of what?"

"Loss. Be reasonable, you child. If through any chance I lost all that money you — you'd never believe in me again."

"Yes I would," replied Holly, calmly taking her scarf and moving toward the door. She had at last intrigued or driven this man into a betrayal of feeling. It was so sweet, so beautiful that she dared not prolong the interview. They followed her out on the porch. Her trust in him then meant something. She had planned this responsibility to see how he would react to it, how he would execute it. Yet she had not gone so far as to hope or dream that he cared deeply for the faith she imposed in him. She must wait until she was alone to ponder that out. The certainty that Frayne entertained something beside indifference to her made Holly strong and calm. She stepped off the porch into the sunlight and waved the red scarf. Scarcely had she sent the long streamer aloft when a puff of white smoke appeared against the green, way down at the apex of the triangle, and it was followed by the report of a gun.

"They're off," declared Britt, with relief. "I see Brazos ridin' hell bent fer election. . . . Go, Frayne. Catch up. . . . Catch up! . . . Thet's the Old Trail word."

Holly lowered the scarf with a whirl that circled it around her neck. That was well, she thought, because her cheeks were hot and red. She extended her hand and smiled up at Frayne, no longer sure of anything except that the parting was poignant. "*Adios,* Renn. . . . Good luck! — Don't forget

— Don Carlos' Rancho!"

"Be it on your head!" he replied, so darkly that Holly did not grasp whether he meant the risk of her money, the risk of her trust, or the risk of some terrible consequence to him that was surely not peril or death. "But don't worry about us. We will come through. . . . Look out for yourself. Don't ride out of sight of the cowboys. . . . *Adios*."

After the blur had left her eyes Holly watched the herd wind the valley toward the gleaming, green-bordered Cimarron. She had always loved to watch a crawling herd of cattle. The yellow dust rose to cloud the sides and rear of the vast wedge of moving red and white. There were two riders in the lead, pointing the herd. One bestrode a big brown horse, and that would be Cherokee. Brazos' white shirt and sombrero shone in the sunlight. She watched until she saw Frayne on his black come into view below, loping swiftly eastward. Upon him she used her field-glass, trying with shaking hands to work him into the magnified circle of her vision. What was that trailing out behind him, like a streamer of red? He had taken her scarf without her being in the least aware of it, though she remembered it last around her neck.

CHAPTER 9

Whit Britt had been captain of the Texas Rangers, hard riding, perilous and perplexing situations, criminals to arrest or kill, rescue of stolen stock, mysterious murders to clear up, settlers to protect from thieving Mexicans and marauding Comanches, all were the order of the day and taken as a matter of course.

But Britt had not then had in his charge a beautiful and imperious young woman whom he loved as his own, and who had no relative, no husband, no one save himself to look after her. It was telling on Britt. In the five weeks since Frayne and the cowboys had driven east with the big herd, enough had happened on the range to keep him awake nights without the several narrow escapes Holly had sustained. She had a habit of riding out alone in spite of orders, protestations, entreaties. There were occasions when the girl was strange, moody, and refused to have an escort. At such times Britt had to watch her or have one of the cowboys do it, and trust to Providence. The arrival of the short, hot, midsummer period put an end to Holly's riding, for which Britt was profoundly grateful. When the cooler weather came Frayne and Brazos would be back, and after that it would not be long until frost and snow. The rustlers holed up in winter; there was no movement of cattle; and some peace and rest might be obtainable until spring.

"By thunder," muttered Britt, "I'm shore goin' to move heaven an' earth to marry Holly off by then!"

Britt did all this soliloquizing in the bunkhouse while he sat at the table, poring over the crude map he had tacked there. The drawing, which had been made by the foreman himself, was not a work of art, but it was accurate to a distance of fifty miles or more beyond Don Carlos' Rancho. The range was now knee-deep in grass and flowers, and black with cattle. The streams had been bank-full until the late hot spell, and with the summer storms still in prospect, the creeks, springs and water-holes would not go dry this season. For Britt this had its good and bad side, the latter being in the fact that many cattle would graze up into the hills and the canyons. Rustlers had become increasingly active. Small bunches of cattle were being driven to Santa Fe and Las Vegas, and to the forts. This rustling of mixed brands did not make much of an inroad upon the Ripple stock, but it would increase and in several years must count heavily. That was calculating without a great raid of thousands of cattle, and the incessant drainage upon the herd of unbranded stock. One of these rustler bands was appropriating unbranded calves and yearlings for the nucleus of a herd. The cowboys had tracked numerous small bunches of young stock toward the hills to the south. Russ Slaughter and his outfit had disappeared, so far as actual sight of them was concerned, but they were well known to be on the range.

With only nine riders and himself, Britt was hard put to it to keep track of stock. They had thirty thousand head in the valley, between the pass and the head of the Cottonwood. Beyond this point a half million cattle roamed the wide plain, and more thousands of these than Britt knew and more than he had calculated before wore the Ripple mark. It was an unprecedented situation and rich pickings for rustlers and unscrupulous cattlemen.

"Wal, let's see," said Britt, as he bent over his map. "Skylark with Stinger an' Gaines air at White Pool. Jim an' Blue an' Flinty air at Cedar Flat. Talman an' Trinidad somewhere in Cottonwood Basin. Rebel is ridin' alone. . . . Nobody heah with me, an' thirty thousand longhorns oot there to be run off. Shore is a hell of a deal!"

Britt had sent Talman and Trinidad to the head-waters of the Cottonwood with a deliberate purpose. This was up in the rough breaks through which the Ute Trail led to the north. Talman had been consistently watched, to no avail. One thing only had Britt noted — Talman's unobtrusive cultivation of Trinidad since the other cowboys had gone and the usually merry Trinidad's preoccupation. As the days and weeks passed Britt grew more convinced that there was something amiss. The crafty indefatigable Rebel had been detailed to keep track of Talman.

These several relays of cowboys had been absent nearly a week, and except the last three Britt had named, were already overdue at the ranch. Britt decided to ride out on the morrow, if none of them returned.

Later, while he was pacing up and down the porch, plodding with his hands behind his back, Holly put in an appearance, slender and graceful in her flimsy white. Her cheeks were without color and her eyes gloomed.

"Cappy, I picked up some riders with the glass. Across the Cottonwood, five miles or so. Three horsemen with two pack animals."

"Thet'll be Skylark," replied Britt, gladly. "Aboot time."

"Frayne is four days late," she said, broodingly.

"What's four days? Why, lass, he might be four weeks late. Reckon he had to wait for the money. . . . Holly, air you worried aboot thet?"

"What do I care about money?" she exclaimed, impatiently.

"Holly, after what you told the man — you couldn't doubt him. . . . In only four days!"

"Doubt him? — Don't insult me, Cappy. . . . I'm worried because there might have been a fight. Brazos *will* fight, you know."

"Anythin' is possible, lass, of course. But thet's not likely. I tell you again Frayne will be along soon now."

"Oh, I hope so! . . . I've watched that Cimarron Trail until my eyes have grown dim. Not a wagon — not a horseman for days on end. . . . It's lonely.

227

. . . Cappy, will you come up to the house after you see Skylark?"

Britt assured her he would come, and almost took advantage of her mood to ask a question about Frayne that he had long pondered. But Holly did not look happy. The old, gay, wilful spirit seemed in abeyance. He watched Holly with misgivings. Any question, save one of the heart, she could master with the Ripple intelligence and courage. But if it was love . . .

In an hour Skylark rode up with Stinger and Gaines, with the white dust sliding in little streams off horses and riders. Begrimed and sweaty, with eyes of fire, they brought a lusty welcome from the old ranger.

"Like May-flowers, you easy-comin' gents! Gosh, I was lonesome. I don't care a damn if you have bad news — I'm shore glad to see you."

"Mebbe we're not glad," replied Skylark, leaning over his pommel. "Any news?"

"Nope. Nobody else in."

"How's Miss Holly? I seen her mopin' up the hill."

"She's wal. But lonesome, too."

"Roll off, Sky," said Stinger. "We'll look after the hosses."

Skylark unlimbered his long frame from the tired and dusty horse and clanked upon the porch, to throw gloves, sombrero, scarf, shirt and gun-belt in a pile beside the wash-bench.

"We got out of smokes," said the cowboy, tragically.

"Ahuh. Is thet dirt or gun-smoke on yore face?"

"Both, I reckon. I pumped my Winchester pretty fast this mornin'."

"Wal, clean up. I'll walk over to the store an fetch you the makin's."

Britt strolled leisurely across the flat to the trading-post. Skylark's few remarks were not reassuring. The Mexican village appeared to be taking its midday *siesta*. Two dusty, well-pointed horses stood at the hitching-rail. Britt encountered a brace of hard-lipped men, strangers who gave him a gruff word and passed on. Britt made his purchases and took his time returning to the bunk-house.

Stinger and Gaines were splashing like ducks in a pond. Skylark was inside, donning a clean shirt. His tanned face, cleaned of grime and beard, appeared somewhat gaunt. He yelled with delight when Britt pitched the package of little tobacco pouches on the table.

"A cowboy without cigarettes is like thet play I read of — with the main hombre left out — jest nothin'." In another moment he was puffing away. "Boss, we drove near four thousand head down out of the canyons to White Pool."

"What? Not our stock! Don't tell me you boys have taken to rustlin' other ranchers' cattle."

"Knew it would floor you, Cap. It shore did us. Say, we have no idee how many cattle we have. These were all wearin' the long ripple. An' there was a load of calves we didn't count."

"Wal, I'll be darned. How you explain thet, Sky?"

"We all had different reasons. Mine is we haven't got enough riders to go around. Stinger knows thet country better than any of us. He says a big percent of this stock has been drifted in them south canyons. I reckon Stinger is right, but dog-gone! I hate to believe it."

"Ah-huh. Stinger seldom makes a mistake, Sky," rejoined Britt, in deep thought.

"If it's so it means a big drive up out of them canyons before the snow flies."

"Where to?"

"South, you ossified little Texan."

"Wal, where south?"

"Seven Rivers — most likelee — or down the Pecos sure."

"By *Paso del Muerte?*"

"No, boss. West of the Pass. You know them little canyons south of White Pool? They were full of our stock an' nobody else's. We cleaned them out. I advise the outfit ridin' over there pronto an' drivin' the bunch down so they'll water on the Cottonwood."

"Good. We'll do thet. Wal, go on. Who did it, Sky?"

"Are you askin' me?"

"I shore am."

"Humph. You better tell me."

"An' what else? Thet doesn't account fer gunsmoke."

"We run onto a funny deal. Or I should say Old

Wasp Stinger did. After we got the herd pointed this mornin' — about sunrise — Stinger took us on a little ride into a draw thet drains into White Pool. Sting didn't say much, but he looked heaps. After we got in the brush he took to his hoofs, an' you can bet Handsome an' me were not so crazy about thet. It shore was hot in thet brush. Finally we get sore an' stops short. 'Whar the hell you takin' us, Sting?' Gaines wanted to know, an' I swore I was near dead. 'Fellars, I got shot at again up here yesterday, an' damn near bored. Look here!' . . . He stripped up his shirt an' showed us a red welt across his side. 'Close shave? — Ha, I should smile.' . . . We saved our wind then an' went on till we come to the big open. There had been a new shack thrown up under the bluff where the spring comes out. We saw smoke an' saddled hosses. Stinger hadn't been very cute about slippin' up, for the bunch was watchin', an' they opened fire on us. We dove for cover, an' they took to their hosses. Sting had a rifle an' I was packin' mine. There were six or seven men in the bunch, all carryin' light packs behind their saddles. Which says a lot. Stinger swears he killed one of them. Saw him pitch out of his saddle. But I was too busy pumpin' lead to watch his shots. I had ten at them, say from four hundred yards on. An' I saw one man who was shootin' back — I saw him drop his gun an' keel over his hoss, an' I'm sure I crippled another. Anyhow, they got away."

"Did you cross the open to see if Stinger had downed one?"

"Not so you'd notice it. Stinger wanted to, but Handsome an' me voted him down."

"Whose ootfit was it, Sky?"

"Stinger swears it was Heaver's. He's seen them, you know. They were workin' thet side of the range. Anyway this job of Stinger's was good. We might have lost thet bunch. Most short horns, cows an' calves, an' tame. . . . Boss, I'd advise, soon as some of the boys come in, to throw thet slow bunch way here along the creek."

"Tomorrer, mebbe, or next day. — Wal, what else, Sky?"

"What do you want for a few days' ridin', Old Timer?"

"I hope thet's all."

"I wish it was. Half way home we saw three riders bob over a rise, an' stand their hosses, waitin' for us. Turned out to be Joe Doane, an' two of his Dad's riders. Joe gave me the stump of his cigarette, which was all he had. Doane lost twenty head of hosses, his best, includin' the blue roan wearin' the Ripple brand. Miss Holly gave thet roan to Ann. Say, wasn't I sore? — Joe said they'd trailed this bunch for three days, till they darn near starved. Along by Dobe Cabin, down to the Cimarron, which the thieves crossed on to the Old Trail."

"How many hawse-thieves?" asked Britt, shaking his head.

"Joe didn't find out. Four shod hosses, he said. . . . Now, boss, wouldn't it be funny if thet bunch run into Brazos an' Frayne comin' back?"

232

"Funny? Aboot as funny as death."

"Cherokee could see thet bunch a long way before they'd see our boys. An' a string of hosses would excite suspicion these days. It just about will happen thet way."

"Brazos would see red."

At this juncture the slim Stinger came in, stripped to the waist, his lean white side marred by an ugly welt.

"Stinger, who's been creasin' you?" asked Britt, jocularly.

"Boss, I've an idee some cowboy took me fer a wild hoss. . . . Mebbe you think thet welt ain't sore? Hurts —— wuss'n a boil."

Jose put his smiling swarthy visage inside the back door. "Eet ees ready, *vaqueros*," which call elicited a wild howl from the two cowboys, and drew Gaines in, mopping his shiny soapy face with a towel.

Early in the afternoon of the next day Jim, Blue and Flinty arrived from Cedar Flat.

This section of the range was quite remote from Don Carlos' Rancho, being a succession of tremendous benches running out from the foothills some sixty miles away. It was favored by cattlemen and cattle alike for spring and summer grazing. Snow fell there in the fall. Jim reported a hundred thousand head of mixed stock on and around Cedar Flats, the largest number of which bore Chisum's famous Long Rail and Jingle-bob brands. There were more Ripple cattle in this herd that Jim was glad to find.

Activity of rustlers had been difficult to uncover and hard to trace. They had encountered half a dozen cowboy outfits, three of which omitted to make clear what connection they had on that range.

Jim's report, however, included other activities that gave Britt food for reflection. San Marcos had more than a year ago begun to feel the influx of new settlers, cattlemen, and the parasites that lived on them, but this summer had seen the sleepy little Mexican village grow in a way that had both gratifying and dismaying reactions for the Ripple foreman.

Horn Brothers had started a new post there, which Jim said was just an excuse to add another saloon and gambling-hall to the already long list. New stores, a hotel, a mining company, and numerous residents, both Mexican and American, had been added since Britt's last visit there. McCoy was reported to have an interest in several new San Marcos business developments. He claimed to be going into partnership with Chisum, but Britt knew this was mere brag, and rather stupid of McCoy, because it was well known that the Jingle-bob cattleman was a lone wolf.

Russ Slaughter and his Seven Rivers outfit had apparently dropped out of sight; and this to Britt was the most significant news. Slaughter had quit Chisum to be a free agent, to be in the thick of the fat pickings for cattle-buzzards that would prevail in central and eastern New Mexico.

"I reckon Slaughter has gone up in the foothills to the north of McCoy's ranch," calculated Britt.

"Some wild nest-holes up there, an' within a day's ride of the trail north to the Indian reservations an' forts."

"Enough said," agreed Jim. "But, boss, dog-gone-me if I think thet's as interestin' as the talk aboot central New Mexico. The Pecos country from Seven Rivers to Roswell an' Lincoln, an' west has poured up the Pecos, an' by the time the rail-road gets to Santa Fe there'll be a million head of stock west of us."

"So much the better."

"Shore, 'cept thet it'll help draw the damndest lot of outfits from all over."

"Rebel ought to be heah soon," replied Britt.

"Where'd you send him?"

"No place in particular. I reckon he'll keep track of Talman an' Trinidad."

"Cap, thet's a big country between Cottonwood Basin an' Ute Hills. Clements has twenty thousand cattle there, Haywood aboot eight, an' Doane, who's on the ridge, aboot five thousand. Or he did have thet many. Doane was pretty much het up when he was heah."

"Wal, countin' six to ten thousand of ours oot there, these hombres have a big bunch to pick from. A big range an' easy ootlets. Jim, it jest makes my blood boil."

"We're doin' all we can. A hundred riders wouldn't be enough. Cattle hev growed too thick an' fast. An' to hev the price bust on us is somethin' onheerd of! . . . Cap, what we ought to do is like Chisum. Help ourselves."

"No. Thet's the cowboy's point of view, Jim," returned Britt, seriously. "Mebbe Chisum takes what comes his way. An' some of the other cattlemen will when this deal comes to a haid. But we cain't double-cross Miss Holly, an' she wouldn't own a steer thet wasn't hers."

"Whoopee!" yelled Blue fiercely, from the porch.

Britt ran out with Jim. A cloud of dust down the road only partially hid a troop of horses being driven up from the Pass toward the village. Flinty joined the others on the porch, where Britt expressed his belief that Frayne and Brazos had arrived home with the horses stolen from Doane.

"By all thet's lucky!" ejaculated Britt. "Gosh, my eyes water! How many, Blue?"

"Aw, two dozen or more. An' thet's our top bunch of riders. There's the chuck-wagon, Britt, comin' down out of the Pass."

"Skylark will be plumb tickled. . . . Wal — wal, I hope Frayne came through safe."

"Outfit's all trailin' home at once," remarked Jim, with satisfaction. "Now, if Rebel would rustle in."

Britt caught the rather significant omission of Talman and Trinidad. It gave him a pang. He had grown attached to every member of this greatest band of cowboys that he had seen.

Stinger appeared in the bunkhouse door, half dressed, and blinking of eye. "What's all the hullabaloo, boss?"

"Ootfit's back, an' I reckon they got Doane's hawses."

"Darn my pictures! Didn't I have a hunch? . . . I'm gonna get into my jeans."

Britt found in the situation another reflection as to his peculiar strain these days. He could hardly conceal either his joy or concern or impatience. How good to have them back — to see Frayne and Brazos — to feel Holly's relief! Would all the cowboys be with them, safe and well? He managed, however, to contain himself while waiting for them to come up. At last when Britt walked off to meet Frayne it ran in his mind that he had never before in his life been so glad to see a man. Britt wondered with a sting of conscience if he had unconsciously harbored a doubt of Frayne. Gaunt, hollow-eyed, unshaven and hard, Frayne had seemed to have about him that something inimically western and stable.

"Howdy, Cap," he said, leaning to meet Britt's eager hand.

"I'm shore glad to see you. Everythin' all right?"

"Now that I'm here — yes," replied Frayne, with his cool laugh.

"How aboot the money?"

"All here," rejoined Frayne, patting the saddle bags which hung over his pommel, instead of the usual place behind the cantle. "That is, except a few dollars to each of the boys."

"What'd they bring?"

"I got forty-two dollars a head."

"Wal, you son-of-a-gun! Thet's great! — But, heah, don't waste another minute on me. Ride up to Holly an' get rid of thet money."

"Britt, you take it up for me. I'm tired. And —"

"No sir. Holly would — Wal, never mind. But she wants to see you. Renn, I'd rather like to be in yore boots. She'll be surprised you're heah."

"She saw us coming, Cap," he rejoined. "Must have been watching with the glass. Cherry saw her wave before we crossed the Cimarron."

"Holly has been on the job with thet glass for the last ten days. Rustle, now."

"But, Cap —"

"There ain't any buts. Go! The girl has worried herself sick. She can't eat or sleep," went on Britt, lying shamelessly.

"Worried herself! — Good God, man! — for fear I'd turn yellow?"

"Hellno! — you're as testy as Brazos. . . . She didn't care a hang aboot the money. She missed you."

Without another word Frayne turned his horse toward the winding road up the green hill. He could not have been a more pondering and dazed man if he had been forced to report loss of the large sum of money.

Britt's conscience did not even smart, and he chuckled to himself as he directed his attention to the approaching cowboys. They had driven the band of horses into a corral. Skylark, Blue, Flinty and Gaines all on foot, were escorting the mounted boys to the bunkhouse. Stinger was on his way to meet them. Britt's fond eye soon missed a familiar figure.

"Where's Brazos?" he yelled, while they were

238

still some distance off.

"He's drivin' the wagon. Be hyar pronto," shouted Laigs Mason.

Britt returned to his chair on the porch. All was well. The outfit had come home. That sombre purple shadow which hung over the foothills could be forgotten for the time being. He watched the cowboys dismount and throw their saddles. Tex Southard appeared to be the only one incapacitated. Skylark took his horse while Blue helped him to the bunkhouse. Tex had a decided limp.

"Wal, I reckon a hawse fell on you," said Britt, dryly.

"Boss, eet es lead bullit, in my laig. Yu mus dig oot," replied the *vaquero*.

"Anybody else hurt?"

"Mason got barked. You'd think he was all shot up, to hear him holler," said Blue.

Britt refrained from more questions at that time. He took out his impatience in listening and watching. They all piled past him with greetings, the vociferous ones of which he noted were made by the cowboys who had remained home. They were merry. Mason glared at Britt as he hobbled up on the porch, and shoved out a dirty hand with a bloody furrow across the back of it.

"Thet's what I get fer not throwin' my gun," he growled, as if Britt had been somehow to blame.

"Wal, it's yore left hand."

"Yass? An' how'm I gonna play cards?"

"Cap, Laigs means he can't stack the deck," said Blue.

"Laigs, when did you an' Tex stop these bullets?" queried the foreman.

"Yestiddy mornin'."

"I reckon it was accident."

"Sorta — fer the hombre who done it."

During the ensuing half hour while Britt went inside to wait for Frayne and Brazos he heard much interesting news, but nothing at all about the rescue of Doane's horses, and the fight which had evidently taken place with the thieves.

Railroad construction had been slow during the spring and summer owing to lack of funds. But now the rails were moving west again and Las Animas was roaring. The construction engineers expected to get to Trinidad before winter set in. Trains were running regularly between Las Animas and Kansas City. One train had been held up for a whole day near Dodge by a herd of buffalo. Another had been stopped recently by bandits. Frank and Jesse James had been blamed for this, but according to railroad men they could not have been implicated because they had been recognized in western Kansas at the time of the hold-up near Newton. This strengthened the rumor of other strong bands of outlaws working westward. Cattle shipments had been large and the price of cattle on the hoof, delivered at the railroad, was expected to increase. The cowboys had passed a large caravan between the Cimarron and the Purgatory Rivers. Laigs Mason had won a hundred dollars in a game of poker, which bit of news appeared to be the most impressive the returning cowboys felt that they had.

Presently the doorway framed the striking figure and face of Brazos Keene. Unlike his comrades, Brazos had that morning taken the trouble to shave and don a clean shirt and scarf. He looked like a handsome imp of Satan.

"Howdy, Old Timer! Yu shore look lonesome. Proves yu don't 'preciate us when we're heah," was his greeting to Britt. "Pards, I had a drink as big as thet. An' who yu think was layin' fer me? Connie! — Did she — was she glad to see me? Wal, yu'd all been green."

"Aw, I was onto you," bawled out Laigs. "You let me drive thet ole wagon all day long, till we get near home. Then you offer to relieve me — all so you could hang behind an' meet the gurls an' have a drink. Dog-gone-you, Brazos! I don't know how'n the hell you make sich a sucker out of me."

Brazos did a jig in the middle of the bunkhouse floor, his fine embroidered boots flying, his spurs jingling, his clustering yellow locks dancing with the rest of him.

"Back home!" babbled Brazos, as he completed his jig. "Lucky trip! — Sweet rest an' good grub an' thet black-eyed slave of mine! Aw, a cowboy's life is hard."

Britt thought that all the marvelous traits of the Texas cowboy, and for that matter of all the range riders in the West, were epitomized in this slender, fair-haired, blue-eyed boy of nineteen. But Britt knew that to look at him and to listen was to court deception. Brazos was never what he seemed. On

241

the surface he was frivolous, carefree, a heedless wild youth, hard as flint, living for the moment, conscienceless and irresponsible. This was true of Brazos, but it had to do with externals. Either Brazos was a youth with many sides or an incomparable actor, or both.

"Wal, how aboot it?" queried Britt, into the first lull.

"How aboot what, boss?" drawled Brazos.

"I want a report, don't I?"

"Dawg-gone if I ever know what yu want," complained Brazos, plaintively. "Anyway, Frayne was haid of this drive."

"You got back Doane's hawses."

"Shore. We didn't know whose they were till I seen thet blue roan with a ripple on his flank. I'd seen Miss Holly on him, an' I recollected thet she gave him to Ann Doane. . . . So things kinda connected up in my dumb haid."

"Ah-huh, I reckon. Wal, tell me aboot what happened?"

"Boss, I ain't feelin' like talkin'," replied Brazos, in cool evasion.

"Laigs, do you want to tell me?" went on Britt, dryly.

"Boss, I'm a cowman what's shy of words. Besides I'm tired an' hurt an' I couldn't talk fer a million."

"Million what?" asked Britt, convinced that he could make Laigs retract this extravagant speech.

"*Pesos*," said Laigs, shortly.

Then Britt called loudly: "Jackson."

"Yas suh. Heah I is."

"Come over heah."

The little bow-legged negro approached Britt with some uncertainty and trepidation, but his eyes rolled till the whites showed, to match with his teeth.

"Air you dumb, too, Jack?"

"I reckon — yas suh, I'se as dumb as Laigs."

"Wal, heah's ten *pesos*."

"Boss! Fer me?" asked Jackson, with a huge grin.

"Yes, if you'll take thet back aboot bein' dumb."

"Sho, suh. I'se not dumb atall. . . . Yo see, Boss, I wuz jes sidin' wif Laigs —"

"*Hyar!*" yelled Laigs, suddenly coming out of his stupefaction. "You darn, hoss-chewin' nigger! Lay off'n me. . . . Boss, I'll take it back. I'll tell you anythin' fer ten —"

"Shet up, Laigs," interrupted Britt. "All of you keep shet up while I get this report from Jackson. Things hev come to a sad pass in an ootfit when the boss has to pay fer a report. . . . Come on, Jack."

"What yu want, suh?"

"Tell me all aboot how you come to get Doane's hawses back."

"Wal, suh, it wuz dis way," began Jackson, eagerly. "Jes befo noon yestiddy mawnin' we wuz ridin' along when Cherry oot ahaid seen dust, an' he held us up. When we all seen it we got to bettin' on what made it. Boss, on dis drive we sho seen things before dey seen us. Cherry bet der wuz a string of hosses comin'. Wal, Cherry won de bet an' Mars Frayne held us dere to wait. It wasn't long den till we seen fo hossmen behind dat string. Wal, den Mars Frayne had us hide round a brushy bend in de road till them riders done come up. Befo all de hosses got by Brazos seen dat blue roan wif our brand, an' den we all knowed sho dey'd been some hoss-stealin'. But, suh, when Frayne rode oot in front of us dem fo men was sho susprised. Dey didn't 'pear sociable an' de leader yelled an' was pullin' his gun when Frayne laid him offen his hoss. De odder riders bolted, shootin' back, an' we rustled after 'em sho burnin' powder. . . . Wal, suh, it wuz soon ober. Laigs an' Tex wuz hit. Dem fo hoss-thieves wuz pore white trash, boss. Dey didn't hev nuthin' much. We trowed dere guns an' saddles in the wagon, den round up de stole hosses, an' rustled along. . . . Dat's all, suh."

"Ten cart-wheels fer thet story," stormed Laigs Mason. "I coulda told it better fer two-bits."

At this junction Britt heard a horse outside, and soon found Frayne there unsaddling. The outlaw had a preoccupied manner. He left saddle and bridle on the ground, and when he turned Britt met a frowning face and bewildered eyes from which the piercing quality had gone into eclipse.

"Wal, Renn?" queried Britt, with a smile.

"Don't grin at me — you Texas chessy-cat," groaned Frayne, with suspended breath.

"What's wrong?"

"Wrong! The whole world is upside down. . . .

I'm locoed, Britt — buffaloed — beat! — Nothing left for me but to go out and get myself shot!"

"Renn, have you been drinkin'?"

"Not yet. But I sure will be pronto."

"Nonsense. Tell me what happened. — Why, man, I was shore Holly would be glad to see you. I'm darn sorry. But I'm only an old fool."

"She *was* glad — to see me," whispered Frayne, huskily, and he looked dazed.

"Aw! — Wal, what could be wrong, then?" went on Britt, smoothly, and drew the unresisting Frayne along to the end of the porch. He felt mightily guilty, yet somehow elated.

"What? — Man alive, it's all wrong."

"Renn, I cain't savvy. Better tell me. What did Holly say?" returned Britt, powerfully.

"She stood in the door — as I rode up," replied Frayne, as if impelled. "But when I got off with the bags she was gone. I went in. . . . There she stood — white — as white. . . . I said, 'Miss Holly. Here I am with the money — more than we figured.' . . . I laid the bag on the table. She waved it aside — as if that money — which damn near drove me crazy — was nothing. Nothing at all! That, and the way she looked — upset me. . . . She took hold of my coat. 'Renn! You're back — safe?' she whispered. I don't know what I said, but I assured her I was all right — that all was well. She shut her eyes. I saw tears slide out from under her tight eyelids. . . . She leaned against me and shook. Then she opened her eyes. The tears were all gone. They shone like black stars

245

— deep in a well. . . . Beautiful! — They will haunt me sleepless — the rest of my life. . . . Then, Cap — she — she kissed me. . . . Not on my cheek! But on my lips — my sun-burnt, alkali-split, tobacco-stained lips!"

"Yeah? An' then what did you do?" queried Britt, feelingly, as Frayne leaned against the cabin wall. This was the moment. The cool hard outlaw did not manifest himself in this moment. He was betraying his true self. A dark terrible pain changed the gray of his eyes.

"Do? — I broke — and ran," he whispered, hoarsely, swallowing hard.

"Ran? — You, Renn Frayne? Wal, wal!"

"Britt, you are a soulless cuss."

"Holly loves you," returned Britt, quietly, sure of Holly, sure of himself, and in this stern broken mood of Frayne's, sure of him.

"My God! — Don't say that!"

"It's true, Renn. I found it out since you left. This is the end of Holly's many flings at the cow-boys. This time — poor kid — she got a dose of her own medicine. Holly is caught. . . . Renn, for heaven's sake —"

"Britt, you needn't say more," interrupted Frayne, coming away from the wall, gray-faced and spent. "Do you think I'm one of these rocks — or a piece of dead wood. . . . I worship Holly Ripple! — That's been true ever since the day she asked me to stay at Don Carlos' Rancho. . . . And it was all right — till now. . . . *Till now!* — My God, who could have foreseen that sweet, beautiful, innocent girl would fall in love with me? *Me!* — Britt, I've got to go out and get myself shot."

"Ah-huh!" ejaculated Britt, in slow scorn. "Thet'd be a fine way to treat Holly. . . . Fer her kindness an' generosity — her faith an' love — you'd reward her by leavin' her heart-broken — by leavin' us heah wuss off than ever. You cain't do thet, Renn Frayne."

"Yes, it's yellow of me," flashed Frayne, passionately. "But what else is there for me? — Cap, she might — she might —"

"Like as not, Renn. Holly not only might. She will! An' then what, man?"

"I'd fall — on my knees."

"Quite appropriate, if you ask me. . . . Frayne, you're worn oot an' overwrought. Let's go in."

"Wait. . . . Cap, I'll take that back — about getting myself shot. Lord knows, I may get it any day. . . . I'll stay on and see you through this rustler war. But I must not go near Holly. And you must swear you'll never betray me."

"Shore, I swear thet, Renn," replied Britt, once more dry and drawling of speech. A happiness tugged at his heartstrings. A moment back panic had assailed him. Britt liked and respected Frayne all the more for his weakness, for his despair, for what must have been honor. The future did not look so dark as formerly for Holly Ripple.

CHAPTER 10

One and all the returning cowboys sought their bunks, after Jose had satisfied the inner man, and in Brazos' case left a dire threat as to what would result if anybody disturbed his repose. Skylark showed remarkable eagerness to undertake the twenty-mile ride to Doane's, to acquaint that individual of the recovery of his horses. This deceived no one, although Laigs made the only audible comment: "My gosh, I'd like to get it so I'd know how it feels!"

Britt, in fear and trembling, yet happy within, went up to the ranchhouse to see Holly. He found her another perfect example of the incomprehensibleness of women. She was the old Holly. It relieved Britt as well as puzzled him. Frayne had been most revivifying medicine. To be sure Holly would never imagine that Frayne had told Britt about the kiss which had been his undoing. And Britt concluded this would be a very inopportune time to break his perfectly unscrupulous promise to Frayne. Somehow, marvelously, Holly had extracted the old fire and joy and mystery, with something sweetly baffling, from those few moments alone with Frayne. Therefore all seemed well.

"Did you hide the money?" asked Britt, recalling Holly's carelessness about this detail. They shared a secret hidingplace, where her father and the Valverdes before him had stored gold and valuables.

"Yes. I counted it. Such a job! You know we told Frayne to fetch small bills."

"How much?"

"Nearly one hundred and twenty-five thousand dollars."

"Wal, it'll hev to last a while, my dear. I can't risk any more drives."

"But you intended to," she protested.

"Shore. Since the ootfit got back I've changed my mind."

"Why?"

"Wal, information. Brazos doesn't like the idee, an' Frayne won't heah of it."

"He won't? — I wonder why."

"Struck me Renn's kinda queer. I reckon it's thet he jest cain't leave you again," rejoined Britt, casually, and he pretended to be blind to Holly's rich red blush. This romance was proceeding to his satisfaction, but he had a warning then not to overdo his part. He would let nature take its course for a while.

"Holly, you remember thet blue roan you gave Ann Doane?" inquired Britt.

"Frisk? Indeed, I do. I loved that pony. But Ann was so taken with him. Why do you ask?"

"Wal, Frisk was stolen by hawse-thieves along

249

with Doane's other hawses. Lo an' behold, our ootfit fetched them back!"

"Today?" exclaimed Holly.

"Shore. When else could they? It was plumb lucky. I didn't get much oot of Brazos an' nothin' oot of Frayne, so I reckon there wasn't much to it."

"Cap Britt! Don't you try any of your old tricks. You know — if these devils of mine captured any horse-thieves they'd hang them."

"I reckon. They're shore het-up aboot things these days. But I know fer a fact thet they didn't capture this bunch of hawse-thieves."

"Good. I'm glad. I pity these poor outcasts who have to steal."

"Wal, lass, I'm not so full of pity as you," drawled Britt. "An' if you didn't have the most dangerous ootfit on this frontier you'd soon lose yore pity."

"Oh, for the days when I was little! The long, lazy, glamorous days of caravans, of the endless *fiestas*, the *fandangos*, the *sombreros* and *chaparagos!*"

"They will never return, lass. But you will always have Mexicans. I rather look ahead, say five years, though thet's awful soon, when we'll have peace on the range — an' the prattle an' patter of children in this great house."

"Oh, yes — romantic," remarked Holly, without flicking an eyelash. "Perhaps Brazos and Skylark — possibly Frayne — will supply you with some of that joy of life soon. . . . By the way, Cappy,

250

are all the men in?"

"No."

"Who's out?"

"Talman, Trinidad an' Rebel."

"Oh. . . . That doesn't look so good, does it?"

"Wal, it might be good. I'm givin' Talman the benefit of a doubt. Cottonwood Basin is a long way an' a big country. It'll take lots of ridin'. But Rebel ought to be heah."

"Is he working alone?"

"Yes. I gave him an odd job."

"Watching Talman! — I should think the boys would hate spying on one another."

"They shore do."

"How *could* any of my men betray me!"

"Wal, Frayne explained thet in his way. I'd say aboot the same. Hail fellar meetin' strangers, or cowmen not in the ootfit, a few stiff drinks, some persuasion — *an'* a big roll of greenbacks. The queer thing is thet cowboys withoot a bit of yellow in them have been known to do it. All the other kind air easy. Slaughter an' McCoy know this as wal as we do. They'd shore pay handsome to corrupt some of our boys. *If* they are goin' crooked."

"Is there any doubt about that?"

"No. But to prove it! Thet'll take hard clever work, unless these men grow bold or careless. Sellin' to crooked cattle buyers they might steal indefinitely heah on this range without bein' caught."

"Britt, I don't believe *any* cowmen, especially

251

on my ranch, could ever fool Brazos or Frayne."

"Wal," rejoined Britt, made thoughtful by this pregnant observation from a woman's intuition, "there might be a heap in thet."

"Anyway, if it happens, don't tell me," concluded Holly, shrinkingly.

At supper that night Britt asked Frayne, "What's this talk aboot the James boys?"

"They were in Las Animas," returned Frayne. "It wasn't known to everybody. But all kinds of talk was going around. I met Jesse and talked with him. I knew him years ago. He wanted me to join his band."

"Wal! — What was he doin' way oot heah?"

"He and Frank had been in California. They came right through Don Carlos' Rancho. They ate at Holly's table one night and she never knew who they were. Cole Younger and others of their gang met them at Las Animas. They had scattered after the robbery at the Kansas City Fair last September. Just before that, somewhere in Missouri, Jesse James had killed three men. Jesse told me that he and Frank had killed six men over a card game in California."

"Nine men!"

"That's nothing for the James Boys. If you cross them one way or another they're tolerable bad hombres. Train robbers, bank robbers! They work on a big scale. Jesse must have twenty men in his outfit altogether. But they travel in small bunches."

"Renn, air them James fellars any punkins with

guns?" inquired Brazos, who had been an absorbed listener.

"Neither would stand much chance with you, Brazos, on an even break. But they're not gunmen. Just plain robbers."

"Gosh! I stood right alongside Jesse James in thet saloon — an' didn't savvy."

"Damn good thing," ejaculated Laigs Mason. "If you had, you'd picked a fight with him."

"Aw, talk sense, yu little tumble-bug! I never picked a fight in my life."

"Frayne, did James ask you what you were doin'?" queried Britt.

"No. I told him I had gone into the cattle business. He said New Mexico had the prettiest ranges he had seen. But that cattle raising was too slow, too tame for him."

"Haw! Haw!" laughed one of the cowboys.

"Too slow an' tame!" ruminated Mason, with scorn.

"Sho he's wrong," spoke up Jackson, seriously. "I done wuz a bank robber once. We stoled de safe oot of de bank, an' sho nuff near busticated ourselves luggin' it oot on de prairiee. Den we wearied ourselves fer two days breakin' dat iron box open. Dere was nuthin' inside but paper."

A roar greeted the negro's laconic exposition of why he considered the bank robbing business undesirable.

"Wal, dawg-gone-it —"

"Lissen!" suddenly interrupted the Cherokee, holding up his hand, his somber, bronze face intent. Jose stopped like a statue over his oven. The room became quiet.

"Cherry, what yu heah?" queried Brazos, sharply.

"Hoss come like hell!"

"Wal, I should smile," agreed Brazos, rising, his face clouded. This cowboy had a penchant for presaging trouble.

"Keep still," ordered Britt. "We all haven't the ears of a jack-rabbit. . . . What if a hawse is comin' like hell?"

That quieted the listening group. The doors were open. The warm summer night was still except for soft sounds of song and guitar in the distance. As Britt listened he swept his glance from one to another of his men. Brazos had heard. The half-breeds nodded. Santone flashed dark eyes at Cherry. Then all the others, almost as one man, exhibited proof of the Indian's marvelous hearing. A second later Britt caught the faint rhythmic roll of the hoofs of a horse coming at a dead run on the hard road. There was nothing in this sound to make that group of cowboys tense and expectant. But it did. It was the moment and the place — the something charged in the atmosphere. Some of the boys went on eating, yet they were very quiet.

"Thet hombre is ridin' in fer cigarettes," burst out Mason.

"Mebbe he wants to keep cool this hyar hot night," vouchsafed a comrade.

"Shore, he's runnin'."

"Jose, shoot me a hot biscuit."

These and other remarks greeted Britt's ears. Outside on the road the swift beat of hoofs slowed to a clatter, then a scraping slide that sent gravel pattering in a shower. Creak of leather, clang of spurs, thud of boots — and hard steps on the porch!

"Rebel!" sang out Brazos. "An' the fire is oot!"

Swift clinking steps thumped through the bunkhouse, to the door of the dining room. A rider entered. Britt recognized Rebel, but only from his unmistakable small stature and his garb. Lather and dust covered him; bits of brush and cedar stuck in his chaps; the odor of the range clung round him. From a gray and black visage blazed two terrible eyes that flashed over the outfit.

"Brazos — Santone — you — all back!" he panted, hoarsely.

"Howdy, Rebel. Shore, we're all heah," replied Brazos, coolly.

"Been ridin', eh?" asked Britt, as he arose.

"Boss, I couldn't have — wuss news. . . . Fellars, finish yore supper. Lemme get — my breath. . . . Water an' some grub. No whiskey. I'm — all right."

"Take it easy, pard. I'll throw yore saddle an' turn yore hawse in," replied Brazos. And scarcely another word was spoken among them, none to Rebel, until a few minutes later, when they all assembled in the bunkhouse.

"Shet doors an' winders," said Rebel, curtly.

255

"Reckon we don't want anybody else heahin' what I got to say."

"Hev a smoke, Rebel," said Laigs Mason, offering one. "An' set down, cowboy. You're shakin' like a fence-wire in a November wind."

Rebel accepted the cigarette and, seating himself on the table, he puffed it a few times while sweeping the semicircle of his comrades with those eyes of fire.

"Captain Britt — an' fellars — I'm darn sorry I hev to report thet — thet Talman an' Trinidad air double-crossin' us," began Rebel, in husky halting voice.

Into the shocked stillness that followed, split the cracking sound of a hard fist in a hard palm. The first treachery under the new regime, since Holly Ripple's endeavor to enroll them in knightly loyalty, grayed the faces and silenced the tongues of these cowboys. Britt's heart sank. He had hoped against hope. And a slow smouldering rage took flame within him.

"All right — Sloan," choked out the foreman. "We all know you hate to squeal as much as we hate to heah you. But as an ootfit we got our backs to the wall."

"I've been ridin' ten days an' in thet time we're oot aboot three thousand haid, rough estimate made at long distance with a glass, an' all grades. Which means shore other brands besides ours."

"Three thousand haid!" ejaculated Britt, thunderstruck.

"Talk low, Cap," interposed Frayne. "Sloan,

you're not a man to overestimate. But. . . ."

"Frayne, I'm underestimatin'."

"Rebel, yu shore ain't drunk or crazy," burst out Brazos in a fierce whisper, his eyes leaping blue flames. "Hev yu been hit on the haid?"

"Aw, Reb!" remonstrated Laigs, who would have corroborated anything stated by Brazos.

"Gospel truth, fellars. An' don't rile me. I'm kinda sick an' so —— mad thet I'm seein' you-all double. . . . Jest the same you know damn well thet Ben Sloan has good eyes. They've watched four drives, all aboot the same size, an' with five riders each. Different riders! Three of these went between west an' south, haided either fer Fort Sumner, Roswell, Lincoln, or Santa Fe, or mebbe Las Vegas. The last drive, with aboot a thousand haid, air due to go north in the mawnin', I reckoned."

"These drives from Cottonwood Basin?" queried Britt, hanging on Sloan's words.

"Three of them. The last bunch must have been picked within sight of the ranch. 'Cause I seen the cattle travellin' west on the other side of the Cottonwood."

"Ha! In the timber?"

"Yes. An' along the edge. Say, less'n thirty miles from where you're settin' now."

"But, Sloan, how could all thet be possible?" demanded Britt, utterly bewildered.

"I don't know shore. My idees may be wrong. But heahs how I figger. Fust, Talman had a field-glass."

"How do you know thet?"

"I seen it. I seen him usin' it from the top of Gray Hill."

"Where'd he get it?"

"Ask me another. Wal, to go on. You sent Talman an' Trinidad off fer the Basin, ahaid of all of us. I was to trail them a day late. Boss, I didn't track them. If I had they'd seen me. 'Cause they never went to the Basin. I figgered they'd do aboot what they did do. So I struck off into the hills from heah, an' worked down. Second mawnin' early I seen smoke come oot of the cedars on Gray Hill. An' thet was my tip. But it took me two days to find oot them campers was Talman an' Trinidad. One of them was there all the time. One of them rode off three times. Two separate bunches of riders made the foot of thet hill, aboot sundown on different days. Wal, Talman is cute. He played to locate when an' where you sent riders. No doubt he seen Skylark ride oot with his men, an' Jim with his. I mustn't forget thet Talman had two kinds of signals, mebbe a piece of mirror, an' the other was regular old Injun smoke-signals."

"Hell you say!" ejaculated Britt, greatly chagrined at becoming the dupe of a cowboy he had not considered at all clever.

"I rode all night an' took up a stand on a high knoll in the Basin. I stayed there two days. Seen the drives from there. I had to get oot fer water. So I left after nightfall, an' come back, an' got on a foothill back of McCoy's ranch. I could see Gray Hill, but too far away to make anythin' oot.

258

I lay low all day. An' thet was yesterday. This mawnin' before daylight I moved back ten miles or so where I could watch Gray Hill. More smoke-signals. Aboot midafternoon I catch some dust risin' above the cottonwoods. I watched thet creep along fer hours. I seen a big bunch of cattle cross the creek an' work toward thet draw west of Gray Hill. Four riders. I watched the cattle oot of sight. An' aboot sundown I seen Talman an' Trinidad ride down to meet them four riders. . . . Aw hell! I knowed their hawses, 'specially thet iron-gray pack-hawse. I watched them go oot of sight up the draw. Then I hit oot fer home an' if my hawse ain't daid by now he's shore got bottom."

"No, it couldn't be wuss," soliloquized Britt, sadness momentarily infringing on anger.

"Reb, it was a hell of a job, but yu done it great," was Brazos' eloquent tribute.

"Rest easy to figger, boss," put in Jim, mildly.

"Sloan, get it over. What's yore angle?" added Britt.

"Wal, I'd say it's all over but the fireworks. . . . There's a fine pasture up thet draw. Oot of sight, an it leads short cut over to the trail to the reservations. Thet's where thet beef is haided. Jest timed nice before the snow flies. Whoever sells them steers to them cheatin' government buyers will get ten dollars or more a haid. — Whew! What a haul! . . . Wal, I don't figger Talman an' Trinidad goin' any farther than thet camp. They're on the way heah. But I figger they had pore fare on thet hilltop. They'll be cocky an' hungry. Mebbe want

259

to talk more business. They might not stay in camp all night an' may be on the way heah now. But I'd gamble not."

"Cap, Talman has sold oot to some big cattle interest fer big money, an' he's made a sucker oot of Trinidad," said Brazos, with terse finality.

"Britt, it's all plain as print now," added Frayne. "Talman's job is to stick with us and be a spy for whoever bribed him to ditch us. Keep these rustlers posted on when and where our outfit rides and the movements of our stock. . . . Damn clever! There's brains behind that deal. . . . Sloan, I congratulate you on the slickest piece of scout work I ever heard of."

"Aw, I was jest lucky. . . . An' onlucky to be the fellar to ketch them."

"Don't talk thet way," returned Britt, sharply. "We air honor an' duty bound in this ootfit. It was a magnificent job. . . . Who's behind this steal?"

"I don't know, boss," admitted Rebel. "Reckon thet's a small matter now, 'cause it's a cinch we're gonna find oot."

"Ah-huh! Thet fetches us down to brass tacks," rejoined Britt, grimly. "Sloan, will you handle the deal?"

"Air you askin' me, or orderin' me, sir?"

"Wal, I leave it to you."

"Reckon I ought to. . . . All right. Gimme six men on fresh hawses. We'll leave pronto an' cut up in the hills the way I went, an' come down on thet draw before daylight. I know right where

260

they'll camp. We'll leave our hawses back a ways an' slip down, aimin' to surprise them."

"Men, I'm callin' fer volunteers, but reservin' right not to accept anyone I want to stay heah," announced Britt.

"Me," spoke up Brazos, coolly, his head bowed. He, the cowboy who had only recently suffered from the treachery of a friend, whom he killed for that treachery, had allied himself with this sinister posse for a like fatal responsibility.

"An' me," growled Laigs Mason.

"I'll go," said Frayne.

"No, Frayne. You stay heah," interposed Britt. "I want to go myself, so I'd rather you stayed heah."

"Me, too," called Tennessee.

"No," objected Britt.

"I'se willin', suh," put in Ride-'Em Jackson. "Dat Talman hombre kicked me once, an' I sho nebber lubbed him."

"Thet's three. Come on, you," called Britt, impatiently.

"Me," replied Santone.

"Wal, I ain't keen to go, but I reckon I'll do it," said Jim, wagging his lean head.

"I'll let you off, Jim," declared Britt. "Rustle, boys. Two more."

Cherokee signified a reluctant willingness to participate, but Britt ruled him out, as also Blue. Then Tex and Mex Southard, slow and impassive as always, chimed in to complete the number Sloan had asked for.

"Couple of you wrangle fresh hawses," ordered Britt. "What else, Rebel?"

"Rifles, water-bags, some grub. We might have a chase."

"Cap, what'll we do if Talman and Trinidad ride in tomorrow?" queried Frayne.

"I was thinkin' of thet. They'd smell a rat, shore. . . . Wal, tie 'em up an' wait for us to come back."

"This must be kept from Miss Ripple."

"Hellyes! So in case they come be shore careful. Holly's worried aboot them cowboys."

"Britt, it'll be most damn uncomfortable for us if Talman and Trinidad come back," said Frayne, ponderingly.

"Let's don't borrow trouble."

An hour later eight horsemen, on bays and blacks, darkly garbed and heavily armed, rode silently away from Don Carlos' Rancho, headed for the foothills to the north.

Down on the range the night was warm and still. Stars shone brightly. Sloan led the single file at a trot until he struck a slow grade, where he put his horse to a walk. The fact that no rider smoked or spoke attested to the nature of this night adventure.

Britt was reminded of his ranger work down on the Rio Grande. How many nights had he ridden out with a grim group of rangers, bent on some such dark quest as this! The fall of Talman, and especially of Trinidad, had hurt him deeply. Still after the first regrets had given way to wrath, he did not think his faith in the other cowboys of his outfit had been impaired. Talman and Trinidad were due for a terrible reckoning.

Once up on the ridge Britt found the air cool and his heavy coat comfortable. Soon Sloan turned west and kept heading the draws that came out from under the bulk of the mountain. From sage they rode on into the cedars, and at last into a fringe of scattered pines reaching down from the timber belt. Deer took the place of cattle, and coyotes and wolves wildly broke the silence. Table Mountain, over in Colorado, loomed square and black above the range of lesser mountains. The gray cedar-dotted ridges ran down to end in hills that sloped off into the range. Between these wide ridges dark timber-choked gullies wound down to merge in the gray. Water splashed with cold tinkle over rocks. Once the lead horses snorted and plunged as a black bear lumbered by insolently. As the country became rougher travel grew slower. Sloan led a tortuous course through thickets of oak and patches of cedar, winding in and out of a jumble of great rocks fallen from above. He crossed a goodly mountain stream, which went tumbling down with shallow roar. This surely was Brush Creek, that had its confluence with the Cottonwood fifteen miles west of the rancho.

In another hour of as rough riding as Britt had experienced Sloan left the dim deer trail and headed down hill. By starlight Britt made out that his watch said one o'clock. The guide knew his way and took his time. It seemed to Britt that the longer the hours the grimmer the men.

A late moon rose, dimming the stars, adding to the weird aspect of the wilderness. It was a pale yellow moon, misshapen, and low over the ramparts. Gnarled and stunted cedars, reaching out with bleached dead snags, added to the spectral scene.

At length Sloan led out of the heavy timber to a marked break in the conformity of the vast slope. Gray, black-dotted ridges ran down, with bare white backs and sides, toward the vast void that was the cattle range. The night spectacle here appeared to Britt grand in the extreme. He was on the backbone of the tableland, between the mountains and the foothills. The great range curved around this corner into an amphitheater walled by the Rockies.

Sloan halted to let his comrades close in around him.

"How long till daybreak?"

"Wal, let's see. My watch says two-thirty. I reckon we hev an' hour an' a half before we can see good."

"Plenty time. Thet camp is tolerable far yet. But in this air a crack of a hoof on a rock would carry a long way. What you-all say?"

"Better be shore than sorry," rejoined Britt. "Pile off, fellars."

"Leave everythin' extra heah but yore rifles — an' ropes," whispered Sloan, as he securely tied his horse to an oak sapling. "Take yore chaps off an' spurs."

In a moment his followers were all ready, dark faces agleam in the pale moonlight.

"Listen, men. I know right where this ootfit will camp. We'll have to go slow an' easy. . . . Now, boss, what's the deal when we slip up on them?"

"Hold them up. If they show fight, wal — thet'd suit us all better. Only —"

"Only we want to find oot who's back of this deal," interrupted Sloan, menacingly. "We wouldn't be so much better off without thet."

"Rebel, you're daid right. We want to force one of them to squeal."

"Jest so thet ain't Talman or Trinidad," said Brazos.

"Britt, you want me to go ahaid with this?" asked Sloan, hoarsely.

"Yes, an' clear through with it."

"All right. Foller me close. Do what I do. When I yell run in with me. Hold them up. Don't shoot unless they go fer their guns. Thet's all."

With a rifle in one hand and a coiled lasso in the other Sloan slipped off under the cedars. He picked his way, walking stealthily, and after proceeding a hundred steps or more he halted to listen. In a moment he pressed on. Britt came last in that file. He had difficulty with his breathing. The altitude bothered him. Patch after patch of dark cedars were passed, and thickets of aspens, rustling in the cool soft breeze, and labyrinthine mazes of lichened boulders. Another bright thread of brooklet meandered down the slope. Beyond it a low incline ran up to a ridge-top where a few rods

265

down on the other side the belt of timber ended. A gray swale extended down into obscurity. Sloan halted at the edge of the trees until all the men were around him. They touched each other and looked, but no one spoke. All heard the cattle down in that swale.

When Sloan started on again he took to an Indian's stealth and slowness. Every few feet he halted. The moon shone fitfully through the spreading branches, casting dark shadows. A cow bawled somewhere. From the opposite ridge a wolf howled. Once again Sloan's followers lined up beside him. He touched his nose. Those nearest him nodded. They smelled smoke or a burned-out campfire.

Then he went on more guardedly than ever. The moon failed or passed behind a peak. This permitted the men to see that the dark hour before dawn had almost passed. Sloan proceeded more slowly, halted oftener, and waited longer, until gloom lightened to gray.

Britt heard horses nipping the grass and presently saw a bunch on the gray slope. Birds began to twitter. The wail of coyotes soared up from the range below. Water trickled somewhere over rocks. Day was at hand, yet the crafty Sloan grew more relentlessly slow than ever. If any of his men snapped a twig, which happened a few times, he paused long. At last when stones and trees could be clearly distinguished he got down to crawl. This method of advance was a relief to Britt, for whom the unusual exertion had been trying. They crawled and they rested. Finally Britt felt a re-straining hand patting his shoulder. He looked up. Santone crouched a little ahead of him. Britt discovered a beautiful glade just below him, the smoking remains of a campfire, prone blanketed forms on the ground, and packs scattered around.

Britt saw Sloan lay aside his lasso and take his rifle in two hands, slowly getting to his knees. His followers did likewise. Britt felt the cold sweat break out over him. He changed his rifle to his left hand, and drew his gun.

On the moment one of the prostrate men rolled over to throw off his blanket, to sit up yawning.

Rebel leaped up to let out that rebel yell for which he was famed. Then rang out a stentorian chorus: *"Hands up!"*

The farthest of these seven men leaped nimbly up, to shoot as swiftly and bound away. A volley of rifle shots answered him. Britt saw him stagger and fall.

Another, unheeding commands or shots, rolled out of his bed, guns flashing red. He was riddled by bullets before he got off his knees. A third, agile and swift, escaped a first fire to make the blunder of wheeling before he reached cover. His gun spouted as the rifles cracked, and he collapsed like a wet sack.

"Hands up, ———— !" bawled Rebel advancing, his rifle at his hip.

Of those remaining one stood paralyzed, his hands aloft, another sat with his hands high as his head, a third lay as if stunned, and the fourth leaned on his elbow, a blanket half concealing him. But his posture, his gray blotch of face, struck Britt as forbidding.

"Yu there. Up with 'em!" rang out Brazos, striding forward.

"Look oot, pard! He's got a gun!" yelled Laigs, leaping and shooting simultaneously. He lunged in front of Brazos just as the rustler fired through his blanket. Mason staggered under the impact of a heavy ball, then shot the man three times, flattening him on the ground.

"My Gawd! — Laigs, air yu hit?" cried Brazos, piercingly.

"Aw — it ain't nuthin'," replied the cowboy, thickly, and turned his rifle on the remaining three men.

"Air yu shore yu're not hurt? I heahed thet bullet hit."

"Never touched me, Brazos. . . . Git yore hands up, thar! . . . Wal, if it ain't pard Talman! — Howdy, Beef. Kinda in the wrong grub-line, ain't you?"

Britt came forward, his gun smoking. He had been in action. The standing rustler was no other than Lascelles, the card-sharp from Louisiana. He looked his fallen estate. Brazos hopped with a wild yell when he recognized the gambler. The second was Talman, on his knees, ghastly livid of face, and petrified with horror. The third was a young, blue-lipped, lean-jawed cowboy who realized his peril.

"Jackson, grab their guns," shouted Sloan,

268

bloody of visage and fearful to behold. He had met a bullet in that melee.

"Anybody else hit?" queried Britt, sharply. Tex Southard sat on a stone, his head down. Mex, with a suspicious red on his hands, was fingering his brother's shoulder.

"Tex bored, but not bad," he called.

"Which one was Trinidad?" queried Brazos.

"I reckon thet one who run first," replied Britt. "Go see. But slow, Brazos."

The cowboy gave the rock a wide berth, and with rifle half up, he sheered around, alert and formidable, to peer ahead. Like a hunter stalking game he started, stiffened, then slowly forged forward to halt and look down. He remained in that posture a long moment.

"Daid!" he called, with the piercing note in his high voice. But he still gazed on. Then in strangled voice he burst out. "Yu —— yellow fool! Game, but yu're daid!"

Brazos came striding back, his hair up like a tawny wave, his eyes narrowed to blue dagger points.

"Jack — Santone. Search these men — an' tie their arms back," ordered Sloan.

Swift hands carried out this command. Brazos poked with the nose of his rifle at the various articles piled on a rock, markedly among them a huge roll of greenback bills which had been taken from Talman.

"Hundred dollar bills," muttered Brazos, his tone and action strangely significant. Then, like a gold-headed striking snake, he leaped to confront Talman. "If yu'd had guts, like Trin, yu wouldn't hev to swing!"

"Swing?" squeaked Talman, his visage like beaded wax. In profound egotism or arrogance or sheer blind folly the cowboy had not counted the cost of failure. "For God's sake! — Brazos!"

The inexorable cowboy turned his back. He bent over Mason who sat humped on a pack. "Laigs, air yu shore yu ain't hurt bad?"

"I ain't hurt — none. . . . Rustle this necktie party — along."

Santone, left-handed and careless, tossed a noose neatly over Lascelles' head, and whipped it tight. Then he made as clever a throw with the other end of his rope, sending it over a branch ten feet up. The gambler, evidently sodden and dazed, awoke to his extremity.

"Lay hold — cowboys!" yelled Sloan, crisply, springing to Santone's side. Brazos was as quick, and Mex Southard left his brother, to participate. One concerted lunge cut Lascelles' hideous blasphemy to a gasping wheeze, and jerked him into the air.

"Make fast."

Britt saw the cowboys hold and tie the rope in a twinkling, and duck to evade the tremendous grotesque kicks of the swinging man. But it was not possible to remove his gaze from Mason, who leaned back with bloody hands pressed to his abdomen and leered up at Lascelles.

"Hey, my caird-sharp galoot. — How you like

thet shuffle? . . . Slip out from under now. Haw! Haw! — Kick, you — ! Stick out yore tongue! . . . Say, you got any jumpin'-jack I ever seen beat to hell an' gone! . . . To hell with you, Lascelles!"

Meanwhile the other cowboys were not idle. The ugly business must be done quickly. Jackson threw a noose over Talman's head and grinned in the act.

"Beef, yo is sho a wonnerful kicker," he shouted. "But yo won't kick no mo niggers on dis green earth."

Talman was sagging down when the ropes strung tight from another branch. His voice had failed; only sickening gasps issued from his lips. Up he shot, six feet above the ground. And Britt turned away. Just then the sun rose, bright and red, over the eastern wall, and flooded the glade with crimson light. Shadows of the writhing victims danced across the sunlit rocks.

Rebel Sloan confronted the pallid third of that trio, and waved a ruthless hand aloft.

"Rustler, you see them?"

The reply was an incoherent affirmative.

"Do you want to save yore neck?"

"Gawd Almighty! — Yes — yes! — Gimme — a chance."

"Will you talk?"

"I — I'll tell — all," he whispered, in eager huskiness, his dark, awful eyes lighting with hope.

"Boss, come heah," called Sloan.

Britt hurriedly got out his pencil and notebook,

and ran over. Brazos joined them.

"Watch them ropes, you cowboys," yelled Sloan. The rustling and threshing of foliage above attested to the violence of the hanged men.

"What's yore name?"

"Jeff Saunders."

"Wal, Saunders, this heah is Britt — Holly Ripple's foreman. What he says you can rely on."

"Britt — if — if I squeal will you let me go?"

"Yes, provided yore information is conclusive, an' you swear to leave the country."

"I know enough, sir, an' I swear. . . . I'm only too glad."

"Who you ridin' fer?"

"Sewall McCoy."

"How long hev you rode fer him?"

"Two years. I come to New Mexico with his outfit."

"Is McCoy back of this deal involvin' my cowboys?"

"McCoy an' Slaughter together," rejoined Saunders, gulping to get his words out quickly. "They joined outfits. Slaughter was the dark hoss. He's got fourteen hands, not countin' this Lascelles. They're located at Aspen Springs, up in the hills."

"What was their game?"

"A few quick drives this fall. Then big deals next spring. McCoy has buyers all over. When the railroad gets heah he aims to ship a hundred thousand cattle, before the law comes."

"How many cattle in his herd?"

"Five thousand. All Texas longhorns. He aims to keep thet herd as is, only addin' branded calves."

"Who's he stealin' from?"

"A little from all cattlemen. But concentratin' on Ripple stock."

"From Chisum, too?"

"No. I reckon McCoy is shy of Jingle-bob cattle."

"Why?"

"I don't know. Mebbe 'cause Chisum will let him alone, so long as he steers clear of the Seven Rivers range."

"How did McCoy corrupt Talman an' Trinidad?"

"Money. Talman was leavin' the range before winter. Trinidad was sore because Talman didn't divvy. Thet's why they camped with us last night. Trinidad refused to go back to your ranch. He cussed Talman mighty hard."

"All right, Saunders. Thet will do. Sign yore name heah. . . . Somebody untie his hands."

After this signature was added to Britt's notebook, Sloan turned Saunders loose. "Grab yore saddle, an' things. Pick oot yore gun. Fork yore hawse an' ride a beeline somewhere far an' wide. Fer yore good luck might not last."

A poignant cry caused Britt to wheel as on a pivot. Brazos was on his knees beside Mason, who had slumped off the pack to the ground and now sat propped there with strange ashen face.

"Laigs!"

Agony rang in that cry. Brazos' nervous hands plucked at Mason's stained shirt.

"It's all — right, pard," replied the wounded cowboy, weakly. "We done fer thet outfit . . . what we come fer! — Funny, how most of these double-crossers show yellow. Pity aboot Trin. . . . I'm glad he cashed game."

"Old man, you've lied to me," exclaimed Brazos, fearfully.

"Wal, it's the — last time," replied Laigs, with a ghost of a smile.

"Fellars, come heah," faltered Brazos, appealing for help, when perhaps he felt instinctively there was none. He opened Mason's wet shirt. In the middle of the cowboy's chest, just below the breast bone, showed an ugly red hole. Only a froth of blood appeared outside. Brazos slipped his hand round to Mason's back.

"Oh — my — Gawd!" he cried, in terror, and when he brought his hand out it was dripping blood. "Laigs! Yu got in front — of me!" Brazos' passionate protest of remorse and sorrow broke at the end.

"Wal, pard — you'd done the same for me. . . . Only I wasn't — quick enough. — I oughta shot — an' yelled afterwards. . . . Don't take on so, Brazos."

Britt bent over to examine Mason's injury. A heavy .45 calibre slug had gone clear through the lad. His moments were numbered.

"Laigs. You haven't got long. . . . Is there anythin'?"

"Don't know what become of — my, people. But thet's no matter. . . . Gimme a smoke."

They gathered around Mason and some one gave him a lighted cigarette. He puffed with difficulty, but composedly. He could not inhale.

"Let's play a hand of draw."

Santone had a greasy deck of cards which he proceeded to shuffle, and dealt to Laigs, Jackson, Mex and himself.

"Dog-gone! I always was lucky," said Mason. "Gimme two cairds. . . . What're you bettin', Jack?"

"I done got you skinned, Laigs. I sho has. . . . It's goin' up."

"Raise you. . . . Rest of you layin' down, huh? You darn black scamp! I'll call an' lay down three aces."

"Thet's good, Laigs. I wuz bluffin'."

"You oughta know better, Jack. . . . Yore deal, Mex. . . . An' rustle. . . . Gettin' kinda dark already."

But the sun was shining bright and gold now, bathing the glade in a glamour of light. A breeze stirred the treetops. Somewhere a raven croaked. The cattle were bawling. Across the golden patch of grass where the cowboys knelt swayed the sinister black shadows of the hanging men — now quiet.

Laigs picked up his cards with steady fingers. Brazos knelt behind, holding him up.

"Thet's dog-gone-funny," said Mason, faintly. "These cairds — sorta blur. . . . Fellars — I cain't see!"

He dropped the cards to the grass and his head fell back against Brazos.

"Pard — sing — Lone Prairiee."

Brazos appeared to quiver through all his lithe frame. He lifted his working face to the sunlit boughs and closed his eyes. In a moment the convulsive quiverings ceased. His features shone with a stern, sad and beautiful light. Brazos was the singer of the outfit. He had a clear tenor voice. It broke and quavered, piercingly sweet. He began again.

"O bury me not on the lone prairie,
The word came low and mournfully
From the pallid lips of a boy who lay
On his death bed at the close of day.

He had wrestled with pain till o'er his brow
Death's shadows fast were creeping now;
He thought of his home and the loved ones nigh
As the cowboys gathered to see him die.

'O bury me not' — and his voice failed there,
But we paid no heed to his dying prayer;
In a shallow grave just six by three
We buried him there on the lone prairie.

Where the dew drops shine —"

Britt reached out to silence the singer. Laigs was dead.

CHAPTER 11

1874, as had been predicted by Buff Belmet and other frontiersmen, ushered in for eastern and central New Mexico the bloodiest era that ever made history for the West.

There were two reasons for this fact — the rich vast grass ranges that had lured venturesome cattle men in the sixties to run cattle over the limitless acres once owned by the Spanish dons; and secondly because there was no semblance of law in all the broad land. Rustlers, desperadoes, wild cowboys, adventurers flocked into New Mexico. At one period, from 1874 to 1879, New Mexico held more desperate and vicious men than ever assembled any other place or time in the settlement of that range country west of Texas and Kansas.

This period saw the inception and development of the Lincoln County War, the bloodiest of all frontier wars, in which three hundred men were killed. It saw the rise of Billy the Kid, Jesse Evans, mere youths in years, but who had no peers in cold nerve, or guncraft, or bloody deeds. At sixteen they were cowboy comrades, riding the same ranch. Before they were twenty they got into different factions and swore to kill each other. But Billy the Kid and Jesse Evans never met face to face. Evans admitted Billy's superiority with a rifle, but claimed he could beat him to a gun. The saloons of Lincoln and Roswell waited and gambled on the meeting of these two cowboys. No doubt Billy and Jesse avoided the encounter that meant a draw on sight.

Don Carlos' Rancho stood at the gateway of the pass through which the Old Santa Fe Trail wound up off the Great Plains. The Mexican village had at one time or another harbored every Western character, good or bad, who passed that way. In the spring of 1875 Holly Ripple closed her famous, hospitable door to the travelling public. The old, leisurely, singing, glamorous Spanish days passed away; and the new day was hard, keen, vivid, uncertain and raw.

Britt saw with regret the snow gradually melt off the uplands of the rolling range. The flowers sprang up as if by magic, and so did riders coming down out of the hills.

May brought the first caravan and the news from outside. Las Animas was teeming. The railroad was forging west. Cattle, stagecoaches, pack-trains, lone, furtive-eyed riders, wagon-trains of settlers, bands of horsemen who asked no questions and said nothing about themselves — movement of all these came upon the heels of the vanishing snow.

Six months had slipped away into the past, quietly for Britt and his outfit, riding less than in the summer, with their enemies holed-up, like groundhogs, until the warm winds would blow again. There had been no rustling of cattle since those raids of last fall. But following Rebel Sloan's round-up of one of these gangs, with report and gossip flying like wildfire over the range, there had been plenty to disturb the peace of the Ripple contingent.

Britt had called a conference in San Marcos of a number of cattlemen within a hundred-mile radius of Don Carlos' Rancho. Doane, Halstead, Clements, his nearest range neighbors, and Bill Wood, the Sedgwick brothers, newcomers in the country, and Hardy Wilson — all these cattlemen had met Britt, to have laid before them the startling facts of the McCoy-Slaughter combine. The result was far-reaching, but very different from what Britt had planned and hoped for. One of these ranchers, in Britt's opinion, no other than Bill Wood, had told of the conference and its purpose, with the result that Britt's hope for a unified front against the rustlers was frustrated. It would have been better if Britt had kept his counsel, as well as the Saunders confession, from everybody except his own men. McCoy was stronger in the range than Britt had estimated; he had powerful friends who were not friendly to Texans. He dominated the ranchers of small herds and little means. Moreover he developed a tendency to go to town and drink and gamble, during which times he was dangerous. He made veiled threats, and in open defiance of Britt and his several notorious cowboys, he attached to his outfit a gunman late from the Kansas border, one Jeff Rankin, whose reputation as a killer came with him and needed no boasting by McCoy. But the loud-mouthed McCoy did brag that he had a man to match Renn Frayne.

After this one blunder Britt kept his mouth closed and his men away from San Marcos. With the Pecos Valley War between bitter factions not wholly ended and the Lincoln County War in its incipiency Britt saw how easily he could be involved in one or the other, or have a private war on his hands.

He and Frayne and Jim talked often and long about how to meet the future. In any case they had a fight on their hands. Doane and his neighbor ranchers feared to ally themselves openly against McCoy. But they ran few cattle compared to the Ripple estate, and knew their own losses would be inconsequential provided they were neutral.

The foreman and his confidants, especially Frayne, worked out a plan that to Britt seemed formidable. They would not make any more cattle drives to the railroad for an indefinite period; they would concentrate all their stock on the thirty mile range between Cottonwood Creek and the hills; they would no longer split up the outfit into small bunches for isolated trips; they would ride and watch the range in a body, sixteen strong, on the swiftest horses. They would be heavily armed and they would shoot first.

Frayne was the genius of this carefully thought-out defense. He did not think Slaughter and McCoy could last out the summer if they resorted to stealing cattle again. Frayne was noncommittal in regard to Jeff Rankin, the gunman imported obviously to kill him and Brazos. Nevertheless it was clear to Britt that Frayne knew beforehand the result of a possible encounter between himself and McCoy's desperadoes. Most significant to Britt had been the constant gun and rifle practice that Frayne insisted upon. The last caravan before winter arrived the preceding year had brought a large consignment of weapons and ammunition Britt had ordered to meet the very contingency that now threatened. New .44 calibre Winchester rifles, and the new 1871 model Colt .45 guns were presented to the Ripple outfit. And Britt, urged by Frayne, had the boys constantly at practice, especially with the rifles. They all became skilled marksmen. The practice of shooting at coyotes and jack-rabbits from a running horse grew to be fun and spirited rivalry, instead of work. Brazos led them all with the six-shooter, but Jackson paired with the Kentuckian Blue, who had been a squirrel hunter as a boy, in preeminence with the rifle. McCoy's riders would possess but few of the long arms, and constant practice with either them or the short arms was out of the question. Ammunition in any quantity cost a good deal of money, an expense to which McCoy and Slaughter would not go. That was a detail they overlooked. McCoy had paid hundreds of dollars to corrupt Ripple cowboys, but he probably never thought of making his own unerring marksmen.

Range gossip this spring had it that Britt's wild outfit of Texans and half-breeds, topped by an outlaw who had killed many men, were intimidated and afraid to frequent the old drinking-saloons and gambling-halls. Gossip from San Marcos came by stage, by rider, and by queer ways that could not be traced. The whole range was buzzing. But what with Chisum about to declare war on rustlers, the Murphy-McSween factions of Lincoln up in arms, the coming of the railroad and the influx of strangers, Holly Ripple's troubles scarcely held first place in popular clamor.

The death of Laigs Mason had changed Brazos Keene. He grieved for months, and when he got over that the boyish, fun-loving, devilish glee had apparently gone forever. Brazos drank a good deal, and drifted toward that fiery, untamed, passionate spirit that had heretofore flared up only seldom and fleetingly. Nevertheless he failed in nothing else.

The tragic end of Talman and Trinidad, as well as Mason's, had likewise worked stern havoc in the devil-may-care minds of the other cowboys. A fatal carelessness which had once marked them almost totally disappeared. They gambled, they drank, they played tricks, but they were changed. They had become cemented in comradeship. Holly Ripple's faith, the spell of Brazos Keene's loss, the creed of Laigs Mason, the example of Renn Frayne — these laid their inscrutable and ineradicable hold upon their primitive minds.

Best of all, and in spite of many adverse conditions, Holly Ripple was happy. Britt, stifling his conscience, hugged that to his bosom. As Holly's

twenty-first birthday approached, she grew love-
lier than she had ever been, more of a woman,
though still capable of girlish fits of temper and
pouts of wilfulness. In those winter months, while
confined mostly to the house, she had lost her tan
and something of the robustness that had come
with a summer's riding, to gain again that pearl
whiteness of face and black brilliance of eye
for which her Spanish mother had been noted.

Holly Ripple was happy. And Britt knew he
dared take the glory of that fact to himself. He
had betrayed Frayne's secret.

Britt often ruminated over the occasion of his
faithlessness to Frayne. When he had an idle hour
in the dusk beside the fire he often saw Holly's
glorious eyes of rapture in the heart of the coals.
Frayne would know some day and bless him for
it. He had played fair, he had kept faith as long
as he could, and that had been until Holly's heart
was breaking. Weeks and months of Frayne's
strange aloofness, his cold, stern avoidance of her,
his inexplicable reaction to that kiss of gratitude
she had given him — these had at last paled her
cheeks and shamed her into seclusion, and would
have destroyed her but for Britt's revelation.

Christmas Eve he had found Holly alone, weeping before her fire, prey to the old memories of
her father and to the hopeless despair of the future.

"Holly lass, I have a Christmas gift for you,"
he said, taking her hands.

"Oh, Cappy — I — I don't want — any gifts."

"Not anythin' from me, or Brazos, or the boys?"

"You are dears — to — to remember me — but I can't care. . . ."

"Not anythin' from Renn?"

A little shock went through Holly, and the fire-bent eyes gazed up hungrily.

"From Renn?" she whispered.

"I reckon."

"Did he send me — ?"

"No, not directly. It has come through me."

"I don't want it then," she replied, moodily.

"Wal, you can heah aboot it, cain't you?" he went on, persuasively, his heart warming, stirring his courage to this momentous and dangerous revelation.

"If it pleases you, Cappy dear."

"Wal, I'll pull up this chair an' set heah beside you. . . . Nice fire, Holly. Cedar wood burns so pretty. You see pictures in the coals. An' it's snowin' oot an' gettin' darker'n the ace of spades. The boys air all in, comfortable as bugs in a holler log, an' comparin' the presents you gave them. . . . All except Frayne. He's by the fire, lone-somer'n ever, with eyes you cain't look into."

"Sad! Lonely! — He might be here — with me," cried Holly, passionately.

"So he might. Wal, if you still care, be patient."

"Still care? — It is killing me," she murmured, hollow-voiced.

"Holly, our friend might be rememberin' his youth — a good home — a lovin' mother — a nice sister. Shore he had them once. . . . Lass, I like the fight Renn's makin'."

She did not answer, but her hands clung to his, and her head inclined to his shoulder.

"Listen, lass. . . . Do you remember the day last summer when Frayne got back from Las Animas?"

"Remember? It haunts me."

"You kissed him!"

"Oh-h!" Holly let out a smothered cry. "How did you know?"

"Renn told me."

"Oh — I thought better of him."

"Wait. I was on the lookout. He came down an' I waylaid him. Renn was not himself. He was dazed. He was like a man between rapture an' despair. Shore I took advantage of this weakness. An' I pumped him, nagged him, till he told me you'd kissed him. He misunderstood thet, Holly. He reckoned you was jest grateful. But thet kiss wrecked him. An' when I cussed him fer not carin' aboot you — then I thought he was goin' to slay me. His eyes were terrible. An' it all come oot in a flood. Love you? Thet was nothin' atall. He worshipped you. Aw, it was all there, in his white face an' burnin' eyes. Then he said: 'Now I've got to go oot an' get myself shot!' "

Holly was on Britt's breast, beating at him, hiding her scarlet face, crying incoherently: "Cappy — darling! — I — Oh! — If you're lying — it'll kill me."

"True as gospel, Holly. He made me swear not to tell you. An' I've kept it. Now be a woman. It'll all turn oot right. This man Frayne comes from fine people. He has good instincts. Honor! Give him time, lass. Time to prove himself. Time to find himself worthy. Thet day he said if you ever kissed him again he'd fall on his knees. So you can bide thet time, long as it may be. Always remember thet you can end it when you choose. Be happy, Holly Ripple — an' wait."

Britt was off at dawn one May morning, bound for Gray Hill, to do some field-glass scouting for his own outfit.

The morning was of that exquisite New Mexican kind which even the old dyed-in-the-wool Texan felt bound to admire. Frost-diamonds glistened on the sage and the blades of grass resembled spears of crystal. The air had an exhilarating tang, cold as ice, and sweet. The sunlight, coming from behind, and just up over the rim of the world, cast long grotesque shadows of himself and his horse ahead over the rippling sage. The cottonwoods along the creek showed a fresh green; the range was black and red with cattle; the hills sloped up bleached gray to the fuzzy dark summits; far off black timber belted the mountains up to the dazzling snow. But it was the range that fascinated Britt — the lap of earth which the cowmen designated as rangeland — level reach on reach and rolling ridge, swale and coulee, the purple vastness on to the dim distance that was obscurity.

At the ranch Britt had left Frayne, Jim, Tennessee and Flinty, Handsome Gaines and Rebel Sloan, all pleasantly engaged in keeping an eye on a herd working westward. The other cowboys were out at the other end of the herd with a scout on the top of Gray Hill.

Disturbing news had initiated this early season vigilance. A stagecoach driver, on the run from Santa Fe to Las Animas, had brought Britt some interesting reminders of the anticipated feud due between the McCoy and the Ripple factions.

McCoy, with some of his men, notably Rankin, had accosted Doane, the rancher, in Blade's Saloon at San Marcos, and had shot him for alleged accusations reflecting upon McCoy's honesty as a cattleman. "Somebody tell Cap Britt that he'll get the same if he shows up in San Marcos," McCoy had loudly proclaimed, standing with smoking gun before the spectators. And the stage-driver repeated another remark, untraceable, to the effect that if Renn Frayne did not untie Holly Ripple's apron-strings from his neck and come to town like a man he might have to face Jeff Rankin on the porch of the Ripple bunkhouse.

Thus the opening gun of the season, fired at an unarmed and defenseless rancher, had to be chalked up in black against the McCoy-Slaughter faction. The cowboys had almost to rope Skylark to keep him home. Brazos rolled his gun with an incredible swiftness. The other cowboys, usually noisy, resentful, volatile, took the news in silence.

Britt rode his fast bay at a swinging lope along the inside trail under the lee of the slope, watchful always. And while he rode his mind was active. This information from San Marcos was three days old. With Russ Slaughter's gang down from the hills, like wolves long famished, and McCoy's outfit in town, it would follow as night the day that a cattle raid might be expected. Britt was well-nigh as eager for a rustler raid as his cowboys. The failure of other range cattlemen to side with Britt had given offense, and the gibes of the Slaughter-McCoy riders rankled deep. In all his career as a Texas Ranger, as a Trail Driver on the Chisholm Trail, as a foreman of hard cattle outfits, Britt had never faced a crisis like the one impending. His Ripple band numbered some of the wildest cowboys and *vaqueros* Texas ever produced, and this did not count the outlaw and gunman Frayne. Brazos Keene was the only one well known to the New Mexico range, though Rebel Sloan's coup the preceding fall had earned him notoriety. But as a matter of fact, Britt's hard outfit had not been tried out. A hard reputation had to be sustained on the frontier. Britt knew the nature of his men. He knew that their tendency to drink, gamble, steal, to ride into town looking for trouble, to run true to their class, had been changed by the extraordinary relation Holly Ripple had given them to her and to the West. Therefore, the cattlemen and rustlers and the desperados of eastern New Mexico had come to the conclusion that Cap Britt's outfit had been overrated. Certain it was that they would be tried out to the limit this summer.

The trail Britt rode branched at Sage Creek, and the left fork wound up in the hills. He followed it to emerge on a long hog-back that dipped to a deep saddle, and then rose to climb Gray Hill. Britt rode two miles of open sage country, up and down, before getting on to the slope he wanted. As he had not been up there before he was not quite sure of his way. At length he espied a landmark he was looking for, a huge split rock standing alone, and from there he soon climbed to the cedars of Gray Hill.

This hill was the highest of the lower foothills, and stood out somewhat isolated, projecting with steep gray bluff over the range below. It had been a favorite lookout for Apaches while waylaying the caravans along the Old Trail, which could be plainly seen, a white road winding over the grassy rolling land. Britt entered the fringy patch of stunted cedars. Presently his horse threw up its ears and whinnied. Britt soon espied a wiry mustang which he took to be Jackson's. Dismounting to tie his horse, he went on. The cedars played out into scrubby brush, at the end of which he found the negro.

"Boss, I seen yu comin'."

"Howdy, Ride-'Em. I don't see how a jack-rabbit could get by you heah."

"He sho couldn't. No suh."

"What's doin'?"

"A lot of bad things doin', boss. A whole lot," replied Jackson, rolling his big ox eyes. He wore a field-glass slung on a leather strap round his neck. He had one of the new .44 Winchesters, and packed his old Colt as well as the new one. And his belt was studded with brass shells. The black *vaquero* did not appear to Britt to be a desirable person to encounter on a lonely hilltop, unless he was friendly.

"Ah-huh. Wal, Jack, let me ketch my breath before you knock me oot," replied Britt.

"Keep yu haid low, boss. Yu can set on my coat. An' I won't spliflicate yu till yu're ready."

This vantage point was the highest from which Britt had surveyed the range. The outlook was grand indeed. He could see across the tops of the uplands to the south and west, which had the effect of shrinking the range below into a three-cornered valley, in shape resembling the ace of clubs. Over to his right the Maxwell grant, consisting of a million and a half acres, resembled a purple sage flat of no great proportions. Cottonwood Basin was a speckled bowl, from which ran a green-lined thread of water. The thirty miles of Ripple range was a hollow in the hand of the vast scene. But the cattle appeared to be too numerous for the space.

The perspective of this immediate valley, which appeared boundless from below, was distorted and reduced by the magnificence and enormous reach of New Mexico to the southwest. The day was clear and bright, rendering visibility perfect. Britt saw the arid breaks running down to the south, a wilderness that amply presaged the termination in the *Llano Estacado*, the Seven Rivers country, and the gray palisades of the Pecos, and farther around the Blood of Christ Mountains, until at length the great white wall of the Rockies loomed south of Las Vegas. Britt had full appreciation then of why New Mexico could graze so many cattle and hide so many rustlers. He made a promise to himself to fetch Holly up there and show her why her father had given up Texas for New Mexico. The strip of Texas here visible was desert, shining far down across the rugged black breaks. Britt disliked to prove traitor to his beloved state, but this vast land of fertile ranges, valleys, hills and plains could not be denied.

Reluctantly the foreman wrenched his gaze from that glorious spectacle to cast it below, on the ten-mile gray strip between the hills and the creek. Cattle were thick down there, thinning out to the west toward the Basin, where in the dim haze they belted the gray with black.

"Wal, Jack, shoot," said Britt, finally.

"Boss, I sho will, befo yu leave dis hill."

Britt flashed a sharp inquiring glance upon his black companion. Jackson had spoken casually, though with conviction. On the moment he had the field-glass fixed upon a point near where Cottonwood Creek sheered toward the hills. Britt saw dust clouds there.

"I ben heah tree days, all de whole day long. Fust day two riders com oot from San Marcos an' stop ober dere on dat yaller ridge. An' dey watch till sundown. . . . Second day de same two com again, an' dis time dey rode ten miles down de crick till I seen dem no mo. Boss, dey wuz scouts lookin' out fer riders. An' sho dey seen dem down

291

whar our cattle is grazin' thick."

"Ah-huh. An' how aboot this mawnin', Jack?" queried Britt, gruffly, as the negro paused.

"Dere's ten rustlers down dere inside de bend roundin' up a fat bunch of our steers. Plumb per-tickler dey air, dis mawnin', boss."

"Hell you say! — Where?"

"Take de glass, boss. . . . Locate de bend of de crick. An' den com oot dis way to dat green swale whar yu see dust pilin'. . . . See dat black patch on de west side of de swale. Dere's a low bluff —"

"Got 'em, Jack. Wal, by — !" interrupted Britt. "Of all the gall!"

The clear magnified circle had showed succes-sively the green border of cottonwoods, the shining pools and gray rocks of the creek, the rolling grassy levels and hollows, and then riders in couples driv-ing cattle down to the natural corral where a goodly herd had already been collected. Britt swore under his breath, and moved the glass back over the same ground to make a count. The rustlers were work-ing in couples. They appeared bold and unhurried. He counted four couples making the round-up. The distance was less than ten miles.

"Thought you said ten riders," said Britt. "I can locate only eight."

"Two lookouts, boss. One on dat little knoll above the swale, an' the other a mile down on dis high ridge. Dat hombre is botherin' Brazos, yu can sho bet yore last dollah on dat."

Britt was silent until he had located both scouts.

Both straddled their horses in any way but that of tense and vigilant spies. The whole procedure had an air of a leisurely execution of well-laid plans.

"Where is Brazos?"

"Aboot half way between de bend of de crick an' whar dat fardest scout is forkin' his hawse. Dey's hid under de bank in dat clump of cottonwoods. Ben campin' right dere dese tree days. I rides oot before sunup an' rides in after sundown. Tree whole long days, boss. But de time is aboot up."

"Jack, air the boys all together in thet place?"

"Sho. Dey's bunched dere."

"Brazos — Skylark — Santone — Cherry — Mex?" muttered Britt, significantly. "An' they're waitin' to see how many steers thet thievin' ootfit will take an' where they'd haid fer."

"Boss, not so much dat as gibbin' dem time to tire oot dere hosses. I heahed Brazos plan dat. It won't be long now till dem hosses will hev dere edge wored off. An' Brazos' hosses hevn't run fer tree days. . . . Boss, if dat bunch don't scatter like a covey of quail dey air gonna be snuffed oot pronto."

"Jack, they won't scatter. . . . But if I was Brazos I'd bust loose on them soon. — I reckon, though, it'll be better to let them line up fer the drive. Which way will they haid?"

"We wuz bettin' on dat de odder night. An' I says dey'd drive square up under dis hill, same as dat McCoy ootfit last fall."

293

"Jack, you're aboot correct, if we judge by the lay of thet swale. There's low ground all the way to the hill — By George, thet would fetch them right heah."

"Boss, if any of dem rustlers run up dat draw dey'll meet hell'n blazes at de top. 'Cause Ride-'Em Jackson will be dere. He sho will!"

"Jack, take the glass an' swing round in a circle, far back an' work closer."

"Nuttin' dere on San Marcos side," returned the negro, presently. And he gave a like report of a survey down the Cottonwood to the east. But when he searched the west he was so long in speaking that Britt grew suspicious and worried.

"Boss, I seen riders come up oot of de crick way far ober. Behind dat scout on de ridge. . . . Den I lost 'em. . . . Dey didn't ride like more rustlers. No suh! — Tree ob dem. Must hev dropped in a wash. . . . *Dere,* — Boss, I see Brazos on his white hoss. As sho as Gawd made little apples! — Two riders wid him. Cherry. I know his hoss. . . . Dere stealin' up behind. . . . Boss, I'se sho sweatin' blood. Brazos is cute. De idee is to rush dem rustlers from de souf an' de west. Dey'll make fo de hills, boss. An' heah we is, waitin', plumb chuck full ob bullets."

"I'm sweatin' some myself, Jack," agreed Britt. It was a wonderful and exciting thing to watch from this high hill, to know what the rustlers did not dream of, to wait for the charge and the fight. Britt had a grim sense of its deadliness.

"Brazos out of sight again," went on the negro,

intent with the glass. "Dawg-gone! Boss, we sho ought to hev a telescope. . . . Dat cain't be far from where I last seen Brazos to de man on de knoll. . . . I got it, boss. I done has. Brazos is off his hoss; crawlin' up on dat hombre. I'm sho glad I'se me 'stead ob him. De odder boys will be holdin' Brazos' hoss, ready to run oot when he shoots. Brazos will be in his saddle again, quicker'n hell. Dat shot will be de signal. Den de bawl is on!"

"Give me thet glass, you bloodthirsty coon! . . . No, take it back. I cain't see clear. My eyes water. Keep close tab, Jack, an' sing oot. I want to know what's goin' on."

"Wal, boss, if dey run dis way yo'll see sho."

Jackson swept the scene again. "All de round-up riders bunched, boss. Got all dey want, I reckon. Hah! dey ain't hawgs atall — O no! — Bet dere's five hundred haid in dat bunch. . . . Boss, dat far scout's ridin' in. . . . It'll be jes like dat Brazos boy to git dere at de right minnit. Dat's Brazos. . . . No sign yit. . . . Ah boss — puff o' white smoke!"

Britt saw that tiny white puff appear against the green.

"Dat fust scout falls offen his hoss, Cap," reported Jackson, with *sang-froid*. "Slides offen de bluff. Dem rustlers bunch sudden. Den dey ride fer de crick. But not straight fer our ootfit. Dat's tough luck. Dey git goin', boss. . . . Awha! Up piles dat ootfit, smokin' dem rifles. . . . I see a rider fall. Dey wheel west. But Brazos an' dem two pards cut 'em off. . . . Boss, dey haid dis

295

way. Dat crick ootfit spreadin'. . . . Dere's Santone on his gray, quarterin' east. Anudder rider close to him. Dat will be Stinger. . . . Boss, dem rustlers pilin' by de steers dey stole. Haw! Haw! Dey won't drive no mo dis day. . . . It's a race fer de hills, boss, an' dem white trash might jes as well fold dere arms an' pray. 'Cause it's all ober but de fireworks."

"Any more shootin', Jack? I cain't see any smoke," cried Britt, eagerly, straining his eyes.

"No mo. Dey's too fur apart. . . . Dere! De rustlin' gents air pilin' under dat ridge. . . . Dey're oot of sight. . . . Dat wash leads right heah, boss. our boys air crossin' de wash. Some of dem stay on dis side. Dey'se on bof sides, boss. All workin' jes as Brazos planned. . . . Boss, now's de time fer us to run back an' haid dat draw."

"Lead, Jack, an' don't run too fast."

Britt snatched up his rifle and started after the negro. Through the brush, back under the cedars, beyond the horses, slanting down the slope they ran until they came out above the saddle that dipped from the back of Gray Hill to the next foothill.

"Boss, dis is de best place to see," said the negro, as he halted. "It's better'n up dere on top."

"Shore is — if they keep on," panted Britt.

"Dis is de only way dey can go. Dey'se cut off. Dey gotta come up de trail dere. See it? Dat's whar McCoy's ootfit drove our cattle last fall. Dere's an easy grade. All de udder slopes air steep."

"Find a place, Jack."

Presently the two were located somewhat lower down on a low bluff which afforded a perfect ambush of the trail and a fan-shaped view of the range below. Britt could now see with his naked eye rising puffs of dust and running horses. There were four riders on each side of the wash and a string of others down inside.

"Boss, dem rustlers hev to com up oot of dat wash," observed Jackson, through the field-glass. "Too sandy. Dey gotta get on hard. Our boys air gainin', boss. An' dey ain't stretched oot, neither. . . . Dere! Up dey come. Dust flyin'. — Away dey'se off, haidin' fer de trail. . . . Wal, now we'll see. I reckon Brazos an' his tree on dat fur side will stay dere. Dat wash peters oot up heah. . . . Aboot even race so fur, boss. An' five miles to come."

"Not so far, Jack. I can see pretty good now. — By Gawd, it looks bad fer thet bunch. One-two-three-four. . . . how many, Jack?"

"Nine, I reckon. But dey're sho pilin' ober each udder. Ebery dawg fer hisself!"

Jackson took the glasses from his eyes and wiped them with his scarf. Britt attended closely to the race. It seemed to him that the distance between Santone, whom they recognized by his gray horse, and the last of the fugitives, was about a quarter of a mile. All horses were running, but apparently not extended yet. If the rustlers had rifles they had a chance to stop their pursuers and escape. If not — ! Britt was keen to ascertain this point.

He had been in many a running race in which the general dislike of most riders for rifles had been their doom.

"Boss, guess I hed dat five miles wrong," said Jackson. "Nebber was no good at distance. . . . Reckon two miles now. An' dey're comin' into dat long sage-flat. . . . Brazos cuts across. His men foller. Dey're behind Santone's bunch. But ketchin' up. . . . Spreadin' again, boss. An' dem rustlers stringin' straight ahaid. By golly, it's like chasin' rabbits into a burro. . . . *Whoopee!* Brazos has cut loose. Dat white hoss is stretchin'. Boss, dere ain't his beat on dis range. . . . An' look at dat Santone. He ain't gonna be left at de post. None of 'em is. . . . Boss, dat space is shortenin' some pronto. See dem rifles shine. . . . Boss, de rustlers air shootin'! . . . Six guns, boss, Haw! Haw! I jes see one damn rifle in dat string. Ob all de white trash fools! . . . Boss, I'se gettin' hot under de collar. I see de dust kickin' up by bullets way in front ob our boys. Aboot tree hundred yards, mebbe. . . . Dey'se comin', boss. Heah dem guns boomin'? . . . Lud, how Brazos can hold dat fire! I'd sho be smokin' 'em. . . . *Awha!* Dey'se shootin', boss. Dem rifles air talkin'! *Whoopee!* . . . Dat last rustler. Hit! He sho takes a lot of killin'. Down! — Dere's a hoss piles up. . . . Anudder rustler down! *Anudder!* . . . Haw! Haw! Youse will steal Ripple cattle. . . . Two hosses down! Tree plungin' off, saddles empty. . . . Boss, *boss!* Heah — dem rifles pingin'? See dat rustler lead fallin' — short?"

"Save yore breath, Jack," ordered Britt, sharply.

"You'll hev to be runnin' to haid some of them off. Two of them air far in front. They're on the grade."

"Look at dem beat dere hosses! — Boss, dey might git away down dere. But nebber up heah."

Jackson laid the glass down and slipped back into the brush. Britt heard his boots thudding. The negro would close the one avenue of escape.

Two of the rustlers were far in advance, out of rifle range. The two behind them, goading their horses, tried to increase the distance between them and their relentless pursuers. Brazos was in the lead, reloading his rifle. Santone came next and his rifle was puffing blue clouds of smoke. The other riders, scattered in a line to the right, were firing at intervals. Suddenly the last rider swerved abruptly off the trail and tore across and down in a daring attempt to pass Brazos. Then began as thrilling a manhunt race as Britt had ever seen. Brazos headed to cut the rustler off before he gained the corner of the slope, some few hundred yards distant. The fugitive, desperately goading his horse, gained perceptibly. But he had farther to go. And Brazos had slowed. Perhaps he wanted to get his rifle fully reloaded. Certainly he did not choose to close in on the rustler, whose bullets were striking up dust beyond him. In a magnificent burst of speed, slanting down the slope, the rustler passed Brazos out upon the flat. But he had not reckoned upon what the crafty cowboy had counted upon. Once on a level, straight in front, the rustler had no hope for his life. He was now reloading. Still at two hundred yards Brazos withheld his fire. The white racer stretched lower, to close up that gap as if by magic. And then as the rustler turned again in his saddle, his arm high, his gun spouting red, Brazos bent his head over his levelled rifle. One blue puff of smoke — another — a third! The rustler pitched headlong out of his saddle, to be dragged by a stirrup at the heel of a terrified horse, to be torn loose by the grasping sage. Brazos kept on.

Britt's gaze came back to the draw, in time to see the rustler farthest behind shot off his horse. He flopped like a crippled rooster. He got up on one knee, and with levelled gun, faced his merciless pursuers. Even as his gun puffed smoke they mowed him down.

That left the two fugitives far up the draw, still goading their horses. When Santone slowed up on the trail, now getting too steep to run a horse, the rustlers did likewise. One of them kept shooting back down the draw. He handed one of his guns to his comrade who proceeded to load it. Santone's followers caught up with them. Brazos' piercing yell floated up from the flat. He put the white to a gallop until he reached the grade.

At this juncture Britt picked up the field-glass. In that hard grim moment he had no pity for these doomed men. They were some four or five hundred yards distant, and still below him. The trail ascended on the far side of this draw. Jackson would be hidden somewhere above.

Britt fixed the glass upon the two rustlers, and

brought them so close that it seemed he might touch them. The taller, a bare-headed, sallow, lead-faced ruffian he had seen in Slaughter's outfit. He mopped back his wet dishevelled hair with a bloody hand, still holding a gun and gazed down the slope, speaking to his companion, who on the instant handed him another weapon. He cocked and levelled it deliberately, to aim long, to fire down the draw. Dust puffed up right in front of the cowboys' horses. They made haste to spread; and harsh yells rang up from them. Britt did not recognize the second rustler. He was a matured grizzled man, his dark face sullenly vague under his black sombrero.

They pushed the dust- and lather-coated horses just to the point of stalling them on the trail. Loud curses pealed down upon their pursuers. Britt clearly saw the bulging jaw of the hatless one, the sombre hawk-head of the other. Then the silence split to the negro's bellow.

"Slow down — white trash!"

Britt's keen gaze, glued to the glass, saw the rustlers whirl with terrific start. Something checked their violence. Something like wind streaked the tall grass beyond them, to strike up dust. Then two Winchester shots pealed almost simultaneously. The rustlers fell together, one upon the other. And the spent horses drooped. Britt realized that he had been witness to an extraordinary sight — that of seeing the impact of two bullets upon grass and ground, after they had passed through the bodies of the men, and before he had heard the shots. Wheeling in grim amaze, Britt espied the little negro out in the open where undoubtedly he had stepped to confront his quarry.

CHAPTER 12

Spring rudely disrupted Holly Ripple's dream. All the long winter months she had been happy, free from the dream of rustler raids and cowboy fights, reading and dreaming in the big sunny living room, before an open fire of cedar logs, and on Saturday nights giving a little *fiesta* with music and dancing. Always she had contrived to see Frayne or to send him a note, and though he always made excuses, the love in her heart kept warm and sweet. He feared to be with her, and Holly feared to be with him, though she yearned for it.

Holly hated the snow, and she could not face the cold wind that whipped down from the heights. Wherefore in winter she could indulge in languishing dreams during her enforced idleness. Holly was ashamed of what she considered a weakness. Always she intended to grow hardy and strong like Ann Doane, to ride in any weather, to exercise the various accomplishments that she possessed, to learn what a pioneer wife should know. But she did not progress far that winter. She blamed it upon love.

The restlessness of spring pervaded her. When the snow melted off the knolls, and it felt good to walk out in sunny protected spots, when the dusty melees began again in the corrals, and the lean riders to sweep over the gray bleached flats, when caravans and stages, horses and cattle began to move, then Holly knew that the thrilling, disturbing, shocking range-life had again come into its own.

The killing of Doane opened Holly's eyes to the true state of affairs on that range. Not right but might was the law of the unscrupulous, and its exponent was the six-shooter. If her father had lived on to this period he might have been as helpless before such a ruthless creed as had been Doane. Britt blamed Doane for talking too much. It came to light after this tragedy that Doane's stock had entirely vanished from the range, and his son and daughter were left in poverty. Holly sent for them. They arrived one day with a wagonload of possessions, and the few horses that had been left them. Joe took up his abode with the cowboys, who welcomed him heartily. Young Doane was no detriment even to the hard-riding Ripple outfit. Ann went up to the big ranch-house to live with Holly.

All the cowboys. especially Skylark, approved of this arrangement, and only Britt demurred. The reason for this, Holly divined, was that Britt would find it harder to keep her in the dark as to what was going on. Ann Doane was younger than Holly in years, but appeared far older. She had been born in a prairie-schooner crossing the plains; she had only the teaching her mother had given her as a child; she was a comely, rose-cheeked, stalwart girl who could ride like a cowboy, throw a rope, and who had at the calloused fingertips of her strong brown hands all the skill of the pioneer girl. And she was as strong in character as she was in body. She was frank, droll, simple, big hearted and wise in the ways of the range. She was Western.

Very soon after Ann arrived Skylark voiced the desire of his heart. He wanted to marry her at once. Ann was willing, though she felt that she ought to wait until a little after her father's death. There was an empty log cabin which could be fixed up comfortably.

"You see, Holly, it's this way," pleaded the tall cowboy. "Ann an' me might as well have each other while we can."

"Meaning what, you persuasive devil?" inquired Holly, dubiously.

"I'm liable to get shot any day," returned Skylark, bluntly.

"Oh, dreadful! — Such an argument for marriage! — You are not going to get anything of the kind."

"Lady, some of us boys will get it this summer — an' it might be me," said Skylark, with the cool inevitableness of his kind, which always stilled Holly's protests.

"Sky, marry Ann whenever she says," replied Holly. "I'll do all I can to start you comfortably."

Whereupon Skylark ran off with a glad whoop, evidently sure of Ann's surrender. She did set a day, not very distant one; then naturally, she grew absorbed in the important details of making a bare log cabin habitable for housekeeping. Holly fell into the spell of this, and helped so much and gave so much that Ann protested.

"Holly, it's shore awful good of you. But I just can't take any more. Save somethin' for yourself."

"Me! — Oh, nonsense," exclaimed Holly, with a blush.

"You'll be gettin' married one of these days."

"Ann, a girl has to be asked," retorted Holly, lightly.

"Holly Ripple! You can't be serious. . . . An' you ought. This marryin' business is serious out heah."

"I'm serious, Ann."

"Thet *is* nonsense. Everybody on this range knows all the single boys an' some of the married men have tried to court you. Didn't my man?"

"You mean Skylark? — No indeed. Sky liked me. He tried to —"

"Wal, Sky told me so himself," interrupted Ann, in her appallingly blunt way. "It's all right. I couldn't be jealous of you. All the boys love you. . . . Holly, ain't you ever goin' to love one of them back?"

"Dear me, I hope so," murmured Holly.

"Wal, you'll just have to. A girl can't go single on this range. It ain't good. It ain't right. . . . These pore, lonely, woman-hungry men! They all need an' want a woman. An' just think, Holly, outside of you an' me there's only five other unmarried white girls in eastern New Mexico. An' hundreds of cowboys. Not quite enough to go round."

"Ann, you make it look terrible. Poor boys."

"How about Brazos, Holly? There's a fellow! — I was crazy over Brazos."

"He's wonderful. I — I like him, Ann. But that's not enough."

"I heah a lot aboot this Renn Frayne," went on Ann, complacently. "Talk goes thet he's turrible sweet on you. Is it so, Holly?"

"He never — told me," faltered Holly, wanting the floor to open and swallow her. Yet she knew this honest Western girl would be good for her.

"Do you like him, too?"

"Yes, indeed."

"He's a man, Holly, no young wild cowboy! — Wonderful lookin' chap. Kinda sad, I thought. I'd hate to have him shine up to me, Skylark or no Skylark. His gun record wouldn't phase me. Dad told me all thet's said aboot Frayne. . . . Holly, out heah you can't afford to be particular. If you are goin' to live in the West you've got to take the West. I know Westerners. Most of them at some time or other weren't so damn good. My Dad rustled calves when he first started in. Yet he shot a man once who stole from him. An' Sky has confessed some pretty bad jobs of his. . . . Holly, you're young, you're rich, you're beautiful, an' everybody loves you. But where are you gettin' with it all?"

"Nowhere, Ann."

"Wal, I say thet's too darn bad. I'm going to

talk to some of these cowboys."

"Don't you dare, Ann Doane."

"I'm goin' to tell thet handsome hombre Frayne somethin'."

"Oh, Ann — please don't," cried Holly, wildly, her dignity dissolving.

"Holly! You shore must like him a lot," rejoined the Western girl, shrewdly. "Wal, in thet case I'll lay off Frayne. But somethin' has got to be done aboot you. I'm shore glad I've come to live at Don Carlos' Rancho."

Holly escaped somehow, but that talk with the Western girl, coupled with all the preparations for the wedding and the furnishing of the little cabin, awakened Holly to her own outcast and deplorable state. She made the discovery that she longed for this very thing herself. It was not that she desired marriage so much: she wanted to be Frayne's wife. She had dreamed of him all winter; she had been happy because he really loved her, and some day it would all work out beautifully. But now something stirred her sluggish blood. If she could have changed places with Ann Doane, provided Skylark were Frayne, she would have given money, jewels, all the old Spanish lace, her ranch and her cattle, just for that cosy little log cabin.

So the old haunting distemper again laid its hold upon Holly's heart. She had been living in a girl's romantic dreamland. Nine years of books, of gentle women, of garden walls, of isolation and protection had ill-fitted her for her part on this hard range. She would have to fight. She had been happy because she had denied realities. She was madly in love with an outlaw who had reformed, but whose fine instincts refused to lay the dishonor of his past upon her. Holly no longer cared what Renn Frayne had been. She wanted his sad, bitter, hard lips to soften to her kisses. Yet her respect for him increased in proportion to his restraint, his strength, his loyalty; and all that mad scheme of coquetry, of stooping to the allurements of Conchita, was as if it had never been.

Ann Doane's wedding day came all too soon. Holly had found the preparations, the interest, the excitement, the companionship of the girl, strangely stimulating. Ann was married in the Ripple living room by the *padre* of the village. Holly gave the bride and groom a *fiesta,* at which only a few of the cowboys could be in attendance. Britt was evasive and aloof. Trouble out on the range! But the event was a happy one for Skylark and Ann. Only after they had gone, and Holly was left alone, did the blank abrupt break seem unendurable.

That night Holly heard the cowboys making the welkin ring around the cabin of the newly wedded pair. Not till morning did these antics cease. But the next day Skylark went back to riding the range and Ann took up the manifold duties of a young housekeeper. Only for Holly was there an emptiness, a desolation, a complexity far removed from the simple happiness of the Western couple.

It seemed to Holly that self-preservation lay in a reversion to the ambition of the preceding summer — to take up her father's work and learn it, to be not only mistress of Don Carlos' Rancho but a worthy daughter of a plain cattleman. Britt had not aided her in this laudable desire, nor had Frayne. Even Brazos, than whom no cowboy could be more ruthlessly frank, had become evasive and elusive. They had sought to spare her the sordid and distressing details of range life. Holly rebelled against this, and especially against the truth she forced from herself — that she had been too soft, too aristocratic, too gentle and girlish to stand up under the hard knocks of the frontier. She admitted it. She scorned it. Her father had been mostly to blame. In his strange need to educate the Spanish out of her he had kept her away from the West, at the formative time of youth and adolescence. And now she was neither Spanish nor Western, nor Southern, nor anything but a highly sensitive, passionate young woman, terribly in love, and despairing of the future.

But Holly did not now torture herself long with indecision. Her spirit rose in revolt, not against the times, nor the trick fate and love had played her, but against that in her which was not of the West. She would know it, she would do battle with it, she would conquer it. Wherefore she magnified all the prophecies Buff Belmet and Britt had ever uttered, and steeled herself against the invisible. But it was that invisible which tortured Holly. She had imagination; she was ignorant, however, of range tendencies, complexities, possibilities. How could she be otherwise when her foreman, her cowboys, when even the man she adored turned his back upon her, and no one would explain and teach her the things she needed to know? Holly forgave them, for they were indeed the knights of the range. She made a resolution, however, that she would be less of a queen and more of a woman.

Holly went out into the spring sunshine. She rode. She walked. Britt stormed at her, and she obeyed. Brazos swore at her, and she listened. Frayne transfixed her with his piercing eyes, and she smiled. The wind stung her white cheeks; the dust choked her, the chill penetrated through her fleece-lined coat. She often stayed hours with Ann and learned to cook, to bake, to sew. She made friends with Conchita and learned much beside gossip from that range belle. She frequented the trading-post to converse with traders, soldiers, Indians, Mexicans, strangers — with any and everyone she met. She went often to the bunk-house, and the cowboys began to look forward to her coming. They betrayed their solicitude. They did not understand, but they felt, they saw the change in her. Yet, of them all, Ride-'Em Jackson was the only one who did not evade her, deceive her. The negro was as simple as a child and he could not lie to her. Holly came to know why Britt or Brazos or Jim always sauntered near when she talked with Jackson. They were aligned against her. They would die for her, but refused to sicken her or blanch her cheek with the truth.

But soon it dawned upon Holly that no one of them, not even Frayne, nor all of them put together, could be a match for her. She was a woman. Her intuitive powers transcended their cunning. And their vulnerable spot was their devotion to her.

Doane's death, apparently, was the forerunner of untoward events out on the range. Holly got an inkling of some fracas that had happened at Gray Hill. Cherokee had been severely wounded out there. But he did not go to bed. Gunshots were nothing to the Indian. He stayed home, somber, brooding, silent, an enigma to Holly, except that she sensed he had the savage's creed of an eye for an eye. Britt seldom ran up to the ranchhouse these spring days. He was a troubled, dark-browed man who adopted a cheerful mask the moment he espied her. Brazos drank hard, but at length, at Holly's earnest importunity, he promised to stop, and kept his promise. It was noticeable that Frayne seldom stayed away over night from the rancho. The cattle, at least thirty thousand head or more, which now constituted two-thirds of the Ripple herd, could be seen in the valley from the hilltop. Brazos and the half-breeds, with Jackson, Flinty and Stinger, rode hard and late, seldom getting back until long after dark, and often staying out all night. But there were no more extended stays away from the ranch. Jim, Gaines, Tennessee, Doane, Rebel, and Frayne patrolled the lower end of the triangle of range that led into the pass. Holly saw them often with her field-glass, riding often, always watching, watching from some height. When she missed Tennessee for several days she had her doubts but kept them to herself. He never came back. And she discovered for a certainty that Stinger nursed a crippled leg, which, when she inquired, he said had been hurt in a fall. But Holly's learning eyes detected a bullet-hole in his chaps.

These were alarming signs, and as the spring days warmed into early summer, they increased. Mex Southard returned one day alone, severely wounded. He had almost bled to death. When Holly saw him, two days later, he was recovering. She did not even attempt to make him talk. A day later, when the outfit got back, Flinty was missing from the ranks.

"Am I losing any cattle?" asked Holly once, casually, of Brazos.

"Yu air not," he drawled, with his old cool smile. "But thet's aboot all yu're not losin'."

"Brazos, you know I prefer to lose my cattle to my cowboys."

"Aw, what's a cowboy now an' then?"

Ann was Holly's greatest source of information. She was not one of the reticent Western girls; she liked gossip; and would linger at the post or the store, or when the stage came in. Outside news did not concern Holly, or she would have added immeasurably to her burden. The Lincoln County War was on, threatening to involve eastern New Mexico in its turmoil. Chisum was not mixed up in that, but the several bands of desperados who were had been stealing his cattle, and he had declared war to the hilt against rustlers. Bandits were

313

operating between Santa Fe and Las Animas.

These items were interesting, but not so thought-provoking as the news of a cattlemen's organization, headed by Sewall McCoy, to protect themselves against cattle thieves. To Holly, who shared Britt's opinion of McCoy, this seemed far-fetched and was very probably merely rumor. But the Western girl had a different point of view.

"Dad was in thet move," she said, "an' he knowed, along with all the ranchers, there was a nigger in the woodpile somewhere. There's bands of rustlers wal known. An' there must be others — one big outfit anyhow — thet only themselves know. Dad's suspicion of McCoy cost him his life. He oughtn't to have spoken out like thet. But Dad was always talkin', an' if he had a drink or two he was loco. People say thet McCoy ain't the man at the head of this secret combine, 'cause if he was he'd not have shot Dad at the drop of a hat. But somebody is. An' thet's what makes the hell. All the cattlemen suspect each other an' are afraid to say so. They'll take it out on some poor cowboys, Skylark says. An' they might be in the Ripple outfit."

"Oh, Ann — impossible!" ejaculated Holly, aghast.

"Wal, Talman an' Trinidad showed yellow, didn't they? An' Dillon before them. No other outfit on the range has thet bad a record. I tell you, Sky is worried. An' he says Britt doesn't sleep at nights."

"But that must be because they are fighting to

save my cattle," protested Holly.

"Mebbe. But not all. What's a few cattle? They don't even know how many you got. They can't count them. You're runnin' too many fer these times."

"That's true. I'd sell half of my stock, and more, if they could be driven to the railroad. But Britt dare not take riders away from here for the drive. It is a dreadful situation, Ann."

"Don't you let it upset you, Holly," rejoined the Western girl. "We women have just got to stand it. An' not let the men know how we feel. Skylark says to me, 'How'n hell can Brazos or Frayne go out an' meet this killer Rankin, when if either of them was bad hurt it'd aboot kill Holly?' "

Holly's heart contracted in her breast.

"Who's Rankin?"

"Jeff Rankin, late of them bad Kansas cattle towns. I seen him the day McCoy shot Dad. A little tan-faced man with eyes like a weasel. You feel queer when he looks at you. I'll always remember him because he told McCoy to wait an' give Dad the benefit of a doubt. But McCoy was full of red-eye an' wild to kill somebody."

"Horrible! — This Rankin. . . . Who is he?"

"Just another bad hombre, only worse. They say he has killed a dozen men. No quiet, sober gunman, like the real ones, but a quarrelsome, ugly, blood-huntin' desperado, quick as lightnin' on the draw, an' a dead shot."

"Why is this Rankin mentioned particularly in

connection with Brazos — and Frayne?"

"Wal, they say Rankin an' Frayne clashed back in Kansas — thet Frayne killed Rankin's pard. Anyway it's common talk in town thet Rankin is lookin' for Frayne."

"Yes? And where does Brazos come in?" asked Holly, strangely disturbed by a totally unknown hot beat and swell along her veins.

"Sky says it's none of Brazos' mix. But Brazos will take up any cowboy's quarrel. An' since Laigs Mason is gone he has cottoned to Frayne. . . . Somethin' will come of it."

"Oh dear! . . . Ann, can't these — these terrible things be avoided?"

"When I was twelve my mother told me Dad had wronged some man somehow or other. An' this man dared Dad to come out to fight. Wal, mother wouldn't let Dad go. An' do you know, Holly, thet ruined Dad with his friends an' neighbors, an' he had to clear out. It was at some fort in Kansas where Dad worked, durin' the war. We moved farther west an' since then I've seen a heap of frontier where men count for what they are."

"If one man is called out by another — to fight — whether it's justifiable or not, he must go or be branded a coward?"

"Thet's it, Holly. An' it's unfair, to my thinkin'. Because a bad man can force a good one to meet him. The moral of it doesn't seem to be considered. Every man has to defend himself with a gun, an' if he can't, he just doesn't belong to the West. Thet applies to all plain Westerners. But it shore

316

applies more to them who have killed others. It's a kind of hideous curiosity. On the part of the fighters to see who can draw quickest! On the part of the crowd to see who gets killed first!"

"So I have to live through that?" queried Holly.

"Wal, dear, it won't be so bad so long as you don't love one of them," declared Ann, with a laugh.

"But suppose I did?"

"What?"

"Why — why love one of them?" Holly faltered.

"Well, you'd have to pray awful hard thet your man beat the other to his gun. . . . There was a girl over here in Roswell who loved both men. They fought over her an' it ended bad."

"What happened?"

"They killed each other, an' she had to go back to an old beau — a no-good cowboy — an' marry him."

"How very sad!" murmured Holly, constrainedly, wanting both to scream and laugh. It was evident that this matter-of-fact Ann would never have understood her poignant agony. Would she be compelled to suffer such suspense — to wait — wait — wait! to see if Renn came home. Worse, she might be with him when this ruffian Rankin contrived to bring about a meeting. These men did not think about women, love, home, children, happiness. The West was in the making. Holly had always to come back to her share in this profound epic — to stifle the cries of her soul and fight to be strong like Ann Doane. But she could not do it. And thinking, pondering, brooding she felt a birth in her of anger at the times, at the men who tortured her.

Holly was haunted by this thing. She vacillated between despair and a dawning strength. She would never wholly conquer her sensitive, poignant emotions, and she could conceive of a West too hard, too unendurable for her if it robbed her of love. But this growing shadow only increased her love — only added fuel to the fire — only brought out her infinite capacity for tenderness and passion. The life of the range out there struck at her heart. Holly awaited something, a trial, the very suggestion of which blanched her cheeks and sent the blood curdling back from her cold skin.

Holly awoke under a strange boding spell. It was not depression, nor the aftereffect of a dreadful dream. She had not before borne the weight of such an inexplicable consciousness, though she had often labored under what her cowboys called "hunches." This was a strong apprehension of an untoward fatality and she could not drive it away.

May with its wind and dust, in melting snows, had passed into June. The golden light that filtered through the foliage over her windows proclaimed the approach of summer. Holly got up and into her riding garb. She had not been on a horse for days, and the reason was because Britt would not allow her to ride out upon the range. But she concluded it would be better to ride up and down the lane rather than not at all. Her Mexican servants were as cheerful and complaisant as usual. Roseta had been down to the village the night before, and prattled of the commonplace happenings. After breakfast, as was her habit, Holly went out on the porch with her field-glass to survey the range. This habit had become fraught with uncertainty and suspense, almost as painful as had been her daily watch for the return of her cowboys from Las Animas. She dreaded to search the wide expanse of grassland for her riders, for there was no telling what they might be engaged in these days.

Far out along the Cottonwood Trail she espied a string of riders coming. That would be Brazos and the outfit with which Britt had been combing the range of late. Not so many riders as usual! They were driving a number of unsaddled stock ahead, probably the *remuda*. She caught a gleam of bobbing packs. The dust clouds rather disputed a leisurely return. These days the cowboys were always in a hurry.

Britt had expected Brazos back and had not been able to hide his concern from Holly. In fact Britt had not been up to see her in the last forty-eight hours, an omission that seemed far from reassuring. Frayne had become more elusive than ever.

Holly reflected on these matters while she slowly moved the glass from the incoming riders along the widening strip of range between the hills and the creek. Cattle blackened the range in spots, and speckled it in others. The cottonwoods were in full foliage, green and beautiful against the gray background. She searched the range beyond the stream as far as San Marcos, shining brightly in the June sunlight, without finding any more riders. Frayne and the cowboys on duty near the rancho could usually be picked up of a morning. But the purple and gray levels out there did not reward Holly's anxious survey. A film of dust, however, hazed her clear vision, and this made her aware that there was movement of cattle or riders closer in to the ranch.

All at once the circle of Holly's glass was filled by a compact group of horsemen. They were on the San Marcos road scarcely a mile from the corrals. Holly looked again, suddenly struck by surprise and dread. These were not cowboys. They did not have that free, easy, graceful look so characteristic of her riders.

"I wonder who they are," she soliloquized, and thought of the bands of rustlers known to ride often in the open. Holly had seen more than one group of that kind. These horsemen gave her the impression of being ranchers and cattlemen on some businesslike errand to the trading-post or the village, possibly her ranch. She left the glass on the porch and faced down the hill in search of Britt, revolving in mind disturbing contingencies.

On the way down the brush and trees obscured view of the range, and when she reached the open she was on a level. In the immediate foreground stood the long bunkhouse, with its adjoining mess-hall and kitchen, Skylark's cabin and several adobe shacks, beyond which Holly could not see.

"Britt," she called anxiously, as she mounted the porch. He did not answer. Holly knocked at the open door. The bunkhouse was empty. She went through to the kitchen, expecting surely to find Jose, but he was gone also.

Holly hurried along the lane toward Skylark's cabin. Ann was never anywhere but home. To Holly's amazement, however, she found the door open, Ann's apron laying upon the threshold, where she had evidently hurriedly flung it. Immediately then Holly connected Britt's absence, and Ann's as well, with that visiting band of horsemen. The road, which was the Old Trail, led between the pastures and the ranch-barns.

The lane appeared long and dusty, and empty. Corral after corral lined the range side, all opening into the big stockyard. On Holly's left towered a dusty green hedge-fence. Inside the irrigation ditch babbled and gurgled on its way like a brook, to pour presently into the high-banked, willow-bordered pool. Ducks and geese swam and squawked in the amber sunlight; blackbirds shone black against the green foliage. The bray of burros, whistle and trample of colts, the bawling of calves, added further to the sense of pastoral ranch life.

Holly reached the last corral on the lane. She heard harsh voices of men, but could not distinguish words. The huge barn loomed above the fence. Holly halted with her hand pressed to her breast. This did not seem a procedure to alarm her prodigiously, yet it did. What if that band of

321

horsemen had not gone on to the post? But where were her riders? What had become of Frayne? And the answer to both was that they were here.

She peeped around the corner of the corral, into the wide court. A score of saddle horses! Holly saw several she thought she recognized. Riders in the road! Men in a circle on the long slant that led up to the wide door! Dark forms outlined against the sunlight beyond the wide floor-space between the walls! She saw women, too.

Holly turned back to run into the open gate of the corral. She followed the fence of peeled poles along toward the barn, past the horses, beyond the groups of riders, as far as she could go. There in the corner she gazed between the fence-poles. Her position was parallel to the line of riders on the runway up to the barn. The great doors had been rolled back on each side.

Britt, bare-headed, his face troubled and dark, paced the entrance to the barn. Frayne occupied the center place. Havoc lined his pale stern features. His eyes appeared to be gray blanks, peering over Britt's head, up at the ranchhouse. Back of Frayne to the left stood grim cattlemen Holly recognized with augmenting fear. But when she swept her gaze to the opposite side and saw Sewall McCoy, heavy-jowled, lowering of face, standing before some cowboys, panic gripped her with petrific power.

"—— ootrage!" Britt cursed fiercely. "I'm tellin' you, Clements. You've been fooled by this slick hombre."

"Thet remains to be seen," declared Clements, a grizzled cattleman, rugged of feature. "We're all gettin' fooled by somebody, thet's shore. Hayward hyar disliked this job as much as me. But we had to organize. McCoy has proof thet three of your riders was crooked. Dillon, Talman an' a cowboy called Trinidad. You don't deny thet, Britt."

"Hellno! I cain't 'cause it was true," retorted Britt, spitting as if he had hot ashes in his mouth. "They're daid, aren't they? Wal, who visited thet crime on their haids? My men! An' they were the last of crooked cowboys in my ootfit."

"Thet's what you think, Britt," spoke up Hayward, a tall, sallow, sharp-eyed rancher. "But you was fooled three times, an' you can be again. McCoy swears he'll prove it."

"We'll show proofs, soon as Slaughter gets here," declared McCoy, loud-voiced and aggressively important. "He an' his outfit ought to be here now."

"By Gawd, he'll *have* to prove it!" hissed Britt. "Listen, Hayward, an' you Spencer, an' you Clements. Cain't you see this means a range war?"

"No, I can't," protested Hayward, testily. "We're not goin' to be drawn into thet Lincoln County mess."

"You'll make a mess of our own, right heah."

"Britt, for an old Texas Ranger you're not showin' much sense," declared Spencer, a short, thickset, bearded man. "Didn't Ripple want you to collect the toughest outfit of cowboys in this hyar whole country?"

"Yes, he did."

"Wal, haven't you got it?"

"You bet yore life I hev," flashed Britt. "An' thet's why I tell you McCoy is skatin' on the thinnest kind of ice. An' if you back him up in this ootrageous deal *you'll* all be —"

"—— it, Britt, this man is an outlaw!" interrupted Hayward, angrily.

"He was, yes. But not heah. Not in New Mexico. He's as honest as I am — an' a damn sight squarer an' finer than any one of you."

"Britt, is it an insult or a threat you're givin' us?" demanded Hayward.

"Both!"

Clements and Spencer shifted uneasily. Britt's passion had told upon them. Hayward appeared to dominate the trio.

"Men," interposed McCoy, insolently, "you're wastin' a lot of breath. This deal is up to Frayne."

That stung Britt as the lash of a whip.

"Shore, you —— lyin' schemer! You play both ends against the middle. Two chances of gettin' rid of the man you hate — the man you fear! You egg on thet gun-slinger Rankin to call Frayne oot. An' thet fails — as shore as death it will fail — you'll throw yore hatched deal on the table. Accuse Frayne of stealin' Holly Ripple's cattle! . . . Gawd Almighty, man, I wouldn't be in yore boots fer a million!"

McCoy grew red and furious under the Texan's piercing tirade.

"Britt, you're a hell of a talker. But this deal is up to Frayne. He has been given two choices. He can meet Rankin, who's over there at the post waitin', an' if he kills him, he can face our proofs of his rustlin'. Or he can fork his hoss an' leave the country."

"Renn Frayne will never leave heah," replied Britt, white-faced with resigned finality, and he turned to Frayne.

"Cap, I've known all along I'd have to meet Rankin," said Frayne, calmly. "I'll do it now. Afterwards. . . ."

Holly's paralyzing emotions gave way to a terror that released her. She slipped through the poles of the fence. She ran up the slant. Ann's scream and the cowboys' excited shouts only lent wings to her feet. Frayne wheeled to see her. The marble relentlessness of his face changed to living color.

"Renn!" cried Holly, wildly, and flung her arms around his neck. A madness possessed her. It was as if the agony of loss had fallen upon her even as she enveloped his flesh with all of mortal passion. "Renn! . . . You can't go! — I love you! . . . I'd die if — if . . . Come. . . . Take me away — from this horrible West. . . . I'll go to the end of the world — with you!"

Frayne clasped her close, drawing her head to his breast, and bent over her. "You poor child! — Oh, Holly, I tried to spare you this."

His look, his sudden powerful embrace, the great

lift of his heart against her bosom, his tender sorrowful words — these seemed to pierce and burn into the very core of Holly's being. He was hers. He loved her. In a rapture that bordered upon loss of consciousness Holly quivered there in his arms. A tremendous storm seemed gathering within her — a whirling maelstrom of thought which love kept from bursting. Then she heard Frayne's voice, as if far away.

"Gentlemen, I shall not meet Rankin. . . . As for McCoy's charge — I am innocent. I demand a fair trial."

Holly's stunned faculties suddenly split like a cloud riven by lightning. Shame leaped with a bursting gush of hot blood. This was the crucial moment toward which she had been cruelly dragged through endless days and nights, cast into the depths and anon lifted up.

"Oh, Renn," she cried, drawing away, "what is it that I have done?"

CHAPTER 13

Britt broke out of his stupefaction to approach them. What indeed had Holly done? Saved or wrecked Frayne! But like the true wonderful girl of generous heart she was she had showed the range what Renn Frayne meant to her.

"Holly, this heah is a man's deal," spoke up Britt, huskily, as he reached her. "You leave it to —"

She silenced him with a flash of her hand.

"Forgive me, Renn," she implored, gazing up at him entreatingly. "I was beside myself. I understand now. . . . I beg of you don't let me — or my love — hamper you in the least. I trust you. I *know* you. . . . Meet these men — as if you had never seen me."

"Holly," he choked, as the slackness, the softness passed out of him. For this girl he would have foresworn the hard manhood of the West, and have accepted a stigma without shame and without bitterness. But he could not speak a word of the passion that consumed him.

Holly, still clinging to Frayne's hand, turned to the gaping cattlemen. Britt stared spellbound. Her loveliness, her race had never shone as then. Out of her proud white face blazed eyes so great, so

327

black, so magnificent that they appeared more than human, flames of a spirit stronger than terror or death.

"Hayward, and all of you, listen. . . . Renn Frayne has been hounded for years by such men as this Rankin. It made him an outlaw. I doubt if he has ever been really bad. But that would not matter to me, since *now* he is honest. I love him and I am going to marry him. Weigh well your antagonism in this hour. We will never forgive more of your biased opinions. Don Carlos' Rancho stands or falls by this man. . . . Sewall McCoy is a contemptible dog. He wanted to marry me. He threatened me with an alliance with Russ Slaughter *if* I refused him. This trumped-up charge against Frayne is not only prompted by jealousy and revenge, but by fear! He is afraid of Frayne. Because, gentlemen, McCoy is the dark horse in this range mystery. *He* is the rustler baron."

"You white-faced, half-breed slut," burst out McCoy, in ungovernable rage.

"Silence!" yelled Britt, leaping out to crouch. "Another word an' I'll kill you! — You dealt this deal. Now, by Gawd, you'll play oot yore hand."

"Hold, Britt! — Steady now," shouted Clements, plainly alive to an unexpected development in the situation. "We'll all play out our hands in this game. . . . Miss Ripple, you use strong words. We can make allowance for your — your — for a most tryin' ordeal. But unless you are beside yourself with fury — you will be called on to prove —"

"Clements," interrupted Holly, "you are hopelessly in the toils of this rustler who *hires* poor cowboys to steal for him. . . . Do you think that *I* would lie? Mr. Clements, I have no doubt that in less than an hour you will be put to the painful ordeal of explaining *your* connection with Sewall McCoy."

"Thet'll do, Holly," spoke up Britt, on edge with the prolongation of this scene. "Go home. . . . Ann, take Holly home."

Ann came forward hastily while Holly turned to Frayne.

"Renn, I'll expect you up at the house soon," she said, coolly, with dark proud eyes upon him. Frayne could not answer. Then as Ann led Holly out of the barn door they were confronted by a tall cowboy.

"Brazos!" cried Holly, in amazement and gladness. "Where have you been?"

"Heah," he rang out.

"Since when? Did you —"

Britt moved to get a good look at Brazos, and did not marvel that Holly faltered.

"I rid in ahaid of the ootfit. Seen yu. An' I follered yu. I been heah all the time."

"Oh, I'm so — so glad," returned Holly, hurriedly, strangely faltering. Did she take Brazos' white face and terrible eyes as indications of unutterable reproach? Britt did not so interpret Brazos' mien. There had been hell to pay out there on the range and would be more here. Ann led Holly away with the other girls, who were Mexicans.

"Renn, I'll go with yu," drawled Brazos. "I shore want to see you bore thet —— beady-eyed little cockroach!"

"You stay heah, Brazos," ordered Britt. "Don't let a single man leave this barn."

"Britt, I'll see to thet," spoke up Clements, darkly. "Reckon I'd like to see Frayne come back. Otherwise we might never find out who this shady rustler is. Haw! Haw!"

"Thet'll do, Clements," yelled Brazos. "Yu'll hev hell swallerin' what yu've said already. Yu're on the wrong side, as yu'll larn damn pronto."

Britt had to run to keep up with Frayne's swift strides, and as he kept pace with the outlaw, he revolved in mind a few pertinent things to say.

"Renn, put Holly oot of yore mind," was the first one.

"No, by God! Do you think any man could beat me to a gun when I remember how she looked — what she said?"

"Wal, I reckon not. . . . Loosen yore belt a little. . . . An' roll thet gun a few times. . . . Ah-huh. An' stick it back sorta light, so it'll come oot quicker'n greased lightnin'. . . . Will this Rankin expect you?"

"Hardly. He's got me wrong. I could have killed him back in Kansas, but I let him bluff me. He was half drunk. McCoy, of course, has his axe to grind and has helped Rankin along in his figuring me. McCoy has reason to know me. But he thinks Holly has made me a four-flush!"

"Wal, I'm damn glad there's goin' to be some action. I'm shore seein' red. An' say, wasn't Holly jest grand? Did she lay it into Clements an' McCoy? Whew! . . . Renn, hev you been practicin' lately?"

"Day and night, Old Timer. I saw this coming."

"You'll hev to marry Holly now."

"Heavens yes!" Frayne threw up his head in exultation. "She disgraced herself — ruined herself! Before them all! — For me! O God, if I could only have gone away!"

"Shore, if you could hev," agreed the wily Britt. "As it is, though, you've got to stay heah an' prove Holly wasn't lyin. . . . An' think, Renn, pretty pronto, when this mess is over you'll be goin' up to the house to see her. An' Holly will be waitin' — all alone. Withoot any pryin' eyes aboot. She was only a tortured girl, fust off, back there at the barn, an' then when thet rotten ootfit made her mad, she was a queen. But, cowboy, this next time you meet her! All thet beauty! All thet blazin' fire — thet sweet love which can never get enough of you — all in yore arms! — Gawd, boy, do you know yore good fortune?"

"Yes, Cap, I know it. No man on earth could know so well!"

"Renn, is this Rankin the real thing?"

"Mean. A scaly rattlesnake. Dangerous if he gets the drop. That's all."

They reached the village. Frayne slowed his stride and kept to the middle of the road. A Mexican in a big straw sombrero passed carrying two pails of water, suspended from a pole across his

331

shoulders. Some Indians lounged in front of the post. Two dusty horses stood haltered to the hitching-rail opposite the entrance to the saloon. For the rest the wide street appeared deserted. Britt saw the crudely painted Mexican designs upon the white-washed adobe walls.

Frayne squared himself before the stained wooden doors, then with a powerful thrust opened them to leap inside. Britt popped in as quickly and sheered to one side. The big saloon smelled of stale rum. Britt's flashing eye gathered in four men before he came to the little man he knew was Rankin. Mean! A scaly rattlesnake! He stood with his back to the bar, his arms stretched along its edge, a position no great gunman would ever have risked while expecting a meeting with a foe.

Britt saw him stiffen in that position. A sombrero shaded his eyes, and that was a circumstance against Frayne, if he needed to read his adversary's intent. But Frayne did not require that. Britt knew that the instant either of Rankin's outstretched hands moved Frayne would be drawing.

The only movement in the saloon was a quick swerve of the bartender to dodge out of line and then run to the far end of the bar.

"Rankin," called Frayne, in cold expectation.

"Howdy. Who air you?" rejoined the other, gruffly.

"You know me. Frayne."

"Aho. . . . Frayne, eh? — Wal, I kind of give you up. Fact is I didn't expect you much. . . .

Wanta tip a bottle with me?"

"No."

"I see. Heerd you'd sworn off drinkin'. — Air yu thinkin' of ridin' away from Don Carlos' Rancho?"

"No."

"Stayin' on, huh?"

"Yes."

"Wal, didn't Hayward invite you to leave the country?"

"He did."

"An' didn't McCoy tell you thet I said fer you to get out?"

"Yes. That's why I'm here."

"Frayne, I'll give you till sundown to leave this range," yelled Rankin, stridently. Anger had succeeded to surprise, but there was no sign of fear in the man. He had grown cunningly conservant of action, increasingly taut of frame. His right hand began to quiver.

"Did I leave Dodge after I shot your stick-fingered pard?" taunted Frayne.

Rankin was game, but he betrayed that he had gotten himself not only into a disadvantageous posture, but into the certainty that he had to meet Frayne alone. Nevertheless he accepted it. He actually bristled. Britt saw his sombrero rise slightly above his opaque formidable eyes. Swift as light then all his frame jerked in downward action.

Frayne's draw was too quick for Britt's sight. But he saw the red spurt — the black burst — then heard the boom.

Rankin's terrific violence sustained a sudden shock. He sagged inward against the bar. His head dropped so that the wide sombrero hid his face. And his hand fell away from his half-drawn gun. A groan rumbled out of him. He lodged there, a shrunken figure, strangely bereft of his sinister menace.

Britt was not loquacious on the march back to the barn. Nor did he allow either the raw gust of passion or the strong feeling of elation and relief to clog his thinking machine. The situation required more than he believed any one man could give it. Moreover he was not in a conciliatory mood. Brazos would run amuck. McCoy did not stand the slightest chance of getting away with his life. Obviously the thing to do was to establish proofs of Frayne's innocence and McCoy's guilt in front of those obsessed cattlemen, and then avoid a general pitched battle. This seemed unlikely. McCoy had a number of cowboys with him and there were half a dozen with the cattlemen. As Britt remembered it Holly's four remaining cowboys were Jim, Skylark, Stinger and Gaines. What had become of Joe Doane and Rebel?

"Frayne, do yu reckon it'll ever get as far as McCoy's charge against you?"

"Never. His trump card is Russ Slaughter. And I've a hunch Slaughter will never get here."

"Brazos!"

"Yes. He's got something up his sleeve."

"Look! — Down the lane! — Frayne, there's

the ootfit. Shore thet must be what makes Brazos so cocky."

"It's likely. Let's rustle along. They're coming at a trot, pack-horses an' all. They might start a fight pronto."

Britt jogged along behind Frayne. They cut short across the field to the barn, coming through the fence near the door. The relative positions of the several groups had not altered much. McCoy sat sullenly aside from his cowboys. The cattlemen ceased a colloquy at Frayne's sudden appearance on the runway. Britt whispered to Jim: "Get back an' be ready fer anythin'."

"Heah yu air, pard!" rang out Brazos, in his lusty piercing tenor. "These heah conscientious cowmen never expected yu back atall. But I knowed yu'd come."

McCoy rose to his feet, livid of face, beginning to manifest a subtle change of front. Brazos would have been disconcerting even to an honest man.

"Frayne, you backed out of meetin' him?" he queried, harshly.

The answer he got from Frayne was a piercing deadly stare. But Britt thought it well to launch a retort.

"McCoy, is yore beady-eyed gunslinger the best you can trot oot?"

"Dead?" gasped McCoy.

"Bored plumb center. Hell, he didn't have a chance."

Brazos reacted to that with a ringing laugh. He dominated the several groups, even Britt and

Frayne backing from his restless front. His gun swung low in its sheath. He had a second weapon stuck into the hip pocket of his jeans. Britt smelled gunpowder on him; then made the observation that his belt was half emptied of shells. All the characteristic red had faded from his face and his pallor enhanced the smear of blood under his clustering hair.

Clements coughed nervously and advanced a step.

"McCoy, press your charge now against Frayne, an' produce your proofs. This deal will begin to look queer if you don't."

"Queer eh?" sneered McCoy. "Look out how queer you make it. I told you Slaughter has the proofs."

"But you told us you knew them," protested Cements, dubiously.

"Will you stop raggin' me an' wait till Slaughter gets here?" yelled McCoy.

Brazos lead out in front of them all with a gun in each hand.

"Wal, here comes Slaughter. . . . Don't nobody move a finger. . . . Yu McCoy hombres, I got eyes in the back of my haid. Somebody is gonna get bored."

Britt saw Brazos' outfit turning from the lane into the barnyard. Jackson was on foot leading a pack-animal with what looked like a man hanging face and feet downward from the saddle. Santone, Cherokee, Tex and Mex Southard rode behind the little negro; and if ever Britt saw a quartet that

336

had been in a fight he saw it then. Black, ragged, dusty, bloody-scarfed, they resembled a crew of pirates. Behind rode Bluegrass, his face like a white splotch, reeling in his saddle.

When this procession neared the runway leading up to the barn door Britt's startled gaze confirmed the first glances at that object over Jackson's saddle. It was a dead man, whose blood dripped down upon the flopping hands that dragged in the dirt.

"Pile off, fellars," called Brazos. "An' come heah. . . . Jack, lead thet cayuse up."

The negro complied, Britt stared in sickening excitement. He could not see the head of the dead man, for that hung on the other side of the horse. But he knew who it was.

"Dump him off, Jack," ordered Brazos.

The negro laid hold of the man's hips and boosted him up so that he slid out of the saddle, to flop suddenly upon the barn floor, spattering blood in all directions. When the horse got out of line Britt confirmed his suspicion as to the dead man. Russ Slaughter presents a hideous spectacle.

"Look, all of yu," pealed the ruthless showman. "But keep back. Take a good look, yu cowboys an' cowmen, so yu'll see what can happen to a cattle-thief. . . . See! He's stretched hemp! — This rustlin' gentleman was shot fust, an' hanged alive, then pumped full of lead!"

In the horrified silence that transfixed the onlookers Brazos leaped over the dead man to align the ghastly McCoy with his several wooden-faced cowboys.

"Heah, McCoy, heah's yore Russ Slaughter,"
went on Brazos, his voice gaining the high-
tensioned ring of cold steel. "He had proofs. Aw,
he shore hed. But of yore rotten deals with
him! Russ must hev been a hombre who didn't
trust yu or his memory. He jotted down every
steer, every calf — every dollar. All in a little book.
An' I got thet book!"

Brazos grew terrible in his cold-blooded fury.
His young clear face had the look of an avenging
god.

"Thet'll be aboot all fer yu, McCoy," he hissed.
"Heah's fer yore insult to Holly Ripple!" One gun
crashed. McCoy, with an awful scream, spasmodically clapped his hands to his abdomen. "An'
heah's fer yore old grudge an' dirty deal to my
pard, Renn Frayne!" The second gun crashed.
McCoy sank behind the cloud of smoke. Brazos
leaped through that to present his smoking guns
at McCoy's men. "Get a move on. Pronto! If yu
ever meet a Ripple cowhand again go fer yore
guns!"

He drove them out of the barn.

"Watch 'em, boys. If they look back — shoot!"

Brazos wheeled to confront the cattlemen, of
whom Clements was the one most obviously
shaken. He quailed before the fire-eyed cowboy.

"Clements; —— yore yellow soul! I cain't be
certain aboot how crooked yu air. But yore name
is in Slaughter's book. Yu bought cattle of him.
How yu explain thet?"

"Unbranded stock, Keene — I swear to Gawd!"

gasped out the cattleman, ashen-hued behind his beard.

"Aw, yu lie! I can see it in yore eyes. An honest man has nothin' to fear. But yu ain't honest. Yu knowed McCoy was crooked."

"No — I swear — I didn't!"

"Wal, yu knowed Slaughter was. . . . Oot with thet before I bore yu."

"Yes — yes. . . . I knew it."

"An' yu bought Ripple stock from him?"

"I shet my eyes. . . . All unbranded calves — yearlings."

"Ah — huh. — Wal, I'll bore yu jest fer luck. . . . But if yu hadn't been mean in yore talk to Miss Ripple, I might hev let yu off."

"Oh my Gawd! — Keene — !"

Brazos' gun crash cut short that impassionate and desperate appeal.

"Rustle, yu conscientious cowmen, before I cut loose. An' in the act. We got McCoy comin' an' goin'. We hev written proofs. We hev Saunders' confession. Mill over thet, yu wise range galoots. . . . An' pack these daid hombres away on their hawses, onless yu want them throwed to the hawgs."

Half an hour later Brazos stepped to the side of a fresh mettlesome horse that Santone had fetched into the court. A light pack and a canteen were significantly bound upon the saddle. Brazos mounted with his slow inimitable grace.

"Whoa, Bounce, or I'll rake yu," he called, as

he pulled the big bay down with iron arm. "So long, Jim, Rebel — all yu sons-of-guns!"

They muttered a farewell that they neither sanctioned nor approved of. Their acquiescence had in it something of Brazos' detachment. Cowboys had to ride away. They bowed to the fate and the greatness of their comrade.

Britt and Frayne crowded close.

"Brazos, you don't hev to go," said Britt, huskily.

"Pard, the man confessed his guilt," protested Frayne. "Hayward, Spencer — all of us heard him."

Brazos lighted his cigarette, and flicking away the match he looked down with his slight enigmatical smile. His wonderful eyes lost their piercing blue hardness behind a shadow that might have been pain.

"Wal, I'm kinda tired of Don Carlos' Rancho," he drawled, in his slow cool speech. "Me fer the Pecos an' the Texas longhorns."

Britt was silent because he could not speak, while Frayne stared up with mute sorrow and a gathering, dark understanding in his gaze.

"Pard, do me a favor," went on Brazos, his lean hand going to Frayne's shoulder. "If yu — an' Holly ever hev a boy — call him Brazos."

Then, with a clink of spurs, and a clatter of hoofs, he was off, swift as the wind. They watched him cross the road and stretch out upon the gray range, headed for the pass, and the long, lonely trail to Texas.

Days passed. June warmed into July. Far and wide spread the fame of Holly Ripple's cowboys. Both factions in the Lincoln County War sought to win them to their side. A month of peace had lulled the riders back into their old lazy ways. They rode, they bet, they played tricks, they watched the cattle, they revelled in their dearly won independence and the respect and aloofness of the range.

Holly's birthday rolled around, and the event this year was to celebrate her wedding. Only the cowboys and her few neighbor friends were invited.

Britt, who felt himself responsible for this great and happy event, left the restless, primping, whispering cowboys to go up to the ranchhouse. There he found Holly radiant at the close of preparations, ready almost to consign herself to Ann and Conchita.

"Oh, Cappy, the girls are going to dress me now," she cried. "Will Renn like me? We made the dress ourselves. . . . Dear old *padre* Augustine is here. Renn swears he wants to marry me twice — the second time by an American preacher. He wants to make sure of me. But my old *padre* would do for me."

At that juncture Ride-'Em Jackson came puffing to the living room door, where he pounded.

"What you want, Jack?" queried Britt.

"Who is it? — Oh, Jackson! You poor fellow! What are you panting about?" exclaimed Holly.

"Missy Ripple — I'se done — powerful — sorry. I sho is," panted Jackson, solemnly rolling his eyes.

"Sorry! What for?"

"I'se de bearer of turrible sad news."

"Jack, get out. This is no time to worry Miss Ripple," protested Britt, angrily. The negro was serious and probably had some dismaying news that might just as well be left until some other time.

"Dis message comes fro Massa Renn."

"Renn! — For goodness sake!" cried Holly, excitedly. "What is it, Jackson?"

"He say to tell yu dat he's turrible sorry dat he cain't marry yu today."

"Oh, mercy! — Britt — Ann, did you hear Jackson? — Heavens, what is it now? Oh, I never felt sure of Renn! He'll ride away — leave me —"

"Nonsense, Holly," interposed Britt. "Don't take on so. It cain't be anythin' serious. Why, less than an hour ago I saw Renn so locoed he couldn't heah the boys. Mad aboot you, Holly. I never saw a man so happy."

"Mad? — Happy! — Then why on earth. . . . Jackson, you staring ebony lunkhead! Why can't Frayne marry me today?"

" 'Cause Missy, dere's a raid on de cattle. Santone jest rode in. He tole us. Oot by Gray Hill. Gosh! I nebber seen Massa Renn so mad. He cuss turrible. 'Hellsfire! Cain't they give me a day to be married?' "

"But, Jack — he didn't ride off?" wailed Holly.

"Yassum, he sho did. Wif de whole ootfit all

dressed up. An' I'll sho hev to rustle to ketch them."

"Did he say — when he'd come back?" asked Holly faintly.

"He say to tell yu he cain't be sho. Mebbe tomorrow. Mebbe not."

Holly fell into a magnificent rage — the first Britt had ever seen her exhibit. At first she was so speechless she could only throw things. But soon she burst out: "Oh, damn the cattle! What do I care for cattle? . . . On my wedding day! He leaves me to chase rustlers! Oh, to hell with my cattle! — I want to be married. I want my husband!"

"Missy, I sho forgot," said the negro. "He say fer yu to wave yu scarf — like yo always do. But yu mus hurry befo dey's oot of sight."

"No. I won't. Wave to him — when he deserts me for some miserable cows? I see myself. . . . Oh, Britt, it must be very bad. A big raid! Renn would not leave me otherwise. . . . Where's my scarf? Ann — Conchita. My scarf, you ninnies!"

Holly ran to and fro, weeping, wringing her hands, wild with mingled emotions. Presently she snatched the scarf from Ann and fled precipitously out on the porch. Britt ran after her. Off the porch she leaped, into the open path, her arm aloft, her beautiful eyes strained.

The range was empty. But in the path, not twenty rods down the gentle slope, Holly espied a procession of marching cowboys, with Renn Frayne at their head, looking handsome, foolish and unutterably happy.

Holly backed with a scream until she reached the porch steps, where she sat down suddenly. The scarf fell to the ground. A flash of joy quickly left her face. Britt was transfixed by the black dilated eyes. She was a tragic savage child.

"Hello, Holly," called out Frayne, as he neared her. "How do I — we look? — We're early. But couldn't wait."

"It's — a trick," panted Holly.

"Trick? Indeed not. This wedding is the most serious, the most beautiful — the most glorious —"

"Devil!" shrieked Holly.

"What?" gasped Renn, blankly.

"Perfidious wretch!"

At that he could only stare down at her. The smile left his face.

"Villain!"

Frayne appealed to Britt in mute consternation. But for once the foreman was equally mute. He had an almost irresistible desire to imitate Jackson, who was rolling in the grass. All of the other cowboys were beginning to manifest terrific and uncontrolled agitation.

"Cowboy! I can think of no more horrible name to call you. . . . *Cowboy!*" cried Holly.

"But, darling, what have I done?" asked the bewildered Frayne, sitting beside her.

"Don't darling me! I hate you! I'll never marry you! . . . Look! Look at your friendly conspirators."

Frayne did look, to be more mystified than ever.

His cowboy comrades, heedless of their best suits, so cleanly brushed and carefully pressed, were rolling over and over in the grass, giving vent to growing sounds of irresistible glee.

"Holly, *whatever* it is — I am innocent," declared Frayne.

"Innocent! When you sent that grinning demon of a nigger up here to tell me you couldn't marry me today? — Rustlers! You had to ride off. You couldn't get back — maybe not tomorrow! — Oh, how could you? Such a horrible trick! Can't you cowboys tell what is fun — and what is cruel? . . . It broke my heart. I — I'll never marry you now."

"Holly! — Don't say that. I didn't know. They played it on me, too. I *thought* something was afoot. But I was loco. In a trance! Honey, don't visit their sins upon my poor head."

"Oh, Frayne! — I warn you. Don't — don't lie. That would be too much."

"Holly, I'll prove it," declared Frayne, and he jumped up to give the rolling Jackson a resounding kick. "You black rascal! Come here! — Tell her, on your knees, or I'll beat you half to death."

He dragged the convulsed negro to Holly's feet, where she regarded him with parting lips and startled eyes.

"Good Lud — Missy Holly. . . . I done knowed — dis would fall on my haid. But Brazos made me do it."

"*Brazos?*" cried Holly, as if stabbed.

"Yes-sum. Brazos. Dat tow-haided debbil. He

345

done it all before he left, Missy Holly. He planned de trick — swored us all in — an' made me tink nobody but me could fool yu. . . . I'se turrible sorry. I is."

"Jackson, get up off your knees," returned Holly. "I forgive you. But only because Brazos trapped you in one of his infernal tricks."

"Thank yo, Missy Ripple. I swear I'll nebber play tricks no mo."

"Jackson, haven't you any heart?" went on Holly, overcome by curiosity. "Were *you* ever about to get married?"

"Yas-sum. I done come orful near such castrophy onct. I *sho* did. But de good Lud who watches ober niggahs saved me. Dat wench runned off wid a long goose-neck niggah who suttinly got let in bad. An' she tooked sixty-nine dollars of mah money."

"Jackson, we will excuse you," said Holly. "Boys, go into the living room and have Roseta brush off your clothes."

They trooped indoors like a lot of schoolboys glad to be let off so easily. Holly leaned her glossy head against Frayne's shoulder.

"Bless their hearts!" she whispered. "I came very nearly letting them see."

"What? Don't tell me you were not furious."

"I was — at first — wild with rage and disappointment. But when I understood and saw their glee — I wanted to shriek."

"You did shriek, Holly," replied Frayne, nodding gravely. "You called me some dreadful

346

names. Didn't she, Cappy?"

"Wal, I should smile she did."

"*You* were tickled, you old reprobate! Renn, once a cowboy always a cowboy!"

As if to corroborate this unique statement Ride-'Em Jackson appeared at the door, his round black head protruding, his solemn black orbs rolling.

"Missy Ripple, it sho might have happened dat way. It sho might. 'Cause me an' Santone seen some rustlers dis mawnin'. An' we didn't say nuffin' to Mars Frayne aboot it."

"Cappy, throw something at that black monster!"

Britt complied with alacrity. "Gosh, they'll shore drive you mad tonight."

"Cap, they've got me buffaloed," admitted Frayne.

"I don't care what they do — *after* —" murmured Holly.

"After what?" asked Frayne, softly, when she left off. But she kept silent. "Holly, I'd feel better if you substituted some nice names for those you called me."

"Renn!" she whispered.

"That's fair."

"Darling!"

"Better. But try again."

"Sweetheart!"

Frayne appeared overcome with her sweet coquetry, under which breathed a passionate tenderness. He could only press her dusky head to his lips.

Holly sprang up. "I'll be calling you husband pronto!" she flashed, with a gay laugh of joy, and ran indoors.

Frayne stood up beside Britt to gaze out over the range. The old foreman did not care to voice his feelings then. But he knew that Holly was safe at last. He knew the West and he knew Westerners. There would still be years of rustling and hard-lipped, hard-eyed men would come and go. He doubted that there was one living who could match Renn Frayne. He thought a moment of that fire-eyed, great-hearted cowboy who had ridden away into the lonely, melancholy wastes of Texas. Britt's loyalty embodied in Brazos all that was great on the range. But on the moment he remembered with a pang those cowboys, molded in the same heroic crucible, who made merry inside Holly Ripple's house, keen to ride out on the moment, ready to die for her as had their comrades — the wild-spirited knights who slept in unmarked graves, out on the lone prairie.

Zane Grey was born Pearl Zane Gray at Zanesville, Ohio in 1872. He was graduated from the University of Pennsylvania in 1896 with a degree in dentistry. He practiced in New York City while striving to make a living by writing. He married Lina Elise Roth in 1905 and with her financial assistance he published his first novel himself, BETTY ZANE (1903). Closing his dental office, the Greys moved into a cottage on the Delaware River, near Lackawaxen, Pennsylvania. Grey took his first trip to Arizona in 1907 and, following his return, wrote THE HERITAGE OF THE DESERT (1910). The profound effect that the desert had had on him was so vibrantly captured that it still comes alive for a reader. Grey couldn't have been more fortunate in his choice of a mate. Trained in English at Hunter College, Lina Grey proofread every manuscript Grey wrote, polished his prose, and she effectively managed their financial affairs. Grey's early novels were serialized in pulp magazines but by 1918 he had graduated to the slick magazine market. Motion picture rights brought in a fortune and, with 108 films based on his work, Grey set a record yet to be equaled by any other author. Zane Grey was not a realistic writer, but rather one who charted the interiors of the soul through encounters with the wilderness. He provided characters no more realistic than one finds in Balzac, Dickens, or Thomas Mann, but nonetheless they have a vital story to tell. "There was so much unexpressed feeling that could not be entirely portrayed," Loren Grey, Grey's younger son and a noted psychologist, once recalled, "that, in later years, he would weep when re-reading one of his own books." More than stories, Grey fashioned psycho-dramas of the human soul in its odyssey to the center of the psyche. They may not be the stuff of the real world, but without them the real world has no meaning — which may go a long way to explain the hold he has held on an enraptured public ever since that first Western romance in 1910.

The employees of G.K. HALL hope you have enjoyed this Large Print book. All our Large Print titles are designed for easy reading, and all our books are made to last. Other G.K. Hall Large Print books are available at your library, through selected bookstores, or directly from us. For more information about current and upcoming titles, please call or mail your name and address to:

G.K. HALL
PO Box 159
Thorndike, Maine 04986
800/223-6121
207/948-2962